The Magic folk Collection

Enid Blyton Collections

The Magic Faraway Tree Collection
The Wishing-Chair Collection
The O'Clock Tales
St Clare's: The First Year

The Magic folk Collection

Enid Blyton

EGMONT

EGMONT

We bring stories to life

The Book of Fairies
First published in Great Britain by George Newnes 1924

The Book of Pixies
First published in Great Britain 1989
Dean edition published 2007

The Book of Brownies
First published in Great Britain 1926

This edition published 2011 by Egmont UK Limited
239 Kensington High Street
London W8 6SA

Text and illustrations ENID BLYTON ® Copyright © 2011 Chorion Rights Limited
All rights reserved

The moral rights of the author and cover illustrator have been asserted

ISBN 978 1 4052 5757 2

5 7 9 10 8 6 4

A CIP catalogue record for this title is available from the British Library

Printed and bound in Great Britain by the CPI Group

48508/4

EGMONT LUCKY COIN

Our story began over a century ago, when seventeen-year-old
Egmont Harald Petersen found a coin in the street.

He was on his way to buy a flyswatter, a small hand-operated
printing machine that he then set up in his tiny apartment.

The coin brought him such good luck that today Egmont has
offices in over 30 countries around the world. And that lucky
coin is still kept at the company's head offices in Denmark.

The Book of Fairies

EGMONT

The Author
Enid Blyton

Enid Blyton is one of the best-loved writers of the twentieth century. Her wonderful, inventive stories, plays and poems have delighted children of all ages for generations.

Born in London in 1897, Enid Blyton sold her first piece of literature; a poem entitled 'Have You . . .?', at the age of twenty. She qualified and worked as a teacher, writing extensively in her spare time. She sold short stories and poems to various magazines and her first book, *Child Whispers*, was published in 1922.

Over the next 40 years, Blyton would publish on average fifteen books a year. Some of her more famous works include Noddy, The Famous Five, The Secret Seven and The Faraway Tree series.

Her books have sold in the millions and have been translated into many languages. Enid Blyton married twice and had two daughters. She died in 1968, but her work continues to live on.

CONTENTS

Fireworks in Fairyland   1

Betty's Adventure   13

Bufo's One-Legged Stool   22

The Wizard's Magic Necklace   33

Lazy Binkity   42

The Lost Golden Ball   51

Pinkity and Old Mother Ribbony Rose   66

The Floppety Castle and the Goblin Cave   80

Two Fairy Wishes   89

The Green Necklace   93

A Fairy Punishment   102

The Search for Giant Osta   110

The Tenth Task   120

Off to the Land of Tiddlywinks   129

The Land of Great Stupids   137

The Prisoners of the Dobbadies   153

Fireworks in Fairyland

Once upon a time there lived in Fairyland a number of little workmen, all dressed in bright green. They had very long legs and very sleepy eyes, and they sat in the grass all day to do their work.

They were the fairies' knife-grinders, and whenever a fairy wanted her knife sharpened you could hear the buuzz-z-z of the blunt knife held

against the little grindstone that each workman had by him.

The fairies used to bring their knives each morning early, and then, as they were being sharpened, they sat on toadstools and talked.

'The North Wind is in a terrible temper today,' said one. 'I met him just now.'

'Ah!' said one of the knife-grinders. '*I* know why. It's because the late roses came out yesterday in the Queen's garden, and she won't let the North Wind blow till they're over!'

'And he says he *must* blow, else he'll burst himself with keeping all his breath in,' went on another workman, stopping his grinding because he was so interested.

'Yesterday I saw Hoo, the White Owl, and he told me a lovely story about those three naughty little gnomes, Ding, Dong, and Dell,' began another fairy.

'Oh, do tell us!' begged all the workmen, stopping work at once to listen.

The fairy told them the story, and the workmen forgot all about their knives. When the story came to an end the sun was high in the sky, and it was nearly twelve o'clock.

'Oh, I'm so sleepy!' yawned a knife-grinder, lying down on his back.

'I *can't* finish these knives!' said another, and fell asleep beside his grindstone.

There those lazy little workmen slept soundly until four o'clock, when the Fairy Queen happened to come along, bringing a crowd of elves with her.

'Oh, your Majesty, look here!' cried one, pointing to a sleeping workman. 'He's fast asleep, and it's only four o'clock!'

'How disgraceful!' exclaimed the Queen. 'And look at all those blunt knives! They ought to have been sharpened long ago! Does this often happen?'

'We don't know,' answered the elves, 'but Hoo, the White Owl, lives near here, and could tell you.'

So Hoo was called and flew silently down to the Queen.

'Yes, your Majesty,' he said, in answer to her question, 'they are good little workmen, but terribly lazy. They are for ever talking with the fairies, and going to sleep any hour of the day.'

'Wake them up,' commanded the Queen to her elves. 'I can't stop to scold them, but you may stay behind and do it for me.'

The Queen flew on and left some of her elves behind.

'We'll give them a fright,' whispered the elves. Then each elf flew down beside a workman and shouted a most tremendous shout in his ear. Then, quick as lightning, they hid themselves behind toadstools.

You should have seen those workmen jump! They all woke up at once, nearly jumped out of their skins, and looked all round in great terror.

'What was it?' they all cried.

Out came the elves from behind the toadstools, looking very stern.

'The Queen has just passed,' they said, 'and found you all asleep with your work not done. She is very cross indeed!'

But the workmen hardly listened. 'Was it *you* who woke us up like that?' they asked, looking very fierce.

'Yes, it was, and it serves you right!' answered the elves.

'Then you are very unkind, and we'll pull your ears!' shouted the workmen, rushing at the elves. But, quick as thought, they spread their wings, and flew away, laughing at the angry little knife-grinders.

'It's a *shame*!' stormed one. 'Those horrid little elves are *always* playing tricks on us and making us jump!'

'Can't we pay them back somehow and give *them* a fright?' asked another.

'Yes, let's! How could we make them jump just like they made us?'

'I've got a glorious idea!' said another. 'Let's go to the world of boys and girls and get some fireworks. It's November 5th tomorrow and there will be plenty about.'

'Yes, and go to the palace and play tricks on those elves with them!' cried all the other workmen, looking really excited.

So it was all arranged. Two workmen were sent off to get rockets, Catherine Wheels, Golden Rain, and jumping squibs from our world. They soon came back with a big sack full of them, and the knife-grinders made all their plans.

Next morning a message came to them from the Queen, saying they must all go to the palace that day, as she was holding a great party and dance for her elves, and wanted all the knives sharpened.

'That's better still!' cried the workmen, and hurried off at once.

They sharpened all the knives very quickly and then asked if they could help lay the table for the feast, and polish the floor for the dancing.

'Certainly!' answered the Head Steward. 'You are very good to help us.'

So those knife-grinders slipped into the banqueting hall, and began preparing their tricks.

They put some crackers in the dishes of sweets and chocolates and some in the middle of a big ice-cream pudding.

'I'm going to put Golden Rain fireworks among all these flowers round the hall!' called a busy workman. 'The elves always smell the flowers!'

'And I'm pinning Catherine Wheels on to the wall!' chuckled another. 'The elves won't know what they are, and they'll be sure to poke about and see!'

'Look, do look! I've had a glorious idea! I've tied rockets to the front legs of every chair! Won't those elves jump?' called another knife-grinder, looking most delighted.

'Isn't it *lovely*? Won't they be cross? They *will* be sorry they made us jump!' called all the workmen.

'Now we'd better hide somewhere and watch. We'll go behind those big curtains. Have you all got squibs in your pockets?' asked the biggest workman.

'Yes,' answered the rest.

'Now, all be quiet whilst I say some magic. We shall have to use some to make the fireworks go off directly anyone touches them.'

Everyone was quiet, and the leader sang some queer words.

'There!' he said. 'Now, directly anyone *touches*

those hidden fireworks, they'll all go off bang! Let's go and hide.'

The knife-grinders ran behind the long curtains, and there they waited till the guests came in to the party.

Soon the elves arrived, all in beautiful dresses and shiny wings. Then came the Queen, and gave the signal for the feast to begin.

Everything went well until an elf asked for some ice-cream pudding. For directly the Head Steward began to put a spoon into it, there came a most tremendous noise!

Crack! Splutter-crack!! Bang!!!

It was the cracker inside the pudding, gone off directly it was touched!

'Oh, oh! What is it?' gasped the Head Steward, looking very astonished.

Then suddenly—

Crack! Bang! Crack!

The elves were helping themselves to chocolates and sweets, and the crackers in the dishes were exploding!

How those elves jumped! And how the naughty little workmen laughed, behind the curtain.

'Someone has been playing tricks,' said the Queen, looking rather stern. 'If you have all finished, get down, and we will start dancing.'

The elves got down, and went into the dancing hall. The workmen followed, making sure no one saw them, and hid behind the curtains there.

'What glorious flowers!' cried the elves, and bent to smell the wonderful roses round the walls.

Fizzle-fizzle-fizz! Whizz-z-z!

Out shot Golden Rain, directly the fairies smelt the roses!

'Oh, what is it?' they cried, falling over one another in their haste to get away. 'It must be some new sort of caterpillar! Ugh, how horrid!'

'Yes, and what are those funny curly things on the walls?' asked the Queen.

An elf went up to a Catherine Wheel and poked it with his finger.

Whirr-r-r-r! Whirr-r-r-r!

The wheel spun round and round and shot off sparks!

'Oh, it's alive! it's alive! What is it, what is it?' shouted the elves, crowding together in frightened astonishment.

'Never mind,' said the Queen, looking sterner than ever. 'Begin your dancing.'

The elves began dancing round the room.

'Throw your jumping squibs on the floor!' whispered the biggest workman. 'That will make the elves jump!'

Quickly the squibs were thrown on the floor of the hall.

Crack! Splutter-jump! Crack! Jump!!

Those squibs were jumping all over the place!

'Oh! Get off my toe, you horrid thing!'

'Goodness me! Go away, go away!'

'Oh, oh, what are they? They jump us and won't let us dance!'

The elves were really frightened.

'Go and sit down,' commanded the Queen, 'and I will find out who has done these naughty things.'

The elves went to the chairs round the hall and sat down.

Whizz-z-z! Whoosh-sh-sh! Bang!!!

All the rockets tied to the chairs shot up in the air directly they were touched by the elves!

'Oh, oh!' cried the elves, nearly jumping out of their skins with fright.

'Keep where you are,' called the Queen, 'and see what else happens.'

Nothing happened, and the elves began to feel more comfortable.

'Lord High Chamberlain,' commanded the Queen, in a dreadfully stern voice, 'go and look behind those curtains over there.'

The Lord High Chamberlain stepped across and pulled the curtains aside.

And there were all the naughty little green workmen, looking very frightened indeed!

'Come here,' said the Queen.

They all came and stood in front of her throne.

'What do you mean by playing such naughty tricks on my elves?' she demanded.

'Please, your Majesty, they made *us* jump the other day, so we thought we'd make *them* jump,' answered the biggest workman.

'You know quite well that that's not the right thing to do at all,' said the Queen. 'I am quite ashamed of you. You are not fit to be in Fairyland. You have spoilt our party and frightened all my elves.'

'Oh, please, we *are* sorry now,' sobbed the workmen, feeling very miserable.

'You don't do your work well and you are lazy,' said the Queen. 'I think it would do you good to do some jumping and stretch those long legs of yours a bit. I am going to punish you, and perhaps you will remember another time that I will have no one in my kingdom who does not do his work well and beautifully.'

'*Please* let us sharpen the fairies' knives for them,' begged the knife-grinders. 'We really *will* do it beautifully now.'

'Very well, you may still do that,' said the Queen, 'and as you are so fond of making people jump, you had better jump a lot too.'

She waved her wand.

And every little workman there turned into a green grasshopper!

'Go into the fields,' said the Queen, 'and do your work properly.'

All the green grasshoppers turned to go, stretched their long legs, and *jumped* out of the hall! Hop and a jump, and a jump, and out they went into the fields.

They still sharpen the fairies' knives for them, and you can hear their grindstones buzzing in the summer somewhere down in the grass. And when you see them hopping you will know why it is they jump instead of run!

Fireworks are forbidden in Fairyland, now, and I really don't wonder at it, do you?

Betty's Adventure

There was once upon a time a little girl who didn't believe in fairies. 'But, Betty, there *are* fairies, because I've seen them,' said her brother Bobby.

'Pooh! You're telling stories!' answered Betty crossly. 'There aren't fairies, or gnomes, or elves, or anything like that, so you couldn't have seen any!'

Now the brownies heard her say this, and they determined to teach her a lesson.

'What can we do to show her she's wrong?' asked one.

'Don't you think it would be rather funny if we took her to the middle of Fairyland, where there's crowds of fairies and elves, and see what she says when she sees them?' laughed a merry little brownie.

'Yes, yes! Let's!' cried the others. So they made their plans and waited.

One day Betty was out for a walk by herself, when she saw a big notice up, which said: 'PLEASE DO NOT WALK THIS WAY.'

'How stupid!' said Betty. 'It doesn't look like a proper notice. I believe it's only a joke. Anyway, I *shall* go that way!'

'We thought she would! We thought she would!' chuckled the brownies, who had put up the notice and were hiding in the bushes.

Betty walked past the notice, and down a little lane. She came to a stream, and by the side of the bank rocked a little golden boat.

'There's no one here! I'll just get in and see how it feels to rock up and down like that!' said Betty. She jumped into the boat and sat down.

Out sprang the brownies, gave the boat a push, and ran back laughing.

Betty didn't see the brownies, and suddenly felt the boat jerk. Then it floated out into midstream, and began going down the river!

'Oh! Oh! Stop! Stop!' cried Betty, feeling frightened. But the boat wouldn't stop. It went by magic. Betty had no oars, and could do nothing.

Presently it passed cottages on each side. Old women in pointed black hats stood at the doors.

'They look just like witches in Bobby's story-book,' thought Betty, 'but I know they can't be.'

On and on the boat went, until Betty, tired with the sun, fell fast asleep. At last the boat stopped with a bump, and Betty woke up. She

found the boat had stopped by some steps, so she got out and ran up them.

'Wherever am I?' she thought. Then she stared in astonishment. She saw a fairy dressed in blue, with long blue wings, coming towards her.

'It can't be a fairy!' thought Betty. 'It must be somebody dressed up for fun.'

'Welcome to Fairyland!' said the fairy.

'Don't be silly!' said Betty. 'There isn't such a place. And what are you dressed up like that for? Is there a fancy-dress party?'

The fairy looked puzzled. 'No,' she said, 'I'm

15

not dressed up. I'm just a fairy!'

'You're telling stories!' said Betty rudely. 'I shan't speak to you any more!' She walked on by herself, turned a corner, and came straight into a noisy market-place, full of fairies, elves, brownies, and gnomes.

'It *is* a fancy-dress party!' said Betty. 'Oh dear! I wish I'd got a fancy dress too, and had been invited!'

'Buy a magic spell?' asked a little brown gnome, running up to her with a tray full of curious packages.

'Oh, don't be silly!' said Betty, getting really cross. 'I know you're not real, so you needn't pretend to be! There aren't any fairies!'

All at once there fell a great silence. No one spoke, but everyone turned and looked at Betty in astonishment. Then a grandly dressed fairy, with great wings, stepped over to her.

'You must be making a mistake,' she said. 'You're in Fairyland, you know, and we think it is very bad manners, besides being very stupid, to say there aren't any fairies when you are surrounded by them.'

Betty began to feel alarmed. After all, it didn't really look like a fancy-dress party! Perhaps Bobby *was* right, and there *were* fairies!

But Betty was an obstinate little girl, and she hated to say she was wrong.

'I don't care *what* you say!' she said. 'I don't believe in fairies!'

The crowd round her looked angry.

'Call for Giant Putemright!' shouted someone, 'and put her in prison till she's a bit more polite!'

Betty felt frightened. She looked round for a way to escape, but there was none. Suddenly there was a shout!

'Here comes Giant Putemright!'

Betty looked and saw a great giant lumbering down the street. She saw everyone was looking at him, and not at her, and she turned and ran away as fast as she could. She ran and ran and ran, till she had no breath left. Then she turned and looked back. Far away she could see a crowd of little people, but they were going a different way.

'They won't catch me after all!' said Betty, sinking down on the grass for a rest. 'Oh dear! I don't like this adventure. I *wish* I'd never said I didn't believe in fairies. Why, here's hundreds and hundreds of them; all sorts!'

Just then she heard a little puffing noise. She looked up, and saw near by her a pair of railway lines, and over them was coming a tiny little train. It stopped near her, and the driver leaned out.

'Are you waiting for the train?' he called. 'We're going to the Glittering Palace.'

Betty jumped up. Yes! She would get in the train, then if the fairies tried to find her any more, she would be far away!

She scrambled into a little carriage and sat down on one of the cushions on the floor. There was a dwarf on another one, but he took no notice of her. The train whistled and went on again.

'What lovely country!' thought Betty as they went through fields of wonderful flowers and past gardens filled with roses.

'Oh! That's the Glittering Palace!' said Betty, as they came in sight of a great shining palace, with turrets and pinnacles gleaming in the sun.

The train stopped and Betty jumped out. 'I'd better ask the way home,' she thought. She went up to the driver.

'Could you tell me the way out of Fairyland?' she asked.

'No, I couldn't,' said the driver. 'But if you go and ask at the Glittering Palace, I dare say someone would tell you.' He blew the engine's whistle, waved to her, and drove away.

Betty made her way to the Glittering Palace. She came at last to some great open gates. There was no one to speak to, so she went through them and up a great flight of steps. At the top she came to a big hall, hung with wonderful blue curtains.

'My goodness!' whispered Betty, stopping. 'Why, I do believe that's the Fairy Queen on that throne, that Bobby talks about such a lot.'

Sure enough it was! Around her was a crowd of fairies, and elves, all chattering excitedly.

'Silence!' said the Queen. 'Sylfai, you tell me what all this excitement is about.'

'If you please, your Majesty,' said Sylfai, 'there's a horrid little girl come to Fairyland, who doesn't believe in us! She's run away from us, and we thought we ought to come and tell you, so we all flew straight here!'

'Oh! Oh! There she is! There she is!' shouted an elf, pointing at poor Betty. She turned to run, but this time she was not quick enough, and the gnomes surrounded her, and dragged her to the Queen.

'Please! Please! I *do* believe in fairies!' wept Betty. 'I'm sorry I said I didn't.'

The Queen looked grave. 'You're a silly little girl,' she said. 'Because you can't leave Fairyland now! No one is allowed to if she comes here and disbelieves!'

'Isn't there any way of going back?' asked Betty. 'I didn't *mean* to come.'

'Yes, there's just one way,' said the Queen. 'And that is this: If you know anyone who really *does* believe in fairies, and loves them, he can take you back!'

'Oh, Bobby does, Bobby does!' cried Betty. 'Please bring him here!'

The Queen looked at her. 'Are you quite sure he does?' she asked. 'Because we don't want *two* people here who don't believe.'

'Yes, he *does*, he's always talking about you, and how he loves you!' said Betty.

The Queen turned to a gnome.

'Go and fetch Bobby!' she commanded. He sped off.

'Let's have a dance while we're waiting,' said a fairy. And they all began dancing in the hall, while the Queen looked on. Suddenly Betty gave a cry of delight.

'Bobby! Bobby!' she called.

And there was dear old Bobby, coming up the hall with the little gnome. He looked delighted to be with the fairies, but most astonished to find Betty there.

Betty told him all her adventures and begged him to take her home again.

'Of course I will, if the Queen will let me,' he answered.

20

'Yes, take Betty home!' said the Queen. 'She has learnt her lesson, but I am sorry she has not had a happy time in Fairyland. Still, it was her own fault. Will you bring her again, Bobby, the next time we have a party, and we'll try to make her love us, as well as believe in us.'

'I'd *love* to!' said Bobby, smiling in delight. 'What fun! Now then, Betty, hold on to me! I know the way home. Shut your eyes, turn round twice—One, two, three!' and down came a great wind, picked them up and set them down in their very own garden.

Betty rubbed her eyes. 'Oh, Bobby!' she said. 'I'm so glad you fetched me. I'll always love the fairies now, and oh! won't it be fun to go to their next party?'

'Let's go and tell Mummy,' said Bobby excitedly. 'My word, *what* an adventure!'

Bufo's One-Legged Stool

Once upon a time the King of Fairyland called all his fairy subjects to his palace. They came flying and running in great excitement, wondering why his Majesty should want them.

The King sat on his beautiful, shining throne, waiting until every fairy was there. Then he held up his hand for silence and spoke to them.

'Fairy-folk,' he began, 'once every year a prize is given to the fairy who thinks of the cleverest idea to make the world more beautiful. Last year, you remember, Morfael won the prize with his golden polish for the buttercups.'

'Yes, we remember!' shouted the fairies.

'Well, this year, I'm going to make a change,' said the King. 'I am going to give the prize to the one who thinks, not of the *cleverest* idea, but of the *most useful!* And please tell the rabbits and frogs and birds about it, because it's quite likely they would think of a good idea just as much as you fairy-folk.'

Well, the fairies were most excited. They rushed off telling everyone about it.

'I'm going to think hard for a whole week!' said one.

'And I'm going to use some old magic that will tell me the most useful thing in the world!' said another.

'Let's go and tell all the animals,' shouted a third.

So they visited the grey rabbits and told them. They called out the news to the grasshoppers. They gave the message to Hoo, the White Owl of Fairyland, and he promised to tell all the other birds.

'Now I do believe we've told everyone!' said the fairies.

'No, we haven't. What about ugly old Bufo the Toad, who lives on the edge of Fairyland?' asked an elf.

'Pooh! What's the good of telling *him*?' cried a pixie scornfully. 'He's so stupid and ugly, he'd *never* think of any good idea. Leave him alone!'

But it happened that next door to Bufo lived a brownie called Bron. He had decided to make a beautiful scarf for fairies to wear when the wind was cold. He thought it would be most useful. He was making it of spiders' webs and thistledown, and as he sat in his little garden at work, he sang a little song:

'Oh! I am very wise,
I'm sure to win the prize,
And when I've won the prize, you'll see
How very, very pleased I'll be!'

Bufo the Toad kept hearing him sing this and at last he got so curious that he crawled out of his cottage and asked Bron what prize he was singing about.

Bron told him. 'The King's giving a prize to anyone bringing him the most *useful* idea this year!' he explained. 'Why don't you try, Bufo?'

'I'm so clumsy!' said Bufo. 'But I'd like to try all the same. Yes, I think I will.'

'I'm making a wonderful scarf for when it's cold!' said Bron proudly. 'It's made of cobwebs and thistledown!'

'My! You are clever!' said Bufo. 'Now I'm going indoors and try to think of something myself!'

He waddled indoors. His cottage was very queer inside. Bufo was so fat and heavy that he had broken all the chairs and his sofa, through sitting on them too hard! So there were none in his cottage at all. He had a big table, and as he really did want something to sit on, he had made himself one large stool. He was so stupid at making things, that he

thought he had better give his stool just one large
fat leg in the middle. He was afraid that if he tried
to make three legs to it like Bron's smart little
stool, he would never get them the same length.
So inside his cottage there was only one table and
a queer one-legged stool.

Bufo the Toad climbed up on to his stool, shut
his great yellow eyes, and thought!

At last he opened his eyes. 'I've got an idea!' he
cried. 'I'll make an eiderdown of pink rose petals!
That will be a most useful thing, and it will smell
lovely!'

So he hopped out into his garden and collected all the largest rose petals he could find. Then he begged some spider-thread from a spider friend and began.

But poor Bufo was clumsy. He kept breaking the spider's thread, and the wind blew half his rose petals away.

'Ha, ha!' laughed the rude little brownie. 'Ha, ha! Bufo! It really is a funny sight to see a great toad sewing rose petals! Don't you worry your stupid old head! *I'm* going to win the prize, I tell you!'

But Bufo wouldn't give up. He went and sat on his stool again and thought. He thought for three days before he found another idea.

That was really rather a good one. He caught a little pink cloud, and decided to stuff a pillow with it. He thought it would be so lovely and soft for fairies' heads.

Bron laughed to see Bufo poking the pink cloud into a big white pillowcase with his great fingers. He called his friends and they came and watched Bufo and teased him.

'Poke it a bit harder, Bufo!' they called over the fence. 'It's a naughty little cloud, isn't it? It won't let you win the prize.'

Bufo took no notice for a whole day. Then he

suddenly got angry, left the half-stuffed pillow on the grass, and hopped to the fence to smack the rude little brownies.

But alas! As soon as the half-stuffed pillow had no one to hold it, the little pink cloud began to rise in the air, to go back to the sky, and it took Bufo's lovely pillow-case with it!

'Oh, oh, now look what you've made me do!' wept Bufo, trying to jump into the air and catch the pillow. But he couldn't, and the naughty little brownies laughed harder than ever.

Bufo went and sat on his stool again. This time he thought for six weeks. When another idea came, he was so stiff with sitting that he could hardly jump off his stool.

'I'll make some wonderful blue paint, to paint the Queen's carriage with!' he decided. 'I know it wants repainting, so that will be useful.'

He lumbered off with a huge sack. He got the dawn fairies to give him a scraping off the blue of the sky. He asked the blue butterflies for a little powder off their wings. He took one bluebell flower and one harebell. Then he lumbered home again with his sack full of all these things.

When he got indoors, he took a blue shadow, mixed it with honey and water, and poured it into a large paint-pot. Then he emptied his sack into it, and stirred everything up well.

'It's the most glorious blue paint ever I saw!' said Bufo, very pleased. '*This* will be useful, I know.'

Now the next day was the day the King had arranged to hold a meeting to judge all the ideas, and everyone in Fairyland was most excited. When the day came, Bufo put his paint outside his cottage door, all ready to take, and then began tidying himself up. Suddenly he heard a terrible yell from Bron, his next door neighbour.

'Help! Help! Arran the Spider is stealing my lovely scarf!'

Bufo rushed out to help, and saw Arran running off with Bron's scarf. He quickly stopped the spider, and took the scarf away.

'He stole some of my thread,' grumbled Arran, running off, frightened. 'I thought I'd come and punish him!'

'Oh, thank you for helping me,' cried Bron. 'If he'd taken my scarf, I wouldn't be able to win the prize.'

'Yes, but it's wrong to take Arran's thread, if he didn't want you to,' said Bufo severely. 'You ought to say you're sorry to him, and give it back!'

He waddled back to his cottage, but, oh! he quite forgot he had put his pot of blue paint outside the door. He walked straight into it, and splish-splash! clitter-clatter! It was all upset.

'Oh! Oh! My beautiful paint!' wept Bufo. 'I've spilt it all, and there's no more time to think of other ideas!'

Some fairies passing by stopped to listen.

'You must take *something*, Bufo,' they called mischievously. 'The King will be cross with you if you don't.'

Bufo believed them. 'Oh dear! Will he really? But what *shall* I do? I've nothing else but my stool and a table!'

'Take the stool, Bufo!' laughed the fairies, flying on.

So poor old Bufo the Toad went indoors and fetched his one-legged stool, and joined the crowd of flying fairies. How they laughed to see him waddling along carrying a big one-legged stool.

At last they all reached the palace, and the King soon came to hear and to see the useful ideas that the fairy-folk had brought.

'Here's a wonderful necklace made of raindrops!' cried a fairy, kneeling before the King.

'It is beautiful, but not useful!' answered the King gently. 'Try again.'

'Here's a new sort of polish for the sunset sky!' said the next fairy.

The King looked at it. 'That's no better than

29

the one we use now,' he said. 'Next, please.'

Fairy after fairy came, and rabbits and birds and other animals.

Some had beautiful ideas that weren't useful, some had stupid ideas, and some had good ones.

At last Bron's turn came. He showed his beautiful scarf.

'It is lovely, Bron,' said the King, 'but it is not warm enough to be useful. Also I know you have been unkind to Bufo, and you took Arran's thread without asking. I am not pleased with you. Go away, and do better!'

Bron hung his head and crept away, blushing and ashamed.

At last everyone had shown their ideas, except Bufo. He crawled up to the King and put his one-legged stool down.

'I thought of many ideas, but they all got spoilt,' he said. 'Is this one any use? It is a good strong stool, easy to make, and quite nice-looking.'

The King looked at it thoughtfully. Then the Queen leaned forward and spoke.

'Don't you think, Oberon,' she said, 'that it is just the thing we want to put in the woods for fairy seats? Think how easy, too, they would be to put up in a ring for a dance!'

'Well now, so they would!' said the King. 'It

really is just what we want. It is certainly the most useful idea we've had given to us today. We could *grow* these one-legged stools by magic in the woods, and use them for tables *or* for stools!'

'Then we'll give Bufo the prize!' said the Queen. 'Three cheers for Bufo!'

How surprised the fairies were to see ugly old Bufo win the prize! And oh! how delighted Bufo was! He could hardly believe his ears. He almost cried with joy. He was given a little golden crown to wear, and though he certainly looked rather queer in it, he didn't mind a bit, because he was so very proud of having won it!

One-legged stools were put all about the woods that very day, and they have been used ever since by fairy-folk. Sometimes you find them growing in a ring, and then you'll know there has been a dance the night before.

They are still called toadstools, although it is many, many years ago since Bufo the Toad won the prize. Not many people know why they have such a funny name, but you will be able to tell them the reason now, won't you?

The Wizard's Magic Necklace

'Oh dear, oh dear!' sighed Gillie. 'I do wish I wasn't so ugly. My nose is so long and my brown suit is so old!'

Gillie looked at himself in a clear pool of water. He was a little gnome living in Fairyland, and he certainly *was* very ugly.

'Hullo, Gillie!' suddenly called a little voice.

Gillie looked round. He saw his friend the grey rabbit, sitting down among the primroses.

'Hullo, Greyears!' he said 'What have you come to see me for?'

'I've got a letter for you,' said Greyears. 'It's to say that the rabbits are giving a party tonight, and they want you to come to it. The pixies are coming too, so be sure and look your best, won't you?'

Gillie took the letter and read it.

'How lovely!' he cried. 'Thank you so much for asking me. But, oh dear, I *wish* I wasn't so ugly, Greyears!'

'Yes, you are rather ugly,' said Greyears, looking at his friend. 'But if you bought a new coat, Gillie, and wore some beads or something, you would look *much* nicer.'

'I can't have a new suit yet,' sighed Gillie. 'I've got to wait till next month. And I haven't any beads at all, have you?'

'No,' answered Greyears. 'But, I say, Gillie! I've got an idea!'

'What is it? Do tell me,' begged Gillie.

'Well, come over here, and I'll whisper,' said the grey rabbit, looking round to make sure that no one was about.

'Listen. You know where that old wizard Coran lives, don't you? Well, he has got a wonderful necklace. It is all made of yellow and red-brown stones. It would look simply *lovely* on your brown suit, Gillie.'

'Oh,' said Gillie, 'but he wouldn't lend it to me, I know. He's a dreadfully cross wizard.'

'Well, if you like, I'll get it for you. I can burrow into the room where he keeps it, and then bring it to you. He will never know. You can easily put it back when you've worn it,' said Greyears.

'All right,' answered Gillie. 'It's very nice of you, Greyears, and I shall look lovely at the party.'

'I'll bring it to you tonight, by this little pool,' called Greyears, hopping off as fast as he could.

Gillie felt very excited. He took off his little brown suit and mended up the holes beautifully with some spider's thread. He washed off a dirty mark and put it in the sun to dry. Then he sat down by the little pool and waited for Greyears to come back with the necklace.

'How lovely I shall look with a string of yellow and brown stones,' he thought. 'Oh, here comes Greyears.'

Greyears lolloped up to Gillie. He held a glittering necklace in his teeth.

'Oh, Greyears, how beautiful!' cried Gillie, taking it into his hands. 'See how the stones shine and glitter. Oh, how beautiful I shall be!'

'Sh!' said Greyears 'Don't talk so loudly, I believe the old wizard heard me. Put on the necklace and come to the party with me, before he finds out it is gone.'

Off they both went, and Gillie had a most glorious evening dancing with the pixies. Everyone thought he looked lovely in his beautiful necklace, and he was very happy.

'It *has* been lovely,' said Gillie to the grey rabbit as they went home.

'Hark, what's that?' suddenly whispered Greyears.

They both crouched down in some bracken and

listened. They heard a curious noise—a sort of panting and groaning.

'It's the wizard,' whispered Greyears.

'Oh dear! Has he missed his necklace?' asked Gillie. 'Whatever shall I do? He'll be dreadfully angry if he finds me here wearing it.'

'Keep still,' said Greyears, 'and perhaps he won't find us.'

They both kept quite still, and presently along came the wizard with his servants. He stopped just by Greyears and Gillie.

'Now then,' he cried to his servants in a queer, panting voice. 'Now then, hurry up and do what I tell you. That necklace *must* be found. You must search in all the homes of the little gnomes for it.'

'Yes, your Excellency,' replied the servants.

'I feel sure one of them has got it. Oh dear! Oh dear! I'm much too old to come out at this time of night, all in the dark!' said the wizard, groaning, as he hobbled off away from the bracken where Gillie and Greyears were hiding.

They waited till he was safely out of sight, then they crept from the bracken and looked around. The necklace glittered in the starlight, and Gillie wondered what to do with it.

'Oh dear!' he sighed. 'How I wish I hadn't borrowed it. Now I must hide it somewhere till

the old wizard has forgotten about it, and then put it back somehow.'

'Where will you hide it?' asked Greyears. 'Don't you think it would be better to go and give it to the wizard and say you're sorry?'

'Oh no! I *couldn't!*' said Gillie. 'I should be so afraid he would be cross with me.'

'Shall I hide it in my burrow for you, Gillie?' asked the grey rabbit.

'No thank you—I know of a much better place. Come with me, Greyears, and I'll show you.' And off went the two friends as fast as they could.

The Book of Fairies

At last they came to an old mossy wall. Gillie climbed up, right to the top, and sat there to get his breath.

'There's a big hole here, Greyears,' he called, 'and I'm going to hide the necklace in it.'

'Can I do anything to help you?' asked Greyears.

'Yes, scrape up some earth with your hind legs, and I'll fill the hole with it so that no one can see the necklace shining, if they fly over the wall.'

Greyears busily scraped some earth loose. Presently Gillie climbed down, and taking off his brown cap he filled it with earth. Then he climbed up again to the top of the wall.

'That's just enough,' he said; 'it covers the necklace nicely.'

'Plant some flowers along the top!' said Greyears, 'then no one will guess what's underneath.'

'How clever you are!' exclaimed Gillie, scrambling down again. He looked about for some flowers, and found some tiny white ones with four petals, growing in a hedge. He pulled them up by the roots and climbing up the wall again, he planted them all carefully along the top. Then he slid down to the ground.

'There! *That's* done!' he said. 'Thank you for helping me, dear Greyears. Now, let's go home, I'm so tired.'

'You can fetch the necklace in a month's time,' said Greyears, 'and put it back again somehow.'

Gillie went to Greyear's burrow for the night, and soon they were both sound asleep.

Gillie didn't go near the old wall at all for a long time. If he had, he would have seen something wonderful happening.

The little white flowers he planted were growing, and were spreading all along the wall—but they were no longer white! They were growing to be great strong flowers, yellow and red-brown like the necklace. They were beautiful in the sun, with their deep colours and soft, velvety petals. They smelt so sweet that some fairies flying by stopped to look at them.

'What lovely flowers!' cried one. 'I've never seen any like them before.'

'And how *did* they come to be growing there!' said the other. 'What a funny place to grow Let's ask the Queen if she has heard of them?'

But when the Queen came *she* didn't know either, and was very puzzled, because of course she knew the names of all the flowers there were in Fairyland.

'They must be magic flowers,' she said at last. 'Bring the old wizard here, and ask him if *he* knows what they are.'

The old wizard was brought, groaning and panting, and leaning on a strong stick. Just behind came Gillie and Greyears, curious to know what everyone was looking at. They were most astonished to find sturdy yellow and brown flowers growing on the wall.

'Good afternoon, Sir Wizard,' said the Queen. 'Can you kindly tell me what those flowers are, up there on the wall?'

The wizard looked.

'Good gracious me,' he cried, 'they're exactly the colour of my lost necklace! That means that they are planted over it, for the stones are magic, and would turn the flowers to yellow and red-brown like themselves.'

'Dear me,' said the Queen, 'but whoever could have put the necklace there?'

'Oh, please, your Majesty, *I* did,' said Gillie, kneeling down in front of the Queen, and beginning to cry. He told her all about the party and how he borrowed the necklace.

'But whatever did you want a necklace for?' asked the Queen.

'Because I am so ugly, and I thought it would make me look lovely,' sobbed Gillie.

'Why, Gillie, you've a *dear* little face!' said the Queen kindly. 'Tell the wizard you're sorry, and I

40

expect he'll forgive you, now he knows where his necklace is.'

'Oh yes, I'll forgive Gillie,' grunted the wizard. 'Only you must climb up and get my necklace for me again.'

'Yes, I will,' cried Gillie, climbing up the wall, and sitting among the flowers.

'What shall we call those lovely flowers?' said the Queen.

'Hm! I should call them *wall*-flowers,' growled the wizard, 'because of where they're growing.'

'Yes, we will,' said the Queen. 'That's a good idea.'

And we still call them wallflowers wherever they grow—on the top of a wall, or in the garden beds—and there are some people who call them '*Gillie* flowers,' because they remember the naughty little gnome who, years ago, planted the flowers on the wall to hide the necklace of yellow and brown, and so made the very first wallflowers grow.

Lazy Binkity

Once upon a time there was a little Brownie called Binkity. He was very lazy and rather naughty, and was always being scolded by the other Brownies.

'Have you tidied up the Oak Tree Wood,' asked Ding, the chief Brownie, one day.

'No, I haven't, and I'm not going to!' answered Binkity rudely, and ran away before Ding could catch him. He curled up inside a hollow tree, and watched Ding looking for him, until he was tired and went away. Then Binkity came out of the tree and looked around for something to do.

'Stupid old Ding!' he said to himself. 'He's always trying to make me work when I don't want to!'

Then he found a squirrel's hoard of nuts hidden under some leaves at the foot of a tree.

'Ha! Ha!' chuckled Binkity. 'I'll hide them somewhere else.'

He dug them up quickly, and put them in a rabbit hole. Then he went to find Bushy the Squirrel, who was asleep in a tree.

'Wake up! Wake up!' he cried. 'It's a lovely day for a scamper!'

Bushy rubbed his eyes and sat up. 'I feel hungry,' he said, and down the tree he scampered.

'I'll eat a nut or two,' said Bushy, scraping up the leaves at the foot of the tree where he had hidden his nuts.

But they weren't there!

'Oh dear, dear, dear!' cried the squirrel. 'Someone's taken them! Whatever shall I do! I

must have something to eat in the winter!'

Binkity sat on a twig and laughed to see Bushy looking for nuts that weren't there.

Just then Ding, the chief Brownie, came by, with a crowd of other Brownies, and asked Bushy why he was looking so miserable.

'Someone's taken my nuts,' explained poor Bushy, 'and that horrid little Binkity keeps laughing at me.'

'Here are your nuts!' called a Brownie, who had accidentally found them in the rabbit hole where Binkity had put them. 'Binkity must have put them there, he's *always* playing tricks!'

Binkity began to feel he had better run away again, and looked round to see where he could go to.

'Binkity!' said Ding very sternly. 'You must be punished. You are lazy and mischievous and never help anyone in anything. I shall send you as a servant to Arran the Spider, and he will make you work really hard and keep you out of mischief!'

Now this was a terrible threat, for Arran the Spider sometimes ate people who didn't work hard enough, and Binkity was dreadfully frightened.

He jumped up, and ran away as fast as ever he could, with all the Brownies after him. It was getting dark, and he hoped that soon they would find it too dark to chase him.

'Catch him! Catch him!' called the Brownies, racing after naughty Binkity.

Binkity rushed right through the wood and out into some fields. Then it began to snow hard, and the snowflakes beat against the Brownie's face till he was cold and tired out. But still he could hear the other Brownies chasing him.

'Ah, there's a cottage!' suddenly panted Binkity, as he saw a light near by. He ran up to the cottage, and quick as lightning changed himself into a puppydog.

All the other Brownies, seeing only a shivering puppy, raced by without stopping.

'Now I'm safe,' thought Binkity, 'but, oh dear, how cold and wet I am!' He began to make a little whining noise, like a puppy.

Presently the door opened and a little girl peeped out.

'Oh, here's a poor little puppy!' she cried, picking Binkity up and taking him in.

She set him down before a fire, and gave him a saucer of milk to lap. When he was quite dry and warm, she took him over to her mother, who was in bed, looking very ill.

'Dear little puppy!' said the mother, stroking

him. 'I wonder where he came from, Jean. We must keep him, if no one comes to claim him.'

Binkity lay down by the fire, warm and drowsy, and listened to Jean and her mother talking. Presently he was astonished to hear the mother crying.

'Oh, Jean darling,' she was saying, 'I am so ill I cannot get up again this winter, and that means you will have all the housework to do, and all the washing. You will have to do most of the sewing too, to make money, for I am too tired even for that!' And the poor woman sobbed as if her heart would break.

'Never mind, Mother,' said the little girl bravely, 'I will do my best. Don't cry, we shall be all right.' But Binkity could see that she looked dreadfully worried, and he was very sorry for her.

'I wonder if I could help her,' he thought, 'she has been so kind to me. I daren't change back into a Brownie in the daytime, in case the other Brownies see me. I must still be a puppy, till they have forgotten I was naughty. But at night! Yes! At night, I will change back into a Brownie, and do all the work!'

Binkity was so excited with his idea, that he could hardly wait until the house was dark and still.

When Jean had gone to bed and everything was

still, Binkity changed into his own shape again. Then he bustled about the house, making no noise at all. He dusted and washed and tidied till the house was as clean as a new pin. Then, just as dawn came in at the windows, he changed into a puppy again and lay down by the fire.

When Jean woke up and looked round, she could hardly believe her eyes.

'Mother! Mother!' she cried. 'Look, look! The house is clean. There is no work to do! I can spend all the day sewing!'

'Jean, it's a Brownie!' said her mother in delight. 'There must have been one near here, working in the night. Leave a saucer of milk on the hearth every night when you go to bed, and don't peep to see what happens when you're in bed.'

All that day Jean sewed at beautiful tablecloths and curtains, which she sold in the town for money, and when night came she put a saucer of milk on the hearth.

'There! That's for you, whoever you are, little Brownie,' she called.

She patted the puppy and kissed him, never dreaming *he* was the little Brownie, and then she went to bed.

All that night Binkity, changed into a Brownie again, did the housework, and even baked some bread for Jean! Then at dawn he changed into a puppy again, and lay by the fire.

'The Brownie's been here again, Mother,' said Jean, next morning, delightedly, 'and he's done all the work! *Isn't* it lovely!'

All through the winter Binkity lived at the little cottage. Jean and her mother loved the little puppy that jumped around them in the daytime, and never guessed he was really a Brownie. And every night, when Binkity became himself again, he did all the housework and worked harder than he had ever worked before in his life. He loved Jean, and was always delighted to see how surprised she was each morning.

In the spring Jean's mother got better, and was able to get up. Binkity began to feel that he would like to live in the woods again, and talk to the birds and animals as he used to do, and to live in his little Tree House.

'I think I *must* go back now!' he said to himself one night as he was washing the floor. 'Perhaps the Brownies will have forgotten they were going to give me to Arran the Spider. Jean's mother can do the housework now, and I'll see that Jean always has plenty of money.'

So when the dawn came Binkity, instead of changing into a puppy again, slipped out of the cottage and ran back to his home in the woods.

'Oh, it's lovely to hear the birds again, and to talk to the rabbits!' said Binkity, thoroughly enjoying himself.

'Hullo, Binkity!' suddenly exclaimed a voice. Binkity turned round, and to his dismay found it was Ding, the chief Brownie.

'Oh, please don't send me to Arran the Spider!' he begged, kneeling down.

Ding smiled kindly. 'Why, Binkity,' he said, 'I'm ever so pleased with you! I know where you were all the winter, and I've often peeped into the cottage at night, and seen you scrubbing the floors.'

'Oh, have you?' cried Binkity, most astonished.

'Yes, often,' answered Ding. 'You used to be lazy and naughty, but you've learnt to work hard, and to help other people now. We're going to have a party tonight to welcome you back to Oak Tree Town again.'

'Oh, how lovely!' cried Binkity, delighted. He ran off to get himself clean and tidy, thinking it was really much more fun to be a good Brownie than a lazy one.

Jean was very astonished and sorry to find the little puppy was gone that morning, but her mother said it *must* have been a Brownie living with them. Binkity kept his word, and often used to go and visit the cottage and see that Jean was quite all right, and sometimes leave a shining gold piece under her pillow, for a surprise.

He's never lazy now, and if ever you come across a very neat and tidy wood, look about for Binkity. He's sure to be hiding somewhere about, watching you with his little twinkling eyes!

The Lost Golden Ball

There was great excitement in Fairyland. The Queen's heralds had just gone through the streets of the chief town, and blown on their silver trumpets, to say that every fairy was to go to the big market-place, and wait there for the Queen to come.

'Oyez, oyez, oyez!' they cried. 'Her Majesty wishes to speak with you all at half-past nine this morning!'

'What *can* it be about!' cried the excited fairies, gathering here and there in little crowds. 'Perhaps someone's been naughty. Or perhaps the Queen wants us to do something for her!'

'Ding, dong, ding, dong!' chimed all the bluebells suddenly.

'Quarter-past nine!' called the fairies to each other. 'Come along to the market-place, everybody. The Queen will be coming in a few minutes!'

Off flew fairies and elves, and off ran pixies, gnomes, and brownies as fast as ever they could. Presently a great crowd was gathered in the marketplace, all wondering what their Queen wanted them for.

'Ding, dong, ding, dong! Ding, dong, ding, dong!' chimed the bluebells round about.

'Half-past nine! Here she comes! Isn't she beautiful? Hip, hip, hurrah!' cheered the fairies as the Queen flew down to the throne set high in the middle of the market-place.

'Good-day to you all!' she said, in her clear silvery voice, when all the fairies were quiet and not a sound could be heard. 'I have come to ask your help. You all know that the Prince of Dreamland has been staying here, and has lately gone back to his own country.'

'Yes, yes, your Majesty!' answered the listening fairies.

'He carried with him a bright golden ball which had, closely hidden inside it, the secret of a new magic spell. It is a wonderful spell which he hoped would make his ill Princess well again. You all know she has been ill?'

'Yes, your Majesty, and we are very sorry,' called the fairies.

'On his way home,' went on the Queen, 'his carriage was drawn by six white rabbits. Suddenly a dog began barking in the distance, and the rabbits were so frightened that they ran away, and in their fear upset the carriage. In the confusion and muddle the golden ball was lost, and the

Prince of Dreamland cannot find it anywhere. Will you help to find it?'

'Oh yes, we'd love to, your Majesty!' answered all the fairies in great excitement.

'Very well. Go now, and seek for it,' commanded the Queen. 'You must find it today, for the spell inside the ball will be no use tomorrow. It must be used before the moon is full.'

Off went all the fairies, helter-skelter, through the woods and lanes.

'I shall look in all the long grass!' said Fairy Rosemary. 'I am sure I shall find it!'

'*I* shall look in all the little pools!' said a yellow pixie. 'It might easily have rolled into one, and be hidden there! Come along and help me, pixie-folk!'

'We are going to hunt in the squirrels' nests!' shouted the frolicking elves. 'We think the squirrels might have found it and hidden it!'

'Where are *you* going to look, Karin?' shouted the brownies, speaking to an ugly little gnome who was sitting on a mossy stone, thinking.

'I think I shall look under the gorse bushes,' said Karin.

'Pooh! Fancy looking there! You'll get pricked all over. You *are* a silly-billy,' sang the brownies, dancing round Karin and laughing.

Karin hated being laughed at. He was a shy

little gnome, ugly and clumsy. He couldn't do the dainty things his comrades did. He looked so funny when he tried to dance, that, although the fairies tried not to, they simply *couldn't* help laughing. And when he began to sing, everybody flew away as fast as they could. This hurt him very much.

'Why don't they love me and want to be with me?' he used to think sadly, going off by himself.

He was too shy to ask the other fairies and gnomes to be his friends and to like him. He was *much* too shy to tell them he loved them, and as nobody ever guessed what he thought, Karin was always left alone, for everyone thought he was cross and surly, and didn't want to make friends.

'Oh dear!' said Karin sadly to himself, as the brownies ran off to look for the golden ball. 'Why does everybody laugh at me and nobody want me to come with them. I *wish* I wasn't ugly and stupid!'

He wandered off by himself, looking for a gorse bush to peep underneath. He found one, and lay down in the grass to wriggle underneath it. It was very prickly and very horrid.

'Ha, ha, ha! Ho, ho, ho!' suddenly laughed someone. 'Karin the Gnome, what in the world

are you doing? Do you want to find out if prickles
are prickly?'

'Bother!' thought Karin, wriggling out again.
'Someone or other is *always* laughing at me.'

He sat up on the grass and brushed away the
bits of gorse that had clung to him. Then he
looked to see who had spoken.

It was Hoo, the White Owl. He was sitting on
a hazel tree, and looking very much amused.

'It isn't nice of you to laugh at me,' said Karin.
'I hate being laughed at. I was only looking for the
golden ball that the Prince of Dreamland lost.'

'A golden ball!' said Hoo. 'Well, now I believe *I* know where that is.'

'Oh, do tell me!' begged Karin excitedly. 'You can't *think* how I'd love to take it to the dear Queen.'

'Well, I'm sorry I laughed at you just now, if you didn't like it,' said Hoo. 'And to show you I'm sorry I'll tell you where I saw the golden ball.'

'Oh, thank you, thank you!' said Karin gratefully. 'Whisper in my ear, Hoo.'

So Hoo flew down and whispered in Karin's ear. 'As I flew by the heath the other night, I saw something gleaming in the moonlight. It was rolling along by itself, and I knew it was magic. I watched where it went, and I saw it roll down beneath a silver birch tree, under a piece of bracken by the bank where Greyears the rabbit lives. You will find it there!'

'Thank you, *ever* so much,' said Karin, jumping up excitedly.

'Tu-whit, tu-whit, don't mention it,' called Hoo, flying off silently into the trees.

'Hurrah! Hurrah! I'll find the ball! What fun!' thought Karin, running as hard as he could over the grass. The bank where Greyears lived was a long long way away, and he knew he would have to hurry.

He came to the heath. It was a big common called Hampstead Heath, stretching away in the distance. To Karin's surprise it was packed with crowds and crowds of people, some walking, some sitting, and some picnicking.

He hid behind a tree and watched. Although he didn't know it, it was Whit-Monday and everyone had come out into the sunshine, away from the shops, away from the busy towns, and from the stuffy offices. There were children everywhere, running, laughing and playing. Mothers sat here and there and fathers played cricket with the boys.

'Dear me, what a crowd of people!' thought Karin, 'and how happy they all look!'

He watched them for some time, then decided he must go on his way. He slipped from bush to bush and tree to tree, unseen, wrapping his green cloak closely round his red jacket and brown knickers. He passed many groups of happy children on his way across the heath, but none of them saw him.

As he glided behind a gorse bush, he stopped suddenly and slipped to the other side. There was a little girl behind it, sitting on the grass and crying. He didn't want her to see him. He was going on his way, when an extra large sob from the little girl stopped him.

'I wonder what's the matter with her!' said Karin to himself, peeping round the bush.

She was a dear little girl. She had short curly hair, big blue eyes filled with tears, and a crying, drooping mouth.

'I want my Mummy,' she kept saying. 'I want my Mummy! I'm so lonely, I *do* want my Mummy!'

Here was somebody else who was lonely besides Karin, and Karin, who knew how miserable it was to feel lonely was dreadfully sorry for the little girl. He wondered if his ugly face would frighten her if he spoke to her. He decided to try.

He slipped out from behind the gorse bush and stood in front of her. She looked up, surprised.

'Oh,' she said, 'what a *dear* little man! I'm sure you're a fairy, aren't you?'

Karin was so astonished to hear anyone call him a *dear* little man that he couldn't say anything, but just stood and smiled delightedly.

The little girl put up her hand and stroked him. 'I'm *so* glad to see you,' she said. 'I was just wishing a fairy or something would come and help me.'

'What's the matter with you?' asked Karin, finding his voice at last. 'I heard you crying!'

'Well, I'm lost!' said the little girl, her eyes filling with tears again. 'I'm Ann, and I've lost my

Mummy in all that crowd, and I can't find her.'

'I'm so sorry,' said Karin.

'But you'll find her for me, won't you?' said the little girl, cheering up. 'Fairies can do anything, you know!'

Karin stared at her. 'I'm afraid I can't stop any longer!' he said. 'You see, I'm doing something very important today. Else I *would* have stopped.'

The little girl began to cry again. 'Aren't I important too?' she sobbed. 'You aren't the nice kind fairy I thought you were. I'm *s'prised* at you. I really am!'

Karin couldn't bear to see her cry. He sat down by her and put his arms round her.

'Don't cry, little girl,' he said, 'I'll give my important business to somebody else to do, then I can stay and help you.'

'Oh, you *darling*,' said Ann, and kissed him. 'I love you ever-so.'

Karin was filled with delight to hear her say so. He never remembered hearing anyone say that to him before. He thought children must be simply lovely, if they went about loving everybody like that.

'I will be dreadfully disappointed not to find the golden ball and to let someone else get it,' he thought. 'But if this little girl wants me, I don't

mind giving up finding it—at least, I don't mind
very much!'

He told Ann to stay where she was, and running
to a pixie he saw by some bracken, he shouted
to him.

'Hoo told me where the golden ball was. It's
under the bracken by the birch tree growing near
the bank where Greyears lives!'

At once the pixie darted off delightedly, and
Karin returned to the little girl.

'I've told someone else my important business,'
he said. 'Now, tell me what your mother's like and
I'll go and find her.'

'She's got curly brown hair and kind eyes,' said
Ann, 'and she's got a lovely purple hat with big
red roses on it, and a purple coat!'

'Oh, I'll be sure to find her easily,' said Karin.
'Stay here till I come back.'

'I'll eat my dinner while you're gone,' said Ann,
opening a little basket of sandwiches. 'Would you
like some to take with you?'

'No, thank you,' said Karin. 'I don't think I
should like your food very much. You eat it all
yourself!'

'You *are* a kind little man,' said Ann, giving
him a hug. 'I really think you've got the kindest
face I ever saw.'

Karin was so delighted to hear anyone praise his ugly face and call it kind, that he almost shouted for joy. He ran off happily.

He searched and searched for a long time, but nowhere did he see a lady with a purple hat and red roses. There were plenty of red roses but no purple hats.

'Oh dear! Oh dear! I *must* find Ann's mother,' said Karin desperately. At last he went back to Ann, to see what she was doing.

She was fast asleep.

'I'll go and have another look,' said Karin, who was getting very tired of searching all over the crowded heath. 'I do hope I find her mother this time.'

As he wandered over the heath again, looking round him as he went, he suddenly saw a very sad-looking lady who was also looking all round *her* as she went. He looked at her hat. It was purple with red roses, and her coat was purple too! It must be Ann's mother.

Karin hurried up to her. 'Please,' he said, 'are you looking for Ann?'

'Yes, yes, I am!' answered the lady, not seeming at all surprised to see Karin. 'Oh, do you know where she is? Pray, pray take me to my little girl quickly! Is she all right?'

'Quite all right,' said Karin. 'Follow me.' He walked off quickly in the direction of Ann's gorse bush, and the mother followed closely behind. On the way a pixie popped his head from behind a piece of bracken and called to Karin:

'I went to the bank where Greyears lives, but I couldn't find the golden ball, Karin.'

'Oh, I'm sorry. I expect someone else found it!' answered Karin, hurrying on.

At last they reached the place where Ann was. She was just waking up. As she heard their footsteps, she looked up and saw her mother.

'Mummy! Mummy!' she cried, flinging herself into her mother's arms. 'Oh, Mummy, I'm so glad it's you. I lost you and I've been so lonely!'

The mother clasped her little girl close, as though she would never let her go, and kissed her curly head again and again.

'That dear, kind little man helped me!' said Ann. 'Oh, you dear fairy, I want to give you something. I found it this morning, and it's *ever* so pretty. I'd love to keep it for myself, but I want to give it to you because you've been so nice and I love you. Look!' and she took something from her little basket and held it out to Karin.

It was the Prince of Dreamland's lost golden ball!

'I found it under some bracken by a birch tree!' said the little girl. 'I want *you* to have it, Karin.'

Karin was so astonished and delighted that he could hardly say thank you. He gave Ann a hug, took the ball, said goodbye, and ran off as fast as he could, thinking that surely children were the very nicest things in all the world.

He ran and ran and ran, hoping he would get to the market-place where all the fairies were to meet, before it was too late. As he came near, he saw hundreds of fairy-folk gathered there and the Queen was speaking.

'Thank you all for looking,' she was saying. 'I am dreadfully sorry nobody found the golden ball, but I expect one of the crowd of people who came to Hampstead Heath today found it instead. I do wish I knew where it was.'

'Here it is! Here it is!' suddenly called an excited voice. All the fairies turned and saw Karin making his way to the Queen, holding in his right hand a wonderful golden ball.

'Karin! Karin's got it! Fancy, Karin's found it!' cried all the fairies to each other.

'Oh, Karin, how lovely!' said the Queen gladly. 'Where *did* you get it?'

Then Karin knelt down and told all the story of the day's happenings.

'You have done well!' said the Queen. 'You gave up something you wanted for the sake of a little girl, and lo and behold, the little girl gave you what you thought you had given up—the golden ball! It was a good reward for unselfishness. Now tell me, what wish shall I grant you for bringing me the golden ball!'

'Oh, please, your Majesty, let me go and play on Hampstead Heath with the children!' begged Karin. 'I believe they'd love me, and I *do* so want to be loved. I don't think they'd mind my ugly face. And I'd love to find their mothers for them when they're lost!'

The Queen smiled. 'We'll all love you, now we know you want to be loved,' she said. 'Yes, you may go and live on Hampstead Heath and look after the children there, Karin!'

And Karin can be found there to this very day. No child need fear being lost, for Karin will be sure to help him somehow, whether the child sees him or not! He is as happy as can be, for all the children love him, and he is happiest of all on Bank Holidays, for then he has so many children to look after, he hardly knows where to begin!

Pinkity and
Old Mother Ribbony Rose

Once upon a time there lived an old witch called Mother Ribbony Rose. She kept a shop just on the borders of Fairyland, and because she sold such lovely things, the fairies allowed her to live there in peace.

She was very, very old, and very, very clever, but she wasn't very good. She was never kind to her neighbour, the Bee-Woman, and never helped the Balloon-Man, who lived across the road, and who was often very poor indeed when no one came to buy his lovely balloons.

But her shop was simply lovely. She sold ribbons, but they weren't just ordinary ribbons. There were blue ribbons, made of the mist that hangs over faraway hills, and sea-green ribbons embroidered with the diamond sparkles that glitter on sunny water. There were big broad ribbons of shiny silk, and tiny delicate ribbons of frosted spider's thread, and wonderful ribbons that tied their own bows.

The fairies and elves loved Mother Ribbony Rose's shop, and often used to come and buy there, whenever a fairy dance was going to be held and they wanted pretty things to wear.

One day Mother Ribbony Rose was very busy indeed.

'Good morning, Fairy Jasmin,' she said, as a tall fairy, dressed in yellow, came into her shop. 'What can I get you today?'

'Good morning, Mother Ribbony Rose,'

answered Jasmin politely. She didn't like the old witch a bit, but that didn't make any difference, she was always polite to her. 'I would like to see the newest yellow ribbon you have, please, to match the dress I've got on today.'

Mother Ribbony Rose pulled out a drawer full of yellow ribbons. Daffodil-yellows, orange-yellows, primrose-yellows, and all shining like gold.

'Here's a beauty!' said she, taking up a broad ribbon. 'Would you like that?'

'No, thank you,' answered Jasmin, 'I want something narrower.'

The witch pulled out another drawer and scattered the ribbons on the counter.

'Ah, here's one I like ever so!' exclaimed Jasmin, lifting up a long thin piece of yellow ribbon, just the colour of her dress. 'How much is it?'

'Two pieces of gold,' answered Mother Ribbony Rose.

'Oh dear, you're terribly expensive,' sighed Jasmin as she paid the money and took the ribbon.

Mother Ribbony Rose looked at all the dozens of ribbons scattered over the counter.

'Pinkity, Pinkity, Pinkity,' she called in a sharp voice.

Out of the back of the shop came a tiny gnome.

'Roll up all these ribbons quickly, before anyone

else comes in,' ordered Mother Ribbony Rose, going into the garden.

Pinkity began rolling them up one by one. He did it beautifully, and so quickly that it was a marvel to watch him.

When all the ribbons were done, he went to the window and looked out. He saw fairies, gnomes, and pixies playing in the fields and meadows.

'Oh dear, dear, dear!' suddenly said Pinkity in a woebegone voice. 'How I would love to go and play with the fairies. I'm so *tired* of rolling up ribbons.' A large tear rolled down his cheek, and dropped with a splash on the floor.

'What's the matter, Pinkity?' suddenly asked a little voice.

Pinkity jumped and looked round. He saw a tiny fairy who had come into the shop and was waiting to be served.

'I'm so tired of doing nothing but roll up ribbons all day,' explained Pinkity.

'Well, why don't you do something else?' asked the fairy.

'That's the worst of it. I've never done anything else all my life but roll up ribbons in Mother Ribbony's shop, and I *can't* do anything else. I can't paint, I can't dance, and I can't sing! All the other fairies would laugh at me if I went to play

with them, for I wouldn't even know *how* to play!'
sobbed Pinkity.

'Oh yes, you would! Come and try,' said the
little fairy, feeling very sorry for the lonely little
gnome.

'Come and try! Come and try *what?*' suddenly
said Mother Ribbony's voice, as she came in at
the door.

'I was just asking Pinkity if he would come
and play with us,' answered the little fairy, feeling
rather afraid of the witch's cross looks.

Mother Ribbony Rose snorted.

'Pinkity belongs to *me*,' she said, 'and he's much
too busy in the shop, rolling up my beautiful
ribbons all day, to have time to go and play with
you. Besides, no one is allowed in Fairyland unless
they can do some sort of work, and Pinkity can
do nothing but roll up ribbons! I'm the only
person who would keep him for that, for no one in
Fairyland keeps a ribbon shop.' And the old witch
pulled one of Pinkity's big ears.

'I should run away,' whispered the little fairy to
Pinkity when her back was turned.

'I wish I could! But I've nowhere to run to!'
whispered back Pinkity in despair.

At that moment there came the sound of
carriage wheels down the cobbled street, and old

Mother Ribbony Rose poked her head out to see who it was.

'Mercy on us! It's the Lord High Chancellor of Fairyland, and he's coming here! Make haste, Pinkity, and get a chair for him!' cried the old witch, in a great flurry.

Sure enough it was.

The Chancellor strode into the shop, very tall and handsome, and sat down in the chair.

'Good morning,' he said. 'The King and Queen are holding a dance tonight, and they are going to make the wood gay with ribbons and hang fairy lamps on them. The Queen has asked me to come and choose the ribbons for her. Will you show me some, please?'

'Certainly, certainly, your Highness!' answered Mother Ribbony Rose, pulling out drawer after drawer of gay ribbons. Pinkity sighed as he watched her unroll ribbon after ribbon, and show it to the Chancellor.

'Oh dear! I'm sure it will take me hours and *hours* to roll up all that ribbon!' he thought to himself sadly.

'This is wonderful ribbon!' said the Chancellor admiringly. 'I'll have fifty yards of this and fifty yards of that. Oh, and I'll have a hundred yards of this glorious silver ribbon! It's just like moonlight.

And send a hundred yards of this pink ribbon, please, too, and I'll have a ribbon archway with mauve lamps made, leading from the Palace to the wood. The Queen will be delighted!'

'Certainly!' answered the witch, feeling excited to think of all the gold she would get for such a lot of ribbon. 'The pink ribbon is very expensive, your Highness. It's made of pink sunset clouds, mixed with almond blossom. I've only just got a hundred yards left!'

'That will just do,' said the Chancellor, getting up to go. 'Send it all to the Palace, please. And don't forget the *pink* ribbon, it's most important, *most* important!'

And off the Chancellor went to his carriage again.

Mother Ribbony Rose, who cared for gold more than she cared for anything else in the world, rubbed her hands together with delight.

'Now then, Pinkity!' she called. 'Come here and roll up all this ribbon I've been showing to the Chancellor, and measure out all that he wants!'

Pinkity began rolling up the ribbon. He did it as quickly as ever he could, but even then it took him a long time. He measured out all the many yards that the Chancellor wanted, and folded them neatly. Then he got some paper and began to make out the bill.

'Hullo,' said Pinkity, 'the inkpot's empty. I must get the ink bottle down and fill it!'

He climbed up to the shelf where the big bottle of black ink was kept, and took hold of it.

But alas! Poor Pinkity slipped, and down fell the big bottle of ink on to the counter, where all the Chancellor's ribbon was neatly folded in piles! The cork came out, and before Pinkity knew what was happening all the ink upset itself on to the lovely ribbon, and stained it black in great patches.

In came old Mother Ribbony Rose.

'Pinkity! Pinkity! Look what you've done! And I haven't any more of that pink ribbon! You did it on purpose, I know you did, you naughty, naughty little gnome!' stormed the witch, stamping up and down.

Pinkity was dreadfully frightened. He was so frightened that, without thinking what he was doing, he jumped clean through the window and ran away!

He ran and ran and ran.

Then he lay down beneath a hedge and rested. Then he ran and ran and ran again, until it was night.

At last he came to a beautiful garden, lit by the

moon, and quite empty, save for lovely flowers. It was the Queen's garden, but Pinkity did not know it.

'I'm free! I'm free!' cried Pinkity, throwing his hat in the air. 'There's a dear little hole beneath this rock, and I'll hide there, and I'll NEVER go back to Mother Ribbony Rose.'

He crept beneath the rock, shut his eyes and fell fast asleep.

Next morning he heard fairies in the garden, and they were all talking excitedly.

'Yes, it was a naughty little gnome called Pinkity, who spoilt all the Queen's lovely ribbon,' said one fairy.

'Yes, and he did it on purpose, old Mother Ribbony Rose says. Just fancy that!' said another.

'And the Chancellor says if anyone catches him, they're to take him to the Palace to be punished, and given back to Mother Ribbony Rose,' said a third.

Pinkity lay and listened, and felt the tears rolling down his cheeks. He had so hoped that perhaps the fairies would help him.

All that day Pinkity hid, and at night he crept out into the lovely garden, and the flowers gave him honey to eat, for they were sorry for him.

For a long time Pinkity hid every day and only

came out at night. One day he heard a group of fairy gardeners near by, talking hard.

'What *are* we to do about those little ferns?' they said. 'Directly they come up, their tiny fronds are spread out, and the frost *always* comes and bites them, and then they look horrid. It's just the same with the bracken over there!'

'It's so difficult to fold the fronds up tightly,' said the fern fairies. 'They *will* keep coming undone!'

'Well, we *must* think of something,' said the gardeners decidedly. 'The Queen simply loves her fernery, and she will be so upset if the frost bites the ferns again this year. Let's go and ask the rose gardeners if they can give us any hints.'

That night Pinkity went over to the baby ferns and bracken and looked at them carefully. It was a very frosty night, and they looked very cold and pinched.

'I know! I know!' cried Pinkity, clapping his hands. 'I'll *roll* them up like ribbons, and then they'll be quite warm and safe, and won't come undone till the frost is gone!'

So Pinkity started rolling each fern frond up carefully. It wasn't as easy as rolling ribbon, for the fronds had lots of little bits to tuck in, but he worked hard and managed it beautifully. The baby ferns were very grateful, and so was the bracken.

'Thank you, thank you,' they murmured. 'We love being rolled up, and we're much warmer now.'

Pinkity worked all night, and just as daylight came, he finished the very last piece of bracken and ran back to his hole to hide.

At six o'clock along came the gardeners. They stared and stared and stared at the ferns.

'Whatever has happened to them!' cried they in amazement. 'They're rolled up just like ribbon!'

'What a splendid idea!' said the Head Gardener. 'But who did it? Someone very kind and very clever must have done it!'

'*Who* did it? *Who* did it?' cried everyone.

Pinkity, trembling with excitement, crept out of his hiding-place.

'If you please,' he said, '*I* did it!'

'Why, Pinkity! It's Pinkity, the naughty little gnome!' cried the fairies.

'I wasn't really naughty,' said Pinkity. 'The ink spilt by accident on the ribbon. I wouldn't have spoilt the dear Queen's ribbon for anything in the world.'

'Well, you've been so kind to our ferns,' said the fairies, 'that we believe you. But how *did* you learn to be so clever, Pinkity?'

'I'm not clever *really*,' said Pinkity, 'but I can roll up ribbons nicely—it's the only thing I *can* do—so it was easy to roll up the ferns.'

The fairies liked the shy little gnome, and took him in to breakfast with them. In the middle of it in walked Her Majesty the Queen!

'*Who* has looked after my baby ferns?' she asked in a pleased voice.

'Pinkity has! Pinkity has!' cried the fairies, pushing Pinkity forward. Then they told the Queen all about him.

'It was quite an accident that your lovely ribbon was spoilt,' said Pinkity, 'and I was dreadfully sorry, your Majesty.'

'I'm quite *sure* it was an accident,' said the Queen kindly, 'and I have found out that all Mother Ribbony Rose cares about is gold, so I am sending her right away from Fairyland, and you need never go back!'

'Oh, how lovely!' cried Pinkity joyfully.

'Your Majesty! Let him look after the ferns and bracken, and teach other fairies how to roll up the baby ones!' begged the fairies. 'He *is* so clever at it.'

'Will you do that for us, Pinkity?' said the Queen.

'Oh, your Majesty, I would *love* it!' answered Pinkity joyfully, feeling happier than ever he had been in his life before.

He began his work that very day, and always and always now you will find that fern fronds are rolled up as tight as can be, just like the ribbon Pinkity rolled up at the ribbon shop.

As for old Mother Ribbony Rose, she was driven right away from Fairyland, and sent to live in the Land of Deep Regrets, and nobody has ever heard of her since.

The Floppety Castle and the Goblin Cave

Once upon a time there was a little boy who wandered into Fairyland quite by mistake.

'Goodness me!' he said to himself. 'Wherever have I got to?'

'Why, you're in Fairyland, of course,' said a tiny voice. 'What's your name?'

'My name's David,' answered the little boy, looking round for the voice.

'Well, here I am, David,' laughed the voice; 'down here, in a buttercup.'

David looked and saw a tiny blue fairy standing up in a buttercup.

'How tiny you are!' he said. 'Please, could you tell me the way out of Fairyland?'

'Why, David, what a funny boy you are! It isn't many children who go to Fairyland, and now you are lucky enough to be here, why don't you look round and see some of the wonderful things?' asked the little fairy, swinging himself in the buttercup.

'Oh, I'd love to,' said David. 'Do tell me which way to go.'

'Well, I should go to that cottage over there, if I were you, and ask for Tom the Piper's Son. He'll go round with you, and show you things,' answered the fairy.

'Yes, I will. Goodbye,' said David. And off he ran.

When he reached the little cottage, he knocked at the door. A boy, dressed in a blue coat and purple knickers, opened it. 'Please, are you Tom the Piper's Son?' asked David.

'Yes,' answered Tom, staring at David. 'What do you want?'

'I've just come to Fairyland,' said David, 'and I'm wondering if you'd show me some of the wonderful things here.'

'Certainly,' answered Tom, looking pleased. 'Just wait till I get my pig.' He ran in, and in a minute came out, carrying a little fat pig under his arm.

David wanted to ask if the pig was the one that Tom stole, but he didn't quite like to. The pig blinked at him, and grunted.

'Now, what shall we see first?' said Tom. 'How would you like to see the Floppety Castle?'

'I'd *love* to,' said David, thinking it sounded lovely.

'All right,' said Tom, putting the pig down.

'Now then, get on his back and hold tight. He'll take us there in a jiffy.'

David was rather astonished, but he got on the pig. The little animal didn't seem to mind their weight at all. He trotted off at a great pace. Presently a queer looking castle came in sight.

'There's the Floppety Castle,' said Tom.

'Why is it called that?' asked David, holding on more tightly to the pig, who was going faster.

'Ah, ha! You'll see when you get there!' said Tom. 'It's a great joke, I can tell you!'

When they reached the castle gate. Tom picked up the pig again and carried him. Into the castle they went.

'I'll wait for you here,' said Tom, and stopped by the door.

David wandered in, looking around him as he went. There were curious pictures of kings and queens on the walls, with heads at the top and at the bottom too. Presently he came to a gnome writing at a table.

'Oh, don't shake, don't shake!' cried the gnome, looking up. 'What clumsy feet you have! You'll bring the castle down, if you don't look out!'

'Don't be silly,' said David, 'I couldn't possibly!' And off he went to another room. Here he found a lot of little gnomes busily sorting out a pile of old books. There were so many left about the floor that David tripped over one and fell bang! on the ground.

'Oh, oh!' cried the gnomes, looking terrified. 'How clumsy you are! You'll break the castle to bits!'

'Why do you say that?' asked David, picking himself up.

'Well, it's only a card castle, you know,' answered the gnomes.

'Goodness me!' said David, looking round. 'How very dangerous! Oh, so that's why there are such funny king and queen pictures on the walls. They're cards!'

David quickly turned to go back to Tom, and ran out of the room, feeling that at any moment such a wobbly sort of castle might fall to bits.

But alas! As he ran, he bumped into a passage wall, and crash! clitter-clatter! Down came the Floppety Castle on top of him! When it had stopped falling, David blinked his eyes, and looked round him. There was nothing but a great mass of higgledy-piggledy cards lying about. The gnomes were busy setting some of them up again.

'Oh dear, oh dear!' cried one. 'That's the third time this week that the castle has fallen down!'

'Well, why do you build it of such silly things?'

asked David, feeling rather cross with fright. 'You know it will only fall down again.'

'Oh, hush!' said Tom, who came up just then. 'You'll hurt their feelings. Do you know why it is called "Floppety Castle" now, David?'

'Oh yes!' said David, beginning to laugh. 'It's really rather funny, you know, to go into a castle and knock it all down!'

'Come on with me,' said Tom, still carrying his pig. 'We'll leave the gnomes to build their castle again.'

He went off with David, talking merrily. Suddenly he stopped and said:

'David! There's the butcher coming that I stole the pig from! Let's run away, quick!'

Off he went, as fast as he could, and David followed him. The butcher saw them, and chased after them, shouting.

Tom jumped over a hedge, and popped a purple berry into his mouth.

'Quick!' he said. 'Eat one, David!'

David ate one—and found himself growing smaller and smaller until he was just as small as the daisies in the grass.

Tom ran down a hole in the bank, and pulled David after him just as the butcher jumped over the hedge.

'Wherever have they vanished to!' they heard him exclaim in wonder.

'I think you ought to have given him the pig back,' said David after a while.

'Bless you, *this* isn't his pig! That's eaten long ago! This is my own pig, but whenever that butcher sees me, he remembers the pig I took long ago, and chases after me to whip me!' explained Tom, hugging his pig under his arm.

'Oh, I see,' said David, feeling glad the pig really wasn't a stolen one. 'Where are we going to?'

'I don't know,' answered Tom. 'The goblins live down here, but they know me, so I don't think we shall come to any harm.'

They soon heard a hammering and a clattering, and came to a great cave, lighted by big star-shaped lamps. In the cave sat hundreds of goblins, making glittering things.

'Why, they're brooches and necklaces!' cried David. 'How lovely they are!'

The goblins looked up and smiled. 'Thank you for those kind words, little Master,' said the chief. 'Choose which you will have.'

'Oh, thank you!' cried David. 'I'd like that tiny brooch shaped like a star, to take home for my mother, please.'

'Here you are!' said the chief gnome, fastening it on his coat. 'It is a magic brooch, and has two wishes for the wearer.'

'How lovely!' said David, as he went out of the cave with Tom and the pig.

Soon the three were quite lost. Cave after cave they wandered through, some brightly lighted, some quite dark. At last, in despair, Tom said, 'Oh, use one of your magic brooch wishes, David! Rub it and wish.'

'That's a good idea!' said David. He rubbed the little brooch. 'I wish we could find our way out,' he said loudly.

Immediately there came a little fluttering sound by them, and David saw an elf, dressed in blue and with mauve wings.

'Come with me!' she cried, and led them up a long dark passage into the open air again.

'Goodbye!' she called, and left them.

'Eat some berries, David, to make you big again,' said Tom, giving one to his pig.

'Oh, it does feel funny to grow big suddenly!' said David. 'It's like going up in a lift! Wherever are we now? I say, the sun is setting and I *must* go home. Do tell me the way, Tom.'

'I don't know it,' said Tom, putting down his pig, 'I'm lost too. Why don't you wish yourself home? You've got another wish. I'm going to get on my pig. He *always* knows the way back to my cottage. Goodbye. See you again another day, perhaps!' And Tom and the pig galloped off, and were soon lost to sight.

'It must be rather nice to have a pig like that,' thought David. 'Now I'll use my last wish. I *wish* I were home again.' And he rubbed the brooch. 'Why, goodness gracious! How *did* I get here? I'm at my front gate, and there's Mother looking for me,' he exclaimed a moment later, rubbing his eyes.

His mother *was* astonished to hear where he had been, and she simply loved the starry brooch that the goblins made. She always wears it at David's parties, and then he tells the other children of all the lovely things he did with Tom the Piper's Son in Fairyland.

Two Fairy Wishes

Jack and Ann were digging in the garden. Ann's spade suddenly struck something hard.

'Oh, Jack!' she said, in an excited voice. 'My spade knocked something! Do you think it is a box of gold?'

'Perhaps it is,' said Jack. 'Dig it up quickly and see.'

Ann dug it up. It was not a box, but a big bottle with a cork. Jack took the bottle and looked at it. Then he pulled the cork out, and

CRASH! BANG! PHIZZ-z-z-z! !

What do you think came out of it? Why, a great long fairy with wings and a crown!

Jack and Ann were too afraid to speak at first. Then the fairy said:

'I have been a prisoner in that bottle for a hundred years. I am very grateful to you both for making me free again; a bad witch put me there, and I could not get out. What would you like me to do for you?'

'Oh,' said Jack, 'could you give us a wish each? We should so like to wish for something and know it would come true.'

'Very well,' said the fairy. He waved his wand, and said some queer, magic words. 'There!' he said. 'I have given you one wish each. Be careful what you wish. Goodbye!' And away he flew.

Ann and Jack were so excited and happy. 'What shall we wish?' asked Ann. 'Let's ask for something lovely, like wings to fly with.'

'Let's think hard,' said Jack. They both sat down and began to think of all the lovely things they wanted.

Then Nurse came down the path towards them. 'Come along, children,' she called. 'It's tea-time, and you must wash your hands.'

'Oh, Nurse, we *can't* come yet,' Jack called back.

'Yes, dear, you must come at once,' said Nurse firmly.

'Oh, I *wish* you'd go right away!' said Jack in a temper.

And all at once, in front of their eyes, Nurse was swished right away into the air! Jack had forgotten that he was wishing. The fairy had promised that whatever he wished should come true, and so it had. Poor Nurse was taken right away somewhere.

Jack and Ann were very unhappy and afraid.

They ran in to tell Mummy all about it, and to ask her what they should do. Mummy looked very sorry and said she hoped Nurse was not feeling unhappy too.

'Did you say the fairy gave you a wish each?' she asked.

'Yes,' said Jack.

'Then Ann has still her wish left. You must

wish for Nurse to be brought back again,' said Mummy.

'Oh, yes,' said Ann, 'of course I can. I *wish* that Nurse would come back again to us,' she said in a loud voice.

And there was Nurse walking into the room! How glad they all were to see her, and Jack said he didn't mind losing the two wishes a bit, now that Nurse had come back again!

The Green Necklace

'Oh dear me!' cried Marjorie sadly. 'I've lost my dear little green necklace! Wherever can it be?'

She ran up and down the field and looked and looked, but it was all no use, she couldn't find the necklace.

'What are you looking for?' asked a deep voice.

Marjorie looked all round in astonishment. Then she saw a large white owl sitting on a gate looking solemnly at her.

'Did you speak?' she asked in astonishment.

'Yes,' answered the owl, blinking. 'I'm Hoo, the White Owl, and I belong to Fairyland. Who are you?'

'I'm Marjorie, and I've lost my green necklace,' Marjorie explained.

'A necklace did you say? Oh, I know who took that,' said Hoo.

'Do you?' cried Marjorie. 'Do tell me who it was!'

'Well, it was a fairy called Briony,' said Hoo. 'He was polishing up the beetles in this field, and suddenly saw your necklace. He was so pleased with it that he took it straight off to Fairyland. He'll give it back if you ask him.'

'Oh, thank you for telling me,' said Marjorie. 'Could you tell me how to find Briony?'

'Certainly,' said Hoo, spreading his big wings. 'Do you see that mushroom growing down there? Well, break off a piece and rub it between your hands. Say "Acrall-da-farray" three times, and see what happens. Goodbye and good luck!' And off went Hoo into the trees.

Marjorie quickly broke a piece off the mushroom and rubbed it between her fingers.

'Acrall-da-farray! Acrall-da-farray! Acrall-da-farray!' she said loudly.

Then suddenly a great wind came round about her, and she gasped for breath and shut her eyes.

'Goodness!' she cried when she opened them again. 'Why, I'm not even as tall as that mushroom! How small I've gone!'

She found she was standing in the middle of a tiny little path. She followed it for some way, between grasses which waved above her head, until she came to a large toadstool. To her surprise, it had a little door, two windows, and a tiny chimney at the top! Lying in the grass was a small ladder.

Marjorie took the ladder and propped it up

against the toadstool. Then she ran up the little sloping ladder and knocked at the door.

'Come in!' cried a voice.

Marjorie opened the door and looked inside. She saw, sitting by the fire, a pixie with large ears and tiny wings. He was playing tunes on a long flutelike pipe.

'Good morning,' said Marjorie politely. 'Could you tell me where I can find Briony?'

'No, I can't,' answered the pixie, 'but if you go to the Big Sleepy Sloo, he'll soon tell you. He's a great friend of Briony's.'

'Where does the Big Sleepy Sloo live?' asked Marjorie, wondering whatever such a creature was like.

'He lives down in the Glittering Cavern,' answered the pixie, getting up. 'I'll show you the way.'

He lifted a mat up from the floor and uncovered a trap-door. He pulled it up, and Marjorie saw a long slanting passage stretching downwards.

'I'll just play a tune on my pipe,' said the pixie.

'What for?' asked Marjorie.

'Well, the only thing that ever wakes the Big Sleepy Sloo is music!' explained the pixie. 'He likes *my* music best of all. I'm the Pixie Piper.'

He put his long pipe to his mouth and blew.

Marjorie thought she had never heard such sweet music. It was like the rippling stream and the rustling trees.

'There!' he said at last. 'He'll be awake now. Sit down and slide. You can't walk down such a slippery passage.'

Marjorie stepped over the trap-door and sat down at the top of the passage. The Pixie Piper gave her a push and down she went, whizzing along at a tremendous pace. Gradually she slid more and more slowly, and in the distance she could see something bright and dazzling.

'I expect that's the Glittering Cavern,' she said. 'I hope Big Sleepy Sloo is awake.'

She slid straight into a large, shiny cave. All the walls glittered and sparkled, and the floor shone like gold. In the middle sat a queer mouse-like creature, blinking its eyes and yawning.

'Hullo!' he said. 'I thought it was the Pixie Piper coming down. What do you want?'

'Please can you tell me where Briony is?' asked Marjorie.

'Yes. He's gone to the Simple Witch to learn how to turn his legs into a tail when he wants to,' answered the Sleepy Sloo. 'He's thinking of staying with the mermaids for a bit.'

'How can I get to the Simple Witch?' asked

Marjorie, beginning to feel she would never find Briony.

'Catch the next train that comes along here,' said the Sloo, pointing to one end of the cave. To Marjorie's astonishment she saw a little pair of rails!

Then puff, puff, puff! Choo, choo, choo! It sounded as if a train were coming already. Sure enough there was! The queerest little engine suddenly appeared, dragging two carriages. It stopped just in the cave.

'Any passengers?' called the engine-driver.

'Yes!' cried Marjorie, hurrying across and jumping into a carriage.

'Get out at Breezy Hill!' shouted the Sleepy Sloo. 'Goodbye!'

'Goodbye!' called Marjorie, sitting down on a fat yellow cushion as there were no seats.

Off went the train into a dark passage. There were only two other passengers. One was a goblin reading a large Fairyland newspaper, and he never spoke a word the whole time. The other was a fat, grey mole, who sat on two cushions.

'Where are you going?' he asked.

'To the Simple Witch,' answered Marjorie. 'Where are *you* going?'

'To the Fiddlestick Field,' said the mole, and fell fast asleep.

The train stopped at a wooden platform on which the name 'Goblin Corner' was painted. The goblin folded up his newspaper and jumped out. On went the train and suddenly came out into green fields and sunshine. The next station was Fiddlestick Field, and Marjorie shook the sleeping mole.

'Get out,' she cried. He woke up suddenly and

climbed out *just* in time, without even saying thank you!

'Well, I don't think much of goblins and moles!' said Marjorie as the train went on.

It climbed up a steep hill, and stopped on the very top. A strong wind blew all round.

'I'm sure this is Breezy Hill!' said Marjorie, and looking out she saw it was.

She jumped out and wondered which way she should go. Then seeing a round hut a little way off, she went up to it, and knocked on the door.

'Come in!' cried a voice.

Marjorie walked in and found an old, old woman stirring something in a pot over a fire. In a corner sat a fairy.

'Good morning,' said Marjorie. 'Is this where the Simple Witch lives?'

'Yes. *I'm* the Simple Witch,' said the old woman, 'and that is Briony.'

'Oh, I'm *so* glad I've found you at last!' cried Marjorie. 'Please, will you give me back my green necklace you found this morning?'

'Rog the Giant has got it,' said Briony. 'I'm so sorry. I gave it to him this morning. Never mind. Would you like a mermaid's tail instead?'

'Oh no, thank you,' said Marjorie. 'I'd much rather keep my own legs.'

'I'm just learning how to get a tail,' said Briony proudly. 'It's great fun. But hark! That sounds like Rog!'

They all ran outside. There stood a huge giant, crying great tears and sobbing bitterly.

'It's broken!' he cried. 'It's broken!'

'Oh dear! He's broken your necklace,' said Briony. 'He wore it as a ring, you know. It just fitted his little finger nicely!'

'Never mind,' shouted the Simple Witch to Rog. 'I'll give you a magic pin instead.'

The giant stopped crying and smiled. Marjorie thought he must be very stupid to cry so easily.

'Where did the necklace break?' she asked Rog. 'In the field,' answered Rog, pointing. Marjorie ran into the field near-by and there, just by the gate, she found her broken necklace. She quickly picked it up and found the beads which had rolled here and there. Then she turned to go back to Briony.

'Good gracious! Where have they all gone?' she cried. 'And where is the Simple Witch's hut?'

'Why, it's the field where I lost my necklace this morning!' she exclaimed.

'Tu-whit, tu-whit!' said someone by her, and turning round, she saw Hoo, the White Owl, sitting on the gate.

'Oh, *do* tell me how I got here like this?' Marjorie begged him, quite puzzled.

'Tu-whit, tu-whit!' answered the owl. And not another word would he say.

'Well, anyway, I've got my necklace back!' said Marjorie, laughing, and ran off home.

A Fairy Punishment

There was once a little girl called Peggy, who didn't always tell the truth. There came a day when she did a foolish and a dangerous thing—she told an untruth to a fairy!

She was playing in the garden, when she saw something lying on the ground.

'Whatever is it?' cried Peggy, as she picked it up. 'Oh, it's a dear little fairy hat! I'll keep it for one of my dolls to wear!' She put it into her pocket, and was just going up the path to fetch her doll, when along came a fairy.

'Please, have you seen my hat anywhere in your garden?' she asked. 'It must have fallen off somewhere about here.'

Now Peggy badly wanted that little hat for her doll. 'Oh no!' she said boldly. 'I haven't seen your hat anywhere.'

Suddenly there arose a faint singing noise from all the flowers round about.

'She has! She has! She has!' they whispered. 'It's in her pocket, look and see.'

Peggy was very frightened when she heard

the flowers speaking and telling the truth. She took the hat from her pocket, and flung it on the ground.

'There's your old hat,' she said angrily.

'Oh, Peggy, did you tell me an untruth?' asked the fairy sadly. 'Don't you know what happens when a mortal child tells an untruth to a fairy?'

'No, I don't know and I don't care!' answered Peggy rudely.

The fairy waved her wand. Immediately there appeared four little gnomes, who caught hold of Peggy, and marched her off down the garden path, singing a queer song:

'To the Land of Pretence she must go,
And there she will more truthful grow.'

Peggy struggled hard to get free and run away, but it was of no use, she couldn't, and at last the gnomes came to the garden wall.

Peggy suddenly saw a door in the wall that she was *sure* had never been there before. The door slowly opened, and Peggy and the four gnomes entered. Instead of going into the field which Peggy knew lay on the other side of the wall, they went down a long narrow passage, lit by swinging lamps.

'Here's Fairyland,' said the gnomes, as they came to the end of the passage and stepped into a cool wood where fairies, pixies, and elves flew about and peeped at them from behind every tree and flower.

The gnomes marched Peggy steadily through the wood, until they came to a wide river on which rocked a yellow boat. Sitting in the boat was a beautiful fairy, dressed in pure white, with silver wings. She had clear blue eyes and the loveliest smile in the world.

'Here is Peggy, Your Highness,' said the four gnomes, bowing low.

'Get into the boat,' said the fairy to Peggy. Peggy stepped into it. The four gnomes turned, waved goodbye, and ran off through the wood.

'Where are you taking me?' asked Peggy.

'To the Land of Pretence,' answered the fairy, as the boat slid off down the river.

'But I don't want to go there, I want to go home!' said poor Peggy, beginning to cry.

'You can go home when you have learnt that truth is the only thing that matters,' said the fairy sternly. 'You have told untruths to your mother and to your nurse, and to your school-fellows, and your teachers. They have all believed you. Now you are going to a land where you will speak the truth and *nobody will believe you!*'

'Then I shan't speak the truth if nobody will believe me!' wept Peggy.

'I am Fairy Truth,' said the fairy. 'If you ever want my help come and look for me by the river.'

'I never want to see you again,' sobbed Peggy. 'I think you're horrid, horrid, horrid! I'll *never* come and look for you.'

Just then the boat bumped against a little landing-place.

'Here you are,' said Fairy Truth. 'Jump out, Peggy.'

Peggy jumped out without another word, and ran down the little path that led away from the river.

Coming towards her was a band of gaudily dressed little creatures, half-fairies and half-dwarfs.

'Are you Peggy?' they asked. 'If you are, we've come to take you to our Palace to stay with us.'

Peggy thought that would be very nice. 'Yes, I am Peggy,' she answered.

The little creatures looked at her.

Then they pointed their fingers at her and laughed.

'No, you're not! No, you're not! We don't believe you! Your eyes are red, and you've come from the Land of Cry Babies! You're not Peggy, you're a Cry Baby!' they shouted.

Peggy turned and ran right away from them. She ran and ran until she came to a little blue house in the middle of a wood.

She knocked at the door.

'Come in,' said a voice. Peggy went in. She saw three little old women, sitting by the fire, knitting red stockings.

'Who are you?' they asked.

'I'm Peggy, and I've come from the land of boys and girls,' said Peggy.

'We don't believe you,' said the old women. 'We believe you're a naughty runaway fairy. You can stay with us if you do our housework for us.'

'Oh dear!' thought Peggy. 'Fairy Truth *said* no one would believe me if I spoke the truth, and no one will. How I wish I'd never told an untruth!'

Peggy stayed with the three old women, and was soon busy making their beds and dusting the room for them.

'Have you dusted the tops of the pictures?' asked the old women.

'Yes,' answered Peggy, quite truthfully.

'We don't believe you!' cried the old women. 'Dust them at once.'

Poor Peggy had to dust them all again.

'Are you hungry?' they asked, after Peggy had worked hard for a long time.

'Yes, very,' said Peggy.

'You're not telling the truth, we know you're not!' cried the old women. 'You say you're hungry just because you're greedy. We shan't give you anything to eat, so there!'

Peggy felt very miserable to think that everything she said was disbelieved. She made up her mind that *next* time the old women asked her anything, she *wouldn't* tell the truth.

'Are you tired?' they asked her, when the night began to fall.

Peggy was dreadfully tired—but she knew they wouldn't believe her if she said so—so she sighed and said, 'Oh no!—I'm not tired at all.'

'We believe you!' cried the old women. 'As you're not tired, you can stay up all night and peel these potatoes.'

'I don't want to,' said poor Peggy, beginning to cry.

'But you must, you must!' said the old women, and they all went to bed, and left Peggy sitting at the kitchen table, with a huge bowl of unpeeled potatoes in front of her.

'I wish I'd never told an untruth in my life,' sobbed Peggy. 'I wish I was at home, where everyone believes me, I'd never, never tell stories again. Nobody's kind to me here.'

She peeled a few potatoes. Then she threw down the knife.

'I'll go and find Fairy Truth. She had a kind face, and if I tell her I'm ever so sorry, perhaps she'll take me back home again,' said Peggy.

She stole out of the cottage and ran through the dark wood. At last she came to a little path, and she ran along this till she came to the shining river. There, sitting in her boat, was Fairy Truth.

'Oh, I'm so glad to see you,' cried Peggy,

jumping into the boat. 'I've come to say I'm sorry I've been rude to you, and sorry I was untruthful. Do take me away from this land, it's awful to tell the truth and not be believed!'

Fairy Truth smiled at Peggy, and kissed her. 'I've been waiting here for you. You have learnt your lesson, and now I will take you home.'

Up the river went the little boat, and Peggy watched the banks slip by.

'Oh,' she cried suddenly, 'this is the river that runs in the fields behind our house! And look! Oh look! There's my home!'

'Jump out, Peggy,' said the fairy. 'Goodbye, and always remember that Truth is the only thing that really matters.'

'I'll never, never forget!' cried Peggy, hugging the fairy and jumping out.

Off she ran, over the fields, up the garden, and into her house. And you can just guess how astonished her mother was to hear of all her adventures.

'I'm never, never going to tell a story again,' said Peggy, 'and I'll never, never go to that nasty old Land of Pretence!'

And you may be quite sure she never did!

The Search for Giant Osta

Sylfai was reading all by herself in the nursery, when there came a knock at the window.

'Goodness me, whoever's that?' thought Sylfai, getting up to see.

The knocking came again. Sylfai opened the window wide and looked out.

'Mind your head!' cried a little voice, and in flew a fairy dressed in yellow.

'I'm Corovell,' she said, 'and I've come to ask you something.'

'What is it?' asked Sylfai, staring at Corovell in astonishment.

'Well, a friend of mine is lying in a magic sleep in Giant Osta's castle. Giant Osta is dreadfully upset, because he's a good giant, and he thinks Peronel, my friend, must have offended someone and had a spell put on her.'

'But why have you come to *me*?' asked Sylfai, looking puzzled.

'Well, because the spell can only be broken by someone called Sylfai, and that's *your* name, isn't it?' asked Corovell.

'Yes, it is. Am I going to Fairyland, then?' said Sylfai, feeling tremendously excited.

'I'll take you now,' said Corovell. 'Shut your eyes and count three, and hold on to me.'

'One, two, three!' counted Sylfai, holding on tight. Then she opened her eyes.

'Oh!' she cried. 'Oh, why I'm in Fairyland! However did I get here?'

She stood in a beautiful wood, with large toadstools standing about here and there. Corovell stood by her side.

'Now listen, Sylfai,' she said. 'I'm not allowed to come with you. You must find the way to Osta's by yourself. But I'll give you a piece of advice. If ever you feel cross with anyone in Fairyland say something nice.'

'I'll try and remember,' said Sylfai, 'but I wish you were coming with me.'

'Goodbye,' called Corovell, and off she flew.

'Dear me, she hasn't even told me which way to go,' said Sylfai, looking around. 'Well, I shall have to sit down on one of these big toadstools, and wait for someone to come along.'

She chose a large toadstool and sat down. Presently, to her astonishment, she saw a large green frog hop up on to another toadstool, and sit down there.

'Please,' said Sylfai, 'will you tell me the way to Giant Osta's?'

The frog blinked at her, but made no answer.

Then Sylfai saw a large green caterpillar crawl up on to another toadstool and curl itself round.

'Will *you* tell me the way?' she asked.

Still there was no answer.

Then on a third toadstool up hopped a great green grasshopper. He stared solemnly at Sylfai, but wouldn't speak a word.

Suddenly a cross voice made Sylfai jump. 'Now then!' it hissed. 'Get off my seat!'

Sylfai looked down and saw a long green snake sliding round about her toadstool.

'This isn't your seat!' she said. 'I got here first.'

Then the frog, the caterpillar, and the grasshopper all spoke at once—'Push her off, push her off, push her off!' they cried in a sort of chorus.

Sylfai was going to say something very cross indeed, when she remembered Corovell's advice, and tried to think of something nice instead.

'Oh, I'm sorry if I am sitting on your toadstool,' she said politely. 'I'll get down.' And off she jumped.

The grass snake wriggled up and curled himself on the top.

'You *are* polite,' he said, 'instead of being cross

and rude. We belong to a Green Club because we are all green and meet here to talk on the toadstools every evening. Can we help you in any way?'

'Well,' said Sylfai, feeling very glad she had been polite, 'can you tell me the way to Giant Osta's?'

The caterpillar raised itself up, and spoke:

'I have eaten cabbages in Osta's garden,' he said. 'I can tell you part of the way.'

'Oh, please do!' begged Sylfai.

'Well, go through the wood until you come to a little wooden house painted yellow. In it there lives a dwarf who will take you part of the way. Tell him Greenskin of the Green Club sent you.'

'Thank you,' said Sylfai, taking a last look at the queer members of the Green Club, and off she went through the wood.

Presently she came to a wooden house, painted yellow. Sylfai walked round it, looking for the door—but to her astonishment there *was* no door! and only one tiny window, very high up.

Sylfai knocked loudly on the walls.

'Come in, come in,' cried a voice.

'I *can't* come in, there's no door,' answered Sylfai.

'Come in, come in!' repeated the voice.

Sylfai was just going to say something cross, when she remembered in time.

'Whatever nice thing can I say?' she thought. 'Oh, I know. What a pretty yellow colour your house is!' she called.

'Oh, do you like it? I'm so glad,' said the voice, sounding very pleased. 'As you like the outside, you can see the inside. Climb up the beech tree by the side of the house and get on the roof.'

Sylfai climbed up the tree and clambered on to the roof. 'Well, dear me,' she said, 'there *is* only one way of getting into this house it seems—and that is down the chimney!'

She climbed into the chimney, let herself go, and whizz! She found herself sitting inside the house, on a big yellow cushion.

'*That's* the way to come in!' chuckled the dwarf. 'I like my house to be different from other people's!'

'Greenskin of the Green Club told me you would show me part of the way to Giant Osta's,' said Sylfai.

'Certainly,' said the dwarf, a queer, bright-eyed little man. 'Follow me.'

He lifted up a trap-door, sat down on the edge, and dangled his legs down. 'Come after me,' he said, and let himself drop.

Sylfai, feeling a little nervous, did the same. She felt herself gliding down a slippery passage—down and down, with little lamps to light the way whizzing past her.

At last she stopped. She found herself by a dark river, which was flowing silently along.

'Here's a boat!' said the dwarf, pulling up a queer-shaped boat to the side. 'Get in—you don't need any oars. I'll give you a push off. Goodbye!'

Sylfai jumped in and off sped the boat, rocking from side to side. It floated past great caves, cast dimly lit passages, and at last stopped by a little wooden platform. Sylfai got out and looked around.

'Wherever do I go now!' she thought. 'Dear me, what's that?'

She heard a queer rumbling noise coming down the passage in front of her, and then there rolled a bright green ball round a corner, right up to her feet.

'Oh,' cried Sylfai, 'you're hurting my toes! Do roll off.'

The green ball pressed harder. Sylfai was just going to lose her temper when she remembered Corovell's advice again.

'If you don't mind, please will you move yourself?' she said politely. 'I'd like to see what you are.'

The ball burst open, and out jumped a peculiar creature, with tiny legs, a round body and a round head.

He waved his funny little arms. 'I'm the Crawly-wawly Bumpty, he said, 'and I always roll on to people's toes, just to see what they say. You're the first person who's ever been polite to me. What can I do for you?'

'What a good thing I was polite!' thought Sylfai. Then she said aloud, 'I don't think you're very kind to hurt people's toes, really, you know. Will you tell me where to find Giant Osta?'

'Oh yes. He lives near here. Go up that passage till you come to a door. Knock and Osta will open it.' The Crawly-wawly Bumpty jumped into his ball again and rolled merrily off.

'What a funny creature!' said Sylfai, as she went along the passage. After a long while she came to a great blue door, with a tremendous handle. She knocked with her knuckles as loudly as she could.

The door swung open, and a giant peered out and said:

'Who is there?'

'It is only Sylfai, come to try and break Peronel's spell,' answered Sylfai, looking in wonder at the huge giant, whose kindly eyes seemed miles above her.

'Oh, splendid!' cried the giant. 'I'll pick you up and take you to Peronel.' And Sylfai suddenly found herself in the giant's hand, being carefully carried along.

Osta put her down in a great high room. At one end lay a beautiful fairy asleep on a couch. Over her hung a purple card, and Sylfai saw written there:

'Here Peronel will have to stay,
Summer, winter, night and day,
Until the spell is killed away
By someone who is called Sylfai.'

'Oh, what a shame!' cried Sylfai, and she gently bent over sleeping Peronel and kissed her forehead. To her delight Peronel opened her eyes and sat up.

'Oh, I've been under a *horrid* spell,' she cried, 'and I'm so glad to wake again. How kind you are, Sylfai, to kiss me. Oh, there is Corovell!'

Sylfai turned round, and sure enough there was Corovell, smiling at them both.

'Brave little Sylfai!' she said. 'I guessed you would break the spell. Now, let's all go and have a lovely time at the Queen's palace. She wants to see you, Sylfai.'

'I'll carry you all there,' laughed Giant Osta, picking them all up, and off he went with big strides—and you can just imagine the lovely time Sylfai had with the fairies, and what a lot of adventures she had to tell when she got safely home again!

The Tenth Task

Jack suddenly saw the little yellow door as he wandered across the moors to pick bilberries. It was neatly fitted into the side of the hill he was climbing, and he *almost* didn't see it.

He thought it must be a magic door of some kind, so he felt rather excited. He went right up to it and looked at it. Just an ordinary door it was, but primrose yellow and small. Jack's head would have touched the top. There was no knocker, but a brightly polished handle seemed to invite Jack to turn it and walk in. He did try to turn it and open the door, but nothing happened.

'It must be locked inside,' said Jack, disappointed. 'What a pity. I can't get in after all.'

He tried again, but it was no use, the door was locked. As he looked at it carefully, he suddenly saw a tiny little card pinned by the door, and on it in beautifully printed letters was:

'OPEN ON THURSDAYS AT MIDNIGHT.'

'Hooray, I'll come then,' cried Jack, 'and see what there is to see. Won't I have a lovely time!'

He raced home to his sister Jean, and told her

all about his find. 'I'm going through that fairy door on Thursday night,' he said, 'and you'll hear some fine adventures when I come back!'

'Oh, *do* let me come with you,' begged Jean. 'I want to have adventures too; and, who knows, I might be able to help you somehow, perhaps.'

'Pooh,' laughed Jack. 'You help *me*! I can take care of myself, thank you! I don't want any silly little girls in my adventures. I'm going all by myself.'

Jean's curly head drooped sadly as she turned away in disappointment. But when Thursday night came, she packed him up some cakes and went cheerfully to the gate to see him off in the dark, for it was nearly twelve o'clock. 'I do hope you'll have some lovely adventures,' she said. 'And I *do* wish I was coming with you.'

'You can next time, perhaps,' promised Jack. 'You're not clever enough nor old enough to come this first time.'

And off he went, whistling loudly.

When he arrived at the little yellow door in the hillside, he found it standing wide open, leading into a narrow passage. This was lighted by a swinging lantern. Jack walked in, feeling just a little bit afraid, but hoping he would have real adventures, with magic in them.

The passage led right into the hill, and suddenly opened out into a large hall, where many kinds of fairy-folk stood about in groups. They were talking and laughing with each other. Jack felt too shy to walk into the hall and speak to the fairies. He hid himself in a little curtained arch at the side of the hall, and watched the fairy-folk in their play.

Soon they began to dance. Jack noticed that they all kept away from one side of the hall, as if they were afraid of something there. He tried to see what it was, but could only catch a glimpse of what looked like a glittering box, standing on a beautifully carved throne. He determined to find out what it was when the fairy-folk had finished dancing. It looked mysterious.

He loved watching the fairies; they were so dainty with their wings outspread and their gossamer frocks, and he was quite sorry when the dancing stopped. One by one the fairies slipped away down the passage and out upon the hillside to their homes, and Jack was left all alone. The hall was dark now, except for one great lamp swinging over the throne on which stood the mysterious box.

Jack crept across to throne, and looked at the box. It was large, and shone in the lamplight like gold. Set around the surface of the lid were rubies and diamonds. The box was locked, but in the lock was a key. Engraven in small letters on the key were these words:

'BEWARE—TURN NOT THIS KEY.'

Jack wondered why the key was not to be turned. What would happen if he *did* turn it? He did so badly want to see what was in the box. Perhaps it was a treasure that he could take home and give to Jean.

He suddenly took hold of the key and turned it. He was just lifting the lid up, when—CRASH! BANG! PHIZZ-Z-Z-Z!!

Out of the box sprang a great spirit, with gleaming eyes and coal-black hair. It was much, much taller than Jack, and, with a kick that sent the box flying across the hall, it sat itself down on the big throne and stared at Jack.

'Do you know who I am?' it said with a horrid smile. 'I am Zani, the chief of the wicked spirits. I can keep you here as my slave for ever.'

Jack threw himself on his knees. 'Be merciful to me,' he pleaded. 'I set you free. Reward me, do not punish me.'

Zani laughed. 'Very well,' he said. 'For ten days you may ask me to do ten things for you, one each day. If you find something I cannot do, you may lock me up in the box again. But if you cannot find a task too difficult for me to perform, then I shall take you for my slave for ever.'

'All right,' said Jack, feeling pleased, and quite sure he could think of things too difficult for anyone to do. 'For today's task I want you to give me a pair of wings which I can put on to fly with, and take off if I like.'

Zani waved his hand. Immediately there dropped a pair of blue wings down at Jack's feet. He was astonished to find his wish granted so soon, and began to fly about gaily for the first time. He flew home to Jean and told her everything. She was very much surprised and wanted to help Jack to choose some very difficult things. He wouldn't let her, for he said she was not clever enough, and *of course* he could think of something which would prove too difficult for Zani to do.

The next day Jack told the Wicked Spirit to build a great palace for him and Jean, with big gardens full of flowers and fountains. That night a tremendous noise of hammering and clattering was heard, and when day dawned there stood a magnificent palace in its own grounds. Jean and Jack could hardly believe it was theirs. They began to think Zani must be very clever indeed.

The third day Jack asked that the great cellars in the palace should be filled with gold, silver, and precious stones. Zani filled them.

The fourth day, Jack wanted a coat that would make him invisible when he put it on. Zani gave it to him.

The fifth and sixth days Jack told the Wicked Spirit to find the most beautiful ring and the most beautiful necklace in the whole world. These he gave to Jean.

Then Jack began to get worried. For the tenth day was drawing near, and if he could not find something which Zani could not do, he would be his slave for ever.

The seventh day he asked for a lake in his palace grounds, thinking that surely Zani would find this too great a task to do in one day. But no, it was quite easy, or so it seemed, for there stretched a blue lake shimmering in the sunshine.

The eighth and the ninth days Jack asked for a magic sword and for magic shoes of swiftness, knowing that these could only be got from the good fairies, and thinking that Zani would not be allowed to have them. But the Wicked Spirit brought them to him.

On the tenth day, Zani came and said, 'What task have you for me today? If you have not one I cannot do, you are my slave, and I shall never let you go.

'I have thought of nothing,' said Jack, trembling. 'Let me have until tonight to think.'

'No,' answered Zani, 'you must tell me now! I will wait no longer. You cannot ask me anything I am not able to do.'

'Let me say goodbye to my sister, then,' cried poor Jack.

'Go, then,' said Zani. 'You will never see her again.' And he laughed horribly.

Jack went into Jean's room and told her that she must say goodbye to him, for he could not think

of anything Zani could not do. He must go and be his slave. Jack trembled as he thought of being in Zani's power.

To his surprise Jean laughed. 'Oh,' she said, 'you thought you were so clever, didn't you? But I can tell you something to ask him which he cannot do.'

'What is it? Tell me quickly!' cried Jack.

Jean pulled out a long curly hair from her head.

'Go and tell him to make this straight,' she said.

Jack took it and ran back to Zani. 'Here is today's task,' he cried. 'Make this hair of my sister's straight if you can!'

Zani laughed. 'What an easy thing to do,' he said 'Look, I will make it straight at once.'

He pulled the hair straight between his fingers but when he let go, the hair sprang back into its curls. He tried again and again, but each time the hair curled, just as curly hair always will.

He wetted it with water. It curled all the tighter! He ironed it with a great iron. It sprang back into such tight curls that he could hardly pull it straight! He smoothed it, he patted it, he stroked it and shook it, but nothing would make that curly hair go straight. All the day he tried, and when night came he knew he was conquered at last.

With a great mournful howl he fled back to the cave in the hillside, with Jean and Jack after him. They were just in time to see him disappearing into the box. Jean ran forward and turned the key, and there was Zani locked up for years and years to come.

You can guess Jack never said again that he was cleverer than Jean.

Off to the Land of Tiddlywinks

John and Polly were climbing up Feraling Hill on a very windy day.

'Goodness! Isn't it windy?' cried John, puffing and panting. 'Hullo! What's that lying there?'

Polly looked. 'Why, it's a lovely kite!' she said, running up to it. 'What a great big one, John. Whoever does it belong to?'

'I don't know. Nobody seems to be here,' said John. 'Let's fly it, Polly. It ought to go beautifully, in this wind!'

The two children lifted the kite and unbound the string.

Puff! The wind swooped down, caught the kite and swept it high up into the air!

'Isn't it lovely, Polly?' cried John. 'Here, hold the kite a minute, whilst I unwind more string!'

Polly held on tightly, but the wind blew and blew, and the kite tugged terribly hard.

'Oh, oh, John, the kite's pulling me off my feet!' cried Polly, running across the grass, dragged by the kite.

'I'll come and help!' shouted John. But alas!

Before he could reach his sister, she was swept off her feet, up into the air, and became a tiny black speck in the distance.

John was dreadfully upset.

'What shall I do? Poor little Polly! What shall I do?' he cried.

'What's the matter?' asked a tiny voice.

John looked round with a jump. He saw a Brownie man sitting on a rock near by.

'Oh, didn't you see what happened to my sister?' he cried. 'She's got whisked off by a kite we found lying here.'

'That comes of touching what doesn't belong to you!' said the Brownie. 'That's a magic kite. It belongs to the Yellow Giant. He *will* be cross when he knows you've used it.'

'Oh dear! How dreadful! But what has happened to Polly?' asked John.

'Oh, I expect the kite's taken her to the Land of Tiddlywinks,' answered the Brownie. 'She'll never come back unless you go and fetch her.'

'*Please* tell me the way,' begged John, 'and I'll go straight off now, and see if I can get her back.'

'Well, go down the Shaking Steps, under that hawthorn bush,' advised the Brownie, 'until you come to the Rollarounds. I expect they'll help you.'

'Thank you!' called John, running to the

130

hawthorn bush. He looked round it, and at last found a very neat trap-door fitted into the green grass and painted green. He lifted it up, and saw a long flight of yellow steps stretching downwards.

'They're all shaky and jerky!' said John in astonishment, looking at the steps which were continually shaking and very steep.

They made no noise, but John felt very uncomfortable as he went down them. First one shook, then another jerked, and then others wobbled, so that he was really rather afraid of tumbling right down them, and he kept tight hold of the hand-rail.

At last he came to the end, and stepped into a dark passage lit by one dim lamp. It hung just above a door marked:

> ROLLAROUNDS. PLEASE KNOCK.

'Good! Perhaps they'll help me!' thought John, and gave the door a thump. It flew open, and out rolled what looked like big india-rubber balls, bumping against his legs, and making a funny squeaking sound.

'What funny creatures!' thought John.

'Please, could you tell me the way to the Land of Tiddlywinks?' he asked politely.

'Yes, yes!' squeaked the Rollarounds, and they rolled off up the passage at a tremendous rate, John running after them.

At last they came to a large cave, in which sat a solemn dwarf dressed in bright red.

'Good morning!' he said as John approached. 'Why have the Rollarounds brought you to me?'

'I asked them the way to the Land of Tiddlywinks,' explained John.

'Can you say your A.B.C. backwards?' asked the dwarf.

'I don't know, I never tried,' answered John, rather astonished.

'Well, no one can go to Tiddlywinks unless they can say their alphabet backwards,' said the dwarf. 'It's one of the rules, you know. Let me see if you can.'

John tried. He began at Z and went backwards to A very slowly indeed, so as not to make a mistake.

'Hm! It's not very good,' said the dwarf. 'But I dare say they'll let you in if you say it a bit quicker. You must go by boat to the Crooked Castle, and ask for Giant Certain-Sure. If you're very polite, he'll hand you across to the Land of Tiddlywinks.'

'Oh, thank you!' said John. 'Where's the boat?'

'Come with me,' said the dwarf, going through an archway into another cave. John saw a bright green river flowing through it.

The dwarf whistled.

Down the river came a beautiful boat of purple with no one inside at all.

'Here you are!' said the dwarf. 'Get in. It goes by magic. Get out at the Crooked Castle. Goodbye.'

'Goodbye!' squeaked all the Rollarounds, nearly rolling into the river.

'Goodbye, and thank you!' shouted John, getting into the boat. Off it floated smoothly, and soon the cave was lost to sight. John was interested in all the other caves they passed. Blue caves, red caves, pink caves, some empty, some full of dancing fairies, some full of sleeping brownies.

At last the boat slipped out into the open air, and floated past fields full of wonderful fairy flowers, which talked to each other and laughed as John floated by.

'Ah! There's Crooked Castle, I'm sure!' suddenly exclaimed John, as he spied a queer, one-sided castle in the distance.

The boat floated on towards it, and at last came to rest beside a little landing-place.

John jumped out. 'Thank you, little boat,' he

said, and ran off to the Crooked Castle. He came to a great open door, and stepped into a cool hall. He looked into all the rooms, but no one was there. At last he came to a big kitchen. There he found a huge giant, sitting by the table with great tears rolling down his face.

'Hullo!' said John. 'What are you crying for?'

'Boo-hoo! I can't learn my A.B.C. backwards!' sobbed the giant. 'I want to go to the land of Tiddlywinks, where my mother lives, but nobody's allowed to unless they can say their alphabet backwards. I'm certain-sure I knew it five minutes ago, and now I don't.'

'Poor Giant Certain-Sure!' said John. 'Let me help you. It's a terribly silly rule, but as it *is* a rule, I'll try and help you learn your A.B.C. backwards.'

'Thank you. You are very kind,' said the giant, cheering up immensely. 'Just let me look over it once more, and then I'll say it to you.'

He looked at his A.B.C. book and frowned hard. At last he smiled, and looked at John.

'I'm certain-sure I know it now!' he cried. 'Z. Y. X. W. ... L. B. A. T. ...'

'No, no! Quite wrong!' cried John.

'Oh dear! I felt certain-sure I knew it!' cried the giant sadly. 'Never mind. I'll try again tomorrow.

134

Can I do anything to help *you* in return for your helping me?'

'Yes, if you don't mind,' said John. 'I want to go to the Land of Tiddlywinks. The dwarf said you could hand me across.'

'I will. Certain-sure I will!' cried the giant. He caught John up in his huge hand, went out into the garden, down a lane, and up to a huge bridge over a great, broad river. He stretched his enormous arm over the river, and put John carefully down on to the other side.

'Goodbye, and thank you, Giant Certain-Sure!' shouted John. He looked around him. He was in the queerest country—the houses were made of tiddlywinks, and the chimneys were tiddly-winks cups!

He was suddenly surrounded by crowds of funny little round-bodied red and white, blue and green creatures—that jumped instead of walked.

'Say your A.B.C. backwards!' cried they.

'Z. Y. X. W.,' began John carefully, and got the whole way through without a single mistake.

'Wonderful, wonderful!' cried the Tiddlywinks. 'What can we do for you?'

'Where's my sister Polly, who came here with a great kite?' demanded John.

'Here she is! Here she is!' cried the funny little

Tiddlywinks as a little girl came running up.

'John! John! I'm so glad to see you!' cried Polly, hugging him. 'Do let's go home quickly!'

'Turn round three times, whistle and wish!' said the Tiddlywinks, dancing round them.

John and Polly turned themselves round three times, whistled and wished, and, hey presto, there they were in their own back garden!

'Oh,' cried John, 'we'll never meddle with anyone's kite again, will we, Polly?'

'No,' said Polly. 'But, my goodness, what a lot of adventures we've had. Let's go and tell Mother!' And off they went, and Mother could hardly believe her ears!

The Land of Great Stupids

Joan and Pat were quarrelling. Pat had been teaching Joan how to bat at cricket, and Joan would keep holding her bat in the wrong way.

'Joan, you're perfectly silly!' said Pat crossly. 'You'll never hit a single ball if you play like that!'

'Well, you're just as silly!' shouted Joan. 'Your balls never hit my wicket even though I *do* miss them, so there!'

'Oh, be quiet!' said Pat. 'You're just a great stupid, that's what you are, just like all girls. You ought to go to the Land of Great Stupids and live there, that's what *I* think!'

He turned to pick up the ball—and when he turned back again he was astonished to find Joan wasn't there!

'Joan! Joan! Where are you?' he called in surprise.

There was no answer.

'Joan! Joan! Don't be silly. Come back and play!' shouted Pat again.

Still there was no answer. Then suddenly Pat heard a little chuckle in the big chestnut tree above him. He looked up in surprise and saw a queer little gnome's face peeping down at him from between the green leaves.

'Call and call!' said the face. 'Call and call! *She* won't hear you! She's gone to the Land of Great Stupids! You said she ought to go there, and she's gone!'

'Oh dear! Oh dear! Poor little Joan!' said Pat. 'I didn't mean what I said. I was only just cross. Oh, *do* tell me how to get her back, please!'

'You'll have to go to the Land of Great Stupids yourself, to do that!' answered the gnome, sliding down the tree and standing beside Pat. 'You won't enjoy it much, I can tell you!'

'Oh, *that* doesn't matter!' said Pat. 'It's my fault Joan went there, and she is my sister, so I *must* look after her. Tell me what to do.'

'The Land of Great Stupids belongs to old Witch Wimple,' said the gnome. 'You'll have to go and ask her if she'll let you go there. I don't expect she will, she's a cross old thing. She may turn you into a spider; you never know.'

'Well, I hope she won't,' said Pat, feeling rather afraid. 'Where does she live?'

'Go to the top of Bracken Hill,' said the gnome, 'and pick the largest toadstool there. Under it is a trap-door. Go down the steps, and walk on till you come to the Underground Lake. Take a red fairy boat to the Gnome Railway. Then take the train to Yellow Chimney Cottage. That's where Witch Wimple lives.'

'Oh, thank you!' said Pat, running off. 'It's awfully kind of you to tell me.'

He ran down the lane and then up Bracken Hill to the very top.

'Oh, here are the toadstools!' he cried. 'I wonder which is the biggest.'

He looked all round and at last found one much bigger than the others. He picked it, and looked in the grass where it had been growing. There he saw a blue ring fixed to the ground.

'I'll pull that ring and I expect I'll lift a trap-door,' said Pat excitedly. He caught hold of the blue ring and tugged. Up came a trap-door well hidden in the grass and bracken. Blue steps stretched downwards into darkness.

'Well, here goes!' said Pat, and began climbing down.

They were funny, narrow steps, and he had to hold on to a rail by the side to keep himself from falling. It was very dark, and Pat could not see where he was going.

At last he came to a green lamp and there he met a pixie.

'Good morning,' said the pixie. 'Where are you going?'

'To the Underground Lake to take a red fairy boat to the Gnome Railway,' answered Pat.

'Oh well, take the first turning on the right,' said the pixie. 'Have you got any money to pay with?'

'No, I haven't,' said Pat.

'Well, give me that big toadstool you're carrying, and I'll give you fairy gold,' said the pixie. 'I can make a spell with your toadstool.'

Pat gave it to him and put three pieces of fairy

gold in his pocket. Then he went on again. He took the first turning on the right, and saw a big stretch of gleaming water lying before him.

'How lovely!' cried Pat. 'It's a fairy lake, and oh, what darling little boats! They're all shaped like birds!'

So they were. There were swan-boats, duck-boats, robin-boats, and all sorts of other bird-like boats!

'I suppose I take a robin-boat,' thought Pat, jingling his fairy gold. 'Hi! You robin-boat, come and take me for your passenger.'

Up came a red robin-boat, steered by a small blue elf.

'Where to?' he asked.

'The Gnome Railway,' answered Pat, jumping in.

'One piece of gold, please,' said the elf. Pat gave it to him and the boat started off, floating smoothly and quickly. It went right across the lake passing other boats full of passengers—elves, pixies, gnomes, rabbits, mice and Pat even saw a hedgehog! He was by himself because he was so prickly.

At last they reached a little pier jutting out from the lake-side.

'Here you are!' said the elf. 'The train will

come right on to the pier. You can get into it there. Goodbye.'

Off he went in his little boat again, looking for another passenger. Pat stood on the pier, waiting. Presently, away in the distance, he saw two little red lights. They drew nearer and nearer, until he saw they belonged to a dear little train, rather like a toy one, coming along quickly and smoothly.

'I suppose it goes by magic as there's no smoke!' thought Pat, as the train ran along the pier and stopped. All kinds of fairy-folk jumped out, and stepped into boats waiting for them. Pat jumped into a carriage and sat down on a cushion on the floor, for there were no proper seats.

The train backed off the pier and then another engine came up and was joined on to the end of the carriages. Off it went into a tunnel, and then through all sorts of lovely caves, and out into the open air. At last it stopped at Dwarf Town Station where lots of dwarfs got in. A little brown dwarf with a long grey beard and twinkling eyes sat on a cushion in Pat's carriage and stared at him.

'What a big hill we're going up!' suddenly said Pat, feeling his cushion sliding down on to the dwarf's.

'Yes, we'll soon be on the top of Blow-away Hill!' said the dwarf. 'We'll run down it then at a good pace, I can tell you! You'll lose all your breath!'

Soon the train came to the top of a very, very windy hill, and began to run down the side of it, between sloping fields of golden buttercups and starry daisies.

Suddenly the dwarf gave a shriek and pointed to something flying through the air.

'Look! Look! There's our driver blown away. I always knew that would happen some day on Blow-away Hill! Now we'll have an accident!' And the dwarf gave another shriek.

Pat clutched the side of the carriage as the train tore down the hill at a terrific speed. Then there came a jolt and a jerk, a tremendous bang, and he found himself rolling head-over-heels on some soft, velvety moss. He got up and felt himself all over.

'Well, I'm not hurt, thank goodness!' he said. 'But I wonder what's happened to the dwarf who was with me!'

He ran up to the tumbled-down train. No one seemed a bit hurt, for everyone had fallen on the soft moss that spread all around the railway track. The dwarfs were busy putting the carriages on the lines again.

'What a good thing there's no one hurt!' said Pat, helping two dwarfs to pick up cushions.

'Oh, but that's why the moss is grown round here,' said a dwarf. 'Didn't you know? The Fairy Queen felt sure there'd be an accident one day, and so she gave orders for moss to be grown at the bottom of Blow-away Hill, just in case!'

Suddenly Pat heard a great noise of crying, and turning round he saw the little dwarf who had been in his carriage.

'Boo-hoo-hoo! Boo-hoo-hoo!' he wept. 'I've lost the necklace I was taking to Witch Wimple! It must have fallen out of my pocket in the accident!'

'I'll help you look for it,' said Pat kindly, and began searching all around. Just as he was thinking the necklace really must be lost for good and all, he saw it half-buried in a big clump of moss.

'Here it is!' he said, and gave it to the dwarf.

'Oh, thank you,' cried the dwarf gladly. 'I'm so glad to have it. Where are you going?'

'To old Witch Wimple's,' said Pat. 'I want to ask her to let me go to the Land of Great Stupids.'

'She won't let you do that,' said the dwarf. 'But look here! I've got an idea. I've got to go there for her, to carry a load of moon beads. I'll ask if you can help me carry it.'

So off the two went, over the fields to Yellow Chimney Cottage which stood away in the distance. Old Witch Wimple was standing at the

144

door, shading her eyes with her hands, looking for the dwarf.

'I'm sorry I'm late,' called the dwarf as he hurried up. 'The Gnome Train had an accident and I nearly lost your necklace.'

'Make haste!' said the witch crossly. 'You'll be too late to take those beads to the Land of Great Stupids if you don't hurry!'

Pat and the dwarf ran up to the door and the dwarf gave the witch her necklace. She handed the dwarf a red sack full of something heavy. He tried to lift it and pretended it was too heavy.

'Oh, I say!' he panted. 'I think the railway accident must have left me rather weak. Can my friend here help me to carry it?'

'No. I don't allow strangers to go to the Land of Great Stupids,' said the witch.

The dwarf tried to lift the sack again, and dropped it.

'Very well,' he said. 'You'll have to wait till tomorrow, when I get my strength back.'

'I *can't* wait till tomorrow, as you very well know,' grumbled the witch. 'Let your friend help you, then. Get on to the Flying Chair quickly.'

The dwarf led Pat to where a big green chair stood in the garden. He sat down on it and made room for Pat. Waving her stick, the witch chanted:

'Acrall-da-farray!
Up and away!
To the Land of Great Stupids,
Take them today!'

Up into the air rose the chair, and Pat held on tightly, afraid he would fall. The chair flew over the hills and fields, across a shining strip of sea, and came slowly down in the middle of a town.

'Here we are!' said the dwarf, getting off the chair. 'Now I must hurry. Goodbye and good luck!' And off he ran down the street.

Pat looked round. The town looked very queer. The houses were crooked and old, and the chimneys were all sorts of shapes.

The windows were very tiny and the doorways very big. Queer looking creatures wandered about, with big heads, big ears, big eyes, and big mouths.

'Well, I suppose these are the Great Stupids!' thought Pat. 'And they look it too! Why ever don't they shut their mouths! They wouldn't look half so stupid then!'

He went up to one.

'Please could you tell me if there is a little girl called Joan here?' he asked politely.

'I can't speak,' said the Great Stupid sadly, and walked off.

'Can't speak!' shouted Pat. 'Why, you've just spoken!'

'No, I haven't!' called back the Stupid, with tears in his eyes.

'My goodness! Fancy poor little Joan being here!' said Pat. 'I'll go and explore, I think. I wonder who lives in that palace place at the end of the street. It looks a bit better built than any of these awful-looking houses.'

He walked up the steps to the palace and into a great hall hung with blue curtains. Then he stood still in the greatest surprise and astonishment. *For there, on a golden throne, sat Joan, his little sister Joan, with a crown on her curly brown hair!*

'Joan! Joan!' shouted Pat, hardly able to believe his eyes. 'Is it really you?'

'Pat! Oh, Pat darling! I'm *so* pleased to see you!' cried Joan, suddenly seeing him and running down the hall to meet him. Then she turned to several Great Stupids standing gaping at her in astonishment.

'Leave me for a minute!' she commanded.

'Yes, Your Majesty,' they answered, and ran out of the room.

'Oh, Pat! Oh, Pat!' squeaked Joan, with her arms round his neck. 'It's lovely to see you! Do take me home.'

'What have you got a crown on your head for?' asked Pat.

'Well, when I came here, these Great Stupids asked me all sorts of questions,' said Joan. 'They asked me why their houses were dark, and I said because they hadn't made their windows big enough. Then they asked me why their houses were so cold, and I told them because they left their big doors open, and of course the wind blew through their houses!'

'What else?' asked Pat.

'They wanted to know why my shoes shone and theirs didn't, and I said because theirs wanted cleaning!' went on Joan. 'And, oh, lots of other silly things. Then last of all they asked me if I could say my twelve-times table, and of course I could, and they thought that was WONDERFUL!'

'Did they make you Queen then?' asked Pat.

'Yes. They thought I was so clever. But, oh, Pat darling! I'd rather be called stupid by you than clever by these Great Stupids! Sh! Here they come again. Ask them to let us go home.'

In came a crowd of excited Stupids and surrounded Pat.

'Do you come from the Queen's land?' they asked. 'Because, if you do, we'll make you King. Come and see if you can answer a difficult question first.'

They dragged Pat off and led him to the seashore where lay a crowd of little boats.

'Our boats always sink when we float them in the sea!' they said. 'Can you tell us why they do?'

'Why, they're full of holes!' said Pat. 'Just look! Of course they get full of water and sink! Have any of you got a cork?'

One of the Stupids gave him one. Pat took

out his knife and whittled it at one end. Then he forced the cork into a hole in a boat.

'Now this boat will float!' he said.

'See! It floats beautifully,' cried the Stupids joyfully. 'We will make you King and you shall stay here always.'

'No, thank you,' said Pat. 'I want to go home with Joan.'

'You shan't, you shan't! There's no way of going back!' cried the Stupids, and dragged Pat back to the palace. They put a crown on his head and sat him by Joan.

'Never mind, Joan! We'll escape when it's dark,' said Pat. 'Look, they're going to give us a feast now! Good! I'm jolly hungry!'

Pat and Joan found it very boring to be King and Queen of the Stupids, for they had to sit and answer questions all day long. They were very glad when night came and they were left alone.

'Quick! Slip out of this window!' whispered Pat.

Both children dropped from the window into a bush, and then ran across the gardens down to the seashore.

'Here's the boat I corked up!' said Pat. 'We'll set off in it!'

They jumped in, and Pat began rowing across the water in the moonlight.

Suddenly there came a shout of rage from the shore and crowds of Great Stupids ran down to the sea.

'Come back! Come back,' they yelled, 'or we'll fetch you back and spank you!'

Then, as they saw Pat was rowing steadily away from them, they jumped into the boats on the beach, and began rowing after Pat's boat. But they had forgotten their boats were full of holes, and before long they filled with water and sank, and the Great Stupids had to wade back to shore, drenched and angry.

'You're too clever for us!' they shouted. 'Oh! Why didn't we mend our boats?'

On and on went Pat's boat, until his arms ached. 'I do *wish* we were home,' he sighed at last.

'Oh! Oh, Pat! What's happening?' suddenly cried Joan. 'The boat's flying through the air!'

'It must be a magic boat, making my wish come true!' said Pat. 'I expect it's taking us home!'

So it was—for some time later it landed with a little splash in the duckpond in Pat and Joan's own garden!

They got out quickly, very glad to be safe again. Then, with a little click, the boat rose into the air again and disappeared.

'It's gone back to the Land of Great Stupids, I

suppose,' said Pat. 'Well, I hope *we* never go there again, don't you, Joan?'

They went indoors, and Mother was so thankful to see them again.

'I don't like the Land of Great Stupids,' she said, when they told her where they had been.

'Oh, look, Mother!' said Pat, feeling in his pockets. 'That pixie in Bracken Hill gave me three pieces of gold, and I only used one! I've got two left!'

'We'll hang them on Joan's gold bracelet!' said Mother and they did. And if ever you see a little girl wearing two fairy-gold pieces on her bracelet, ask if her name is Joan, and if she has ever heard of the Land of Great Stupids!

The Prisoners of the Dobbadies

When Peter was just finishing his lessons at twelve o'clock, Nurse came running in at the front gate, looking very red.

'Whatever is the matter, Nurse?' asked Mummy.

'Oh dear, oh dear! I've lost Pamela!' said Nurse, sinking down into a chair and looking very miserable.

'Lost Pamela! Where?' exclaimed Mummy.

'We were in the wood together, and Pamela wanted to play at ball. I threw the ball to her and she missed it. She laughed and ran behind a tree to get it, and then,' said poor Nurse, 'she didn't come back. I looked and called, but it wasn't any good.'

They all set off to look for Pamela, but although they called and called, they got no answer, and had to come home without her.

'She must have gone with the fairies,' said Peter. 'Mummy darling, do let me go and see if I can find her.'

Mummy looked at Daddy.

'Shall we let him go and see?' she asked. 'He really does see fairies, you know.'

'Yes, let him try,' said Daddy.

'Oh, thank you, Daddy!' cried Peter, catching up his hat. 'I'll go now, and I'm sure I'll bring Pamela back again. Goodbye, Mummy!' and, after a hug, Peter ran out into the garden.

He went straight to the wood, and made his way into the darker parts where the trees grew close together. He came to a little clearing at last, and in the middle grew a ring of white toadstools.

'I'll sit down in the middle of this ring,' he said, 'for there must be fairies somewhere about here.'

He sat down and looked around. Presently he heard a little voice.

'Hullo, Peter!'

'Hullo!' he said. 'Where are you? I can't see you.'

'Here I am!' laughed the voice, and, looking round, Peter saw a little yellow fairy peeping from behind a tree.

'Come and talk to me,' begged Peter. 'I want to ask you something.'

The fairy came and sat on one of the toadstools. 'I'm Morfael,' she said. 'What is it you want to know?'

'Can you tell me where Pamela is?' asked Peter.

'Yes, Caryll took her off to Fairyland this morning,' answered Morfael.

'Whatever for?' asked Peter in surprise.

'Well, you see, the Princess of Dreamland is very ill, and the Wise Elf says she will only get better if she hears the laugh of a little mortal girl. We knew Pamela had the sweetest laugh in the world, so Caryll had orders to take her to Dreamland for a time,' explained Morfael.

'Well, I'm going to fetch her back,' said Peter, getting up. 'Mummy wouldn't mind her making the Princess better, I know, but Pamela is too little to be all alone without anyone she knows. Which is the shortest bay to Fairyland from here?'

'Down Oak Tree House,' answered Morfael.

'Knock three times. Goodbye! I hope you'll find Pamela,' and away she flew.

'Oak Tree House!' said Peter, looking round. 'Wherever's that?'

All around him grew beech trees, and he walked about a little, until he came to a big oak tree.

'This must be it,' he thought to himself, and knocked three times loudly. A little voice sang a queer little song:

> *'If a fairy's standing there*
> *Enter in, and climb the stair.*
> *If a mortal child you be*
> *Eat an acorn from the tree.'*

Peter looked for an acorn, and ate the nut inside the shell.

Immediately everything round him seemed suddenly to grow tremendously big, and made him gasp for breath.

'Goodness me!' said Peter, most astonished. 'Why, I've gone small. And oh, how funny! I'm holding on to a grass!'

He looked up at the oak tree. It seemed simply enormous, and its branches looked as if they must touch the sky.

Just in front of him was a little door. It was

fitted into the oak tree so beautifully that it was difficult to see it.

Peter pushed at it, and it opened. To his surprise he saw a staircase going up inside the tree.

'What fun!' he said, and carefully shutting the door behind him, he ran up the winding staircase.

At the top he came to a queer little room, rather like an office, in which sat a gnome with a very big head.

'Good morning,' said Peter politely, 'and thank you for telling me to come in.'

'Good morning,' said the gnome. 'I'm Garin. It isn't often I get a visit from a little boy.'

'I'm Peter, and I'm looking for my sister,' said Peter. 'Could you tell me the way to Fairyland?'

'Yes, certainly. The Yellow Bird will take you straight there,' said Garin. 'But he doesn't come till two o'clock. I'm just going to have my dinner. Will you have some with me?'

'I'd *love* to,' answered Peter. 'I haven't had any, and I'm terribly hungry.'

'Sit down then,' said Garin. He bustled about, and soon had the queerest-looking dinner ready. Peter enjoyed it thoroughly and told him all about Pamela, and how he was going to look for her.

'Well, I don't think you'll find it quite so easy as you think,' said Garin, looking grave. 'The

Dobbadies don't like the Princess of Dreamland, because she won't let them live in her country, they're too mischievous. And if *they* hear that Pamela is going to cure the Princess, they may take it into their heads to capture Pamela before she gets to Dreamland.'

'Oh dear! Do you really think so?' asked Peter, putting down his glass of honey-dew drink in dismay.

'Well, I don't know,' answered Garin, 'but the Yellow Bird will tell us all the news when he comes. Anyway, I'll give you a piece of advice, which will always be of help to you in Fairyland.'

'Oh, thank you!' said Peter gratefully. 'I'll be sure to remember it.'

'Well, it's this,' said Garin. 'Whenever you feel impatient, or cross, don't think about it, and instead, look round you and see if you can find something beautiful. If you do that you'll be all right—but if you don't, things will go wrong and you won't find Pamela.'

'Well, that sounds easy enough,' said Peter.

'Hark! What was that?'

A noise of footsteps was heard on the stairs.

'Oh, that's only the people who want to go to Fairyland at two o'clock,' explained Garin, clearing away the dinner.

Then into the little room came all sorts of fairies and gnomes, talking and laughing with each other.

Suddenly a little bell tinkled.

'There's the Yellow Bird,' exclaimed Garin. 'Come along, everybody.'

He opened a door, and Peter saw leaves waving in the wind.

'Why, it's the outside of the tree,' he exclaimed.

Everyone walked along a broad branch until they came to where a large and beautiful yellow bird was waiting.

'Good afternoon,' said the Yellow Bird. 'Is everybody here?'

'Yes,' said Garin. 'Get on, Peter. Any news, Yellow Bird?'

'Yes,' answered the bird. 'The Dobbadies have captured the Princess of Dreamland, and a little girl called Pamela, who was with her, and nobody knows where they've gone.'

'Oh dear! Oh dear!' said Peter. 'That's just what you said might happen, Garin. *Now* what am I to do?'

'Are you Pamela's brother?' asked the Yellow Bird. 'Well, get on my back, and I'll try and think of a plan for you as we go along.'

Peter got on, and all the fairies and gnomes climbed up too. It was a very good thing the

Yellow Bird had such a broad back, Peter thought.

Just as they were going to start, someone came running across the branch.

'Stop, stop!' she cried. 'I'm coming too.'

'Hurry up, hurry up, Little Miss Muffet,' called Garin. 'You're very late.'

'I'm *so* sorry,' panted Miss Muffet, a little girl about the same size as Peter, 'but that horrid spider came and frightened me again and I dropped my bowl and spoon, and had to go back and find them.'

She sat down beside Peter. The Yellow Bird spread his wings and off he flew into the air.

'Goodbye, goodbye!' called Garin.

Peter clung on to the bird's feathers, and thought flying was simply glorious. He was sorry when the Yellow Bird kept stopping at various places, to let the fairies, the gnomes, or the rabbit get down.

At last only he and Miss Muffet were left.

'Have you thought of a plan yet?' asked Peter.

'Yes. I think you had better go to the Hideaway House, and ask the Wise Elf there to help you. He will know what to do,' answered the bird.

'I'll go with you,' said Miss Muffet. 'I've got to get off near there.'

At last the Yellow Bird slowed down and came to a stop.

'Here you are,' he said. 'The Hideaway House is in that wood over there.'

'Oh, thank you,' said Peter, getting off. He helped Miss Muffet off, and they both went into the wood.

Suddenly Miss Muffet gave a scream.

'Oh! Oh! There's that horrid spider again!'

Peter saw an immense brown spider coming towards Miss Muffet.

'Quick, run!' he shouted, catching hold of her hand and dragging her behind a tree.

Then he bravely caught up a dead tree-branch, and turned to face the spider.

'I'm going to *kill* you if you frighten Miss Muffet any more,' he said, and lifting up his stick, he brought it down on the spider's hairy back with a tremendous whack.

To his great astonishment, the spider sat down and began to cry.

'Oh, oh, oh!' he sobbed. 'You are unkind to me. I'm not really a spider, I'm a fairy changed into one. And I love Miss Muffet, but directly I sit down beside her, I'm so ugly, I frighten her away. And now you've hurt me dreadfully.'

'I'm awfully sorry,' said Peter, 'but how *was* I to know that you weren't a spider? Wait a minute, and I'll tell Miss Muffet.'

He ran to where she was hiding.

'It isn't a spider, it's a poor fairy changed into one,' he told her, 'and he loves you and doesn't want to frighten you.'

'Is it *really*?' asked Miss Muffet. 'Then I don't mind so much. I'll go and stroke the poor thing.'

She ran to where the spider was still crying large tears on to the grass, and stroked him. He stopped crying at once, and cried out:

'A thousand thanks to you, little boy. You have done me a great kindness in making Miss Muffet friends with me. Any time you want help, clap your hands three times, and call for Arran the Spider.'

'Thank you, I will,' said Peter, 'but now, goodbye, I'm going to the Wise Elf in Hideaway House.'

'We'll stay and help you catch it, then,' said Miss Muffet, who seemed to have lost all fear of the spider.

'*Catch* it! Whatever *do* you mean?' exclaimed Peter, astonished.

Miss Muffet laughed. 'Ah! You'll see,' she said.

'There's Hideaway House,' said Peter, running towards a queer little wooden house. But just as he got near to it, it disappeared!

'Oh!' cried Peter, amazed and stopping still. 'It's gone!'

'It's behind you, Peter,' laughed Miss Muffet. Sure enough it was.

'However did it get there?' said Peter, going towards it again. But just as he reached the front door, it vanished again.

'I don't like this sort of house,' said Peter, looking puzzled. 'Where's it gone to now?'

'Over in that corner,' said the spider, pointing to it with one of his eight legs.

'I'll try again,' said Peter, and ran over to the little house, but no—directly he reached it, it disappeared once more.

'This is stupid,' stormed Peter, feeling quite cross.

'We'll help you,' said Miss Muffet. 'Directly it comes near us, we'll catch hold of it.'

But try as they would, the Hideaway House always got away, and when they looked round, there it was, standing behind them somewhere.

'It's got a very good name,' said Peter, 'but it's the stupidest house I *ever* saw.'

He stared at the house and frowned hard. He felt very impatient and cross. Then he suddenly remembered Garin's advice.

'He said I was to look round for something beautiful whenever I felt cross,' said Peter to himself. 'Very well, I will.'

He looked all round the wood, and his eye caught sight of something blue.

'What's that?' he said, and ran to see. 'Oh, 'tis a perfectly lovely little flower!' he called to Miss Muffet. 'Come and look, it's the prettiest I ever saw.'

Miss Muffet looked at it.

'It's the rarest flower in Fairyland,' she said. 'What a good thing you saw it! Now, all you've got to do is to pick it, and stand in the middle of the clearing here and shout out to the Wise Elf that you've found the blue Mist-flower! He's always wanting it for his magic spells.'

Peter picked it, and stood upright.

'Wise Elf in Hideaway House!' he called. 'I've found the blue Mist-flower! Do you want it?'

At once the door of Hideaway House opened, and an Elf with large wings, large eyes and large ears stood on the doorstep.

'Come in! Come in,' he called, 'and bring the Mist-flower with you.'

'Goodbye,' cried Miss Muffet and the spider. 'We're so glad you've got the Hideaway House at last!' and off they went into the wood.

Peter ran across to the Hideaway House, and to his delight it stood still this time and didn't disappear. He went inside the front door and found himself in a dark room at one end of which sat the Wise Elf.

'Good afternoon,' he said. 'I am glad to see you.'

'Good afternoon,' said Peter. 'This is a funny sort of house to live in. If I hadn't remembered Garin's advice to stop being cross and look round for something beautiful, I would never have got here.'

'Possibly not,' said the Wise Elf, nodding at Peter. 'Being impatient and cross never did *anybody* any good. Give me that Mist-flower, please.'

Peter handed it to him.

'Please could you tell me how I can find the Dobbadies?' he asked.

'Well,' said the Wise Elf, putting on a large pair of spectacles, and taking down a book. 'Well, I can tell you which way to go, and as you've been clever enough to find exactly the flower I've been wanting for six months, I shall be glad to show you part of the way. Let me see. Let me see!' and he turned over the pages of his book.

'Ah, here we are,' he said at last, coming to a page on which was a queer map. 'Yes, I thought so—the Dobbadies live on the north side of Dreamland—now, how can you get there? Ummm-m, um-m-m, let me see. Yes, I think I can tell you.'

'Oh, thank you,' said Peter gratefully.

'You had better go through the Underground Caves to the Sleepy Sloos, then you must get them to take you to the Rushing Lift to Cloudland. From Cloudland you can get straight down to Giant Roffti's, and he will carry you across to where the Dobbadies live. Then you must find out how to rescue Pamela.'

'It sounds rather hard,' said Peter, feeling a little dismayed.

'If you make up your mind to do it, you *will* do it,' said the Wise Elf, looking over the tops of his spectacles at Peter.

'Then I'm *going* to do it,' said Peter, jumping up. 'Would you mind showing me part of the way, Wise Elf?'

'Certainly,' answered the Elf. 'I can take you as far as the entrance to the Underground Caves.'

'Thank you,' said Peter. 'I'm really awfully obliged to you.'

The Wise Elf bent down and pulled a mat up from the floor. A trap-door lay underneath.

'Help me pull it up,' said the Elf. He and Peter tugged it upright, and Peter saw a long flight of steps stretching downwards.

The Wise Elf ran down the steps, and Peter followed. After they had gone down about a hundred, they came out into a large passage, which was lighted with green lamps.

'Oh, I do believe it's an underground railway. How lovely!' cried Peter.

'Quite right,' said the Elf. 'Ah, look! The lamps have changed to red. That means the train is coming.'

Then suddenly, gliding out of the darkness, came such a small engine that Peter thought it must be a toy one.

'It's run by magic,' explained the Wise Elf. 'It's stopping for us, so we must get in quickly.'

He helped Peter into a funny-looking carriage. There were no seats, but just fat cushions on the floor.

'Good afternoon,' said the Wise Elf politely to the folk inside. He chose a fat green cushion to sit on, and pointed out a mauve one.

The carriage was full of fairy-folk of all kinds. Goblins, gnomes, fairies, and pixies were there, all chattering gaily to each other.

'Where are you going to?' they asked Peter.

'To the Underground Caves,' he answered. 'Where are *you* all going to?'

'We're all going to the Gnome King's party,' answered a very beautifully-dressed fairy.

The train ran along quietly, past big bowl-shaped lamps lighting up the passage, and at last came to a stop at a little platform.

'Here we are!' said the Wise Elf. He and Peter got out, and the train went on into the darkness.

'Goodbye, goodbye,' called all the folk who were going to the party.

The Wise Elf went to a door on the platform and opened it. It led into a dark cave, lit only by one lantern in the middle.

'Here I must leave you,' said the Elf. 'If you wait here for a little while, you will see the entrance to the Underground Caves. I hope you will find Pamela. Goodbye.'

'Goodbye!' called Peter, feeling rather lonely as he saw the Elf run back to the platform to catch the next train back.

He waited in the dark cave for about ten minutes and then suddenly saw a shiny silver rope coming slowly down from the ceiling.

'This must be something to do with the cave's entrance,' said Peter, and as the rope reached him, he caught hold of it and gave it a pull.

Immediately one side of the cave split open and formed a great archway, leading into another cave!

'Hurray!' cried Peter, running through. 'Here's the entrance at last!'

He looked all round him, and found he was

in a tremendously large cave, lighted with pink lights. No one was there. There was an archway leading into another cave. Peter ran into it. It was lighted with mauve lights, and was smaller than the first.

'Why, *this* one's got an archway leading into another cave,' cried Peter, 'and they're all empty.'

He ran into the next one and looked all round. It had orange lights and was still smaller.

On and on Peter went, into smaller and smaller caves, each lighted differently. At last he came to the smallest cave of all, which had big blue lamps swinging from the ceiling.

'Oh, there really *is* somebody here!' said Peter, feeling very pleased.

All around the cave were lying mouse-like creatures with large ears, and all were fast asleep.

'Hullo! Are you the Sleepy Sloos?' asked Peter loudly.

No one stirred.

'I say! I want to go to Cloudland,' called Peter, 'so will you help me, please?'

Still no one stirred, but Peter somehow felt quite certain some of the Sleepy Sloos were awake, but were too lazy to help him.

'Wake up! Wake up!' shouted Peter, shaking the one nearest him.

But it was all no good. Peter felt very cross and most impatient, and was just going to stamp round the cave in a temper, when he suddenly remembered Garin's advice again.

'Oh dear, there *isn't* anything beautiful to look at here!' he grumbled. But he determined to have a good look round the cave all the same.

'Hullo! What's that?' he said, tugging at something that twinkled in a crack of the cave rock. 'What a beautiful stone! It's a diamond, I do believe.'

'What?'

'What's that?'

'What have you got?'

All the Sleepy Sloos had suddenly waked up and were shouting at Peter.

'Hurray! He's found the magic stone we lost last week! How lovely!' cried they, and crowded round Peter.

'Oh,' said Peter, 'so you've waked up at last! What a good thing I took Garin's advice! If I give you back your stone, will you stay awake long enough to show me the Rushing Lift to Cloudland?'

'Yes, yes, yes!' cried the Sleepy Sloos.

Peter gave them the stone, which glittered and twinkled just as though it were alive.

The Sleepy Sloos took paws and danced in a ring and sang:

'Rushing Lift
You must come down
And take this boy
To Cloudland Town.'

Then crash! The roof of the cave split open and down there came a bright orange chair, swinging on purple ropes.

'Get in, get in,' cried the Sleepy Sloos. 'We want to go to sleep. Goodbye!' and they all settled down again and began to snore.

Peter got into the orange chair, and whizz-z-z! He shot right up into the air at a most tremendous pace! When it stopped, he got out and found himself on a great soft cloud.

'Goodness me! *Now* where do I go?' he said.

'Where would you like to go?' asked a voice.

'Who are you speaking?' asked Peter, looking all round.

'I'm the cloud. I'll take you wherever you like,' answered the voice.

'Then take me down to Giant Roffti's, please,' said Peter, feeling most astonished to hear a cloud speak.

'Very well. Sit down and hold tight,' commanded the cloud. Peter did so, and felt the cloud slowly sink down, down, down, through the air. It seemed simply ages before it stopped.

'Here we are!' at last said the cloud. 'We're in Roffti's backyard. He'll be in the kitchen, I expect. Goodbye!' And as Peter scrambled off the cloud, it swiftly rose again up into the sky.

Peter was in a huge backyard, full of the largest dustbins he had ever seen. Near by

was a great open door.

'I suppose that's the kitchen,' thought Peter, and walked boldly in.

Inside he found a huge giant busy putting tremendous cakes into an oven. The giant looked very hot and very tired, Peter thought.

'Please,' said Peter, 'could you take me to the Dobbadies?'

'Bless me! Bless me!! Bless me!!!' exclaimed the giant, dropping a tray of cakes in amazement. 'How you made me jump!'

'I *am* so sorry,' said Peter, feeling very uncomfortable as he saw the cakes rolling all over the floor.

'Oh, never mind,' puffed the giant, looking hotter than ever. 'Accidents *will* happen!'

'Are you very busy?' asked Peter politely.

'Yes. There's a grand party on in Giantland today and I'm baking some extra cakes,' answered the giant, picking up the dropped cakes.

'What a lot of parties are on today!' said Peter.

'Yes, the Dobbadies are going to this one,' said the giant. 'So it's no good my taking you to see them today.'

'Oh, good!' cried Peter. 'You see, I want to rescue my sister and the Princess of Dreamland from the Dobbadies, and it would be much easier if they're not there!'

'Right! Come along, quickly!' cried Roffti, catching Peter up in one hand. He rushed out into the garden, jumped across a large pond, ran down a dark lane, and into a broad drive. At the end stood a great sparkling palace, with thousands of windows.

'That's where the Dobbadies live!' said Roffti. 'Now, what's your sister's name?'

'Pamela,' said Peter, still dangling in the giant's huge hand.

'Pamela! Pamela! Pamela!' roared the giant.

At a tiny window near the roof a little girl's curly head peeped out.

'There she is!' shouted Peter excitedly. Roffti lifted Peter up and put him on the window-sill. To Peter's great delight there was Pamela, lifting her arms to him in joy.

'Peter! Oh, I *am* glad you've come!' she cried. 'And here's the Princess, she's a prisoner too.'

Peter clambered into the room, and saw a beautiful lady sitting on a chair, and looking very miserable.

'Cheer up!' he cried excitedly. 'I've come to rescue you while the Dobbadies are at the party!'

'Come on, then,' said Pamela, running to the door.

All three raced down the stairs and out into the garden. 'Hush!' suddenly cried the Princess as a queer cloppity noise reached them.

'Oh, oh, it's the Dobbadies!' whispered Pamela.

Sure enough it was! There they were, little gnome-like creatures, but with three legs instead of two, pouring into the garden, back from the party early.

'Oh dear! What *can* I do?' thought poor Peter, looking desperately around. 'I can't fight them *all*!'

Suddenly he remembered Arran the Spider.

'*He'll* help me, of course!' he cried, and clapping his hands three times loudly, he cried, 'Arran, Arran the Spider! Come and help me, Arran!'

All the Dobbadies crowded round shouting: 'They're escaping! Catch them!'

Then, just as they caught hold of Pamela and the Princess, Peter gave a shout:

'Hurrah! Here's good old Arran! And he's brought Miss Muffet, too!'

Arran, the huge spider, ran rapidly into the garden, carrying Miss Muffet on his back. The Dobbadies let go Pamela and the Princess with cries of alarm. 'What is it? What is it?' they cried.

'Something that will *eat* you!' cried Arran, as he jumped at them.

'Oh, oh, oh!' cried the Dobbadies, and fled into the palace for all they were worth.

'Quick!' cried Arran. 'Run whilst you've a chance. Miss Muffet will show you the way, and I'll come last and eat up the Dobbadies that follow!'

Little Miss Muffet ran down a passage into a large cave, and the others followed her. A river ran through the cave, and there was a little boat moored to a yellow post.

'Jump in, jump in!' cried Arran. 'The Dobbadies are coming again.'

All of them jumped in the little rocking boat, and just as a crowd of three-legged Dobbadies came rushing into the cave, Arran pushed off.

'Now we're safe,' he said, as the boat raced off on the underground river. 'There's no other boat for the Dobbadies to take.'

So the Dobbadies were left behind, shouting and screaming because the prisoners had escaped.

'Oh, thank you for coming to our help, Arran,' said Peter, stroking the huge spider.

'Very pleased to,' said Arran. 'You made little Miss Muffet friends with me, and I could never forget that.'

'Where do you want to go to?' asked Miss Muffet.

'Oh, *home*, please,' said Pamela. 'I've made the Princess well now, and I want my mummy.'

The boat went on and on until at last the river flowed out into open fields.

'Why, we've come to a pond!' exclaimed Peter, as the boat came to a stop.

'And it's *our* pond, in *our* garden!' cried Pamela. 'But I *know* there isn't a river into it!'

'Ah, it's magic, you see,' said Arran. 'It'll be gone tomorrow. Now, goodbye; you'll see us again sometime. I'm going to take the Princess back to Dreamland.'

'Goodbye, goodbye!' shouted Pamela and Peter, running up the garden path.

'Mummy, Mummy!' cried Pamela, as Mummy and Daddy came running to meet them.

'Oh, Peter, you *are* clever and brave!' said Mummy, when all the story had been told, and everyone had been hugged and kissed a hundred times over.

'Come and look at the magic river, Daddy,' begged Peter, running into the garden.

But alas! It was gone.

'Never mind,' said Peter, 'we've had some *glorious* adventures, and when the river comes again one day, we'll have some more!'

The Book of Pixies

EGMONT

CONTENTS

Dame Quickly's Wash-Tub	183
The Three Wishes	189
It Was The Wind	194
The Bed That Took a Walk	201
He'll Do for a Sweep!	208
The Spell That Didn't Stop	212
It All Began With Jinky	218
Muddle's Mistake	224
Dame Topple's Buns	232
The Train That Went to Fairyland	238
Little Mister Sly	246
The Brownie's Magic	252
Little Connie Careless	260
The Three Bad Imps	265
Silky and the Snail	272
Mr. Topple and the Egg	279
The Angry Pixies	287
Binky the Borrower	293
The Birthday Party	299
He Wouldn't Take the Trouble	307
A Puddle for the Donkeys	313
The Very Lovely Pattern	318
Dame Lucky's Umbrella	326
The Yellow Motor Car	332
The Little Hidden Spell	338
The Forgotten Pets	347

Dame Quickly's Wash-Tub

One day when Tickle the pixie was going home, he passed by Dame Quickly's cottage. He thought he would peep round and see what he could see. Dame Quickly often used magic spells, and it was fun to watch her.

But there was nobody in the cottage. On the table, by itself, stood something that made Tickle's eyes gleam. It was a wash-tub, a bright yellow one, as magic as could be.

Everyone knew Dame Quickly's wash-tub. You had only to put your dirty clothes in it, and say, 'Alla malla, wash-tub, get to work!' and the wash-tub would swish the clothes round and round, clean them beautifully, and then wring them out and throw them on to the table.

'I wish I could borrow that wash-tub,' thought Tickle, thinking of the big wash he had to do that afternoon. 'What a pity Dame Quickly is out. I suppose she has gone to her sister's for the day. She always does on Monday.'

He looked and looked at the wash-tub. Then he climbed in at the window and picked it up.

'It can't matter borrowing it,' he thought. 'I know I ought to ask – but if I wait till tomorrow and ask Dame Quickly, she might say no. So I'd better borrow it now. I can take it back before she comes home tonight. She won't even know I borrowed it!'

He ran off with it on his shoulders. When he got home he filled it with warm water, put some soap into the water, and then threw in all his dirty clothes and linen.

Then he tapped the tub three times and cried, 'Alla, malla, wash-tub, get to work!'

And my goodness me, you should have seen that wash-tub dealing with those clothes! It swished them round and round in the soapy water and got all the dirt out as quickly as could be.

Then it tossed them out on to the table, with all the water wrung out, ready for Tickle to rinse. It was marvellous.

Tickle took them to rinse in the sink. The wash-tub made a curious whistling noise, and suddenly the curtains flew from the window and put themselves into the water. Then the washtub set to work on them.

'Hi!' cried Tickle. 'Don't do that. Those curtains were only washed last week. Now I shall have to dry them and iron them all over again. Stop, you silly wash-tub.'

But the wash-tub took no notice. It tossed the washed curtains out of the water, and then whistled again.

And into the tub jumped all the rugs and mats off the floor! It was most annoying. Tickle shouted crossly. 'Will you stop behaving like this? I don't want my mats washed. Stop it, you silly wash-tub.'

Out came the rugs and mats as clean as could be – and then the wash-tub whistled again. All the cushions threw themselves into the tub! But that was too much for Tickle.

'I won't have my nice feather cushions soaked with water! Now, stop it, wash-tub!'

The tub whistled again – and, oh dear, poor Tickle found himself jumping into the wash-tub too! He was swished round and round, well-soaped, squeezed, and tossed out on to the table.

'You wicked wash-tub!' he cried, wiping the soap from his eyes. 'You wicked—'

The tub whistled, and into the water went Tickle again! This was a fine game, the wash-tub thought, a very fine game indeed. It waited till Tickle had been thrown out once more, then whistled again – and in went poor Tickle, splash!

When he was tossed out for the third time he

fled to the door. He ran down the road to meet
Dame Quickly's bus. Oh, oh, oh, she must get her
horrid wash-tub as soon as she could! Who would
have thought it would behave like that?

Dame Quickly stepped off the bus. Tickle ran
up to her, dripping with water.

'Dame Quickly, dear Dame Quickly, please,
please come and get your wash-tub from my
house!' begged Tickle. 'It is behaving so badly.'

'From your house?' said Dame Quickly, in
surprise. 'How did my wash-tub get into your
house?'

Tickle felt rather awkward. 'Well, you see,' he

said, 'I – er – I wanted to borrow it – but you were out – so I er – I – er—'

'You took it without asking!' said Dame Quickly, looking very stern. 'Don't you know that's a very wrong thing to do? You knew I wouldn't lend it to you if you asked me – so you took it without asking. That's next door to stealing, you know that. You bad little pixie. Well – keep the wash-tub. I can make myself another.'

'Oh!' squealed poor Tickle, 'I can't keep it. I really can't. It keeps on whistling me into the water, and washing me. Oh, do, do come and get it.'

Dame Quickly laughed. 'What a strange lovely punishment for you,' she said. 'No – I tell you I don't want my tub back.'

'But I shall spend the rest of my life being whistled into the water and washed!' wailed Tickle.

'That's quite likely,' said Dame Quickly. 'Good-bye.'

Tickle caught hold of her skirt, and wept big tears down his cheeks. 'Please, I'll never borrow without asking again, please, I'm sorry. What can I do to show you I am sorry?'

'Ah, now you are talking properly,' said Dame Quickly. 'If you are really sorry, and want to make up for what you have done, I'll come and get the tub. But for the next three weeks, I shall expect you to come and do my ironing for me.'

She went back to Tickle's cottage, spoke sharply to the tub, which had begun to whistle as soon as it saw Tickle again, and then put it on her shoulder.

'Now, remember,' she said to Tickle, 'come each Tuesday for three weeks to do my ironing. And maybe at the end of that time you will have made up your mind that it really isn't good to borrow without asking! Goodbye!'

Poor Tickle. He'll be very careful now, won't he?

The Three Wishes

Elsie and Bobby were sitting in the meadow, and, as usual, they were quarrelling.

They were brother and sister, but to hear them quarrelling with one another, you might have thought they were enemies!

'I didn't want to come to this wood. I wanted to go up the hill,' said Elsie. 'You always do what you want. You never do what I want.'

'Oh, you story-teller!' said Bobby. 'You are the most selfish girl I know – I'm always having to do what you choose. I don't like you a bit.'

'Well, I don't like—' Elsie began, and then she stopped. She had seen something moving in the buttercups near her. She put out her hand quickly and caught the thing that was moving.

To her enormous surprise, it was a pixie! The little creature gave a scream, and wriggled hard. But Elsie didn't let go. She held the little creature very tightly.

'Look!' she said to Bobby, in an excited voice. 'Look! I've caught a fairy!'

'Let me go!' squealed the little thing. 'You are hurting me.'

'Make her give us three wishes,' said Bobby, suddenly. 'Go on – tell her. We might get three wishes that would come true!'

Elsie squeezed the poor little pixie till she cried out.

'Give us three wishes and I'll let you go,' she said. 'Three wishes! Then we can make ourselves rich and happy and wise.'

'I'll give you three wishes,' said the pixie. 'But they won't do you any good! Children like you can't wish for the right things! But I'll give you three wishes if you want them.'

Elsie let the pixie go, and the little thing fled away among the bluebells, laughing as if she had heard a joke.

'What's she laughing at?' said Bobby. 'Oh, well, never mind. Now, what shall we wish?'

'I want to wish for a budgerigar that can talk,' said Elsie, at once. 'I've always wanted one.'

'What a silly wish!' said Bobby. 'No – let's wish for a little aeroplane that will take us anywhere we want to go.'

'I'm sure I don't want to fly in the air with you as the pilot,' said Elsie. 'No, you're not to wish that.'

'Well, I shall,' said Bobby, and he wished it. 'I wish I had a little aeroplane of my own, that I could fly off in.'

At once a most beautiful little aeroplane flew down from the air and landed beside Bobby. He was simply delighted. He got into it and grinned at Elsie, who was very angry.

'You bad boy, to waste a wish on a thing like that!' she said, and she got up to shake him. She caught hold of his shoulders, and tried to pull him out of the aeroplane.

'I wish you were miles away!' she shouted. 'You're a horrid brother to have!'

The aeroplane's engine started up, and the propeller began to whirl round. Elsie's wish was coming true!

Bobby dragged Elsie in beside him as the aeroplane flew off. 'You horrid girl!' he said. 'That's the second wish gone. Now goodness knows where we shall land.'

They flew in the air for a long way and then the aeroplane landed on a little island. The sea splashed all round it, and except for a few strange trees and sea-birds there was nothing to be seen.

'Now see what you've done!' said Bobby. 'You made us come here!' He got out of the aeroplane and walked round the little island. He came back looking gloomy.

'We can't stay here. There is nothing to eat. We should starve. We must go back home.'

'How?' said Elsie.

'In the aeroplane,' said Bobby. 'Come on, get in. We'll fly back, and then we'll be very, very careful about what we wish for our last wish.'

They got into the aeroplane – but it didn't fly off. It just stood there, its engine silent and its propeller still.

'I'm afraid we'll have to use our last wish to get back home,' said Bobby, sadly. 'How we have wasted them! Aeroplane, I wish you would take us back home.'

The aeroplane flew up into the air and soon the children were back in the meadow again. They got out and looked at the nice little plane.

'Well, anyway, we've got an aeroplane,' said Bobby. But even as he spoke the little pixie ran up, jumped into the plane, set the engine going, and flew off.

'What did I tell you?' shouted the pixie, leaning out of the aeroplane. 'I said that three wishes would be wasted on children like you – and so they were! People who quarrel always do stupid things – what silly children you are!'

Bobby and Elsie watched the little aeroplane as it flew above the trees. They were very sad.

'If we hadn't quarrelled, we'd have been able to talk over what we really wanted,' said Elsie. 'We could have wished for some lovely things.'

'Well – we will next time,' said Bobby.

But there won't be a next time. Things like that don't happen twice!

It Was The Wind

Tricky and Dob lived next door to one another. Dob was a hard-working little fellow, always busy about something. Tricky was a scamp, and he teased the life out of poor old Dob.

He undid the clothes from Dob's washing-line, so that they dropped into the mud and had to be washed all over again. He crept through a hole in his fence and took the eggs that Feathers, Dob's white hen, laid for him. He borrowed this and he borrowed that – but he always forgot to return anything.

Dob put up with Tricky and his ways very patiently, but he did wish Tricky didn't live next to him!

He didn't like Tricky at all, but he didn't tell tales of him or complain of him, so nobody ever punished Tricky or scolded him.

Still, things can't go on like that for ever, and one day a very funny thing happened.

It was an autumn day, and the leaves had blown down from the trees, spreading everywhere over Dob's garden.

They were making Tricky's garden untidy, too, of course, but he didn't mind a bit. Dob did mind. He was a good little gardener, and he loved his garden to be tidy and neat.

So he took his broom and began to sweep his leaves into a big heap. He swept them up by the fence between his garden and Tricky's. There! Now his garden was tidy again. Dob went to fetch his barrow to put the leaves into it to take down to the rubbish heap.

Tricky had been watching Dob sweeping up his leaves. He grinned. Here was a chance to tease Dob again, he thought. Dob had put the pile of leaves just by the hole in his fence! Tricky slipped out as soon as Dob had gone to fetch his barrow, and went to his fence.

He wriggled through the hole into the middle of the pile of leaves. Then he scattered all the leaves over the grass; what fun he was having. When he had finished, he crept back unseen through the hole.

'Dob *will* be surprised!' he thought. And Dob was. He was annoyed as well. What had happened? A minute ago the leaves had been in a neat pile – now they were all over the place again!

He saw Tricky looking over the fence. 'Good-day, Dob,' said Tricky politely. 'It's a pity the wind blew your leaves away just as you got them into a pile, wasn't it?'

'The wind?' said Dob, puzzled. 'But there isn't any wind.'

'Well, it must have been a sudden, mischievous breeze, then,' said Tricky, grinning. 'You know – a little young wind that doesn't know any better.'

'Hmm!' said Dob, and he swept up all his leaves into a pile again. It was dinner-time then, so he left them and went indoors. But he did not get his dinner at once. He just watched behind his curtain to see if Tricky came into his garden to kick away his pile of leaves.

Well, he didn't see Tricky, of course, because that mischievous fellow had wriggled through the hole in the fence that was well hidden by the pile of leaves. He was now in the very middle of the pile – and to Dob's enormous surprise his leaves suddenly shot up in the air, and flew all over the grass.

'What a very peculiar thing!' said Dob, astonished. 'I've never seen leaves behave like that before. Can it be that Tricky is right, and that a little breeze is playing about with them?'

He thought about it whilst he ate his dinner. It couldn't be Tricky, because Dob hadn't seen him climb over the fence and go to the pile. One minute the pile had been there, neat and tidy – and the next it had been scattered all over the place.

'I'll sweep up the leaves once more,' thought Dob. 'And I'll put them into my barrow before that wind gets them again.'

But, of course, Tricky got into the next pile too, through the hole in the fence, and Dob found his leaves scattering all round him. He was very cross and very puzzled.

Soon Tricky called to him. He had wriggled out of the pile, through the hole in the fence and was now back in his own garden, grinning away at

Dob. 'My word – are you still sweeping up leaves? There's no end to it, Dob.'

'I think you must have been right when you said that the wind is playing me tricks,' said Dob. 'But the thing is – what am I to do about it?'

'Catch the bad fellow and make him prisoner!' said Tricky.

'But how can you catch the wind?' asked Dob.

'Well, haven't you seen how the wind loves to billow out a sail, or blow out a sack or a balloon?' said Tricky. 'Just get a sack, Dob, put the wind in it when it comes along, tie up the neck and send him off by carrier to the Weather Man to deal with. He'll give him a good telling off, you may be sure!'

'Well – if I *could* catch the wind that way I would certainly do all you say,' said Dob. 'But I'm afraid it isn't possible.'

All the same he went and got a sack and put it ready nearby in case the wind did come along again. Tricky watched him sweep up his leaves once more, and he simply couldn't resist creeping through the hole to play the same trick on poor Dob again!

But this time Dob was on the watch for the wind, and as soon as he saw the leaves beginning to stir, he clapped the sack over the pile. He felt something wriggling in the leaves, and gave a shout.

'I've got him! I've caught the wind! He's filling up my sack! Aha, you scamp of a wind, I've got you!'

Tricky wriggled and shouted in the sack, but Dob shook him well down to the bottom of it, together with dozens of leaves, and tied up the neck firmly with rope.

'It's no good wriggling and shouting like that!' he said sternly. 'You're caught. It's a good thing Tricky told me how to catch you! Now, off to the Weather Man you're going, and goodness knows what he'll do with you!' He wrote a big label:

'*To be delivered to the Weather Man by the Carrier – one small, mischievous breeze. Suggest it should be well spanked before it is allowed to blow again.*'

And when the Carrier came by with his cart, Dob handed the whimpering Tricky to him, tightly tied up in the sack. The Carrier read the label and grinned.

'I'll deliver him all right,' he said. 'The Weather Man isn't in a very good temper lately – I'm afraid he'll be very cross with this little breeze.'

Dob went to look over the fence to find Tricky

and tell him that his good idea had been carried out – but Tricky was nowhere to be seen, of course! And he was nowhere to be seen for three whole days! Dob was puzzled.

He came back the evening of the third day. He looked very solemn indeed. The Weather Man had told him off well and truly, and had sent him to do all kinds of blowing errands, which made Tricky very much out of breath.

'Hallo, Tricky! Wherever have you been?' cried Dob.

Tricky wouldn't tell him. He wouldn't tell anyone. But everyone agreed that his three days away had done him good – he wasn't nearly so mischievous, and ever since that day he has never played single trick on old Dob.

'I can't imagine why!' said Dob. How he would laugh if he knew!

The Bed That Took a Walk

The pixie Miggle was always late for everything. If he went to catch a train he had to run all the way and then he would miss it. If he went to catch a bus it had always gone round the corner before he got there.

'It's just as easy to be early as to be late,' said his friends. 'Why don't you get up a bit sooner, then you would be in time for everything?'

'Well, I'm so sleepy in the mornings,' said Miggle. 'My wife comes and calls me, but I go off to sleep again. I really am a very tired person in the morning.'

'Lazy, he means!' said his friends to one another. 'Never in time for anything! It's shocking. One day he will be very sorry.'

In the month of June the King and Queen of the pixies were coming to visit Apple Tree Town, where Miggle and his friends lived. The pixies were very excited.

'I shall get a new coat,' said Jinky.

'I shall buy a new feather for my hat,' said Twinkle.

'I shall have new red shoes,' said Flitter.

'And I shall buy a whole new suit, a new hat and feathers, and new shoes and buckles with the money I have saved up,' said Miggle. 'I shall be very grand indeed!'

'You'll never be in time to see the King and Queen!' said Jinky, with a laugh.

'Indeed I shall,' said Miggle. 'I shall be up before any of you that day.'

Well, the day before the King and Queen came, Miggle was very busy trying on his new things. The coat didn't quite fit, so he asked his wife to alter it. She stayed up very late trying to make it right.

It was about midnight when Miggle got to bed. How he yawned! 'Wake me up at seven o'clock, wife,' he said. 'Don't forget.'

Mrs. Miggle was tired. 'I shall call you three times, and then, if you don't get up, I shan't call you any more,' she said. ' *I* have to call myself – nobody calls *me* – and I am tired tonight, so I shall not be very patient with you tomorrow if you don't get up when I call you.'

'You *do* sound cross,' said Miggle, and got into bed. He fell fast asleep, and it seemed no time at all before he felt Mrs. Miggle shouting in his ear, and shaking him.

'Miggle! It's seven o'clock. Miggle get up!'

'All right,' said Miggle, and turned over to go to sleep again. In five minutes' time Mrs. Miggle shook him again, and once more he woke up, and went to sleep again.

'This is the third time I've called you,' said Mrs. Miggle, ten minutes later, in a cross voice. 'And it's the last time. If you don't get up now, I shan't call you any more.'

'Right,' said Miggle. 'Just getting up, my dear.' But he didn't. He went to sleep again. Plenty of time to get up and dress and go and see the King and Queen!

Mrs. Miggle kept her word. She didn't call Miggle again. She got dressed in her best frock and went to meet the King and Queen. Miggle slept on soundly, not hearing the footsteps going down the road, as all the pixies hurried by to meet the royal pair.

Miggle's bed creaked to wake him. It shook a little, but Miggle didn't stir. The bed was cross. It thought Miggle stayed too long in it. It knew how upset Miggle would be when he woke up and found that the King and Queen had gone.

So it thought it would take Miggle to the Town Hall, where the King and Queen would be, and perhaps he would wake up there.

The bed walked on its four legs to the door. It squeezed itself through, for it was a narrow bed. It trotted down the street, clickity-clack, clickity-clack.

Miggle didn't wake. He had a lovely dream that he was in a boat that went gently up and down on the sea, and said 'clickity-clack' all the time.

'Gracious! Look, isn't that Miggle asleep on that bed?' cried Jinky, with a squeal of laughter. 'The bed is wide awake, but Miggle isn't – so the bed is taking him to the Town Hall!'

'Clickity-clack, clickity-clack,' went the four legs of the bed. Miggle gave a little snore. He was warm and cosy and comfy, and as fast asleep as ever.

The bed made its way into the Town Hall just as the King and Queen came on to the stage to speak to their people. The pixies jumped to their feet and cheered loudly.

The bed jumped up and down in joy, because it was enjoying the treat too. Miggle woke up when he heard the cheering, and felt the bumping of the bed. He sat up and looked round in the greatest surprise.

'Ha ha, ho ho, look at Miggle,' shouted everyone, and the King and Queen had to smile too. Miggle was full of horror and shame!

What had happened! Had his silly bed brought him to the Town Hall? Oh dear, and he was in his pyjamas too, instead of in his lovely new clothes!

Miggle could have wept with shame. Mrs. Miggle saw him and went over to him.

'Really, Miggle! To think you've come to see the King and Queen in bed, not even dressed! I'm ashamed of you! What *can* you be thinking of?'

Miggle slid down into bed and pulled the clothes over his head. Mrs. Miggle pulled them off.

'Now you get up and bow properly to His

Majesty the King and Her Majesty the Queen,' she said.

'What, in my pyjamas?' said poor Miggle.

'Well, if you've come in pyjamas, you'll have to bow in them,' said Mrs. Miggle. So Miggle had to stand up on the bed in his pyjamas and bow to the King and Queen. How they laughed!

'What a funny man!' said the Queen. 'Does he often do things like this?'

Miggle didn't know what to do. He lay down again and ordered the bed to go home. But the bed wasn't a dog, to be ordered here and there. It wanted to stay and see the fun.

So Miggle had to jump out and run all the way home in his pyjamas. 'How dreadful, how dreadful!' he kept thinking, as he ran. 'I can't bear it! I'd better put on all my fine clothes, and go back and let the King and Queen see how grand I really am!'

So he did – but alas, when he got back to the Town Hall, the King and Queen had just gone. Everyone was coming away, pleased and excited. Miggle's bed trotted with them, 'clickity-clack'.

'Hallo, Miggle? Going to ride home asleep in bed?' cried his friends. 'Oh, how you made the King and Queen laugh! It was the funniest sight we've ever seen.'

Miggle frowned and didn't say a word. His bed tried to walk close to him, but he wouldn't let it. Horrid bed! 'I'll never be late again!' thought Miggle. 'Never, never, never!'

But he will. It's not so easy to get out of a bad habit. Won't it be funny if his bed walks off with him again?

He'll Do for a Sweep!

Dick was such a dirty little boy. His face was always grimy, he never washed his neck, or behind his ears, and as for his knees, well, you would think he walked on them, they were so dirty.

'I wish you didn't always look so dirty,' said Miss Brown. 'Don't you ever have a bath, Dick? Don't you ever wash your face? And look at your clothes! What have you been doing to them?'

Dick stared at his teacher. He didn't see why she should make such a fuss about dirt. What did it matter?

'It matters a lot,' said Miss Brown. 'A dirty person catches an illness more quickly than a clean one – and it looks so horrid to be dirty. It isn't polite to other people to go about looking so grimy and ugly.'

Even then Dick didn't try to be clean. He never even cleaned his nails, and they looked really horrid.

'You look as if you've been sweeping chimneys!' said Miss Brown, in disgust, one day when he came to school. 'No, Dick – I really will not allow you to come to school in this state. You have soap and water at home, and I am sure you have some clean clothes somewhere. Go home, please, and come back clean.'

Dick was cross. He walked out of school and went into the woods. He had to go through them to go home.

He hadn't gone very far before a little man rushed out of the trees and caught hold of him. 'Here's one!' he cried, in excitement. 'Here's one.'

'Don't,' said Dick, half-afraid. 'Let me go.'

Some other little men came running up. 'Good!' they cried. 'Come on – bring him along. Quick! Has he got any brushes?'

'He doesn't seem to have,' said the first little man. 'Never mind – he can borrow mine.'

'What do you mean? Where are you taking me?' yelled Dick, getting angry.

'We want you to sweep our chimney,' said the first little man. 'It's smoking terribly. Our own sweep has gone away, and we really must get the chimney done.'

'But I'm not a sweep!' said Dick, crossly. 'Can't you see I'm not?'

'You are! Sweeps are always grimy and dirty, they can't help it,' said the little men. 'You're grimy and dirty, so you must be a sweep. Come along!'

They dragged him along, though he didn't want to go. They came to a little cottage set in the heart of the wood. They took Dick inside. The fire was out, but it had been smoking very much, for the room was full of smoke, and Dick's eyes began to smart.

'Here are the brushes,' said the little men, and they pushed a collection of poles and strange round brushes into Dick's hands. 'Now sweep the chimney.'

'I'm *not* a sweep!' wailed Dick.

'Well, you'll do for one. You can't get much dirtier than you are already,' said the little men. 'We will shut and lock the door, and we shan't let you out till you've swept our chimney for us!'

They locked the door and poor Dick was left in the smoky room. He stamped and raged. It was no good. The little men were not going to let him out till he had swept that chimney!

So he fitted the brush on top of a pole and pushed it up the chimney. Then he fitted another pole to the end of that one and pushed it up still farther. Soot fell down in a cloud, and he coughed and choked. How dirty he got!

At last the brush stood out at the top of the

chimney and all the soot was cleared. 'Hurrah!' cried the little men, and opened the door. Poor Dick! You should have seen him. He was covered in soot from head to feet, and how he coughed and choked.

The little men let him go. 'You aren't a real sweep, but you'll do for one, you're always so dirty,' they said. 'We will come and get you next time our chimney wants sweeping. We shall always know you, because you are such a dirty boy.'

Dick got into dreadful trouble when he went back home. His mother wouldn't believe that he had swept the chimney of all the little men. She thought he had got himself into more dirt than usual.

'No wonder Miss Brown sent you home!' she scolded. 'Take off your clothes. Get into a hot bath. And keep yourself a bit cleaner in future, or I'll send you to bed each Saturday, and know that for one day at least you will have to keep clean.'

Dick is much better now – not because he is afraid of being punished by his mother, but because he doesn't want those little men to use him for a sweep again. He's happier now he's cleaner – and he looks so much nicer!

The Spell That Didn't Stop

Old Dame Quick-Eye put her head round the kitchen door, and lazy little Yawner jumped up at once.

'What! Reading again in the middle of the morning before you've done your work!' scolded Dame Quick-Eye. 'Do you want me to put a spell on you and make you grow two more arms and hands? Then you'd have to do twice as much work!'

'Oh no, no,' cried Yawner, shutting his book and beginning to bustle round at once. 'Don't do that.'

'I have three friends coming to dinner,' said Dame Quick-Eye. 'There are all the potatoes and apples to peel and the cabbage to cut up. I shall be very angry if everything isn't ready in time.'

Yawner was very frightened when Dame Quick-Eye was angry. As soon as she had gone he rushed into the kitchen.

'The potatoes! The potatoes! Where are they? And what did I do with those cabbages? Did I fetch them from the garden or didn't I?

212

Where's the potato knife? Where is it?'

The potato knife was nowhere to be found. Yawner looked everywhere.

'Oh dear, oh dear – the only sharp knife I have! I can't peel the potatoes with a blunt one. I'll never have time to do all this peeling!'

The front door slammed. Yawner saw Dame Quick-Eye going down the path. He stopped rushing about and sat down. He yawned widely. 'Oh dear, what am I to do? I'd better get a spell from the old Dame's room. A spell to peel potatoes and apples! She'll never know.'

He tiptoed upstairs to the strange little room where Dame Quick-Eye did her magic and her spells. There they all were, in boxes and bottles on the shelf. 'Spell for making things Big'. 'Spell for making things Small'. 'Spell for curing a Greedy Person'. 'Spell for growing more Arms and Hands'. 'Spell to cure Yawner of being Lazy'.

'Oh dear,' said Yawner, staring at the bottle with his name on the label. 'I'd better not be lazy any more. Now – where's the spell to Peel Things Quickly?'

'Ah, here it is – good,' he said at last, and picked up a box. In it was a green powder. Yawner hurried downstairs and took up an ordinary knife. He rubbed a little of the green powder on the blade.

'Now peel!' he whispered. 'Peel quickly, quickly. Don't stop!'

He rushed upstairs again and put the little box of powder back on the shelf. Then down he went. Dame Quick-Eye would never know he had taken a bit of her Peeling Spell.

The spell was already working. The knife was hovering over the bowl of potatoes in the sink, and one by one the potatoes rose up to be peeled, falling back with a plop. 'A very pleasant sight to see,' thought Yawner, and he bustled about getting ready the things he needed to lay the table.

The knife peeled all the potatoes in about two minutes. Then it started on the apples. Soon long green parings were scattered all over the draining-board and a dozen apples lay clean and white nearby.

Yawner shot a glance at the busy knife. 'Splendid, splendid! Take a rest, dear knife.'

He rushed into the dining-room to lay the lunch. He rushed back into the kitchen to get the plates – and how he stared! The potato knife was peeling the cold chicken that Yawner had put ready for lunch. It was scraping off long bits of chicken, which fell to the floor and were being eaten by a most surprised and delighted cat.

'Hey!' cried Yawner and rushed at the knife.

'Stop that! You've done your work!'

He tried to catch the knife, but it flew to the dresser and peeled a long strip from that. Then it began to scrape the mantelpiece and big pieces of wood fell into the hearth.

Yawner began to feel frightened. What would Dame Quick-Eye say when she saw all this damage? He rushed at the knife again, but it flew up into the air, darted into the passage and disappeared.

'Well, good riddance to bad rubbish, I say,' said Yawner loudly, and ran to put the potatoes on to boil. He heard Dame Quick-Eye come in with her friends and hurried even more. Lunch mustn't be late!

Then he heard such a to-do in the dining-room and rushed to see what the matter was. What a sight met his eyes!

The potato knife had peeled all the edges of the polished dining-room table. It had peeled every banana, orange, pear and apple in the dishes. It had peeled the backs of all the chairs, and even peeled the top off the clock.

'Look!' cried Dame Quick-Eye in a rage. 'What's been happening? This knife is mad!'

'Bewitched, you mean,' said one of her friends, looking at it closely. 'I can see some green powder on the blade. Someone's been rubbing it with your Peeling Spell.'

'It's that wretched tiresome lazy little Yawner then!' cried Dame Quick-Eye. 'And there he is — peeping in at the door. Wait till I catch you!'

Yawner didn't wait to hear any more. He ran out into the garden. He kept his broomstick there, and he leapt on it at once.

'Off and away!' he shouted and up in the air rose the broomstick at once.

The broomstick soon became tired of going for miles and miles. It turned itself round and went home again. It sailed down to the yard. Yawner leapt off and rushed to the coal-cellar. He went in and slammed the door. Then he sank down on the coal and cried. Why had he been lazy? Why had he ever stolen a spell? Wrong deeds never, never did any good at all. Dame Quick-Eye looked in at the cellar window. She felt sorry for Yawner.

'Will you be lazy again?' she asked.

'No, Mam,' wept Yawner.

'Will you ever steal my spells again?'

'No, Mam,' said Yawner. 'Never.'

'Then come out and wash up the dirty plates and dishes,' said Dame Quick-Eye, opening the door. 'I've caught the knife and wiped the spell from it. You did a silly and dangerous thing.'

'Yes, Mam,' said Yawner mournfully, and went off to do the dishes.

Dame Quick-Eye hasn't had to use the special 'Spell to cure Yawner of being Lazy'. In fact, she has only to mention spells to make Yawner work twice as hard as usual.

It All Began With Jinky

Once upon a time Jinky the pixie looked over his garden wall into the garden next door.

'Dear me,' said Jinky. 'It does want digging up! I wonder why old Miss Tip-Tap doesn't get it done.' So he asked her, and she told him.

'I've got a bad leg and I can't dig. I'm too poor to pay anyone. So I can't dig my garden and grow the lovely flowers that my bees like.'

Jinky was kind. 'We must help one another,' he said. 'I am strong. I will dig your garden for you, even though you cannot pay me.'

So he dug Miss Tip-Tap's garden, and she planted flowers that made plenty of honey for her bees to collect. They buzzed in them all day long.

They put the honey in their hive and Miss Tip-Tap collected it and put it into jars. It was lovely honey, sweet and golden. It was a pity Jinky didn't like honey, or Miss Tip-Tap would have given him a jar or two.

'I'll give some to poor Dame Cough-a-Lot,' she said. 'She has such a bad throat. It will make it better.'

So she went to Dame Cough-a-Lot and gave her three jars of the honey. It did Dame Cough-a-Lot's throat so much good that she was able to get up and go to wash and mend all Flitter-Wing's curtains and chair-covers.

'Oh, thank you!' said Flitter Wing. 'Now I can have a party here for old Sir Dimity-Dot, who is staying with my aunt, and is feeling very dull since he had the flu.'

So she gave a jolly party for Sir Dimity-Dot, and he was so pleased. He danced with Flitter-Wing, he ate four of her chocolate buns and had two slices of her iced cake, and he played hide-and-seek with everyone.

'Well!' he said, at the end of the party, 'I don't know when I have enjoyed myself so much. Thank you, dear Flitter-Wing, thank you. You went to a lot of trouble for an old man, and I did enjoy it. Is there anything I can do for you? Or for your village? I should be very glad to, because I have enjoyed myself so much.'

'Well,' said Flitter-Wing, pleased, 'could you see that we have a policeman of our very own? You see, we have to share Mr. Plod, who lives in the next village, and whenever we want him, he can't come. If we could have a policeman of our own, it would be lovely.'

'Right,' said Sir Dimity-Dot, who could do anything like that. 'I'll send you a policeman the very next day.'

So he did, and the policeman came along, looking very smart and clever. It was a good thing he came, too, because the next week Dame Treasure's jewels were stolen, and somebody was needed to catch the thief.

The policeman caught the thief, and put him into prison. But he didn't get back the jewels. So he wrote out a very big notice, and this is what it said:

Dame Treasure's jewels have been hidden by the thief, and he won't tell me where they are. A reward of one hundred pounds is offered to anyone who finds them.

Well, you can guess everyone hunted about for those jewels. Jinky hunted too, because he was very poor just then – so poor that he couldn't even buy jam to eat with his bread. It would be lovely, Jinky thought, to find the jewels and be rich for a change!

And suddenly Jinky found the jewels! He was trotting down Sandy Lane, when a rabbit popped his head out and spoke to him.

'Jinky! You once helped me when I hurt my paw. Now I'll help you. There's something in a bag down my hole that you might like to have. I've tried to eat what's inside, but it doesn't taste nice. Maybe you can cook it for your dinner.'

Jinky bent down, and put his arm into the rabbit-hole. He pulled out a cloth-bag – and in it were all Dame Treasure's stolen jewels!

'Good gracious! I certainly shan't cook these!' said Jinky, in delight. 'Why, they are jewels – and there is a reward offered for them too! Oh, Bobtail, what a darling you are. I shall take them straight to the policeman.'

He did, and the policeman was glad. He gave Jinky the hundred pounds. 'There you are,' he said. 'That's your reward. Spend it well.'

'Oh, I shall!' said Jinky. 'I shall put some in the bank. I shall buy myself a nice cake to eat and a pot of jam. I shall buy old Mother Shivers a warm black shawl. I shall—'

'Go along now and do a bit of spending then,' said the policeman, and Jinky ran off in glee.

'Aren't I lucky, oh, aren't I lucky!' he sang as he went on. Miss Tip-Tap, who lived next door, heard him. She popped her head over the wall.

'No, you're not lucky!' she said. 'You earned

that money, Jinky – and I'll tell you how. Now you just listen to me, and see how your little bit of help to me went all the way round the village, and came back to you.'

'Whatever do you mean?' said Jinky, surprised.

'Well, you dug up my garden for me, and I planted flowers for the bees. They made honey, and I gave some to old Dame Cough-a-Lot, and it made her throat so much better that she was able to go and wash curtains and covers for Flitter-Wing.

222

'And that meant that Flitter-Wing could give a party for old Sir Dimity-Dot, because then her house was nice and clean. And he was so pleased with the party, that he gave our village its new policeman.

'And when Dame Treasure's jewels were stolen, the new policeman caught the thief, and offered a reward for the jewels. And you found them, Jinky, and got the reward! So your little bit of help went all the way round and came back to you!'

'Oh, good!' cried Jinky. 'I'll start it off again, shall I? I'll give a warm shawl to old Mother Shivers. Miss Tip-Tap, isn't it lovely to help one another!'

It is, isn't it? Let's think hard and see what we can do for somebody this very day!

Muddle's Mistake

There was once a brownie called Muddle. I expect you can guess why he had that name. He was always making muddles! He did make silly ones.

Once his mistress, the Princess of Toadstool Town, asked him to take a note to someone who lived in a fir tree. But Muddle came back saying that he couldn't find a tree with fur on at all!

Another time she asked him to get her a snapdragon – and he said he didn't mind fetching a dragon, but he didn't want to get one that snapped.

So, you see, he was always making muddles. And one day he made a very big muddle. The Princess always said he would.

'You just don't use your eyes, Muddle,' she would say. 'You go through the world without looking hard at things, without listening well with your ears, without using your brains. You are a real muddler!'

Now once the Princess was asked to a party given by the Prince of Midnight Town. She was very excited.

'I shall go,' she told Muddle. 'You see, this prince gives really wonderful midnight parties, and he lights them by hanging glow-worms all over the place. It's really lovely!'

'Shall I go with you?' asked Muddle. 'I expect you will need someone to look after you on your way to the party, because it will be dark.'

'I think I shall fly there on a moth,' said the Princess. 'That will be nice. You get me a nice big moth, and you shall drive me.'

'Very well, Your Highness,' said Muddle, and he went off to get a moth. He hunted here and he hunted there, and at last he found a beautiful white-winged creature.

'Ah!' he said, 'just the right moth for the Princess. I must get it to come with me. I will put it into a beautiful cage, and feed it on sugar and honey, so that it will stay with me until the night of the party.'

So he spoke to the lovely creature. 'Will you come home with me, White-Wings? I will give you sugar and honey. You shall stay with me until next week, when you may take the Princess of Toadstool Town to a party.'

'I should like that,' said White-Wings. 'I love parties. Get on my back, brownie, and tell me which way to go to your home.'

Muddle was pleased. He got on to White-Wings' back, and they rose high in the air. It was fun. They were soon at Muddle's house, which was a sturdy little toadstool, with a little green door in the stalk, and windows in the head.

'Shall I put you in a cage, or just tie you up, White-Wings?' asked Muddle. White-Wings didn't want to be put into a cage. So Muddle took a length of spider thread and tied her up to his toadstool. He brought her honey, and she put out her long tongue and sucked it up. Muddle watched her.

'What a wonderful tongue you have!' he said. 'It is a bit like an elephant's trunk! I like the way you coil it up so neatly when you have finished your meal.'

'It is long because I like to put it deep down into flowers, and suck up the hidden nectar,' said White-Wings. 'Sometimes the flowers hide their nectar so deep that only a very long tongue like mine can reach it.'

Muddle told the Princess that he had found a very beautiful moth to take her to the midnight party. The Princess was pleased. 'Well, I am glad you haven't made a muddle about that!' she said. 'Bring White-Wings to me at twenty minutes to midnight and we will fly off. Make some reins of spider thread, and you shall drive.'

Muddle was so pleased to be going to the party too. It was a great treat for him. He had a new blue suit made, with silver buttons, and a blue cap with a silver knob at the top. He looked very grand.

When the night came, Muddle went out to White-Wings. The lovely insect was fast asleep.

'Wake up,' said Muddle. 'It is time to go to the party.'

White-Wings opened her eyes. She saw that it was quite dark. She shut her eyes again. 'Don't be silly, Muddle,' she said. 'It is night-time. I am not going to fly in the dark.'

'Whatever do you mean?' asked Muddle in surprise. 'It is a midnight party! You *must* fly in the dark!'

'I never fly at night, never, never, never,' said White-Wings. 'Go away and let me sleep.'

'But moths always fly at night!' cried Muddle. 'I know a few fly in the day-time as well – but most of them fly at night. Come along, White-Wings. The Princess is waiting.'

'Muddle, what is all this talk about moths?' asked White-Wings in surprise. 'I am not a moth. I am a BUTTERFLY!'

Muddle lifted up his lantern and stared in the greatest surprise at White-Wings. 'A-b-b-b-

butterfly!' he stammered. 'Oh no – don't say that!
No, no, say you are a moth!'

'Muddle, sometimes I think you are a very silly
person,' said the butterfly crossly. 'Don't you know
a butterfly from a moth? Have you lived all this
time in the world, and seen hundreds of butterflies
and moths, and never once noticed how different
they are?'

'I thought you were a moth,' said Muddle,
and he began to cry, because he knew that the
Princess would be very angry with him. 'Please be
a moth just for tonight and let me drive you to the
midnight party.'

'No,' said White-Wings. 'I am a butterfly and
I don't fly at night. If I were you, I'd go and find
a moth now, and see if you can get one that will
take you.'

'But how shall I know if I am talking to a moth
or a butterfly?' said Muddle, still crying. 'I might
make a mistake again.'

'Now listen,' said the butterfly. 'It is quite easy
to tell which is which. Do you see the way I hold
my wings? I put them neatly back to back, like
this, so that I show only the underparts.'

The white butterfly put her wings back to back.
'Now,' she said, 'a moth never holds her wings like
that. She puts them flat on her back – like this; or

she wraps her body round with them – like this; or she just lets them droop – like this. But she certainly doesn't put them back to back.'

'I'll remember that,' said poor Muddle.

'Then,' said the butterfly, 'have a look at my body, will you, Muddle? Do you see how it is nipped in, in the middle? Well, you must have a look at the bodies of moths, and you will see that they are not nipped in, like mine. They are usually fat and thick.'

'I will be sure to look,' promised Muddle.

'And now here is a very important thing,' said the butterfly, waving her two feelers under Muddle's nose. 'A *most* important thing! Look at my feelers. What do you notice about them?'

'I see that they are thickened at the end,' said Muddle. 'They have a sort of knob there.'

'Quite right,' said White-Wings. 'Now, Muddle, just remember this – a moth never has a knob or a club at the end of his feelers, never! He may have feelers that are feathery, or feelers that are just threads – but he will never have knobs on them like mine. You can always tell a butterfly or moth at once, by just looking at their feelers.'

'Thank you, White-Wings,' said Muddle, feeling very small. 'All I knew was that butterflies flew in the day-time, and moths mostly flew at night. I didn't think of anything else.'

'Now go off at once and see if you can find a moth to take you and the Princess to the party,' said White-Wings. 'I'm sleepy.'

Well, off went poor Muddle. He looked here and he looked there. He came across a beautiful peacock butterfly, but he saw that it held its wings back to back as it rested, and that its feelers had thick ends. So he knew it wasn't a moth.

He found another white butterfly like White-Wings. He found a little blue butterfly, but its feelers had knobs on the end, so he knew that wasn't a moth, either.

Then he saw a pretty moth that shone yellow in the light of his lantern. It spread its wings flat. Its feelers were like threads, and had no knob at the tips. It *must* be a moth. It left the leaf it was resting on and fluttered round Muddle's head.

'Are you a moth?' asked Muddle.

'Of course!' said the moth. 'My name is Brimmy, and I am a brimstone moth. Do you want me?'

'Oh yes!' said Muddle. 'Will you come with me at once, please, and let me drive you to the midnight party, with the Princess of Toadstool Town on your back?'

'Oh, I'd love that,' said the moth, and flew

off with Muddle at once. The Princess was cross because they were late, and Muddle did not like to tell her why.

They went to the party and they had a lovely time. Muddle set White-Wings free the next day, and gave her a little pot of honey to take away.

'You have taught me a lot,' he said. 'I shall use my eyes in future, White-Wings!'

Now let's have a game of Pretend! I am the Princess of Toadstool Town and you are just yourself. Please go out and see if you can find a moth to take me to a party! If you point out a butterfly to me instead, do you know what I shall call you?

I shall call you 'Muddle' of course!

Dame Topple's Buns

In Cherry Village there lived a small goblin called Pop. It was a funny name, but he was very greedy, you see, and his friends kept thinking he would one day eat too much, and go pop. They kept telling him this.

'You'll go pop! Why are you so greedy? It is disgusting. We shall call you Pop, because we are sure you will go pop!'

But even being called Pop didn't stop the little goblin from being greedy. Greedy people are always selfish, so Pop was not very much liked by the people of Cherry Village.

He always wanted the best of everything. He always wanted the biggest apple or the finest plum. He was quick too, so he could snatch or grab before anyone else could.

Now it is all very well to snatch and grab when you do it among people who can scold you, or can take back from you what you have grabbed. But it is very bad to do it to people who cannot stop you grabbing.

And that is what Pop began to do. He stopped

little Flitter the pixie in the street when he saw her carrying home a bag of sweets and he made her give him the very biggest. She had to because she was afraid of the fat little goblin.

Another day he helped old Mr. Limp across the road, and when Mr. Limp thanked him and said Pop could come into his garden and pick a few apples, what did Pop do but take his biggest basket and pick every apple off Mr. Limp's little tree!

That was greedy and unkind – but poor old Mr. Limp couldn't get them back because he couldn't run fast enough to catch the bad goblin.

'This sort of thing won't do,' said the folk of Cherry Village, when they met in the street and talked about Pop's bad ways. 'We must teach Pop a lesson. We must show him that it is not good to be greedy. He is getting more and more selfish, fatter and fatter, and horrider and horrider.'

So they went to Dame Topple, who was a very clever old woman, and asked what to do with Pop.

She laughed. 'I'll make some Balloon Buns,' she said. 'That will soon stop him from being greedy. You leave it to me.'

'What are Balloon Buns?' said Jinky, in surprise.

'Well you can eat three with safety,' said Dame Topple. 'At the fourth you begin to swell up. At the fifth you almost burst your clothes. At the sixth you feel like a balloon. I don't know what happens at the seventh bun, because I have never seen people eat seven. I should think they would go pop.'

'Can we all come to tea with you when you have made the Balloon Buns, and watch the fun?' asked Jinky, and Dame Topple said yes.

So the next Monday Pop and a good many of his friends were asked to tea at Dame Topple's. Pop was pleased about the invitation.

'She's a very good cook,' he told the others. 'She makes the finest cakes I know, and the loveliest pies. As for her buns and biscuits, well! I've never tasted anything like them. How I shall enjoy myself.'

'Please don't be greedy,' said Jinky. 'I'm warning you, Pop. Please don't be greedy. You know we hate to see you taking the best of everything. It isn't nice. We don't like you when you are greedy.'

'I don't care,' said Pop, crossly. 'I'm always hungry. And someone has got to have the biggest and best, so why not me, if I'm clever enough to get them?'

Nobody said any more. Pop had been warned. If he took no notice, it was his own fault.

You should have seen the table of goodies at

Dame Topple's on that Monday afternoon! There was fruit salad and cream, all kinds of jellies, a great big chocolate cake, some ginger biscuits and, of course, the plate of Balloon Buns.

'Oooh,' said Pop, taking a biscuit even before he sat down. 'Ooooh! What a feast! Shall we begin?'

Well, of course, Pop had three times as much as anyone else. He took the biggest helping of everything, and he took the most cream, and more biscuits than anyone.

The Balloon Buns looked gorgeous. They were all different colours, just like small balloons. They shone strangely and they were scattered with sugar. Dame Topple said they were to be left till last.

Then everyone had three each – and oh, how delicious they were! 'They taste of strawberries and pineapple and ice-cream and ginger pop all mixed together!' said Jinky.

'There are four left,' said Pop. He took one and ate it. He meant to finish them all up, he was so greedy. Everyone watched him.

He was fat, but when he had finished that fourth Balloon Bun he was much fatter! He took a fifth bun, and ate it quickly. How delicious it was!

Pop! A button flew off his coat. 'You're bursting

out of your clothes,' said Jinky. 'Be careful, Pop. Goodness, there goes another button – and look, the seam of your coat has burst all down your back!'

Pop took no notice. He was so afraid that someone else would eat the last two buns that he put them both on to his own plate. He ate the sixth one, and then he looked round at everyone.

'I feel a bit funny,' he said. 'Rather like a balloon. I feel sort of light and poppish.'

'You'll go pop,' said Jinky, alarmed. 'Oh, don't eat any more!'

But Pop was not going to miss that last Balloon Bun. He put it into his mouth and chewed it. And then a most peculiar thing happened. He floated up into the air! He went up like a little balloon and there he floated, bumping his head against the ceiling.

'What's happened?' he shouted in alarm. 'Get me down, quick!' But as soon as someone pulled him down by his fat legs, he floated up again.

'You really would go pop now if anyone stuck a pin in you!' said Jinky. 'You are just like a balloon. Whatever will happen to you?'

Well, they all got him down to the ground, and tried to take him home. But as soon as he got out of doors, up he went into the air again, and floated out of sight!

'He's gone,' said Jinky. 'Poor old Pop. He's gone above the clouds, out of sight. What an awful punishment for being greedy.'

'If he falls into a holly-bush, he really will go pop now,' said Dame Topple. 'Well, well – Balloon Buns for Greedy People ought to be sold all over the country. I think I'll do that – it will soon stop greediness, I'm sure!'

She's right, too! I don't expect you're greedy, but if you are, don't eat more than three Balloon Buns, will you? You might go and join poor Pop, wherever he is, if you do!

The Train That Went to Fairyland

Once, when Fred was playing with his railway train in the garden, a very strange thing happened.

Fred had just wound up his engine, fastened the carriages to it, and sent them off on the lines, when he heard a small, high voice.

'That's it, look! That's what I was telling you about!'

Fred looked round in surprise. At first he saw no one, then, standing by a daisy, he saw a tiny fellow dressed in a railway guard's uniform, but he had little wings poking out from the back of his coat! He was talking to another tiny fellow, who was dressed like a porter. They were neither of them any taller than the nearest daisy.

'Hallo!' said Fred, in surprise. 'Who are you and what do you want?'

'Listen,' said the tiny guard. 'Will you lend us your train just for a little while, to go to Goblin Town and back? You see, the chief goblin is taking a train from Toadstool Town and our engine has broken down. We can't get enough magic in time to mend it – the chief goblin is getting awfully angry.

'Lend you my train?' said Fred, in the greatest astonishment and delight. 'Of course I will, but you must promise me something first.'

'What?' asked the little guard.

'You must make me small and let me drive the train,' said Fred.

'All right,' said the guard. 'But you won't have an accident, will you?'

'Of course, not,' said Fred. 'I know how to drive my own train!'

'Shut your eyes and keep still a minute,' said the guard. Fred did as he was told, and the little guard sang out a string of very strange words. And when Fred opened his eyes again, what a surprise for him! He was as small as the tiny guard and porter.

'This is fun!' said Fred, getting into the cab. 'Come on. Will the engine run all right without lines, do you suppose?'

'Oh, we've got enough magic to make those as we go along,' said the little guard, and at once some lines spread before them, running right down the garden to the hedge at the bottom. It was very strange and exciting.

'Well, off we go!' said Fred. 'I suppose the

engine has only got to follow the lines, and it will be all right!'

He pulled down the little handle that started the train, and off they went! The guard and the porter had climbed into the cab of the engine too, so it seemed rather crowded. But nobody minded that, of course.

The lines spread before them in a most magical manner as the train ran over them, down the garden, through a hole in the hedge, and then goodness me, down a dark rabbit-hole!

'Hallo, hallo!' said Fred in surprise. 'Wherever are we going?'

'It's all right,' said the little guard. 'This will take us to Toadstool Town. We come up at the other side of the hill.'

The engine ran through the winding rabbit-holes, and once or twice met a rabbit who looked very scared indeed. Then it came up into the open air again, and there was Toadstool Town!

'I should have known it was without being told,' said Fred, who looked round him in delight as they passed tiny houses made out of the toadstools growing everywhere. 'Hallo, we're running into a station!'

So they were. It was Toadstool Station. Standing on another line was the train belonging to the little guard. The engine-driver and stoker were trying their hardest to rub enough magic into the wheels to start it, but it just wouldn't go!

On the platform was a fat, important-looking goblin, stamping up and down.

'Never heard of such a thing!' he kept saying, in a loud and angry voice. 'Never in my life! Keeping me waiting like this! Another minute and I'll turn the train into a caterpillar, and the driver and stoker into two leaves for it to feed on!'

'What a horrid fellow!' whispered Fred. The

guard ran to the goblin and bowed low.

'Please, your Highness, we've got another train to take you home. Will you get in?'

'About time something was done!' said the goblin, crossly. 'I never heard of such a thing in my life, keeping me waiting like this!'

He got into one of the carriages. He had to get in through the roof, because the doors were only pretend ones that wouldn't open. The little guard slid the roof open and then shut it again over the angry goblin.

'Start up the train again quickly!' he cried. So Fred pulled down the handle again and the little clockwork train set off to Goblin Town. It passed through many little stations with strange names, and the little folk waiting there stared in the greatest surprise to see such an unusual train.

Fred was as proud and pleased as could be! He drove that engine as if he had driven engines all his life. He wished and wished he could make it whistle. But it only had a pretend whistle. Fred wished the funnel would smoke, too, but of course, it didn't!

Suddenly the train slowed down and stopped. 'Good gracious! What's the matter?' said the little guard, who was still in the engine-cab with Fred. 'Don't say your train is going to break down, too? The goblin certainly *will* turn us all into something unpleasant if it does!'

The goblin saw that the train had stopped. He slid back the roof of his carriage and popped his angry face out.

'What's the matter? Has this train broken down, too?'

Fred had jumped down from the cab and had gone to turn the key that wound up the engine. It had run down, and no wonder, for it had come a long, long way! It was surprising that it hadn't needed winding up before.

The goblin stared in astonishment at the key in Fred's hand. He had never seen a key to wind up an engine before. He got crosser than ever.

'What are you getting down from the engine for? Surely you are not going to pick flowers or do a bit of shopping? Get back at once!'

But Fred had had enough of the cross goblin. He tapped him hard on the head with the key, and slid the roof back so that the goblin couldn't open it again.

'Now you be quiet,' said Fred. 'The pixies and elves may be frightened of you, but *I'm* not! Here I've come along with my train to help you and all you do is to yell at me and be most impolite. I don't like you. I'll take you to Goblin Town with pleasure, and leave you there with even greater pleasure, but while we are on the way you will please keep quiet and behave.'

Well! The little guard and porter nearly fell out of the cab with horror and astonishment when they heard Fred speaking like that to the chief goblin! But Fred only grinned, and wound up the engine quickly.

There wasn't a sound from the goblin. Not a sound. He wasn't used to being spoken to like that. He thought Fred must be a great and mighty wizard to dare to speak so angrily to him. He was frightened. He sat in his roofed-in carriage and didn't say a word.

The train went on to Goblin Town and stopped. Fred got down, slid back the roof of the goblin's carriage and told him to get out.

The goblin climbed out quickly, looking quite scared.

'What do you say for being brought here in my train?' said Fred, catching hold of the goblin's arm tightly.

'Oh, th-th-thank you,' stammered the goblin.

'I should think so!' said Fred. 'I never heard of such a thing, not thanking anyone for a kindness. You go home and learn some manners, goblin.'

'Yes, yes, I will, thank you, sir,' said the chief

goblin, and ran away as fast as ever he could. Everyone at the station stared in amazement.

'However did you dare to talk to him like that?' said the little guard in surprise. 'Do you know, that is the first time in his life he has ever said, "Thank you"! What a wonderful boy you are!'

'Not at all,' said Fred, getting back into the engine-cab. 'That's the only way to talk to rude people. Didn't you know? Now then, back home we go, to my own garden!'

And back home they went, past all the funny little stations to Toadstool Town, down into the rabbit-burrows and out into the field, through the hedge and up the garden, back to where they started.

'Shut your eyes and we'll make you your own size again,' said the little guard. In a trice Fred was very large indeed and his train now looked very small to him!

'What would you like for a reward?' said the little guard. 'Shall I give your train a real whistle, and real smoke in its funnel? Would you like that?'

'Rather!' said Fred. And from that very day his clockwork engine could whistle and smoke exactly like a real one.

Little Mister Sly

Mister Sly lived in a small cottage at the edge of Lilac Village. He kept hens and sold the eggs, but he never gave any away. He was a mean little man, and was only generous when he thought he would get something out of it.

Now one day Sly found six eggs that one of his hens had laid away from the hen-house. He felt sure they had been laid weeks ago, because for at least seven weeks he had shut up his hens carefully, and not let them stray.

'What a pity! They will be bad!' he said to himself. 'All wasted!'

Then he thought hard. 'I could give them away. I'll give them to old Mister Little-Nose. He can't smell anything bad or good since he had the flu last year. Maybe he will give me some honey from his bees then.'

So Sly put the eggs into a round basket and took them to Mister Little-Nose.

'Oh, thank you!' said Mister Little-Nose. 'That's kind of you, Sly. I will give you some honey in the summer-time.'

After Sly had gone, Mister Little-Nose heard someone knocking at his door again, and dear me, it was the carrier, bringing twelve eggs for him from his sister.

'Well, well – I've too many eggs now,' he thought. 'I'll send some to the pixie Twinkle.'

So he sent his little servant round to Twinkle with the six eggs that Sly had given him. But before Twinkle could use them she had to leave in a hurry to go and see her aunt, who was ill.

'I'll take the eggs to old Dame Groan,' she thought. 'She's been ill and needs feeding up.'

So she took them to Dame Groan's house and left them outside the door, because Dame Groan was asleep. Twinkle could hear her snoring.

Dame Groan grumbled when she saw the eggs. 'Twinkle might have known that the doctor has said eggs are the one thing I mustn't eat!' she said. 'What a pity! Well, Twinkle is away, so I can't give them back to her. I'll give them to old Miss Scared. She can do with a bit of good luck, she's so poor.'

Miss Scared was simply delighted with them. 'Oh, thank you, dear Dame Groan,' she said. 'I do hope you are feeling better now. Thank you very much.'

But before Miss Scared could eat any of the

eggs, there came another knock at her door. She opened it. Outside stood Mister Sly, a horrid mean look on his face.

'I lent you fifty pence last week,' he said. 'And you said you would pay me sixty pence back this week. Where is the money?'

'Oh, Mister Sly, I haven't got it. Won't you wait till tomorrow?' said Miss Scared. 'Please do.'

'Can't wait,' said Mister Sly. Then he caught sight of the six eggs. 'Hallo – you've got six eggs! Give me these six eggs, and I'll let you off.'

'All right,' said poor Miss Scared with a sigh, for she had badly wanted an egg for her tea. 'Take them.'

Mister Sly went off with the eggs. He didn't know they were the very same old eggs he had taken to Mister Little-Nose that very morning.

'I'll have bacon and eggs for tea,' he said, and got out his pan. He put in his bacon and it sizzled well. He put in a few mushrooms – and then he cracked an egg on the side of the pan, and let it run in, among the bacon and mushrooms.

But oh dear, it was bad! Mister Sly managed to scrape it out, and tried another egg. That was bad too. They were all bad! The worst of it was that his bacon tasted of bad egg when he ate it, and the whole kitchen smelt dreadful.

Mister Sly felt very sick.

He was very, very angry. 'That dreadful Miss Scared!' he said. 'How dare she give me bad eggs! This is a matter for the police. I will call Mr. Plod in and tell him all about it. He will give Miss Scared a good talking-to, and that will scare her properly.'

So he went to Mr. Plod and told him. Then he and Mr. Plod went to Miss Scared's cottage, and he knocked on the door.

'You bad woman! You gave me rotten eggs!'

said Sly, angrily. 'Where did you get them from?'

'Oh, Dame Groan sent them to me,' said Miss Scared, as frightened as could be. 'Please, please, don't blame me. I didn't know they were bad. I really didn't.'

'Ha – Dame Groan,' said Mr. Plod, and wrote the name in his notebook. 'Come along – we'll go and see her.'

So they went to Dame Groan. 'Those eggs you gave Miss Scared were bad!' scolded Sly. 'How dare you give away rotten eggs?'

'I didn't know they were bad,' said Dame Groan, in a rage, 'and don't you talk to me like that, Sly. Twinkle sent me those eggs – she said that Mister Little-Nose had given them to her.'

'We'll go to Mister Little-Nose then,' said Mr. Plod. 'Ah – there he is, just over there! Hi, Little-Nose, I've got something to ask you.'

'What?' said Little-Nose.

'Well, Sly here is trying to trace a batch of bad eggs he had given to him,' said Mr. Plod. 'It seems that Miss Scared gave them to him, and Dame Groan gave them to her, and Twinkle gave them to Dame Groan, and you gave them to Twinkle. Now – did your hens lay them? And what right have you to send out bad eggs?'

'I've got no hens,' said Mister Little-Nose, in

surprise. 'and as for who gave them to me – well, Sly should know, for he sent them round himself!'

'What!' cried Mr. Plod, and snapped his notebook angrily. 'What! Did you give him six bad eggs, Sly? And you have dared to come and complain to me about them and waste my time, when they were your eggs! You must have known they were bad, too. How dare you, I say?'

Sly hadn't a word to say for himself. Little-Nose looked at him in disgust.

'He always was mean,' he said. 'He'd never give away anything good. I might have guessed they were bad. Well, I'm glad they came back to you, Sly, very glad. Serves you right!'

And so it did.

The Brownie's Magic

One night the snow came. It fell quietly all night through, and in the morning, what a surprise for everyone! The hills were covered with snow. The trees were white. The bushes were hidden, and the whole world looked strange and magical.

Bobbo the brownie looked out of his cave in the hillside. The path down to the little village was hidden now. The path that ran over the top of the hill had gone too.

'Snow everywhere,' said Bobbo. 'Beautiful white snow! How I love it! I wish I had watched it falling last night, like big white goose feathers.'

He saw someone coming up the hill, and he waved to him.

'Ah!' he said, 'there is my clever cousin, Brownie Bright-Eyes. I wonder what he has brought to show me today. He is always bringing me wonderful things.'

Brownie Bright-Eyes walked up the hill in the snow, making deep footprints as he came, for he carried something large and heavy.

'What have you got there?' said Bobbo, when

Bright-Eyes at last came to his cave. 'You are always bringing me something strange and wonderful to see, Bright-Eyes.'

'I have made a marvellous mirror,' panted Bright-Eyes, bringing the shining glass into the cave. 'I do think I am clever, Bobbo. I made this magic mirror myself. I think I must he the cleverest brownie in the world.'

'Don't boast,' said Bobbo. 'I don't like you when you boast.'

'I am not boasting!' cried Bright-Eyes crossly. 'Wait till you do something clever yourself, and then scold me for boasting. It's a pity you don't use your own brains.'

'I do,' said Bobbo. 'But you are always so full of your own wonderful doings that you never listen to me when *I* want to tell you something.'

'I don't expect you would have anything half so wonderful to tell me as I have to tell you,' said Bright-Eyes. 'Now – just look at this mirror.'

Bobbo looked at it. It was a strange mirror, because it didn't reflect what was in front of it. It was just dark, with a kind of mist moving in the glass. Bobbo could see that it was very magic.

'I can't see anything,' said Bobbo.

'No, you can't – but if you want to know where anyone is – Tippy the brownie for instance

– the mirror will show you!'

'What do you mean?' asked Bobbo, astonished.

'Now look,' said Bright-Eyes. He stroked the shining mirror softly. 'Mirror, mirror, show me where Tippy the brownie is!'

And at once a strange thing happened. The mist in the glass slowly cleared away – and there was Tippy the brownie, sitting in a bus. The mirror showed him quite clearly.

'Isn't that wonderful?' said Bright-Eyes. 'You couldn't possibly have told me where Tippy was, without the help of the mirror, could you?'

'Yes, I could,' said Bobbo. 'I knew he was in the bus.'

'You didn't!' said Bright-Eyes.

'I did,' said Bobbo.

'Then you must have seen Tippy this morning,' said Bright-Eyes.

'I haven't,' said Bobbo. ' *You* found out where he was by using your magic mirror, but *I*, Bright-Eyes, *I* found out by using my brains! So I am cleverer than you.'

Bright-Eyes didn't like that. He always wanted to be the cleverest person anywhere. He frowned at Bobbo.

'I expect it was just a guess on your part that Tippy was in the bus,' he said. 'Now – can you tell me where Jinky is – you know, the pixie who lives down the hill?'

'Yes,' said Bobbo at once. 'He's gone up the hill to see his aunt, who lives over the top.'

Bright-Eyes rubbed the mirror softly. 'Mirror, mirror, show me where Jinky is!' he said. And at once the mirror showed him a pixie, sitting in a chair, talking to a plump old lady. It was Jinky, talking to his aunt!

'There you are, you see – I was right,' said Bobbo, pleased. 'I am cleverer than your mirror. It uses magic – but I use my brains. I can tell you a lot of things that you could only get to know through your magic mirror but which I know by using my very good brains. Ha, ha!'

'What can you tell me?' asked Bright-Eyes.

'I can tell you that Red-Coat the fox passed by here in the night, although I did not see or hear him,' said Bobbo. 'I can tell you that six rabbits played in the snow down the hill this morning. I can tell you that Mother Jane's ducks left the frozen pond today and went to her garden to be fed.'

'You must have seen them all. That's easy,' said Bright-Eyes.

'I tell you, I have not seen anything or anyone today except you,' said Bobbo. 'I know all this by using my brains.'

'What else do you know?' asked Bright-Eyes, thinking that Bobbo must really be cleverer than he thought.

'I know that the sparrows flew down to peck crumbs that Mother Jane scattered for them,' said Bobbo. 'I know that Crek-Crek the moorhen took a walk by the side of the pond. I know that Mother Jane's cat ran away from Tippy's dog this morning. And I know that Tippy's cow wandered from its shed, and then went back to it.'

Bright-Eyes stared at Bobbo in wonder. 'You are very clever to know all this, if you did not see anyone,' he said. 'I shall ask my magic mirror if what you say is true!'

He stroked the glass and asked it many things – and each time the glass showed him that what Bobbo said was true! There was the cat chasing the dog. There was the moorhen walking over the snow. There was Tippy's cow wondering all about!

'Please tell me your magic,' said Bright-Eyes to Bobbo. 'It must be very good magic to tell you all these things.'

'Well – come outside and I will show you how I know them all,' said Bobbo, beginning to laugh. They went outside, and Bobbo pointed to the crisp white snow. There were many marks and prints in it, as clear as could be.

'Look,' said Bobbo, pointing to some small footprints that showed little pointed toes. 'Tippy always wears pointed shoes – and do you see how deep his footprints are? That shows that he was running. Why was he running? To catch the bus! That's how I knew where he was, without having seen him.'

'How did you know about Jinky going to see his aunt?' asked Bright-Eyes.

Bobbo pointed to some very big footprints. 'Those are Jinky's marks,' he said. 'He has enormous feet. The footprints are going up the hill, and the only person Jinky goes to see over the top is his aunt. So I knew where Jinky was!'

'Very clever,' said Bright Eyes.

'And I knew that Red-Coat the fox had passed in the night because there are his footprints,' said Bobbo, pointing to a set of rather dog-like marks that showed the print of claws very clearly. 'I knew it was Red-Coat because I saw the mark his tail made here and there behind his hind feet – see it?'

Bright-Eyes saw the mark of the fox's tail in the snow, and the line of footprints too.

Bobbo took Bright-Eyes farther down the hill. He showed him the rabbit-prints – little marks for the front feet and longer, bigger ones for the strong hind feet. He showed him where

Mother Jane's ducks had walked from the pond to her garden.

'You can see they were ducks because they have left behind them the mark of their webbed feet,' he said. 'And you can see where the sparrows fed because they have left little prints in pairs – they hop, you see, they don't walk or run – so their prints are always in pairs.'

'And there are the moorhen's marks,' said Bright-Eyes. 'He has big feet rather like the old hen at home, although he is a waterbird. But he runs on land as well as swims on water, so he doesn't have webbed feet. Look how he puts them one in front of the other, Bobbo, so the footprints are in a straight line!'

'And there are the marks made by Tippy's cow,' said Bobbo. 'You can tell each hoof-mark quite well. And Mother Jane's cat ran *here* – look at the neat little marks. And Tippy's dog ran *here* – you can tell the difference, because the cat puts her claws *in* when she runs, so they don't show in her footprints, but the dog doesn't – so his *do* show!'

'Bobbo, you are very, very clever,' said Bright-Eyes. 'You are cleverer than I am. It is better to use your eyes and your brains, than to use a magic mirror! I think you are the cleverest brownie in the world!'

Would you like to be as clever as Bobbo? Well, go out into the snow, when it comes, and read the footprints you find there! You will soon know quite a lot.

Little Connie Careless

There was once a little girl whose name was Connie. Everyone called her Connie Careless, and you can guess why.

Oh, she was careless! She lost something nearly every day. She lost her hankies, she lost her hats, she lost her books, she even lost her dear little watch that her father gave her for Christmas.

'It's no good giving Connie anything,' said her mother. 'She never takes care of a thing. She's so careless. I do wish I could cure her.'

But Connie didn't try to be cured. She didn't try to remember where she had put anything, she didn't try to think at all.

'I've lost my gloves!' she would wail. 'I don't know where I put them! I must have left them in the bus.'

'I've lost my pencil, and it was a new one! I've lost the ten pence Daddy gave me, and I wanted to buy some sweets. I've lost my ruler too.'

The things Connie lost! She once lost her lovely teddy bear. She lost the clockwork clown that her aunt gave her, and she even lost a box of skittles, though how she did that she couldn't think! You see, she had been carrying them home when her shoe came undone. She had put the box of skittles on a wall, whilst she did up her shoe – and when she stood up again, she forgot about the skittles and went home!

'It's no good lending Connie a book, she will never remember to give it back,' said Bob.

'It's no good lending her anything,' said Lily. 'She always loses everything.'

'She's lost her umbrella again,' said Ronnie. 'That's the fourth one she's lost.'

'And last week she lost her mackintosh,' said Margery. 'I should think her mother must get very cross with her.'

Her daddy was very cross too. 'What is the good of my working hard and earning money to spend on nice things for you, if you don't care enough for them to keep them?' he said, angrily. 'I wanted to buy myself some new books this week, and now I must use that money to buy you another mackintosh to replace the one you lost. You are a bad, careless unkind little girl.'

Connie went into the garden and cried. She hadn't thought before that her carelessness might rob her daddy of something he badly wanted himself.

'I wish I had a cure for the way I lose things,' she wept. 'I wish I had.'

'I can give you one,' said a little voice, and a small green imp popped his head up from behind a pansy. Connie stared at him. She didn't know that imps played tricks, and should never be trusted.

'I wish you would give me a cure,' she said. 'Please do.'

'Eat this,' said the imp and threw her something that looked like a small sweet. 'Eat it, and say, "I wish all the things I ever lost would come back

again. I wish I was cured of being careless!'"

Connie ate the sweet, and the imp popped down behind the pansy. Nothing happened. Connie was disappointed. Then her mother called her and sent her down to the shops for something.

Now, as she came back, Connie heard a funny pattering noise behind her, and she turned to see what it was – and what do you think she saw?

All the things she had ever lost were coming after her! There were hundreds and hundreds of them in a long, long line. There were gloves and hats, hankies and shoes, her mackintosh, four little umbrellas, a coat, all kinds of money, books and papers, the skittles all jumping along out of their box, the big teddy bear carrying her watch in one hand, the clockwork clown and a rabbit.

Connie was frightened. She turned and ran, and everything tore after her. She couldn't get rid of them. They galloped along, the teddy bear now at the very front.

'Stop!' he cried. 'We belong to you! Stop!'

But Connie wouldn't stop. Everyone stared and how they laughed!

'Look at all that Connie has lost in her seven years!' they said. 'What a careless child!'

She rushed in at her garden gate and slammed it. The teddy bear couldn't open it. The little green imp popped his head up and grinned.

'Shall I let them in?' he said. 'They belong to you. Don't you like my magic?'

'No, I don't, it frightens me,' wept Connie. 'Make them go away. I never saw so many things in my life. I don't like them. I'll never, never lose anything else if only you'll make them go away!'

'Ping!' said the imp, making a noise like a bell – and at once all the lost things vanished! Where they went to, Connie didn't know. She only knew that they were gone. She hurried indoors, sobbing.

'What's the matter?' said Mummy, and Connie told her the whole story. Mummy really couldn't believe it, so Connie took her out into the garden to show her the green imp behind the pansy plant.

But he wasn't there. Mummy shook her head. 'You've been imagining it all,' she said. 'If it was really true, Connie, I know you would be careful in future, and would never lose anything else!'

'Well, I never shall!' said Connie. 'So you'll know it's all true!'

It's a very funny thing, but Connie has never lost anything since, and now we call her Connie Careful instead of Connie Careless. Nobody has ever seen that green imp again, but he certainly managed to cure Connie, didn't he?

The Three Bad Imps

There was once three bad imps. They were called Snip, Snap and Snorum, and they really were very naughty. They were very small – not even as tall as a daisy. They had all kinds of jobs to do, and they did them very badly.

They were supposed to help the moths when they crept out of their cocoons – but they pulled them out so roughly that sometimes they spoilt the wings of the little creatures. They had to polish the little coppery beetles that ran through the grasses – and sometimes they polished the beetles' feet too, so that they slipped and slid all over the place!

They were always up to naughty tricks, and nobody could ever catch them to punish them. They were so small, and could hide so easily.

'Nobody will ever catch *me*!' Snip would boast, as he swung up and down on a grass-blade.

'And I can always hide where nobody can find me!' said Snap.

'We're as clever as can be!' said Snorum. And so they were. They got into trouble every day, but they slipped out of it as easily as worms slip out of their holes!

But one day they really went too far. They had been told to brush the hairs of a furry caterpillar who had fallen into the mud and got very dirty. And instead of brushing his hairs and making him nice and clean again, Snip, Snap and Snorum cut off all his hairs to make themselves little fur coats!

Well, of course, the caterpillar complained very loudly indeed, and the pixies set off to find and catch the three bad imps.

'We'll punish them well!' said the biggest pixie. 'I shall spank each of them with a good, strong grass-blade!'

But nobody could catch those naughty imps. They hid here, and they hid there – and even when they were found, they slipped away easily.

'They have polished themselves all over with the polish they use for the beetles,' said the biggest pixie. 'So, even if we get hold of them, we can't hold them! They slip out of our hands like eels.'

'What shall we do, then?' asked the smallest pixie. 'How can we catch them?'

'Well, first we must find them,' said the biggest pixie. 'Now – where can they be?'

'Send the ants to find out,' said another pixie. 'They can run here, there and everywhere, and they will soon find where they are hiding.'

So the little brown ants were sent hurrying through the wood, between the grasses, to find the hidden imps. One ant found them and came hurrying back.

'They are asleep in the leaves of the honeysuckle, where it climbs high,' said the tiny ant. 'If you come now, you could catch them.'

'They will slip out of our hands as soon as we touch them,' said the pixies. 'If only we could trap them. Little ant, where could we find a trap that will hold the imps?'

'Only the spiders make traps,' said the ant. 'You might ask *them.*'

So the pixies called the spiders, and they came running over the grass on their eight legs, their eyes looking wisely at the pixies.

'Come with us,' said the pixies. 'We want you to make a trap for some naughty imps.'

So, all together, the pixies and the spiders ran to the honeysuckle, where it climbed high. Softly they all climbed up the twisted stems, and came to where the imps were lying fast asleep among the honeysuckle leaves.

'Can you make a trap to catch them?' whispered the pixies. The spiders looked at one another. Yes – they could!

'There are six of us,' said a fine big spider. 'We can make a cage, if you like – a six-sided cage of web, that will hold the three naughty imps as long as you like!'

'Oh yes!' cried the pixies. 'Make six webs, in the form of a square – four for the sides, one for the top and one for the bottom. That will be a splendid cage. But be careful not to wake the imps.'

The spiders began their work. The pixies watched them. The spiders were very clever indeed. Underneath each spider were little lumps, and from them they drew the thread for their webs.

'These are our spinnerets,' said a big spider to a pixie. 'We spin our web from them. The thread isn't really made till it oozes out of our spinnerets, you know. It squeezes out like a liquid, and the air makes it set, so that we get threads to work with.'

'It's like magic,' said the pixies in wonder. They watched the spiders pull the thread from their spinnerets, more and more and more – as much as they needed.

'Feel the thread,' said a spider. 'It's so fine – and yet so strong.'

'Yes, it is,' said the pixies. 'We would like some to sew our party frocks with! Hurry, spiders, or the imps will wake.'

Each spider chose a leaf, stalk or twig to

hang her outer threads on. It was marvellous to watch them.

After they had fixed their outer threads, they began to make threads that ran to the middle and back, like spokes of a wheel. The three imps slept soundly all the time, for the spiders made no noise at all.

'See how the spiders use their clawed feet to guide the thread,' whispered a pixie. The pixies watched in delight. 'Oh look – now the spiders are running a spiral thread round and round the spokes!'

So they were. They had finished all the spokes, and were now moving round their webs, letting out a thread that went round and round in smaller and smaller circles.

'The imps will never, ever be able to escape from this trap,' said a pixie.

'We will make the web sticky too,' said a spider. 'If we hang tiny sticky drops along the threads, the imps will find themselves caught fast if they try to break through!'

'I have seen flies caught in webs,' said a pixie. 'I suppose the stickiness holds them fast, spider?'

'Of course,' said the spider, pulling a thread tighter. 'Now – we have finished. Shall we go and hide under leaves, and watch what happens?'

'Yes,' said the pixies. So the spiders ran up to some leaves, and hid themselves there, waiting silently, just as they did when they waited for flies to come.

Soon the imps awoke and stretched themselves – and they saw the trap they were in! They jumped to their feet in alarm.

'What's this! We're in a cage!'

'It's a cage made of spider's web!'

'Break it, break it!'

The three imps flung themselves against the webby walls of the strange cage. They broke the threads – but in a trice the sticky web fell on their arms and legs and heads – and they were caught!

They struggled, and they wriggled, but it was no use. The strong, sticky threads held them as tightly as they could hold flies. Down rushed the spiders and, pouring out more thread from their spinnerets, they rolled the imps round and round in it, until they were helpless.

'Thank you, spiders,' said the pixies. 'We are very grateful to you. Now at last we have caught these bad little imps! They will be well punished!'

'If you want our help again at any time, just let us know,' said the spiders. 'We'll come running to you on our eight long legs!'

The imps were carried off by the pixies – and

dear me, didn't they get a telling off! They sobbed and they cried, and they promised they would be as good as gold.

And so far, they have – you'll find that the caterpillars have their hairs well brushed, and the ladybirds and beetles are well polished now.

But the imps keep away from the spiders. They have never forgotten how they were caught in a webby trap, spun by the six clever spiders!

Silky and the Snail

Silky was a pixie. She lived under a hawthorn hedge, and often talked to the birds and animals that passed by her house.

One day a big snail came crawling slowly by. Silky had never seen a snail, and at first she was quite afraid. Then she ran up to the snail, and touched his hard shell.

'How clever you are!' she said. 'You carry your house about with you! Why do you do that?'

'Well, you see,' said the snail, 'I have a very soft body that many birds and other creatures like to eat – so I grow a shell to protect it.'

'What a good idea,' said the pixie. 'Can you put your body right inside your shell, snail?'

'Watch me!' said the snail, and he curled his soft body up quickly into his shell. There was nothing of him to be seen except his spiral shell.

'Very clever,' said the pixie. 'Come out again, please, snail. I want to talk to you.'

The snail put his head out and then more of his body. He had four feelers on his head, and the pixie looked at them.

'Haven't you any eyes?' she said. 'I can't see your eyes, snail.'

'Oh, I keep them at the top of my longer pair of feelers,' said the snail. 'Can't you see them? Right at the top, pixie – little black things.'

'Oh yes, I can see them now,' said the pixie. 'What a funny place to keep your eyes, snail! Why do you keep them there?'

'Well, it's rather nice to have my eyes high up on feelers I can move about here and there,' said the snail. 'Wouldn't *you* like eyes on the ends of movable feelers, pixie? Think what a lot you could see!'

'I should be afraid that they would get hurt, if I had them at the end of feelers,' said Silky.

'Oh no!' said the snail, and he did such a funny thing. He rolled his eyes down inside his feelers, and the pixie stared in surprise.

'Oh, you can roll your eyes down your feelers, just as I pull the toe of my stocking inside out!' she said. 'Sometimes I put my hand inside my stocking, catch hold of the toe, and pull it down inside the stocking, to turn it inside out – and you do the same with your eyes!'

'Yes, I do,' said the snail. 'It's rather a good idea, don't you think so?'

'Oh, *very* good,' said Silky. 'Where's your

mouth? Is that it, under your feelers?'

'Yes,' said the snail, and he opened it to show the pixie. She looked at it closely.

'Have you any teeth?' she said. 'I have a lot.'

'So have I,' said the snail. 'I have about fourteen thousand.'

Silky stared. 'You shouldn't tell silly stories like that,' she said.

'I'm not telling silly stories,' said the snail. 'I'll show you my teeth.'

He put out a long, narrow tongue, and Silky laughed. 'Don't tell me that you grow teeth on your *tongue*,' she said.

'Well, I do,' said the snail. 'Just look at my tongue, pixie. Can't you see the tiny teeth there, hundreds and hundreds of them?'

'Oh *yes*,' said the pixie in surprise. 'I can. They are so tiny, snail, and they all point backwards. It's like a tooth-ribbon, your tongue. How do you eat with your teeth?'

'I use my tongue like a file,' said the snail. 'I'll show you.'

He went to a lettuce, put out his tongue, and began to rasp away at a leaf. In a moment he had eaten quite a big piece.

'Well, you really are a strange creature,' said Silky. She looked closely at the snail, and noticed a strange little hole opening and shutting in the top of his neck.

'What's that slit for, in your neck?' she asked. 'And why does it keep opening and shutting?'

'Oh, that's my breathing-hole,' said the snail. 'Didn't you guess that? Every time that hole opens and shuts, I breathe.'

'Why don't you breathe with your mouth, as I do?' asked Silky.

'All soft-bodied creatures like myself, that have no bones at all, breathe through our bodies,' said the snail. 'Now, if you will excuse me, I must get into my shell. I can see the big thrush coming.'

He put his body back into his shell and stayed quite still. The thrush passed by without noticing him. The pixie went into her house, and came out with a tin of polish and a duster.

'Snail, I am going to polish up your shell for you,' she said. 'I shall make you look so nice. Everyone will say how beautiful you are!'

'Oh, thank you,' said the snail, and he stayed quite still whilst Silky put polish on her cloth and then rubbed his shell hard.

'I rather like that,' he said.

'Well, come every day and I'll give you a good rubbing with my duster,' promised the pixie.

So, very soon, the two became good friends, and

the snail always came by the pixie's house for a chat whenever he was near.

One day Silky was sad. She showed the snail a necklace of bright-blue beads – but it was broken, for the clasp was lost.

'I wanted to wear this at a party tomorrow,' said Silky. 'But I can't get anyone to mend it for me.'

'I know someone who will,' said the snail. 'He is a great friend of mine. He lives in a tiny house the fifth stone to the left of the old stone wall, and the fifteenth up. There's a hole there, and Mendy lives in it, doing all kinds of jobs for everyone.'

'I would never find the way,' said Silky. 'I know I'd get lost.'

'Well, I will take the necklace for you tonight,' said the snail. 'But I know Mendy will take a little time to do it, so you would have to fetch it yourself some time tomorrow.'

'But I should get lost!' said Silky.

'I will see that you don't,' said the snail. 'I will take the necklace to Mendy, give it to him, and come straight back here. And behind me I will leave a silvery trail for you to follow!'

'Oh, snail, you are kind and clever!' said Silky, delighted. She hung the beads over the snail's feelers, and he set off towards the old wall he knew so well. It was a long way for him to go, because he travelled very slowly.

It was a dry evening and the soft body of the snail did not get along as easily as on a wet night. So he sent out some slime to help his body along, and then he glided forwards more easily.

The slimy trail dried behind him, and left a beautiful silvery path, easy to see. The snail went up the wall to the hole where old Mendy the brownie lived, and gave him the broken necklace.

'It will be ready at noon tomorrow,' said Mendy. 'Thank you,' said the snail, and went home again, very slowly, leaving behind him a second silvery trail, running by the first.

Silky was asleep, so he didn't wake her, but he told her next morning that her necklace would be ready at noon.

'And you can't get lost,' he said, 'because I have left two silvery paths for you to follow. It doesn't matter which you walk on — either of them will lead you to Mendy.'

So Silky set off on one of the silvery paths, and it led her to the old wall, up it, and into Mendy's little house. Her necklace was mended, so she put it on ready for the party. She was very pleased indeed.

'Thank you,' she said. 'Now I know the way to

your house, I'll bring some other things for you to mend, Mendy!'

She went to find her friend, the snail. 'Thank you for leaving me such a lovely silvery path,' she said. 'I do think you are clever!'

I expect you would like to see the snail's silvery path too, wouldn't you? Well, go round your garden any summer's morning – you are sure to see the snail's night-time trail of silver gleaming in the sunshine here and there.

Mr. Topple and the Egg

Mr. Topple lived next door to Mr. Plod the Police-man. Mr. Topple was a brownie, and a very nice fellow too, always ready to help anyone he could.

One day his Aunt Jemima was coming to tea, and he wanted to make a little cake for her. So he got everything ready, and then, oh dear, he found that the egg in his larder was bad.

'I must have an egg for my cake,' said Mr. Topple to himself. 'I wonder if Mr. Plod the Policeman would sell me one. I'll ask him.'

Mr. Plod kept hens in his garden, and they laid very nice eggs. Mr. Topple went to ask him, but he was out. Still, Mr. Topple knew where he would be. He would be at Busy Corner, directing the traffic there.

So off he ran to Busy Corner, and told Mr. Plod what he wanted. The big policeman nodded his head. 'Of course you can have an egg from my hens. Run back, look in the hen-house, and take the biggest and brownest you see there.'

So Mr. Topple went back home. He climbed over the wall and jumped down into Mr. Plod's

279

garden. He went to the hen-house, looked round, saw one big brown egg in a nesting-box there, and came out with it in his hand.

He climbed back over the wall again, and went indoors to make his cake. He made a lovely one, and cut a big slice out of it to send to Mr. Plod for his tea.

Now, as Mr. Topple was climbing over the wall to get into Mr. Plod's garden, little Mrs. Whisper was passing by. She saw him jump down, and she watched him go into the hen-house. She saw Topple come out with an egg in his hand, and jump back down over the wall into his own garden again.

'Well!' said Mrs. Whisper. 'Well! The nasty, horrid thief! He knows Mr. Plod is down at Busy Corner, and so he thought he would get over and steal an egg. Well!'

Mrs. Whisper hurried on and soon she met Mr. Talky. 'Good morning, Mr. Talky,' she said. 'Do you know, I've just seen a most dreadful thing – I saw Mr. Topple creeping into Mr. Plod's hen-house and stealing an egg! What do you think of that?'

'What a thing to do!' said Mr. Talky, shocked. 'I'm surprised at Mr. Topple, really, I am. Dear, dear, dear – and he seems such a nice fellow too.'

Mr. Talky went on his way. Soon he met Miss Simple, and he stopped to speak to her. After a bit he said, 'Do you know, I've just heard a most dreadful thing. I met Mrs. Whisper and she told me that she saw Mr. Topple creeping into Mr. Plod's hen-house today and stealing an egg!'

'Well, well – would you believe it!' said Miss Simple, her eyes wide open in surprise. 'You wouldn't think Mr. Topple would do such a thing, would you?'

Miss Simple hurried on her way, longing to tell somebody about Mr. Topple. What a bit of news!

Fancy Mr. Topple daring to steal an egg from the village policeman!

Miss Simple met Dame Listen. 'Dame Listen!' she said at once, 'I've just heard such a bit of news! Mr. Topple – you know that nice Mr. Topple the brownie, don't you – well, do you know, he's been stealing eggs out of Mr. Plod's hen-house! What do you think of that?'

'Shocking!' said Mrs. Listen. 'Really shocking! Something ought to be done about it!'

She went away and soon met Mr. Meddle. She told him the news. 'Mr. Meddle! Would you believe it, that brownie, Mr. Topple, is a thief! He steals eggs. Fancy that! He was seen creeping into somebody's hen-house stealing eggs! He's a thief. He ought to be in prison.'

'So he ought, so he ought,' said Mr. Meddle, banging his stick on the ground. 'And, what's more, I shall complain about this to Mr. Plod the policeman. Why, none of our eggs or our hens either will be safe, if Mr. Topple starts stealing. There's Mr. Plod over there, at Busy Corner. I'll go and tell him now.'

So Mr. Meddle, feeling very busy and important, went over to Mr. Plod. 'Mr. Plod,' he said, 'I've a complaint to make, and I expect you to look into it. I hear that Mr. Topple is a thief. I think he ought to be in prison.'

Mr. Plod was so surprised to hear this that he waved two lorries on at the same moment and there was very nearly an accident. He stared in astonishment at Mr. Meddle.

'Mr. Topple a thief!' he said. 'Nonsense! I've lived next door to him for years, and a kinder, more honest fellow I never met. Who says he's a thief – and what does he steal?'

'Mrs. Listen told me,' said Mr. Meddle. 'She said he steals eggs.'

Mr. Plod left Busy Corner, and, taking Mr. Meddle with him, walked off to find Mrs. Listen. 'What's all this about Topple stealing eggs?' he said.

'Oh,' said Mrs. Listen, 'well, Miss Simple told me. You'd better ask her where she got the dreadful news from. There she is, in the baker's.'

Mr. Plod called Miss Simple. 'What's all this about Topple stealing eggs?' he said.

'Well, I heard it from Mr. Talky,' said Miss Simple. 'He told me all about it. Dreadful, isn't it?'

'Come along,' said Mr. Plod to Mr. Meddle, Dame Listen and Sally Simple. 'We'll all go to find Mr. Talky. I'm going to get to the bottom of this.'

They found Mr. Talky at home. 'What's all

this about Topple stealing eggs?' said Mr. Plod, beginning to look rather stern.

'Isn't it a shocking thing?' said Mr. Talky. 'I've told ever so many people, and they were all surprised. It was Mrs. Whisper that told me.'

Mrs. Whisper lived across the road. Mr. Plod took them all to her house and banged on her door. She opened it, and looked surprised to see so many people outside.

'What's all this about Topple stealing eggs?' said Mr. Plod.

'Oh, have you heard about it?' said Mrs. Whisper. 'Well – I saw him take the egg!'

'When and where?' asked Mr. Plod, taking out his note-book.

'This very morning,' said Mrs. Whisper. 'I was passing your backgarden, Mr. Plod, and I happened to look over the wall – and what did I see but Mr. Topple going into your hen-house, and coming out with one of your eggs in his hand – and then he jumped back over the wall again! What do you think of that? I think he ought to be in prison.'

Mr. Plod shut his note-book with a snap. He looked round so sternly that everyone began to feel afraid.

'This morning,' said Mr. Plod, in a loud and

angry voice, 'this morning, my friend, Mr. Topple, came to me at Busy Corner, and said his aunt was coming to tea, and he was making her a cake. And as his egg was bad, could he have one of mine?'

There was silence. No one dared to say anything. Mr. Plod went on. 'I said of course he could, and so, I suppose, he went back, and got the egg. And now, all round the town, there are people saying that Topple is a thief – a kind, honest fellow like Topple.'

'I'm sorry I said such a thing,' began Mr. Talky, 'but I believed Mrs. Whisper when she told me.'

'Don't make excuses,' said Mr. Plod, in a thundery sort of voice. 'It's all of you who ought to be in prison, not poor Mr. Topple! How dare you say a man is a thief, Mrs. Whisper, when you don't know at all whether he is or not? How dare you, Mr. Talky, and all you others too, repeat this wicked story, when you don't know at all whether it is true or not?'

Miss Simple began to cry. 'Now, one more word of this kind from any of you, and I'll be after you!' said Mr. Plod. 'You will all go round and tell everyone that you've made a sad mistake, and are ashamed of yourselves. Go now – for I've a very good mind to put you all into prison!'

Miss Simple gave a scream and ran away. The

others ran too, because Mr. Plod looked so stern. 'I just won't have people taking somebody's good name away!' said the policeman, and he stamped back to Busy Corner. 'I just won't. It's as wicked a thing as stealing!'

Well, so it is, isn't it? I think Mrs. Whisper and the others will be very careful in future, don't you?

The Angry Pixies

The children loved to go for a picnic in Pixie Wood. It was such a beautiful place. Primroses shone there by the hundred, violets smelt sweetly, and bluebells made a wonderful carpet in May time.

One day, when the primroses were out, Joan, Harry, Peter and Lucy went to the woods to have a picnic. They took with them packets of sandwiches and cakes, a big bar of chocolate, two bottles of lemonade, and some plastic cups to drink from.

'We shall have a lovely picnic,' said Harry. 'My mother has made egg and cress sandwiches.'

'And mine has made jam ones,' said Joan. 'We can share them all out and have some of each.'

They found a beautiful dell in the woods, and sat down to have their picnic. How good the food tasted. The children sat and looked round them as they ate.

Primroses shone pale and yellow all about them. Anemones nodded in the breeze. Violets nestled close to the primroses, and birds sang all round. The green moss was as soft as smooth velvet.

A robin sat in a bush and looked at them. He was hoping for a crumb. Harry saw him. He picked up a stone and threw it at the robin.

'Don't!' said Joan. 'Poor little thing – you hit it!'

The robin flew away with a cry of pain. It did not come back again. A tiny rabbit peeped at them from behind a tree. 'Isn't he sweet?' said Lucy. But he didn't peep long because Peter threw a stick at him. He ran into his hole and didn't come back again.

'I've finished my dinner,' said Harry. 'Let's put these lemonade bottles up on that stone over there, and throw stones at them. We'll see who can break them first.'

So they did. Harry was the best. He broke both bottles, and bits of glass flew all over the primroses and green moss. Peter began to throw bits of moss at the others.

'Don't' said Lucy. 'Let's play a proper game, Peter. Don't let's throw any more things.'

So they played 'It', and in their excitement they trampled on the primroses and violets, and crushed the anemones.

The wind came into the dell and blew the sandwich papers about. But nobody bothered to pick them up. The plastic cups were trodden on and lay in the dell too.

Soon Peter looked at his watch. 'Almost time to go,' he said. 'Shall we dig up a few primroses to take home?'

They dug up the best ones and then they went home, thinking what a lovely picnic they had had.

Now, the next day, Harry went into the woods again. He was on his way to see his uncle, who lived on the other side of the woods. He hadn't gone very far before he heard a loud and angry voice.

'I shall tell the policeman! It's a wicked shame! I shall go and tell the policeman now!'

Harry peeped to see who was speaking. He saw a small pixie-man, and he was surprised and pleased, for he had never seen one of the little folk before.

'What's the matter?' said Harry. 'Can I help you?'

'What do you think has happened?' said the pixie angrily. 'I had a most beautiful home in these woods, and the prettiest garden you ever saw, with primroses, violets and anemones growing all round. And I had a robin for a friend, and a little rabbit too. I had moss for a carpet, and I kept everything as neat as could be. And now somebody has spoilt it all!'

'What a pity!' said Harry.

'Yes – they've stolen some of my primroses, trampled on all my flowers, and dug up my moss,' said the pixie, angry tears running down his cheeks. 'And do you know, one of them has broken my robin's leg? Think of that!'

'Oh,' said Harry.

'And they frightened away my little rabbit and he won't come and talk to me,' said the pixie. 'But worst of all, they left broken glass all over the place, and when I got back late last night in the dark, I trod on it, cut my shoes to pieces and hurt my foot!'

Harry saw that the pixie's foot was bound up in a white rag. The little man went on, getting more and more upset as he talked.

'They left their rubbish there too – bits of paper and things like that. How dare they? What would they say if anyone did all that in *their* gardens?'

'Perhaps they didn't know it was your garden,' said Harry, very red in the face.

'Well, even if they didn't, surely they had the sense to know that other people might want to come and enjoy the beauty of the woods!' cried the pixie. 'Why should people spoil beautiful things? They must have very ugly minds if they can't see these woods are lovely. They must be horrid, selfish people, and I am going to the policeman who lives in the heart of the woods, to tell him to punish them. He's a pixie policeman who knows all kinds of magic. You come and tell him too.'

'I must get home, thank you,' said Harry, and before the pixie could say another word, he ran all the way home. He found Joan, Peter and Lucy, and told them about the angry pixie and all he had said.

'He was quite right,' said Joan, looking ashamed of herself. 'We did spoil that lovely dell – and oh, Harry, that poor, poor little robin! Did you really break its leg?'

Lucy had tears in her eyes. She loved birds. She didn't like to think of the frightened rabbit either. How *could* they have behaved like, that?

'We'll go and tell that pixie that we're very sorry and we'll never behave like that again,' said Lucy. So they all went to find him. But he wasn't there. The dell lay silent in the sunshine, spoilt and trampled.

'The pixie must have moved,' said Lucy.

'Let's pick up our rubbish. What a pity we can't say we're sorry and won't ever do such a thing again. I wish we could see the pixie.'

But they never did. Still, they kept their word, and now, when they go for a picnic, they never spoil anything, never throw stones, and always take their rubbish back in a bag. So they should, shouldn't they?

Binky the Borrower

'Please will you lend me your ladder?' said Binky the pixie, to Dame Lucy.

'Yes, but bring it back tomorrow,' said Dame Lucy. Binky didn't. He stood the ladder in his shed, meaning to take it back day after day, but he didn't remember.

'Please will you lend me your barrow? Please will you lend me a book? Please will you lend me your shovel? Please will you lend me a box of matches?' Binky was always saying things like this.

The little folk of Up-and-down Village were kind and generous, so they always lent Binky the things he asked for. But he hardly ever remembered to bring them back.

'Binky! Where's my lamp?' Twinkle would shout. 'I want it back!'

'Binky! Where's my carpet? Do bring it back!' Feefo would call. And Binky would always answer the same thing.

'I'll bring it back tomorrow.' But he never did.

'It's too bad,' grumbled the little folk of

Up-and-down Village. 'It's really too bad. Binky is always borrowing things and never bringing them back.'

'Borrowing is not a good thing,' said Feefo. 'It's stealing, if the things aren't given back. It is really.'

'So it is,' said Twinkle. 'Isn't that dreadful? Does Binky know he is a thief, if he doesn't give us back our things?'

'We'll tell him,' said Dame Lucy. So they told him, and he was very upset.

'How can you say such a thing about me? You know I am a very honest pixie. I wouldn't steal for anything! I will sort out all the things I have borrowed and send them back tomorrow. I think you are all very horrid.'

The next day Binky had a cold and stayed in bed, so nothing was sent back. The little folk of the village really did not know how to get back their things.

Then Dame Lucy had a good idea. 'I'll go to my aunt, the Wise Woman, and ask her for a Get-back Spell. She knows how to make them. Then we can get back all our things!'

So off she went to the Wise Woman and asked her for a Get-back Spell. The Wise Woman gave one to her. It was in a little box. It was a yellow powder, and it had to be blown into the air when the wind was in the south.

'Say these magic words when you blow the powder,' said the Wise Woman, and she told Dame Lucy some very powerful magic words. Dame Lucy hoped she would be able to remember them all.

She took the powder back to her village and showed it to everyone. 'When the wind is in the south we will use it,' she said. 'Then all our things will come back again.'

The next day the wind was in the south. Good! Dame Lucy opened the box and faced the wind. She blew the yellow powder into the breeze and then called out the magic words.

The Get-back Spell went into Binky's house. It got into everything he had ever borrowed in his life. He was most astonished when he saw his carpet get up, shake itself and rush out of the door. He was even more surprised when he saw the clock jump off the mantelpiece and the shovel hop out of the fender! They all went out of the door.

The people of the village were watching nearby to see if the Get-back Spell was going to work. As soon as they saw the carpet come rushing out, they knew the spell was a very good one.

'Here comes my carpet!' cried Feefo, in delight, and rolled it up under his arm.

'Here's my clock!' cried Dame Lucy, and took it gladly.

'Here's my shovel!'

'Here's my lamp!'

'Here's my armchair!'

'Here's my ladder!'

One by one the things came rushing and tumbling out of Binky's house. Each one went to its owner, but some of them raced off down the road to the next village.

'Look at that,' said Dame Lucy, in surprise. 'I suppose those are things that Binky borrowed in the next village before he came to live here – and they are all going back to their proper owners! Good gracious, what a lot of things he has borrowed!'

He certainly had! Curtains, tables, a ladder, pails, kettles, lamps, books, pencils, a coal-scuttle, all of them came scurrying back out of Binky's house in a great hurry to obey the Get-back Spell. The little folk began to laugh, because it really was a funny sight to see.

Binky couldn't understand what was happening. Why, all his belongings were going away! He hadn't anything left. His house was bare!

He rushed out into the street, and shouted to the others there. 'What's happening? Everything has gone! My house is empty!'

'Empty!' said everyone in amazement. 'What do you mean? Haven't you anything left at all?'

'Not a thing,' said Binky, beginning to cry. 'Oh, do tell me what's happening! Get my things back for me.'

'They are not your things,' said Dame Lucy, suddenly looking very stern. 'They belong to others. They are the things you have borrowed.

How dreadful to think that your whole house was made up of things you had borrowed!'

'Stolen, you mean!' said Feefo, fiercely. 'He never meant to give them back. He's a thief! He borrows things and never returns them. That's dishonest. He's a thief!'

'I'm not, I'm not,' wailed Binky, watching his pictures hop down the road to the next village. 'Oh, what am I to do? Can somebody lend me a bed to sleep in and a rug to cover me?'

But nobody would. No, they knew Binky by now, and they were not going to help him to be dishonest. It would be different if he always gave back what he borrowed, but he didn't. Let him sleep out in the fields!

So he did, and then he had to go and find some work to do to buy himself the things he needed.

Wouldn't you have liked to see the Get-back Spell at work? I would!

The Birthday Party

Once upon a time Bron the Brownie wanted to give a birthday party.

'It shall be the most wonderful party ever given,' said Bron. 'I shall give it in the field that runs down to the stream, then those who want to can go for a sail in the moonlight.'

'What will you have to eat,' asked Jinky.

'Honey cakes, daisy-jelly, bilberry buns, and the most delicious ice-creams ever made,' said Bron. 'And I shall have lemonade to drink, made of dewdrops shaken off the grass.'

'It does sound nice,' said Tippitty.

'And I shall ask the Princess Peronel,' said Bron. 'She loves a party. She will be staying with her aunt, quite near here, on my birthday. I am sure she will love to come.'

Everyone in Cuckoo Wood felt excited. A moonlight party near the stream, with lots of nice things to eat and drink. What fun!

Bron was very busy. He wrote out cards to tell everyone to come. He got the grey squirrel to take them to his friends, and everyone wrote back at once to say they would come.

He began to make jellies and cakes, biscuits and buns. He ordered himself a new suit of red and gold, with a pointed hat that was set with bells. 'They will ring whenever I walk,' said Bron. 'Then people will know I am coming.'

'Where will you get all the glasses and cups and plates and dishes from?' asked Tippitty. 'You won't have nearly enough.'

'The oak tree is giving me acorn-cups,' said Bron. 'I am borrowing all the other things from Jinky and Gobo – and perhaps you would lend me a few glasses, Tippitty dear.'

It was to be such a big party. Bron went down to the meadow and had a look at it. He had asked all the little folk he knew – the brownies, the elves, the pixies, and a few of the nicely-behaved goblins.

'The Princess Peronel says she will come too,' he told everyone. 'So you must all wear your very *best* dresses and suits, and polish up your wings nicely.'

'Where are you going to get all the chairs and tables you want?' asked Jinky. 'I can lend you mine, Bron, but I haven't very many.'

'Oh, I've thought about all that,' said Bron. 'I have written to the enchanter Heyho, and asked him to make me hundreds of little chairs and tables, and to send them here by midday, before the party. Then I shall have plenty of time to arrange them before midnight comes, and we begin the party.'

'How is he going to send them?' asked Jinky.

'His black cats are going to bring them,' said Bron. 'He is going to pack them all up neatly, and put them on the backs of his big cats. Then they will bring them to me by midday. I shall arrange them in the meadow then. Won't it be fun?'

The day of the party came. Bron's new suit was ready, and his hat with little bells. He looked very fine. He hurried about, looking to see if the jellies were all right, and the lemonade was sweet enough.

Midday came – but no black cats! Bron looked out for them, and wondered why they were late. One o'clock came – two o'clock. Still no black cats with all the tables and chairs.

Then, at three o'clock, a poor, limping cat came mewing to Bron. The cat was much bigger than little Bron. He looked up at her in surprise.

'Where are the other cats?' he asked. 'You are one of Heyho's cats, aren't you? Where are the little chairs and tables you were to bring?'

'Oh, Bron, a dreadful thing happened,' said the cat. 'As we were going down Breezy Hill, with the piles of little chairs and tables tied safely to our

backs, a big brown dog came trotting by. He saw
us and chased us all.'

'Oh dear! What happened?' asked Bron.

'Well, we rushed up trees,' said the cat, 'and all
the little chairs and tables caught in the boughs
and were smashed to bits. Oh, Bron, I'm so sorry.'

'This is dreadful,' said Bron.

'I got down the tree first, and came to tell you,'
said the cat. 'The dog chased me again, and I hurt
my paw. The other cats have gone back to our

master. But he will not be able to send you any more chairs and tables in time for your party.'

Bron felt as if he would burst into tears. 'How can I have a party without tables and chairs?' he wailed. 'I can't put the cups and plates on the ground! Oh dear, oh dear, this is a dreadful thing to happen just before the party! Whatever am I to do?'

The cat didn't know. She ran back to her master and left poor Bron looking very sad. Jinky came to see him, and he listened to the dreadful news.

'Bron – don't worry too much. I believe I know what we can do!' he said. 'Let's *grow* our own tables and stools!'

'What do you mean – grow them?' said Bron. 'I don't know enough magic for that.'

'Let's put a mushroom spell on your meadow!' said Jinky. 'Then mushrooms will grow up all over it.'

'What's the good of that?' asked Bron. 'You know what a long time plants take to grow – weeks and weeks. Don't be silly!'

'No, Bron, no – mushrooms are not like green plants that take a long time to grow,' said Jinky. 'They are quite different. They grow very, very quickly – in a night! You know how quickly toadstools grow, don't you? Well, mushrooms grow very quickly too, and they have very nice broad tops that will do well for tables and stools. Do let's come and try it.'

Bron began to cheer up. He went with Jinky to the meadow. Jinky began to dig about in the ground a bit, and he showed Bron some small white threads here and there. 'Just a bit of mushroom magic and hundreds of mushrooms will grow!' he said.

'I don't know mushroom magic,' said Bron. But Jinky did. He fetched his best wand and did a little waving and chanting. Bron thought he was really very clever.

'And now we'll just see what happens!' said Jinky, when he had finished.

Well, it really was very surprising. Before long, wherever there were the white threads that Jinky had found, the ground began to move a little, and to heave up.

'Jinky! Jinky! The mushrooms are growing!' cried Bron in delight. 'Here's one – and another – and another! Oh, what fun! There will be hundreds of them. Wherever I tread I can feel them growing.'

Well, by the time that it was nearly midnight, the meadow was covered with mushrooms! They grew very quickly indeed, as mushrooms always do, and Bron was full of joy when he saw what fine little tables and stools they would make.

He and Jinky and Tippitty quickly set out the goodies on the biggest mushrooms. By the time the guests arrived, everything was ready, and there was Bron, jingling his bells and giving the pretty little Princess Peronel and all his guests a great welcome!

'What marvellous tables and stools!' said the Princess. 'I do like them. Aren't they nice and soft to sit on – and oh, do look underneath the tops, everyone – there are the prettiest pink frills there, as soft as silk. Bron, I think they are the nicest tables and stools I have ever seen!'

Everyone else thought so too. The tables couldn't be knocked over, because they grew from the ground. There were so many of them that everyone could sit down at once if they wanted to.

It was a splendid party. The things to eat and drink were really lovely. There were tiny boats on the stream, made of curled-up water-lily leaves, with a white petal for a sail. The Princess had a wonderful time.

'This is the nicest party I have ever been to,' she said to Bron. 'The very nicest! As it is your birthday I would like to give you a present, and please wear it.'

She gave him a little shiny brooch in the shape of a mushroom! She had made it by magic and Bron was very pleased with it. 'I shall always remember this party when I wear it,' he said. 'Thank you, Princess Peronel.'

At dawn the guests all went home. Jinky and Bron cleared away the dishes and cups. Only the mushroom stools and tables were left.

'It's a pity they will all be wasted,' said Bron. 'They are so pretty, with their frills underneath, and they smell so nice!'

But they were not wasted – for, when the little folk were all sound asleep in the early morning sun, children came into the fields with baskets.

'Mushrooms!' they cried. 'Mushrooms for breakfast! Oh look! There are hundreds, all with pretty frills, and nice white caps. Mushrooms! Mushrooms!'

They picked them all – and for their breakfast they ate the stools and tables that the little folk had grown so quickly the night before. They did enjoy them!

It's strange that mushrooms and toadstools always grow so quickly, isn't it? There must be some of Jinky's magic about!

He Wouldn't Take the Trouble

Oh-Dear, the Brownie, was cross.

'I ordered two new tyres for my old bicycle ages ago,' he said, 'and they haven't come yet! So I have to walk to the village and back each day, instead of riding. It's such a nuisance.'

'It won't hurt you,' said a friend Feefo. 'Don't make such a fuss, Oh-Dear! Everything is so much trouble to you, and you sigh and groan too much.'

Feefo was right. Oh-Dear did make a fuss about everything. If his chimney smoked and needed sweeping he almost cried with rage – though if he had had it swept as soon as it began to smoke, his rooms wouldn't have got so black.

If his hens didn't lay eggs as often as they should, he shouted angrily at them – but if only he had bothered to feed them properly at the right times, he would have got all the eggs he wanted.

Now he was angry because his new bicycle tyres hadn't come. It was really most annoying.

The next day he walked down into the village again to ask at the post office if his tyres had come. But they hadn't. 'They might arrive by the next post,' said the little postmistress. 'If they do, I will send them by the carrier.'

'Pooh – you always say that and they never do come!' said Oh-Dear rudely. He walked out of the shop. It was his day for going to see his old aunt Chuckle. He didn't like her very much because she laughed at him – but if he didn't go to see her she didn't send him the cakes and pies he liked so much.

Oh-Dear walked in at his aunt's gate. He didn't bother to shut it, so it banged to and fro in the wind and his aunt sent him out to latch it.

'You just don't take the trouble to do anything,' she said. 'You don't bother to shine your shoes each morning – just look at them – and you don't trouble to post the letters I give you to post – and you don't even take the trouble to say thank-you for my pies and cakes. You are so lazy, Oh-Dear!'

'Oh Dear!' said Oh-Dear, sulking. 'Don't scold me again. You are always scolding me.'

'Well, you always need it,' said his aunt, and laughed at his sulking face. 'Now cheer up, Oh-Dear – I've a little bit of good news for you.'

'What is it?' said Oh-Dear.

'I've heard from my friend, Mr. Give-a-Lot, and he is having a party tomorrow,' said Aunt Chuckle. 'He said that if you like to go, he will be very pleased. So go, Oh-Dear, because you love parties, and you know that Mr. Give-a-Lot always has a lovely tea, and everyone goes away with a nice present.'

'Oh!' said Oh-Dear, pleased – but then his face grew gloomy. 'I can't go. It's too far to walk. No bus goes to Mr. Give-a-Lot's – and I haven't got my new bicycle tyres so I can't ride there. Oh dear, oh dear, oh dear – isn't that just my luck?'

'Well – never mind,' said Aunt Chuckle. 'I should have thought you could walk there – but if

it's too far, it's a pity. Cheer up. Look in the oven and you'll see a pie there.'

Oh-Dear stayed with his aunt till after tea. Then he set out to walk home. It was quite a long way. He groaned.

'Oh dear! It will be dark before I get home. Oh dear! What a pity I can't go to that party tomorrow. Oh dear, why isn't there a bus at this time to take me home?'

He went down the hill. A cart passed him and bumped over a hole in the road. Something fell out of the cart and rolled to the side of the road.

'Hi, hi!' shouted Oh-Dear, but the driver didn't hear him. 'Now look at that!' said Oh-Dear, crossly. 'I suppose I ought to carry the parcel down the road and catch the cart up – or take it to the police station.'

He picked up the parcel. It was too dark to see the name and address on it, but it was very heavy and awkward to carry.

'I can't be bothered to go after the cart or carry this all the way to the police station!' said Oh-Dear to himself. 'I really can't. And what's more I won't. Somebody else can have the trouble of taking it along!'

He threw the parcel down at the side of the road and went on his way. He wasn't going to take the trouble of finding out who it belonged to, or of handing it over safely. There the parcel lay all night, and all the next morning, for no one came by that way for a long time.

About three o'clock Cherry the pixie came along. She saw the parcel and picked it up. 'Oh!' she said, 'This must have been dropped by the carrier's cart yesterday. Somebody didn't get their parcel. I wonder who it was.'

She looked at the name and address on it. 'Master Oh-Dear, the Pixie,' she read. 'Lemon Cottage, Breezy Corner. Oh, it must be the bicycle tyres that Oh-Dear has been expecting for so long. Well – the parcel is very heavy, but I'll carry it to him myself.'

So the kind little pixie took it along to Oh-Dear's cottage and gave it to him. 'I found it lying in the road,' she said. 'It must have dropped off the cart last night.'

'Yes, I saw it,' said Oh-Dear, 'but I wasn't going to be bothered to carry it all the way after the cart.'

'But Oh-Dear – it's for you,' said Cherry, in surprise. 'I suppose it was too dark for you to see the name on it. It's your very own parcel – I expect it's the tyres you wanted.'

'Gracious! It is!' said Oh-Dear, in excitement. 'Perhaps I can go to Mr. Give-a-Lot's party after all.'

He tore off the paper and took off the lid of a big cardboard box. Inside were all the things he had ordered for his bicycle – two new tyres, a pump, a basket and a lamp.

Oh-Dear rushed to put them on his bicycle. He forgot to thank Cherry for her kindness. He worked hard at fitting on his tyres, but it was very very difficult.

At last he had them on – but when he looked at the clock, it was half-past six! Too late to go to the party now!

'Oh dear, isn't that just my bad luck!' wailed Oh-Dear. 'Why didn't you bring me the parcel earlier, Cherry?'

'Why didn't you take the trouble to see to it yourself last night, when you saw it in the road!' said Cherry. 'Bad luck, indeed – nothing of the sort. It's what you deserve! You won't bother yourself about anything, you just won't take the trouble – and now you've punished yourself, and a VERY GOOD THING TOO!'

She went out and banged the door. Oh-Dear sat down and cried. Why did he always have such bad luck, why, why, why?

Well, I could tell him the reason why, just as Cherry did, couldn't you?

A Puddle for the Donkeys

One day Dame Bonnet set out to catch the bus to the market. And, at the same time, Dame Two-Shoes set out to get the bus, too. They met on the common that leads down to where the big green bus stops three times a day.

'Good day to you, Dame Bonnet,' said Dame Two-Shoes. 'And where are you off to this fine morning?'

'To the market to buy me a good fat donkey,' said Dame Bonnet.

'What a strange thing!' said Dame Two-Shoes. 'I'm going to market to buy the very same thing.'

'Well, well, there will be plenty of good fat donkeys for sale,' said Dame Bonnet. 'Will you ride home on yours?'

'That I will,' said Dame Two-Shoes. 'I'm taking the morning's bus there, but I'm riding home on my own donkey, so I am.'

'And that's what I shall do, too,' said Dame Bonnet. 'I'm taking a carrot for my good donkey. Look!'

'Well, well, how do we think alike!' said Dame

Two-Shoes, and she held out a large carrot, too. 'I've got a carrot as well.'

'I expect our donkeys will be thirsty this hot day,' said Dame Bonnet, looking round. 'There's a nice big puddle near here, left by the rain. I mean to let my donkey drink it up.'

The two old dames looked at the puddle of water. 'I had that idea, too,' said Dame Two-Shoes, frowning. 'That puddle is only enough for one donkey. You must let mine share it, or mine will have none. Let them have half each. That will be fair.'

'If my donkey is here first, he shall have all the puddle,' said Dame Bonnet at once. 'I spoke about it first.'

'Don't be so mean,' cried Dame Two-Shoes. 'Would you have my donkey die of thirst?'

'Well, I shall not let mine die of thirst, either,' said Dame Bonnet. 'I don't care about yours. I have to think of my own good fat donkey. I don't go to market to buy donkeys and then let them die of thirst on the way home. The puddle is for my own donkey. So make up your mind about that!'

The old horse who lived on the common came wandering by, wondering why the old dames were talking so loudly. He saw the gleaming puddle of water and went over to it.

'Now look here!' said Dame Two-Shoes, angrily. 'For the last time, Dame Bonnet, will you let my donkey share that puddle? For the last time I ask you.'

'And for the last time I say that I shall look after my own good fat donkey, and not yours,' said Dame Bonnet, in a rage.

Then they heard the sound of gulping, and they turned to see what it was. It was the old horse drinking up every scrap of the puddle. There wasn't a drop left at all.

'Look at that!' cried Dame Two-Shoes in a fine

old temper. 'That greedy horse has been drinking up our donkeys' puddle! You bad horse!'

'Who do you belong to?' said Dame Bonnet. 'I'll go and tell your master. That puddle belonged to our two good fat donkeys. Now, when we ride them home tonight, there will be no puddle for them to drink and they will both die of thirst.'

'Hrrrumph!' said the horse, and backed away in alarm.

There came the sound of rumbling wheels and the old dames looked down to the road at the bottom of the common.

'The bus, it's the bus!' they cried. 'It's coming! Hurry, hurry! We shall never get to the market in time!'

So off they ran over the common path, the old horse looking after them in astonishment. How they ran! They panted and they puffed, they pulled their skirts away from the prickly gorse bushes and tried to hold them, they skipped over the rabbit-holes, and ran like two-year-olds.

The bus stopped. Nobody got out. Nobody got in. The driver looked round, but didn't see Dame Bonnet and Dame Two-Shoes scurrying along.

They had no breath left to shout at him. They ran and ran. But the bus went off without them, down the country road, out of sight.

'Oh!' said Dame Bonnet, almost in tears. 'Now we can't get to the market in time.'

'We can't buy our donkeys,' said Dame Two-Shoes. 'We shall have to walk home,' said Dame Bonnet.

'If we hadn't quarrelled about the pool of water that isn't there, we should be halfway to market now, we should buy good fat donkeys, and we should ride home on them,' wept Dame Two-Shoes.

'And we would have given them a drink before we started so that they wouldn't have wanted the puddle at all,' said Dame Bonnet.

They went slowly back home again. The old horse saw them and stared after them.

'Now what do they want with donkeys?' he said to himself. 'Donkeys themselves, that's what they are! Hrrrumph!'

And I rather think he was right.

The Very Lovely Pattern

Betty was sitting in her seat at school, trying very hard to think of a lovely pattern to draw and colour.

'I'm no good at drawing,' said Betty to herself. 'Not a bit of good! I never shall be. But oh, I do wish I could think of a pattern to draw on this page, so that Miss Brown would be pleased with me!'

'Betty! Are you dreaming as usual?' said Miss Brown. 'Do get on with your work.'

'I'm trying to think of a pattern,' said Betty. 'But it's very hard.'

'No, it isn't. It's easy,' said Harry. 'Look, Betty – do you see my pattern? I've made a whole row of little rounds, with squares inside them, and I am going to colour the squares yellow, and the bits inside the rounds are going to be blue. It will be a lovely pattern when it's finished. I shall make it all over the page.'

'Yes – it *is* lovely!' said Betty. 'I think I'll do that pattern too!'

'No,' said Harry. 'You mustn't. It's *my* pattern,

the one *I* thought of. You mustn't copy it.'

'No, you must think of one for yourself,' said Peggy. 'Look at mine, Betty. Do you like it?'

Betty looked at Peggy's. She had drawn a pattern of ivy-leaves all over her page, joining them together with stalks. It was really lovely.

'Oh dear – I do, *do* wish I could think of a lovely pattern too,' said Betty.

But do you know, by the end of the lesson poor Betty still sat with an empty page before her! She hadn't drawn anything. Miss Brown was cross.

'That is really naughty, Betty,' she said. 'You must take your pattern book home with you, and think of a pattern to bring me tomorrow morning. You have wasted half an hour.'

Betty was very upset. She badly wanted to cry. She worked very hard in the next lesson, but all the time she was thinking of whether or not she would be able to bring Miss Brown a lovely pattern the next day. She was sure she wouldn't be able to.

'It's snowing!' said Harry suddenly. 'Oh, Miss Brown, look – it's snowing!'

Everyone looked out of the window. Big white snow-flakes came floating down without a sound.

'The snow is so quiet,' said Betty. 'That's what I love so much about it.'

'It will be lovely to go home in the snow,' said

Harry. 'Miss Brown, isn't it fun to look up into the sky when it is snowing and see millions and millions of snow-flakes coming down? Where do they come from?'

'Well,' said Miss Brown, 'when the clouds float through very cold air, they become frozen. Sometimes, you know, the clouds turn into rain-drops. But when there is frost about, they turn into tiny ice-crystals instead – and these join together and make a big snowflake. It has to fall down, because light though it is, it is too heavy to float in the sky.'

'Snow-flakes look like pieces of cloud,' said Harry. 'Bits of frozen mist – how lovely!'

Betty thought it was lovely too. As she went home through the snow, she looked up into the sky. It was full of falling flakes, silent and slow and beautiful.

The little girl lost her way in the snow. She suddenly knew she was lost, and she leaned against a tree and began to cry.

'What's the matter?' said a little voice, and Betty saw a small man, dressed just like a brownie, all in brown from top to toe.

'Everything's gone wrong today!' said Betty, sobbing. 'I've lost my way in the snow – and Miss Brown was very cross with me because

I couldn't think of a pattern.'

'What sort of pattern?' asked the brownie in surprise. 'Why do you have to think of patterns?'

Betty told him. 'It's something we do at school. We make up our own patterns, draw them and colour them. It's fun to do it if you are clever at thinking of patterns. But I'm not.'

'But why do you bother to think of them?' asked the brownie. 'There are lovely patterns all round you. A daisy-flower makes a lovely pattern – so does a pretty oak-leaf.'

'There aren't any daisies or oak-leaves about now,' said Betty. 'I can't copy those.'

'We'll, look – you've got a most wonderful pattern on your sleeve!' said the brownie suddenly. 'Look! Look!'

Betty saw a snow-flake caught on the sleeve of her black coat. She looked at it hard.

'Have you got good eyes?' said the brownie. 'Can you see that the snow-flake is made up of tiny crystals – oh, very tiny?'

'Yes, I can,' said Betty, looking hard. 'Oh, what lovely patterns they are, brownie! Oh, I do wish I could see them get bigger!'

'I'll get my magic glass for you,' said the brownie, and he suddenly opened a door in a tree, went inside, and hopped out again with a round glass that had a handle.

'It's a magnifying glass,' said Betty. 'My granny has one when she wants to read the newspaper. She holds it over the print and it makes all the letters look big, so that she can easily read them.'

'Well, this will make the snow-crystals look much bigger to you,' said the brownie. He held the glass over Betty's black sleeve – and the little girl cried out in delight.

'Oh! Oh! They are beautiful! Oh, Brownie, they are the loveliest shapes!'

'But they are all alike in one way, although they are all quite different,' said the brownie. 'Look at them carefully, and count how many sides each little crystal has got, Betty.'

Betty counted. 'How funny! They all have six sides!' she said. 'All of them. Not one of them has four or five or seven sides – they all have six!'

'Ice-crystals always do,' said the brownie. 'But although they always have to have six sides, you won't find one ice-crystal that is like another. They all grow into a different six-sided pattern. Isn't that marvellous?'

'It's like magic,' said Betty. 'Just like magic. Oh – the snowflake has melted into water! The ice-crystals have gone. Quick – I want to see some more. I'll catch another snow-flake on my black sleeve.'

Soon she was looking at yet more tiny crystals through the glass. They all had six sides, each one was different and they were beautiful.

'Brownie,' said Betty suddenly, 'I shall choose these ice-crystals for the pattern I have to do for Miss Brown. Oh, they will make a most wonderful pattern! I can make a different pattern for every page in my drawing book – patterns much lovelier than any of the other children draw. Oh, I do feel excited!'

'I'll show you the way home,' said the brownie. 'I'm glad you are pleased about the ice-crystals. It's funny you didn't know about them. You'll be able to make fine patterns now!'

Betty went home. She thought of the lovely six-sided crystals she had seen, and she began to draw them very carefully.

She drew a page of this pattern. Then she turned over and drew a page of a second pattern, choosing another ice-crystal whose shape she remembered.

Mother came to see. 'Betty, what a lovely pattern!' she said. 'Quite perfect! How *did* you think of it!'

'I didn't,' said Betty. 'I saw it on my black sleeve, out in the snow. It's a six-sided ice-crystal, Mother. Oh, Mother, where is Granny's magnifying glass? Do take it out into the snow and look through it at a snow-flake on your sleeve! Then you will see how different all the ice-crystals are – and yet each one has six sides. There is no end to the shapes and patterns they make.'

Miss Brown was full of surprise when she saw Betty's patterns the next day. 'You didn't do these, dear, surely!' she said. 'Why, even I couldn't think of patterns like this. They are wonderful.'

'I'll show you where to find them,' said Betty happily. 'It's snowing, Miss Brown. Come out with me – and all the others too – and I'll show you where I found these beautiful patterns!'

She took them out into the snow, and they saw what she had seen. You will want to see it too, of course. So remember, next time it snows, go out with a bit of black cloth and catch a snowflake. You'll get such a surprise when you see the beautiful six-sided crystals in the flake.

Dame Lucky's Umbrella

Dame Lucky had a nice yellow umbrella that she liked very much. It had a strange handle. It was in the shape of a bird's head, and very nice to hold.

Dame Lucky had had it for her last birthday. Her brother had given it to her. 'Now don't go lending this to anyone,' he said. 'You're such a kindly, generous soul that you will lend anything to anyone. But this is such a nice umbrella that I shall be very sad if you lose it.'

'I won't lose it,' said Dame Lucky. 'I shall be very, very careful with it. It's the nicest one I've ever had.'

She used it two or three times in the rain and was very pleased with it because it opened out wide and kept every spot of rain from her clothes.

Then the summer came and there was no rain to bother about for weeks. Dame Lucky put her umbrella safely away in her wardrobe.

One morning in September her friend, Mother Lucy, came to see her. 'Well, well, this is a surprise,' said Dame Lucky. 'You've been so ill that I never thought you'd be allowed to come all this way to see me!'

'Oh, I'm much better,' said Mother Lucy. 'I mustn't stay long, though, because I have to get on to my sister's for lunch. She's expecting me in half an hour.'

But when Mother Lucy got up to go she looked at the sky in dismay. 'Oh, goodness – it's just going to pour with rain. Here are the first drops. I haven't brought an umbrella with me and I shall get soaked.'

'Dear me, you mustn't get wet after being so ill,' said Dame Lucky at once. 'You wait a moment. I'll get my new umbrella. But don't lose it, Lucy, because it's the only one I have and it's very precious.'

'Thank you. You're a kind soul,' said Mother Lucy. Dame Lucky fetched the yellow umbrella and put it up for her. Then off went Mother Lucy to her sister's, quite dry in the pouring rain.

She had a nice lunch at her sister's – and, will you believe it, when she left she quite forgot to take Dame Lucky's umbrella with her because it had stopped raining and the sun was shining!

So there it stood in the umbrella-stand, whilst Mother Hannah waved goodbye to her sister Lucy.

In a little while it began to pour with rain again. Old Mr. Kindly had come to call on Mother

Hannah without an umbrella and he asked her to lend him one when he was ready to go home.

'You may take any of the umbrellas in the stand,' said Mother Hannah. 'There are plenty there.'

So what did Mr. Kindly do but choose the yellow umbrella with the bird-handle, the one that belonged to Dame Lucky! Off he went with it, thinking what a fine one it was and how well it kept the rain off.

When he got home his little grand-daughter was there, waiting for him. 'Oh, Granddad! Can you lend me an umbrella?' she cried. 'I've come out without my mackintosh and Mummy will be cross if I go home wet.'

'Yes, certainly,' said Mr. Kindly. 'Take this one. I borrowed it from Mother Hannah. You can take it back to her tomorrow.'

Off went Little Corinne, the huge umbrella almost hiding her. Her mother was out when she got in, so she stood the umbrella in the hall-stand and went upstairs to take off her things.

Her brother ran down the stairs as she was about to go up. 'Hallo, Corinne! Is it raining? Blow, I'll have to take an umbrella, then!'

And, of course, he took Dame Lucky's, putting it up as soon as he got out of doors. Off he went, whistling in the rain, to his friend's house.

He put the umbrella in the hall-stand and went to find Jacko, his friend. Soon they were fitting together their railway lines, and when Pip said goodbye to Jacko he quite forgot about the umbrella because the sun was now shining again.

So there it stayed in Jacko's house all night. His Great-aunt Priscilla saw it there the next morning and was surprised because she hadn't seen it before. Nobody knew who owned it. What a peculiar thing!

Now, two days later, Dame Lucky put on her things to go out shopping and visiting. She looked up at the sky as she stepped out of her front door.

'Dear me – it looks like rain!' she said. 'I must take my umbrella.'

But it wasn't in the hall-stand. And it wasn't in the wardrobe in her bedroom, either. How strange! Where could it be?

'I must have lent it to somebody,' said Dame Lucky. 'I've forgotten who, though. Oh dear, I do hope I haven't lost it for good!'

She set out to do her shopping. It didn't rain whilst she was at the market. 'Perhaps it won't rain at all,' thought Dame Lucky. 'I'll visit my old friend Priscilla on my way back.'

She met Jacko on the way. 'Is your Great-aunt

Priscilla at home?' she asked him.

'Oh, yes,' said Jacko. 'She was only saying today that she wished she could see you. You go in and see her, Dame Lucky. You might just get there before the rain comes?'

She went on to the house where her friend Priscilla lived. She just got there before the rain fell. Dame Priscilla was very pleased to see her. Soon they were sitting talking over cups of cocoa.

'Well, I must go,' said Dame Lucky at last. 'Oh dear – look at the rain! And I don't have an umbrella!'

'What! Have you lost yours?' asked Priscilla. 'How unlucky! Well, I'll lend you one.'

She took Dame Lucky to the hall-stand and Dame Lucky looked at the two or three umbrellas standing there. She gave a cry.

'Why! Where did *this* one come from? It's mine, I do declare! Look at the bird-handle! Priscilla, however did it come here?'

'Nobody knows,' said Dame Priscilla in astonishment. 'Is it really yours? Then how did it get here? It has been here for the last two days!'

'Waiting for me, then, I expect,' said Dame Lucky happily. 'Isn't that a bit of luck, Priscilla? I shan't need to borrow one from you. I'll just take my own umbrella! Goodbye!'

Off she went under the great yellow umbrella, very pleased to have it again. And whom should she meet on her way home but her brother, the very one who had given her the umbrella!

'Hallo, hallo!' he cried. 'I see you still have your umbrella! I *would* have been cross if you'd lost it. Let me share it with you!'

So they walked home together under the big yellow umbrella – and to this day Dame Lucky doesn't know how it came to be standing in Dame Priscilla's hall-stand, waiting for her.

The Yellow Motor Car

Brian had a yellow motor car, just big enough to take his teddy bear for a drive. It was a clockwork car, and Brian had to wind it up with a large key. It said, 'Urrr, urrrr, urrrr' whenever it was wound up. It ran quickly across the floor, from end to end of the big nursery, and looked really fine.

It hadn't a hooter. It hadn't a brake. Its lamps were only pretend ones, with no glass and, of course, Brian couldn't switch them on, because they were only pretend-lamps. Still, they looked very fine.

Now one night a surprising thing happened to Brian. He was awakened by somebody pulling so hard at his sheet that the bedclothes nearly came off the bed. Brian sat up, quite cross.

'Who's pulling off the clothes! Stop, please!'

And then a small, growly voice spoke rather humbly to him.

'Brian! It's Bruiny, your teddy bear. Please wake up and come into the nursery very quietly. Something's happened.'

'Are you real, or am I dreaming that you

are walking and talking?' Brian asked.

'You're not dreaming,' said the bear. 'Oh, do come, Brian. The King of the Brownies is in the nursery and he is getting so cross.'

'Good gracious!' said Brian, more astonished than ever. 'The King of the Brownies! I can't believe it! I'm just coming – where are my slippers?'

He went into the nursery with the bear. Bruiny pulled at his pyjamas to make him go more quickly, and there he saw a most peculiar sight.

A small man with a long beard was pacing up and down the nursery, muttering to himself. He wore brown and green clothes, and a small golden crown. Beside him, trying to calm him down, were two more brownies.

'I tell you, it was a great mistake to get the black bats to draw my carriage!' shouted the King in a high, squeaky voice. 'What happens? They see flying beetles, go after them, turn upside down to catch them, and I am flung out of my carriage, bumpity-bump!'

'Well, Your Majesty, it's a good thing you were not hurt,' said the little servants, hurrying beside him as he paced up and down the nursery carpet.

'Hurt! I don't mind being hurt! What I do mind is that those stupid, silly, tiresome bats have gone off to eat their beetles and taken my carriage with them! And how I am going to get to the Pixie's Ball by midnight, I *do* not know! I, who have never been half a minute late for anything in all my life!' The brownie king stamped on the floor, took off his crown, and flung it down.

The servants picked it up, dusted it, and put it back on his head. All the toys watched, quite frightened, for they had never seen such an angry person before. Brian stared in surprise. The king was so small, so fierce, and so very surprising.

'Well! Anyone any suggestions to make?' stormed the brownie king, looking round at his servants and the toys. 'Isn't there a toy train I can ride to the ball in? Or a toy aeroplane I can fly off in?'

'Please, Your Majesty, the train is broken, and the aeroplane won't fly,' said the teddy bear. 'But look, I've brought you Brian. I thought maybe he could help you.'

The brownie king saw Brian for the first time. He bowed, and so did Brian. Then the king flew off into a temper again.

'It's too bad!' he squeaked, in his funny high voice. 'I can't go to the ball, and if I do I'll be late. Oh, I'm so annoyed!'

He took off his crown again and flung it down on the floor. The servants picked it up at once.

Brian really couldn't help smiling.

'Now look here,' he said. 'I've thought of something that might help. I've a toy motor car that would just about fit you and your servants. Look, here it is. Would you like to go to the ball in it?'

The king looked at it. He screwed up his nose. He frowned.

'No lights,' he said. 'No brake. No hooter. Silly sort of car this!'

'Well, it's only a toy one you know,' said Brian. 'I wish it *had* got a real hooter, and brake, and lamps. But toy cars like this never do have them.'

'A little magic would put that right,' said the teddy bear to the king.

'Of course, of course!' said the king. He took a wand from his pocket and waved it over the car, touching the lamps, the steering-wheel, and the inside of the car. And at once there was a small hooter on the wheel, a brake inside the car, and the lamps shone! Just like a real car!

Brian's heart beat fast. This was very exciting indeed. Still grumbling, the brownie king got into the yellow toy motor car and took the wheel. The servants wound it up with the key. 'Urrr, urrrrrrr, urrrr!' it went.

The car shot across the floor, with the lamps

shining brightly, hooted loudly at the clockwork
mouse who was in the way, and disappeared out of
the door! Brian heard it go down the passage, and
hoped that the garden-door was open.

'Well,' he said, 'that was a very funny thing to
happen in the middle of the night! I do hope I'll
get my car back again all right.'

'Of course you will,' said Bruiny. 'No doubt
about that at all. What a temper the brownie king
has, hasn't he? Flinging his crown about like that!
Well, you'd better go back to bed, Brian. You
must be tired. Thank you so much for your help.'

Brian did go back to bed, for he was dreadfully sleepy. And in the morning, of course, he was certain that it was all a dream.

But do you know, when he got out his toy yellow motor car to play with it, it had a hooter, a brake, and the lamps were real! There was a tiny switch by the steering-wheel that turned them off and on. Brian could hardly believe his eyes.

And now when his friends come to tea they have great fun with that yellow motor car. They put Bruiny into the car, wind it up, and send it off with the lamps alight. Bruiny is *very* clever at hooting and putting on the brake – you should just see him!

The Little Hidden Spell

Once upon a time Jinky came running into Tiptoe's cottage in great excitement.

'What's the matter?' asked Tiptoe. 'You do look pleased.'

'Well, I am,' said Jinky. 'What do you think? I have made a most wonderful spell! It is a spell that will make sad people smile – and, as you know, anyone who can be made to smile does not feel so sad! Isn't that marvellous?'

'Yes, it is,' said Tiptoe. 'Where is the spell? Show it to me.'

Jinky took it out of his pocket. It was so small that it looked no bigger than a poppy seed. It was bright blue, and twinkled as Jinky held it in his hand.

'That's all it is,' he said. 'Just that. But if any sad person holds it in his hand for just one second, he will smile at once.'

'Be careful that Tangle the goblin doesn't hear of it,' said Tiptoe. 'He would take it away from you and sell it to Tall-Hat the enchanter for a lot of money.'

'I'm afraid Tangle does know about it,' said Jinky. 'You see, Tiptoe, I was so pleased that I couldn't help making up a little song about my new spell – and I sang it on the way here.'

'Oh dear – and I suppose Tangle heard it,' said Tiptoe sadly. 'Oh, Jinky – quick – here comes Tangle now! I am sure he is after your new spell. Hide it quickly!'

'Where? Where?' cried Jinky.

'It's no good putting it into my pocket, no good at all. He'd find it there!'

Tiptoe picked up a bag from the table. In it were a good many little brown things. She picked one out and gave it to Jinky.

'Stuff the spell in one of these tiny bulbs,' she said. 'Go on, hurry! Stuff it right down at the top end. That's right.'

'I am sure Tangle would never think of looking there,' said Jinky. 'I'll put the little bulb in my pocket, and I'll bury it deep in my garden, Tiptoe. Then no one will know where it is but me. I can dig it up when Tangle has forgotten about it, can't I?'

'Yes,' said Tiptoe. 'Ah – here he is!'

Tangle walked into Tiptoe's kitchen. He was called Tangle because his hair always wanted brushing and combing. He was a very untidy goblin.

'Where's this spell I heard you singing about?' he said to Jinky.

'Spell? What spell?' said Jinky, opening his eyes very wide.

'It's no good pretending to me that you don't know about the smiling-spell,' said Tangle angrily. 'I know you brought it to show Tiptoe.'

He caught hold of poor Jinky and put his hand into every one of Jinky's pockets. He found a red handkerchief, an old bit of toffee, a piece of string, two stones with little holes in them – and the tiny bulb.

'What's this?' said Tangle, holding it up.

'That's one of my snowdrop bulbs,' said Tiptoe, showing Tangle the bag of them. 'I'm going to plant them under my lilac tree. I gave Jinky one for himself.'

Tangle gave Jinky back all the things he had taken from his pocket. Then he searched Tiptoe's kitchen well, even looking into her two teapots. She was very cross.

'You've no right to do this!' she said to Tangle. 'No right at all. I shall never, never ask you to come to any of my parties.'

'Pooh! I don't like parties,' said Tangle. He went off in a temper, and banged the kitchen door so hard that a plate fell off the dresser and broke.

'Horrid thing!' said Tiptoe, almost in tears. 'Look – now he's peeping in at the window! Jinky, don't take the spell out of the bulb, whatever you do, or he'll see it. Hurry home, and bury it in your garden tonight, when it's dark and Tangle won't see you.'

Jinky waited until Tangle had gone away. Then he hurried home as fast as he could. He didn't sing any song about his smiling-spell as he went. He ran indoors and shut and bolted his door.

Tangle came along, but Jinky wouldn't open his door, so Tangle had to go away. That night, when it was dark, Jinky opened his door and crept softly outside.

He went to his big garden, and found a trowel. He dug a little hole, popped the snowdrop bulb into it, and covered it with soil.

'Now I've hidden my spell, and no one will know where it is!' thought Jinky to himself.

Now, soon after that, Tangle went away to live somewhere else. Jinky was delighted.

'Now I can dig up my smiling-spell again, and use it!' he said. So out he went and got his trowel.

But dear me, he couldn't think where he had put the little bulb! He stood there in the middle of his big garden and frowned hard.

'Did I put it by the wall over there? Or did I put it under the hedge? Or could I have put it into the rose-bed?'

He didn't know. He began to dig here and there, but he couldn't find it. It was no good trying to hunt for it. He might have to dig up the whole garden before he found it!

'Oh dear!' said Jinky, very sad. 'Now I've lost it. I shall never find it again. My wonderful, marvellous smiling-spell is gone, quite gone!'

He went to tell Tiptoe. But she didn't seem at all sad. She smiled so widely that Jinky wondered if someone had given *her* a smiling-spell to hold in her hand for a second.

'Don't worry, Jinky dear,' she said. 'You will find your spell again in the early springtime. It's only just past Christmas now – you wait for a few weeks, and you will find your spell. I promise you that!'

'But how can I find it?' asked Jinky. Tiptoe wouldn't tell him.

'I've always told you that you are very, very stupid about things like seeds and flowers and bulbs and trees,' she said. 'You don't know anything about them at all, and it is very wrong of you. You have a lovely big garden, Jinky, and yet you don't grow anything in it but grass and weeds!'

'Just tell me how I can find my wonderful spell again,' said Jinky. 'Please do, Tiptoe.'

'If you knew anything at all about plants, I wouldn't need to tell you!' laughed Tiptoe. 'Now go away, Jinky, and watch your garden well this spring-time. If you see anything strange in it, come and tell me.'

Jinky watched his garden, as Tiptoe had told him. It was bare and brown in January. At the beginning of February there came a little snowfall. It made the garden look very pretty. Jinky went out to look at it.

And then he saw two straight green leaves growing up from the earth beneath the snow. He saw a tight little bud pushing up between the two leaves. He was astonished.

'A flower so early in the year!' he said. 'How lovely! I must watch it.'

So he watched it each day. He saw the flower-stalk grow long. He watched the bud shake itself free of its covering and droop its pretty head. He saw the flower open into a pure-white bell, its three outer petals as white as snow itself.

He went to tell Tiptoe. She smiled. 'I thought you would soon be coming to tell me about the snowdrop,' she said. She put on her hat and went back to Jinky's garden with him. 'Yes – that's the snowdrop which is growing from the tiny brown bulb you buried,' she said. 'You buried your spell – but you planted a snowdrop, Jinky! And it grew, as you see!'

'How can it grow in such cold weather?' said Jinky, amazed. 'Where have the leaves come from, and the beautiful flower?'

'Out of the bulb!' said Tiptoe. 'The bulb is a little store-house of food, Jinky. It can send up leaves and flowers very early in the year. When the flower has faded, dig up the old bulb – and you will find your spell still there in safety!'

So Jinky waited till the pretty flower had died, and then he carefully dug up the old bulb, which by now was dried up, because the growing leaves and flowers had used up the food it had held. In it was still his wonderful spell. He took it out, twinkling blue, and ran off to Tiptoe with it.

'I shall sell my spell to a doctor for a lot of money!' he cried. 'And, Tiptoe, with some of the money I shall buy hundreds and hundreds of bulbs! I shall plant them in my garden – and then, early in the year, I shall have the joy of seeing them grow!'

'Get daffodils and hyacinths too,' said Tiptoe, smiling. 'They all store up food in their bulbs, and send up leaves and flowers early in the year.'

'I think a bulb is just as much a magic thing as my smiling-spell,' said Jinky.

And I really think he was right!

The Forgotten Pets

Eileen and Fred had a good many pets, but they didn't love them very much. They had a rabbit in a big hutch. They had a yellow canary in a cage. They had a dog and a nice kennel for it. But not one of the pets was happy.

'My hutch smells,' said the rabbit. 'It hasn't been cleaned out for days!'

'I haven't any water in my pot, in my pot, in my pot,' trilled the canary. 'Eileen has forgotten again.'

'I want warm straw in my kennel because the nights are cold,' barked the dog. 'Wuff, wuff – bring me warm straw!'

But the children didn't look after their pets as they should, because they didn't love them. They shouldn't have had pets, of course, because they weren't the right kind of children for them.

One day the rabbit sent a message to a pixie friend of his. 'Come and help me. I am unhappy. The children who own me don't look after me at all.'

The pixie went to two or three of his friends,

and they made a plan. The next day, when the two children were coming back from school, the pixies met them.

'Would you come and stay with us for a day or two?' said Twinkle, the chief pixie. 'We don't see many little boys and girls in Fairyland, and we would like to give you a little house to stay in, and we would be so glad if you would let all the fairies, pixies and brownies have a look at you.'

The children thought this sounded lovely. 'Yes,' said Eileen, 'of course we'll come. Fancy having a little house of our own.'

'You shall have plates and cups with your names on too,' said Twinkle.

'How lovely!' said Fred. 'We shall be just like pets.'

'You will,' said Twinkle. 'We will look after you well, and not forget you at all.'

They took the children to Fairyland. They showed them into a dear little house with two rooms. A good fire burned in one room, for it was cold. There were two beds in the bedroom, but they had only one blanket on each.

'We'll be cold with only one blanket,' said Fred.

'Oh, we'll bring you more,' said Twinkle. 'Now see – aren't these dear little cups and plates and dishes – all with your names on!'

They certainly were nice. The children were very pleased. They went into the garden of the little house. It was wired all round, and there was a gate, tall and strong, with a padlock on it.

'We'll lock you in, so that no bad brownie or pixie can get you,' said Twinkle. 'Now we'll just go and tell everyone you are here, and then they can come and look at you through the wire, and you can talk to them.'

The first day was great fun, and the meals were delicious, served in the cups and dishes with their names on. But when night came, and the children went into the little house, they found that it was very cold.

The fire had gone out. There was no coal or wood to be seen. And dear me, Twinkle had forgotten to bring the extra blankets for their beds!

They shivered. 'We'll call for Twinkle, or go and find him,' said Eileen. So they called. But nobody came. They tried to open the gate, but it was locked. They went back to the cold house and hoped their little candle would last till the daylight came.

They were so cold that night, they couldn't sleep. The wind howled round. Eileen was thirsty, but she couldn't find any taps in the house at all.

She felt cross with Twinkle. 'I do think he might look after us better,' she said. 'He promised to bring us warm blankets, and he didn't. And there isn't a drop of water to drink! After all, if he wants us to be like pets here, he ought to treat us well. We can't look after ourselves!'

The next day the children waited for Twinkle to come. He came at last – but he didn't bring them much breakfast.

'I'll bring you a better dinner,' he said. 'What's that – you want a drink? All right, I'll bring that later. I'm rather busy at the moment. And yes – I'll bring those blankets. How stupid of me to forget!'

But he didn't come again that day. Other pixies came and stared through the fence, but as the gate was locked they could not get in to give the children any food or water. They grew angry and frightened.

Twinkle came about six o'clock. 'So sorry not to have been able to come before,' he said. 'I had such a lot to do. Oh dear – I've forgotten the water again – and the blankets. Still, here is some bread and butter. I'll go back for the other things.'

'Only bread-and-butter,' said the poor children, who were now dreadfully hungry. 'Oh dear! Bring us something else, please. And we think we'd like to go home tomorrow.'

Twinkle went off. He didn't come back that night! Eileen and Fred were so thirsty that they cried. They didn't undress because they were too cold. They sat huddled on their beds, feeling miserable.

'It's raining,' said Eileen. 'Let's go out and open our mouths to drink the rain – then we shall get a drink.'

They did – but they also got soaked through which made them colder than ever. There was still no fire, because Twinkle had forgotten to bring them wood or coal. The candle had burnt out. It was dark and horrid in the little house, which could have been so cosy and comfortable.

'I don't call this being pets!' sobbed Eileen. 'We're forgotten. They don't love us a bit – they don't remember to give us water or proper food, or to keep us warm. They don't deserve to have us as pets!'

Fred was quiet for a moment. Then he spoke in a serious voice. 'Eileen – I think the pixies have done this on purpose! This is how we keep our pets! We forget to give them proper food – we forget to give them fresh water – we don't clean out their cages when we should – and you know we didn't give poor old Rover any warm straw in his kennel those cold nights.'

'Oh,' said Eileen. 'Oh, poor Rover! Fred, I know what it feels like now, don't you, to be in a cage, not able to look after ourselves or get food – and then to be forgotten. It's dreadful. It's wrong. I'll never do such a thing again. I'll always love my pets and look after them.'

As soon as she said that a strange thing happened. She felt warm and cosy and comfortable – and as she felt round, she gave a loud cry.

'Fred! I'm not in that little house – I'm in my own bed at home! How did it happen?'

They never knew how it was that they had gone from Fairyland to their own beds, and I don't know either – all I know is that as soon as they had learnt their lesson, they were back home again.

They didn't forget what they had felt like when they had been forgotten pets in Fairyland. They love their pets now, and care for them well.

The Book of Brownies

CRAB-APPLE
COTTAGE

EGMONT

CONTENTS

Hop, Skip and Jump Play a Naughty Trick   359

Their Adventure in the Cottage Without a Door   378

Their Adventure in the Castle of the Red Goblin   389

Their Adventure in the Land of Giants   405

Their Adventure in the Land of Clever People   423

Their Adventure in the Land of Clever People
(continued)   436

Their Adventure on the Green Railway   447

Their Adventure in Toadstool Town   460

Their Adventure with the Saucepan Man   472

Their Adventure with the Labeller and the Bottler   491

Their Adventure in the House of Witch Green-eyes   507

Their Very Last Adventure of All   526

GOODBYE!   532

Waiting for the postman

Hop, Skip and Jump Play a Naughty Trick

Hop, Skip and Jump were just finishing their breakfast one morning when they heard the postman rat-tatting on all the knockers down the street.

'Dear me!' said Hop. 'Everybody seems to be getting a letter this morning! Perhaps we shall too.'

The three brownies leaned out of the window of Crab-apple Cottage and watched the postman come nearer. Next door but one, rat-tat! And a large letter fell into the letter-box. Next door, rat-tat! Another large letter, just like the first.

'I wonder whatever the letters are!' said Skip. 'They're all the same and everyone is having one, so there'll be one for us too!'

But there wasn't. The postman walked right past Crab-apple Cottage.

'Hey!' called Jump. 'You've missed us out! Come back, postman!'

The postman shook his head.

'There isn't a letter for you,' he said, and rat-tatted on the knocker of the cottage next door.

Well, Hop, Skip and Jump *were* upset. No letter for them, when everyone else had one! Whoever could be writing letters and missing them out!

'Let's go and ask Gobo next door what his letter's about,' said Hop.

So the three brownies hopped into Gobo's. They found him looking very pleased and excited, reading his letter out loud to Pinkie, his wife.

'What's it all about?' asked Skip.

'Listen! Just listen!' said Gobo. 'It's an invitation from the King. This is what he says: "His Majesty, the King of Fairyland, is giving a Grand Party on Thursday. Please come".'

'Oh!' cried the brownies. 'Then why haven't *we* been asked?'

Gobo looked surprised.

'Haven't you had a letter?' he asked. 'Oh well, there must be a reason for it. Have you been good lately?'

'Not *very*,' said Hop.

'Not *much*,' said Skip.

'Not at all,' said Jump, who was the most truthful of the three.

'Well, there you are,' said Gobo, folding up his letter. 'You know the King never asks bad brownies to his parties. You can't expect to be invited if you *will* be naughty.'

The brownies went out crossly. They ran back into Crab-apple Cottage and sat down round the table.

'What have we done that was naughty lately?' asked Hop.

'We painted Old Mother Wimple's pig green,' said Skip.

'Yes, and we got on to Gillie Brownie's cottage roof and put fireworks down her chimney,' said Jump.

'And we put a bit of prickly gorse in that horrid old Wizard's bed,' said Hop. 'Oh dear – perhaps we *have* been a bit naughtier than usual.'

'And someone's told the King,' sighed Skip.

'So we've been left out of the party,' groaned Jump. 'Well, it serves us right!'

Everybody except the three bad brownies had got an invitation. Brownie Town was most excited.

'It's going to be a *very* grand party!' said Gobo next door, who was busy making himself a new suit. 'There's going to be dancing and conjuring, and presents for everybody!'

This made Hop, Skip and Jump feel more disappointed than ever.

'Can't we go somehow?' wondered Hop. 'Can't

we dress up and pretend to be someone else, not ourselves?'

'We haven't got a card to show,' said Skip mournfully.

'Look, there's Gobo's wife,' said Jump, pointing through the window. 'What's she looking upset about? Hey, Pinkie, what's the matter?'

'Oh, a *great* disappointment,' answered Pinkie. 'The conjurer that the King was going to have at the party can't come after all, and the Lord High Chamberlain can't get anyone else. *Isn't* it disappointing?'

'Not so disappointing for us as for you!' said Hop. Then a great idea came to him, and he turned to Skip and Jump.

'I say!' he said, with his naughty little eyes twinkling. 'I say, couldn't we pretend we were conjurers and get the Lord High Chamberlain to let us in to the party?'

'What a fine idea!' cried Skip and Jump in delight. 'You can be the conjurer, Hop, and we'll be your assistants!'

'But what tricks shall we do?' asked Hop. 'We don't know how to do any yet!'

All that morning the brownies tried to think of conjuring tricks to do at the party, but although they tried their hardest to make rabbits come out of hats, and ribbons come out of their mouths, it wasn't a bit of good, they just couldn't do it.

They were having dinner, and feeling very unhappy about everything, when a knock came at the door.

'Come in!' cried Hop.

The door opened and an old woman with green eyes looked in.

'Good afternoon,' she said, 'do you want to buy any magic?'

'She's a witch!' whispered Jump. 'Be careful of her.'

'What sort of magic?' asked Hop.

'Oh, any sort,' said the witch, coming into the room. 'Look here!'

She took Hop's watch, rubbed it between her hands, blew on it, and opened her hands again. The watch was gone!

'Buttons and buttercups!' gasped Hop in astonishment. 'Where's it gone to?'

'You'll find it in the teapot,' said the witch.

Skip lifted the lid of the teapot, and there, sure enough, lay the watch, half covered in tea-leaves. He fished it out with a spoon. Hop was very cross.

'I call that a *silly* trick!' he said. 'Why, you might have spoilt my watch!'

'Do something else, Miss Witch,' begged Jump.

363

'Give me your tea-cup,' said the witch.

Jump gave it to her. The witch filled it full of tea, covered it with a plate, whistled on the plate, and took it off again.

'Oh,' cried Jump, hardly believing his eyes, 'it's full of little goldfish!'

So it was – the tiniest, prettiest little things you ever saw! The brownies thought it was wonderful.

Then the witch emptied Jump's tea into Skip's cup. And, hey presto! all the fishes vanished.

The brownies began to feel as if they were dreaming.

'If only we could do one or two tricks like that!' sighed Hop. 'Why, we could get into the King's party as easily as anything.'

'Oho, so you want to go to the party, do you?' asked the witch. 'Haven't you been invited?'

'No,' answered Skip, and he told the witch all about it. She listened hard.

'Dear, dear!' she said at the end. 'It really is a shame not to invite nice little brownies like you! Listen – if I get you into the Palace as conjurers, will you do the trick I want you to? It's a very, very special one.'

'Show us it!' said the brownies, beginning to feel most excited.

The witch went outside and came back carrying

a round green basket, with a yellow lid. She put it on the floor.

'Now you,' she said, pointing to Hop, 'jump into this basket!'

Hop jumped inside. The witch put the lid on. Then she tapped three times on the top of it and sang:

'Rimminy, romminy ray
My magic will send you away;
Rimminy, romminy ro
Ever so far you will go!'

Skip and Jump looked at the basket. It didn't move or creak!

'Take off the lid and look inside,' said the witch.

Skip took off the lid and almost fell into the basket in surprise. 'Oh!' he shouted. 'Oh! Hop's gone, and the basket's empty.'

So it was. There was nothing in it at all.

'Now watch,' said the witch, and putting the lid on again, she began singing:

'Rimminy, romminy ray
Hear the spell and obey;
Rimminy, romminy relf
Jump out of the basket yourself!'

Immediately, the lid flew off and out jumped Hop, looking as pleased as could be.

'Good gracious!' gasped Jump, sitting down suddenly on a chair. 'Where have you been, Hop?'

'In the basket all the time,' said Hop.

'But you *weren't*, we looked!' said Skip.

'You couldn't have,' said Hop, 'or you'd have seen me!'

'We *did* look, I tell you,' said Skip crossly.

'Be quiet,' said the witch. 'It's the magic in the basket that does the trick. Now listen – I'll lend you that basket if you'll promise to do the trick at the party in front of the King and Queen.'

'Of course we will, of course we will!' cried the brownies. 'But why do you lend it to us for nothing?'

'Oh, just because I'm kind-hearted,' said the witch, grinning very wide indeed. 'But mind – when you've got into the basket and have vanished, and been brought back, you've got to offer to do the same thing with anyone else. Perhaps the King will offer to get into the basket, or the Queen, or the Princess!'

'My!' said Hop, 'do you think they will?'

'They're almost sure to,' said the witch. 'So mind you let them try. But you must remember this. If any of the Royal Family get in, tap seven times, not three times, on the lid when you sing the magic verse. Three times for ordinary folk, but seven times for royalty – see?'

'Yes, we'll remember,' promised Skip, 'and thank you very much for lending us such a lovely trick.'

When the witch had gone, leaving behind her the green basket with its yellow lid, the three brownies were tremendously excited. They began to plan their clothes for the next day, and spent all the afternoon and evening making them.

Hop looked very grand in a black velvet suit with a long red cloak and peaked hat. Skip and Jump were dressed like pages and were just alike in bright green suits.

When the party day came they all went out very early with the magic basket and hid in a nearby wood, for they didn't want any of the brownies to see them and guess what they were going to do.

'I hope they have lots of lovely things for tea,' said Hop. 'I'm getting very hungry.'

'It will soon be time to go,' said Skip. 'Listen! There are the drums to say that the first guests have arrived!'

'Come along then,' said Jump. 'We'll arrive too!'

'Now remember, I'm Twirly-wirly the Great Conjurer from the Land of Tiddlywinks,' said

Hop, 'and you are my two assistants. Don't forget you've got to be polite to me and bow each time you speak to me!'

Off they went, all feeling a little nervous. But Hop, who was bigger than the others and rather fat, looked so grand in his red cloak, that Skip and Jump soon began to feel nobody could possibly guess their secret.

At last they reached the Palace Gates.

'Your cards,' said the sentry to Hop, Skip, and Jump.

'I am Twirly-wirly, the Great Conjurer from the Land of Tiddlywinks,' said Hop, in such a grand voice that Skip and Jump wanted to laugh. 'I am here to take the place of the conjurer who could not come.'

The sentry let them pass.

'Go straight up the drive,' he said, 'and at the top of the first flight of steps you will find the Lord High Chamberlain.'

The three brownies went on. Hop was enjoying himself. He told the others to walk behind him and bow to him, whenever they saw him turn their way.

'You're getting a great deal too grand,' grumbled Jump, who began to wish he was the conjurer instead of Hop, for he was carrying the basket and finding it rather heavy.

The Lord High Chamberlain was very surprised to see them. He was even more surprised when he heard Hop telling him who he was.

'Twirly-wirly, the Great Conjurer,' he said, pretending to know all about him. 'Dear me, what an honour to be sure! Very kind of you to have come, *very* kind. Pray come this way!'

He led them to a tea table and gave Hop a chair. Skip and Jump stood behind him, and looked longingly at the cakes and jellies, tarts and custards spread out on the table in front of Hop.

Little pages ran up and offered all the nicest things to the conjurer. He took some of each, and Skip and Jump looked on enviously.

'Aren't *we* going to have any?' whispered Skip in Hop's ear. 'You're not going to leave us out, are you?'

'Hush!' said Hop. 'You are only my servants today. If you don't keep quiet I shall keep turning round to you and you'll have to bow till your backs ache!'

Hop had an enormous tea. Then he announced to the Lord High Chamberlain that he would now come and do his famous trick with his magic basket, if Their Majesties the King and Queen would like to see it.

Their Majesties at once sent a message to say they would be very pleased to see it.

'Come this way,' said the Chamberlain, and led the three brownies to where the King and Queen sat on their thrones. In front of them was a square piece of grass, and round it sat scores of fairies and gnomes, brownies and elves, all waiting to see Twirly-wirly the Great Conjurer.

Hop stepped grandly up to the King and Queen, and bowed three times. So did Skip and Jump.

'I will now do my wonderful basket trick' said Hop in a very loud and haughty voice. Then he turned to Skip.

'Bring me the basket,' he ordered. Skip rushed forward with it in such a hurry that he tumbled over, and everyone began laughing. Jump helped him up, and together they picked up the magic basket.

'Get into it,' commanded Hop, pointing at Skip. Skip jumped in.

'Put the lid on!' Hop commanded Jump. Jump did so. Then Hop tapped three times on the lid and sang:

'Rimminy, romminy ray
My magic will send you away;

370

Rimminy, romminy ro
Ever so far you will go!'

Everybody listened and watched, and wondered what was going to happen. The King and Queen bent forward to get a better view, and the little Princess Peronel stood up in her excitement.

'Take the lid off!' ordered Hop.

Jump took the lid off. The basket was empty!

'Ooh!' said everyone in the greatest surprise. 'Ooh! He's gone!'

'Roll the basket round for everyone to see that it's empty,' commanded Hop, who was now thoroughly enjoying himself.

Jump rolled the basket round so that everyone could have a good look. Then he brought it back to Hop.

'Put the lid on!' said Hop. Jump put it on. Everybody stopped breathing, to see whatever was going to happen next.

Hop tapped three times on the lid and sang the magic song:

'Rimminy, romminy ray
Hear the spell and obey;
Rimminy, romminy relf,
Jump out of the basket yourself!'

371

Just as he finished, the lid flew off and out jumped Skip in his little green suit, looking as perky as anything! He capered about and bowed to everyone.

'Oh look! Oh look! He's come back again!' shouted the fairies and brownies. 'Oh, what a wonderful trick! Do it again, do it again!'

Hop bowed very low. 'Would anyone care to come and get into the basket?' he asked. 'I will do the trick with anyone.'

'Oh let *me*, let *me*!' cried a little silvery voice, and who should come running on the grass but the Princess Peronel!

'Come back, Peronel!' cried the King. 'You're not to get into that basket!'

'Oh please, oh, please,' she begged. 'It's my birthday and you *said* I could have anything I wanted.'

'No, no!' said the Queen. 'You mustn't get into that basket! Come back!'

'I shall cry then!' said Peronel, screwing up her pretty little face.

'Oh dear, oh dear!' said the King, who couldn't bear to see Peronel cry.

'You'd better have your own way then, but make haste about it!'

Peronel jumped into the green basket, and Skip

clapped on the lid. Hop remembered what the witch had told him – he must tap the lid seven times for royalty. So, very solemnly, he did so. Then he and Skip and Jump all chanted the magic rhyme together.

'Rimminy, romminy ray
My magic will send you away;
Rimminy, romminy ro
Ever so far you will go!'

But, oh dear, oh dear, oh dear! Whatever *do* you think happened?

Why, just as the magic rhyme was finished, the basket rose into the air, and sailed right away! Higher and higher it went, over the trees and over the palace, towards the setting sun.

'Oh! Oh!' cried the Queen, jumping up in terrible distress. 'Where's my Peronel gone to? Bring her back, quickly!'

But Hop, Skip and Jump were just as surprised as anyone! What an extraordinary thing for the basket to do!

'Arrest those conjurers!' suddenly said the King, in an awful voice.

Six soldiers at once ran up and clapped their hands on the brownies' shoulders.

'Now, unless you bring Peronel back *at once*,' said the King, 'you go straight to prison, and I'll have your heads cut off in the morning!'

'Oh, no, no!' cried the brownies, very frightened indeed. 'Please, please, we aren't conjurers! Only just brownies!'

'Nonsense!' stormed the King. 'Ordinary brownies can't do tricks like that! Now then, are you going to bring Peronel back again?'

'I can't, I can't,' wailed Hop, big tears beginning to pour down his cheeks. 'I'm only a naughty brownie dressed up like a conjurer, because you didn't ask me to your party!'

Suddenly a watching brownie gave a shout of surprise. It was Gobo. He ran up to Hop and pulled off his peaked hat and red cloak.

'Why, it's Hop!' he cried, in astonishment. 'Your Majesty, these brownies are Hop, Skip and Jump, the three naughty brownies of our town.'

'Goodness gracious!' said the King, in a terribly upset voice. 'This is more serious than I thought. If they are really brownies, then they cannot bring back Peronel. But where did you get the basket from?' he asked Hop sternly.

Hop dried his eyes and told the King all about the witch's visit, and how she had left the basket with them.

'Oh, it's Witch Green-eyes!' groaned the King. 'She's often vowed to steal Peronel away and now she's done it through you, you naughty, stupid little brownies.'

'My goodness!' said Hop. 'Do you think the witch has *really* stolen her for always?'

'Yes!' sobbed the Queen, who was terribly distressed. 'We shall never get her back again, the darling!'

'Oh my goodness!' said Skip, in a frightened voice.

'Oh my goodness!' wailed Jump, in a miserable voice.

'Oh your goodness!' roared the King suddenly, in a temper. 'What do you mean, oh your *goodness*! You ought to say, "Oh your badness," you mischievous little brownies! You haven't a bit of goodness among the three of you. And now see what you've done! I've a good mind to cut off your heads!'

'Oh my goodness!' wept Hop again. He didn't mean to say it, but he couldn't think of anything else.

The King grew angrier than ever.

'Where *is* your goodness?' he demanded.

'Yes, where *is* it?' shouted everybody.

'We d-d-don't know,' stammered the brownies in dismay.

'Well, go and find it!' stormed the King. 'Go

along! Go right out of Fairyland, and don't come back till you've found your goodness that you keep talking about! Make haste before I cut off your heads!'

'Oh, oh, oh!' cried the three brownies in a great fright, and they all took to their heels and fled. Down the steps they went and down the drive, and out through the palace gates past the astonished sentries.

Even then they didn't stop. They rushed down the road and into the Cuckoo Wood, as if a thousand soldiers were after them!

At last, out of breath, tired and unhappy, they sat down under a big oak tree.

'Oh my goodness!' began Hop.

'Don't be silly!' said Skip. '*Don't* keep saying that. We're in a terrible, terrible fix.'

'To be turned out of Fairyland!' wept Jump. 'Oh, what a terrible punishment! And how can we find our goodness? Of course we never shall! People don't have goodness they can find!'

'It's just the King's way of banishing us from Fairyland altogether,' wept Hop. 'He knows we'll never be able to go back. And, oh dear, whatever's happened to poor little Peronel?'

What indeed? None of the brownies knew, and they were very unhappy.

'The only thing to do now is to go and see if we can find Peronel and rescue her,' said Jump. 'We'll sleep here for the night, and start off in the morning, on our way to Witchland.'

So all night long they slept beneath the big oak tree, and dreamed of horrid magic baskets, and packets of goodness that would keep running away from them.

Their Adventure in the Cottage Without a Door

Next morning the brownies set out on their journey. They soon passed the borders of Fairyland and found themselves in the Lands Outside. For a long, long time they walked, and met nobody at all.

'I *am* getting hungry!' sighed Hop.

'So am I!' said Skip.

'Well, look! There's a cottage,' said Jump. 'We'll go and ask if we can have something to eat. Have you got any money, Hop?'

Hop felt in his pockets.

'Not a penny,' he answered.

'Oh dear, nor have I,' said Skip.

'What *are* we to do then?' asked Jump. 'Perhaps there's someone kind living in the cottage, who will give us some breakfast for nothing.'

The three brownies went up to the little cottage. It was surrounded by trees and its front door was painted a very beautiful bright blue.

Hop knocked loudly.

'Who is knocking at my door?' asked a deep voice.

'Three hungry brownies,' answered Hop boldly.

'Come in!' said the voice.

Hop opened the door and the brownies went in. Clap! The door swung to behind them, and made them jump. Hop looked round to see who had shut the door.

But to his enormous surprise, he could see no door at all – and yet they had just come in by one.

'Good gracious!' he cried. 'Wherever has the door gone!'

'He, he!' chuckled a deep voice. 'It's gone where *you* won't find it! I've got you prisoners now. Three nice little servants to work for me all day!'

Hop, Skip and Jump looked most astonished. This was a fine sort of welcome!

Then they saw an old wizard, huddled up by the cottage fire, laughing at them.

'We're not your prisoners, so please let us go,' said Hop.

'All right, go!' laughed the wizard.

But search as they would, the brownies couldn't find any door at all. There were blank walls all round them. Then they knew that they were prisoners indeed.

'Now, listen,' said the wizard. 'I will give you your meals, and in return you must work for me. I have a great many spells I want copied out. Sit down at that table and begin work at once.'

The three brownies obeyed. They knew that it was best not to anger such a powerful wizard.

He brought them each a great book of magic, and set it down beside them.

'Begin at page one,' he said, 'and if you make me a fair copy of all the books, without one single mistake, perhaps I will let you go.'

'Oh dear!' groaned Jump. 'Why, the books have got about a thousand pages each.'

The three brownies set to work, and very difficult it was too, for the wizard wrote so badly that they could hardly read his writing in the big magic books.

All day they wrote, and all the wizard gave them to eat was a large turnip, which tasted just like India-rubber. The brownies kept looking round to see if the door came back again, but alas, it didn't.

That night, when the wizard was snoring on his bed, the three brownies began whispering together.

'We *must* escape somehow!' said Hop.

'But how?' whispered Skip and Jump.

None of them could think of a plan at all.

'It's no good thinking of escaping until we find out about that disappearing door!' groaned Hop.

'The wizard's barred the window right across. We'd better go to sleep.'

So off to sleep they went, and were wakened up very early the next morning by the wizard, who wanted his breakfast.

After that they had to sit down and copy out the magic books again. It was dreadfully dull work.

But suddenly Hop found he was copying out something that made his heart beat with excitement. It was about Disappearing Doors.

'A Disappearing Door will come back if a wizard's green stick is swung three times in the air and dropped,' said the book. Hop's hand shook as he copied it out.

'If only the wizard's stick is green, and I could get hold of it whilst he's asleep!' he thought.

He turned round to look at the stick. Yes, it was green, sure enough – but the wizard was holding it tightly in his hand.

'But when he's asleep, he'll put it down!' thought Hop, longing to tell Skip and Jump what he had discovered.

That night he watched the wizard carefully – but oh, how disappointed he was to see that he went to bed with his stick still held in his hand.

'I'd be sure to wake him if I tried to get his stick!' thought Hop, and he whispered to Skip and

Jump all that he had thought of during the day.

They were most excited. 'Oh, do let's try to get his stick!' whispered Skip. 'If only we could get out of this horrid cottage!'

'And if only we could go back to dear old Fairyland!' whispered Jump, with tears in his eyes.

Now Hop was the bravest of the brownies, and he couldn't bear to see Jump crying.

'I'll go and see if I can possibly get the stick!' he said. 'Stay here and don't make a sound.'

Then the brave little brownie crept quietly across the floor till he reached the wizard's bed.

'Snore – snore!' went the wizard. 'Snore – snore!'

Carefully, Hop put up his hand and felt in the bedclothes for the green stick. But oh my! No sooner did he catch hold of it, than what do you think happened?

Why, that stick jumped straight out of bed by itself and began to chase Hop all round the room. Poor Hop began to yell in fright. That woke the wizard up. He sat up in bed and chuckled.

'He, he,' he laughed, 'so you were trying to steal my stick, were you! Well, well! You won't do it again in a hurry!'

Poor Hop was running all over the place trying to get out of the way of the stick, which gave him the biggest chase he'd ever had in his life.

'Come back, stick!' at last said the wizard, and the stick jumped back into bed with him. Hop ran over to the others.

'This all comes of our last naughty trick at the King's Palace,' he sobbed. 'If only we could go back to Brownie Town, I'd never be bad again!'

After that the brownies knew it was no good trying to get the stick away from the wizard. They were much too afraid of it.

'We must think of something else,' sighed Skip.

Each night the brownies whispered together, but they couldn't think of any plans at all. Then one day the wizard had a visitor.

He was a red goblin, and the ugliest little fellow you could think of. He didn't come in by the vanished door, nor by the window, so the brownies thought he must have jumped down the chimney.

'Good morning,' he said to the wizard. 'Have you those spells you were going to give me?'

'They are not ready yet,' answered the wizard, so humbly and politely that the brownies pricked up their ears.

'Oh, ho,' they thought, 'this red goblin must be someone more powerful than the wizard, for the wizard seems quite frightened of him!'

'Not ready!' growled the goblin. 'Well, see that they are ready by tomorrow, or I'll spirit you away to the highest mountain in the world.'

The wizard shivered and shook, and told the goblin he would be sure to have the spells ready by the next day.

'Mind you do,' said the goblin, and jumped straight up the chimney.

The brownies stared open-mouthed. Then Hop had a wonderful idea. He turned to the wizard.

'That goblin is much more clever than you, isn't he?' he said.

'Pooh!' growled the wizard, angrily. 'I can do things he can't do.'

'Can you really?' asked Hop, opening his eyes very wide. 'What can you do?'

'Well, I can make myself as big as a giant!' said the wizard.

'That's a wonderful thing,' said Hop. 'Let's see you do it!'

'Yes, let's,' said Skip and Jump, seeing that Hop was following out an idea he had suddenly thought of.

The wizard muttered a few words, and rubbed his forehead with some ointment out of a purple box. All at once he began to grow enormously big. Bump! His head touched the ceiling, so the wizard sat down on the floor. Still he went on growing, until once again his head touched the ceiling, and he filled the cottage from wall to wall. The three brownies had to jump on the window-sill to get out of his way.

'Wonderful! Wonderful!' cried Hop, clapping his hands. 'You're a giant now!'

The wizard looked pleased. He muttered something else and quickly grew smaller, till he reached his own size again.

'He, he!' he said. 'That will teach you to say that the goblin is more clever than me!'

'Oh, but perhaps the goblin can make himself *smaller* than you can!' said Hop.

The wizard snorted crossly.

'That he can't!' he said. 'Why, I can make myself small enough to sit in that pudding-basin!'

'Surely not!' said Hop, Skip and Jump together.

'I'll just show you!' said the wizard. He rubbed some ointment on his forehead out of a yellow box. At once he began to shrink!

Smaller and smaller he grew until he was the size of a doll.

'Put me on the table!' he squeaked to the brownies. Skip put him there. He jumped into the pudding-basin and sat down.

'Wonderful! Wonderful!' cried Hop. 'You can't grow any smaller, of course.

'That I can!' squeaked the wizard.

'Small enough to sit in a tea-cup?' asked Hop.

The wizard rubbed some more ointment on his forehead. He grew smaller still, and jumped into a tea-cup.

'Simply marvellous!' said Hope, Skip, and Jump.

'I can grow smaller still,' squeaked the wizard.

'What, small enough to creep into this tiny bottle?' asked Hop, pretending to be greatly surprised, and holding out a very small bottle.

The wizard laughed, and at once became very tiny indeed – so tiny that he was able to creep through the neck of the little bottle and sit in it easily.

Then, quick as a flash, Hop picked up the cork and corked up the bottle!

'Ha!' he cried, in the greatest excitement. 'Now I've got you! Now you can't get out! Now you can't get out!'

The wizard shouted and yelled in his bottle, and struggled and kicked against the cork, but it wasn't a bit of good, not a bit.

'You're a wicked wizard,' said Skip, 'and now you've got your punishment!'

'Where's the wizard's stick?' asked Jump, looking round. 'Oh, there it is, leaning by his chair. Perhaps the wizard is powerless now and his stick will be harmless to us!'

He picked it up. It did nothing at all, but behaved just like an ordinary stick.

'Now to get out of here!' said Jump.

He swung the green stick three times into the air, and then let it fall on the ground.

At once the blue door appeared in one of the walls.

'Hurray!' cried Skip, and flung it open. 'Now we're free again!'

But, dear me! What a surprise they got when they ran out of the cottage — for, instead of being among the trees in the wood, it now stood on a sandy beach, and in front of the three brownies stretched a calm blue sea!

'Good gracious!' cried the brownies. 'What an extraordinary thing! The cottage must have been travelling for days!'

They looked out over the blue sea. Not a sail was to be seen.

'Well, I don't want to go exploring along this part of the country any more,' said Jump, 'in case we meet any more unpleasant wizards. I wish we could sail away on the sea!'

'I know,' cried Hop, 'let's get the table out of the cottage, and turn it upside down!'

'And use the table-cloth for a sail!' shouted Skip. 'And the magic stick for a mast!'

So into the cottage they went again, and dragged out the big table. They turned it upside down on the water and it floated beautifully. Then they set up the mast and fastened the table-cloth for a sail.

'Bring some of that purple and yellow ointment!' called Hop to Skip. 'It might come in useful!'

So the two boxes of ointment were fetched, and Hop put them into his pocket. Then, picking up the bottle with the angry little wizard inside, he pushed off their table-boat, jumped on it, and there were the brownies safe and sound on the calm, blue sea.

A tiny little breeze took them along, and they watched the wizard's cottage grow smaller and smaller in the distance.

'We'll keep the wizard with us,' said Hop. 'He might come in useful somehow, and so long as he's corked in the bottle, he's quite harmless.'

So he slipped the little bottle into his pocket along with the boxes of ointment.

On and on they went, rocking softly over the sea, till one by one they grew drowsy, and soon in the afternoon sun they fell asleep, whilst their strange little boat went sailing dreamily on.

Their Adventure in the Castle of the Red Goblin

As the sun was setting, the three brownies awoke and rubbed their eyes.

The sea was still very calm. Hop looked all round. Then he pointed excitedly to the left.

'Look!' he cried. 'Land!'

Skip and Jump looked.

'An island!' said Skip. 'I wonder who lives there.'

'That's a very grand castle on the top of that hill,' said Jump. 'Someone grand must live there, I think.'

'Well, it isn't a very big island,' said Hop. 'What about landing, and seeing if we can find anyone and get something to eat?'

Just as he said that, the table-boat changed its course and floated with the tide towards the island.

'Good!' said Skip, 'The boat thinks it would like to visit there!' And he patted the table kindly.

As they floated nearer they saw that there were trees near the edge of the sea, and directly behind them rose the steep hill on the top of which was set the castle. It was built of red stone, and gleamed oddly in the setting sun.

'I don't much like the look of it,' said Hop suddenly. 'Goodness knows who lives there! Don't let's go!'

But Jump was curious to see what was on the lonely little island.

'Oh, let's go!' he begged. 'I tell you what we'll do – we'll just land for a few minutes, and have a look round. Then if we see anything we don't like, we'll jump on to our table-boat again, and sail off!'

'All right,' said Hop, 'only don't blame *me* if anything happens.'

The boat reached the shingle and grated against the stones. Off jumped the three brownies, pulled their boat higher up the beach and looked round.

No one was there at all. The trees grew right down to the beach, and whispered and sighed, as if they could tell many secrets, if only they knew the brownie language.

The brownies went into the wood. It was gloomy there. No birds sang, and no little animals frisked and rustled about. Hop, Skip and Jump thought it was a horrid place.

Then suddenly they heard the sound of crying.

'Whoever's that?' said Hop, peering between the whispering trees.

'Look! It's a little girl!' said Jump, in the greatest astonishment. 'Whatever is she doing here?'

'She's lame,' said Skip. 'She can't walk properly.'

'Let's go and comfort her,' said Hop, who couldn't bear to see anyone cry.

So, very quietly, they walked through the trees towards the little girl. She had sea-blue eyes, golden hair that floated around her, and a dress made of tight-fitting scales, just like a fish's coat. Her feet were big and ugly.

'What's the matter, little girl?' asked Hop in his kindest voice.

The little girl jumped. She looked up at him in fright, and then stared at him and the other brownies in astonishment.

'Oh,' she said, 'brownies, however did *you* come here, to this dreadful island?'

'Dreadful island?' said Skip, feeling rather uncomfortable. 'Why is it dreadful?'

'Oh, don't you know who it belongs to?' asked the little girl. 'It belongs to that horrid red goblin, and he's so powerful he can work nearly all the magic spells there are.'

'Oh my!' said the three brownies, feeling very upset indeed. 'The red goblin! Oh my!'

'It was he who came and frightened the wizard so much!' said Hop. 'Fancy having the bad luck to float to his island! We'd better sail away quickly!'

Then he turned to the little girl.

'But how is it *you're* here?' he asked. 'And what were you crying for?'

'Well, I don't belong here,' she said sadly. 'I'm a little mermaid really, and I used to have a tail. Then one day the red goblin caught me and changed my tail into these horrid feet, because he knew I wouldn't be able to swim away then. And I've been here a whole year, keeping his red castle clean for him. Oh dear, oh dear!'

She began to cry again. Hop couldn't bear it. He put his arm round her.

'Never mind!' he said. 'I'll tell you something lovely. We've got a boat on the beach near here, and we'll take you away from this horrid island this very night!'

'Oh! oh! oh! how lovely!' cried the little mermaid, and clapped her hands so loudly that the brownies were afraid someone would hear.

'Come along!' said Skip, nervously. 'The sun's gone down, but the moon's coming up and there's quite enough light to set off on our voyage again. *Do* come on!'

'Yes, quick!' said Jump. And the three brownies and mermaid made their way through the trees to the shore. They looked along the beach for their boat – but, oh dear me – where *was* their boat?

It was gone. Quite gone.

'Buttons and buttercups! Where's the boat gone?' whispered Hop, feeling his heart beat very fast.

'Look!' said Skip in dismay. 'The tide's taken it out to sea again! There it is, ever so far out!'

Sure enough it was. The three brownies stared at the table bobbing far away in the moonlight.

'We can swim out to it!' said Jump.

'But the mermaid can't swim now she hasn't got a tail,' said Hop, 'and we can't leave her alone here.'

'No, we can't!' said Skip and Jump decidedly.

'But whatever *shall* we do!' wondered Hop.

'Come back to my cottage for the night,' said the mermaid. 'And in the morning perhaps we shall think of something.'

She led them through the trees to a little tumble-down hut and gave them dry bracken to lie on for a bed. Then she made some bread-and-milk, and they all ate it and tried to think of a plan.

But soon they felt so sleepy that their eyes closed, and they slept on their bracken beds until morning.

No one had thought of a plan. Hop frowned and wondered what to do. At last he made up his mind.

'There's nothing for it but boldness,' he said. 'We must just march up to the castle, and demand a boat to take us away.'

'That would never do,' said the mermaid. 'The red goblin would laugh at you and turn you into beetles or something. He's only polite to wizards, and that's because he thinks they know a magic spell that he doesn't know!'

'Very well then,' said Hop, an idea coming into his head. 'If he's only polite to wizards, we'll pretend to be wizards, and trust to luck to get away *somehow*. Don't talk to me for a minute, and I'll think of a plan.'

Everybody was very quiet whilst Hop thought hard.

'Listen,' he said. 'We'll all go up to the castle with the mermaid. She must hide you two somewhere in the castle. I'll meet the red goblin alone, and if he's nasty, I'll clap my hands three times, and you must come running in. He'll think then I've called you by magic, for he won't know where you've come from – and perhaps he'll be polite then and hope to get some new spells from me!'

So it was arranged. The mermaid led them up to the back door of the castle by a secret way through the woods. Then she went to see what the red goblin was doing.

'It's all right,' she whispered, when she came back. 'He's having a bath. I'll take Skip and Jump into the big hall, and hide them each in a chest there. The goblin *will* be surprised when they jump out! You go round to the castle door and ring the big bell in ten minutes' time, Hop!'

Skip and Jump crept off with the mermaid, feeling very nervous indeed. She put them safely into two chests and closed the lids.

Then Hop went boldly round to the castle door. He saw a great bell-rope hanging by the side. He took hold of it and pulled it sharply three times.

Jangle-jangle-jangle, it went. Hop waited.

'Who's there?' came the angry voice of the red goblin, and the great castle door slid open, to show the goblin standing in the doorway.

'A wizard come to see you!' said Hop, bowing low.

'Come in,' growled the goblin, and led the way into the great hall.

'Who are you?' he asked.

'Ah, that is a secret,' answered Hop.

'Oh!' said the goblin, wondering who he could be. 'How did you get here?'

'That is also a secret!' answered Hop. 'I do not give my magic spells away for nothing!'

'Ho,' said the goblin again, thinking this must

be a very clever wizard. 'Will you stay here for a day or two, and perhaps we can exchange spells?'

'Certainly!' answered Hop. 'Allow me to call my servants to wait on me!'

He clapped his hands three times and, to the goblin's tremendous astonishment, up popped the lids of two chests nearby, and out jumped two brownies. They ran up to Hop and bowed.

'Master, we come from the ends of the earth to greet you,' they said.

'How did they come into those chests then?' demanded the astonished goblin.

'That is a secret,' smiled Hop.

The goblin thought there were a great deal too many secrets about this peculiar wizard. He was quite determined to find them all out.

'Come to breakfast,' he said, and invited Hop to a big table on which were set all kinds of food. Hop sat down. He was very hungry, and he knew Skip and Jump were too. How could he manage to get them food?

'Servants, get under the table,' he said suddenly. 'Take off my shoes and tickle my feet whilst I eat.'

The goblin stared in surprise.

'I enjoy my food better when my feet are tickled,' explained Hop.

The goblin said nothing, but he thought this

wizard was one of the most peculiar he had ever met. He was astonished, too, at the way he ate. No sooner was his plate full than it was empty! He didn't know that half of it was dropped down to Skip and Jump under the table.

'Dear me!' he said at last, when Hop had taken three apples and apparently eaten them in one minute. 'Tickling your feet seems to give you a great appetite, Sir Wizard.'

'You should try it too,' answered Hop. 'Take off his boots, servants, and tickle him!'

In a second Skip and Jump slipped off the goblin's shoes and began tickling his feet. The goblin gave one yell, and fell off his chair.

'Don't, I can't bear it!' he shouted, rolling about on the floor. Skip and Jump giggled, and tickled him all the more.

Suddenly, to Hop's horror, the red goblin gave a yell of rage and shouted some magic words. Immediately Skip and Jump disappeared, and in their places were two brown mice!

'How dare you let your servants do that!' raged the goblin. 'See how I have punished them!'

Hop went pale with fear. Poor Skip and Jump changed into mice! Then he faced the goblin.

'Change my servants back at once,' he commanded in his biggest voice.

The goblin laughed.

'Change them back yourself, if you're such a wonderful wizard,' he grinned.

Hop looked round wildly for something to help him. Then he quickly put his hand into his pocket – yes, the little bottle with the wizard in it was still there.

'Do you know what I do to people who annoy *me*?' he asked the goblin. 'I don't change them into mice – that's a *very* ordinary trick – I put them into bottles like this!'

And he drew out the bottle, and showed it to the goblin. The goblin looked at it and saw the wizard sitting inside.

'Ow!' he cried. 'It's the wizard I visited yesterday! Good gracious! Look at him! As small as a beetle, sitting in one of his own bottles. Oh, what a wonderful wizard *you* must be to have done that to him!'

'Yes, I *am*,' said Hop, 'and I'll put *you* into a smaller bottle if you don't do what I say! Change my servants back to their own form!'

The goblin muttered some magic words, and the two mice disappeared. In their place stood Skip and Jump again, looking as frightened as could be!

'Thank you,' said Hop. 'I'm glad I didn't have

to bottle you up. You'd have made the fifty-fifth bottled person in my cupboard at home, if I had!'

The goblin trembled.

'Of course I don't wonder that you bottled up *that* wizard,' he said. 'He's a nasty little person! Not a bit truthful and *very* stupid!'

The wizard inside the bottle heard what he said, and was as angry as anything. He jumped about in his bottle, and kicked and struggled, and shook his tiny fist at the goblin.

'Ha, ha!' said the goblin 'You can't get at me, you tiny little thing! I always thought you were silly and stupid, but I really didn't think you were stupid enough to get put into a *bottle*!'

The tiny wizard grew so angry that Hop began to be afraid he would break the bottle, so he hastily slipped him into his pocket again.

'Now,' said the goblin, 'let me show you round my castle. I collect all sorts of magic things, and they may interest you.'

Hop thought they certainly would, and he went with the goblin.

He was shown all kinds of things.

'This,' said the goblin, 'is a witch's cauldron. I can make powerful magic in it. And this is a fairy's wand. I stole it from a sleeping fairy one day.'

Hop thought he was an even nastier goblin than

he had thought before. But he said nothing. He just looked, and wondered if he would be shown anything that might help them to escape.

The goblin showed him his magic books, which read themselves out loud – magic seeds that grew shoots, leaves, flowers and fruit, whilst you watched – magic table-cloths that spread themselves with food. Hop began to feel quite dizzy with all the wonders shown him.

Then he saw something that made his heart beat fast.

'This,' said the goblin proudly, 'is a witch's broomstick!'

'Will it fly?' asked Hop.

'Oh yes,' said the goblin. 'But it only flies when you say the magic words – and that's a secret – ho, ho!'

'Pooh!' said Hop. 'You only say it's a secret because you can't make it fly, or you don't want me to know you can't! *You* don't know the magic rhyme!'

'I do, then!' cried the goblin, in a temper. 'Listen:

Onaby O
Away we go,
Onaby Eye
Up in the sky!'

Immediately the broom rose in the air, and flew towards the window. The goblin clapped his hands. It flew back again, and stood still in its place.

'There you are,' said the goblin. 'Did I know the magic rhyme or didn't I?'

'You did!' said Hop, grinning to himself to think that he and Skip and Jump now knew it too. 'I beg your pardon. You are more clever than I thought.'

That pleased the goblin, and he became quite friendly. After dinner he went away by himself to practise magic, and Hop, Skip, Jump and the mermaid went to the kitchen to make their plans.

'We'll creep tonight into the room where the broomstick is,' planned Hop, 'and jump on it. We'll say the magic rhyme, and off we'll go.'

They wandered about the castle till night fell. Then, when the goblin had shown them their room and bade them goodnight, they crept to the kitchen again to fetch the mermaid. Then Hop went to see if the way was clear.

He tiptoed into the room where the broom was kept – but, oh my! There was a light there, and the red goblin was sitting at the table, reading a magic book.

'He may be there all night,' sighed the mermaid.

401

'Well, we *must* go tonight,' decided Hop, 'because any minute tomorrow I might give myself away; I nearly did lots of times today.'

Just at that moment he felt the little bottle in his pocket jerking about. He took it out, and saw the tiny wizard knocking on the glass.

'Let me out!' he squeaked in a voice like a mouse. 'Let me out! Let me get at that red goblin.'

'Well now, that's an idea!' said Hop, staring at him.

He ran up into the room above the one in which the red goblin sat, and kicked and thumped on the floor, and made a terrible noise. Then he loosened the cork in the wizard's bottle, and set the bottle down in the middle of the floor. Then he ran and hid behind a curtain.

After a bit up came the red goblin, wondering whatever in the world all the bumping and thumping was. He was very much surprised to see the bottle on the floor. He went up and looked at it.

As soon as the wizard saw him, he began kicking and banging at the loosened cork. Then Pop! out it flew, and out came the wizard like a beetle on the floor. Immediately he grew bigger and bigger, until he reached his usual size.

And then, oh my! He went for the red goblin

and gave him a big push. The goblin went over like a skittle.

Hop didn't wait to see any more. He ran downstairs and called the others. Together they went into the broomstick room.

'Now quickly!' said Hop. 'Jump on whilst those two up there are fighting. They've forgotten all about us!'

The mermaid jumped on. Skip jumped on, and so did Hop – but oh dear, there wasn't any room for Jump! The broomstick only held three!

'It'll break if we have four!' groaned Hop. 'Now what are we to do?'

'Leave me behind, of course!' said the mermaid, and jumped off again.

'Certainly *not*!' said all the brownies at once, and pulled her on again.

Then Jump made a brave speech.

'I'm not coming,' he said. 'It was my fault that we came to this island. I wanted to see what was on it. So I'm going to be the one to stay behind.

Well, there was no time to be lost in arguing, so poor Jump *was* left behind.

'Onaby O,
Away we'll go,
Onaby Eye
Up in the sky!'

said Hop. And off went the broomstick out of the window, while Jump stood on the ground, and watched them fly away from him, up into the moonlit sky.

Their Adventure in the Land of Giants

The broomstick went sailing away in the air, and Hop, Skip and the mermaid clung to it tightly. They were all very sad, thinking of poor Jump left behind. They didn't know *what* might happen to him.

'Poor Jump,' said the mermaid.

'Poor, poor Jump,' said Skip.

'Poor, poor, poor –,' began Hop – then he stopped.

'I say!' he said hopefully.

'What?' asked the other two.

'Supposing I rub some of the ointment that makes people bigger on to the broomstick! It might make it grow bigger!'

'Then we could go back and fetch Jump!' cried the mermaid.

So Hop got out the yellow ointment and rubbed some of it on to the end of the broomstick.

It immediately grew much smaller, and Hop nearly fell off! He just managed to hang on round Skip's waist.

'Oh, you silly!' cried Skip. 'That's the wrong ointment.'

Quickly, he took the purple ointment from Hop's pocket, though he nearly tumbled off in reaching it.

Immediately it grew enormously large.

'Gracious!' giggled Hop, who was now sitting down firmly again. 'There's room for twenty people at least!'

They turned the broomstick back to the island, and soon after arrived at the castle again. They landed at the front door.

There was a terrible noise going on, and dust flew in clouds out of the windows of one of the upstairs rooms.

'They're still trying to settle who's the strongest!' said Hop. 'I'll run and fetch Jump!'

He jumped off and ran indoors. There he found Jump, looking very scared indeed. How astonished and glad he was to see Hop!

'Come on, you brave little brownie!' called Hop. 'We've made the broomstick bigger, and there's room for you!'

Jump scurried out with Hop and mounted the broomstick with the others. Then once more the magic rhyme was said, and the broomstick rose into the air.

'Oh, I *am* glad to be with you!' said Jump, sighing gladly. 'The wizard and the red goblin were behaving in a terrible manner. They kept changing each other into different things, and chasing about all over the place!'

'Well, they're both about as strong as each other,' said Hop cheerfully, 'so they'll probably have a jolly time fighting each other for a good many days yet!'

The broomstick went sailing on and on over the sea in the bright moonlight, and soon left the island far behind.

Suddenly the mermaid gave a shriek of joy.

'There is my home!' she cried. 'There is my home!'

The brownies looked down, and saw two or three brown rocks sticking up out of the sea. On them lay mermaids and mermen.

'Quick! Turn the broom downwards!' cried the mermaid. Jump turned it, and soon they were gliding down to the rocks.

Splash! Splash! All the mermaids and mermen slid into the water and disappeared when they saw the broomstick gliding down to them.

Bump! It came to rest on one of the rocks.

'Come back! Come back!' called the mermaid. 'It's the little mermaid Golden-hair come back! I've been rescued!'

Up popped all the mermen and mermaids again, and as soon as they saw that it *really* was Golden-hair, *what a fuss* they made! The cried over her and laughed over her, and patted her and kissed her.

Then one of the mermen brought a shell full of sea-water, and said a spell over it. Golden-hair put her goblin feet into it, and to the brownies' astonishment, they changed into a beautiful glittering tail.

Then, flick! Golden-hair slipped into the water and swam about joyfully with the others.

'Stay with us!' she cried. 'We will give you a lovely time!'

'No, thank you,' answered Hop. 'We'd very much like to, but we are in search of a stolen Princess, so we must go.'

The brownies hopped on to the broomstick again, waved goodbye to the merfolk, sang the magic rhyme, and were soon off again.

'I'm glad we were able to rescue Golden-hair,' said Jump. 'I do wonder where we'll go to next!'

'We mustn't any of us go to sleep,' said Hop, 'else we'll fall off the broomstick into the sea! Hold on tight till the morning!'

All night long the broom sailed over the sea. Soon the moon went down, and the brownies grew very sleepy indeed.

As the sun rose, they saw that they had left the sea behind at last, and were flying over a wooded country.

'Let's go down here,' said Hop, yawning. 'I'm longing to go to sleep.'

So they turned the broom downwards, and were soon among the trees.

'What enormous trees!' exclaimed Skip in astonishment. 'I've never seen such big ones before.'

They *were* enormous. When the brownies had landed safely on the ground they craned their necks backwards to try to see the tops of the trees – but they couldn't.

'And just look at the grass!' cried Hop. 'It's as tall as a house! And goodness me, is this a buttercup? Why, I could easily go to sleep in one of the buds!'

'I could go to sleep *anywhere*!' yawned Jump, lying down on a daisy-leaf that was as big as a bed. 'Goodnight, everybody!'

'Well, we'll explore the country when we wake,' said Hop, and he chose a leaf too. Skip climbed into a bud and very soon all the brownies were fast asleep.

Suddenly they were awakened by an enormous noise.

Crash, crash, crash, crash!

Hop woke up with a jump, and looked round him. To his amazement, he saw walking by him the biggest pair of boots he had ever seen. They seemed as large as two small trees. Hop looked above them.

'Gracious!' he said. 'There's legs in the boots!'

The brownies looked above the legs, and then, with a shout of fear, saw that the legs belonged to a body, and that the body had an enormous head with eyes like little lakes.

'Ow!' cried Hop. 'It's a giant! We've come to Giantland!'

'Quick!' said Skip. 'Hide before he sees us!'

But it was too late. The giant had seen them, and was staring at them in just as much astonishment as they had stared at him. Before they could run and hide, a great hand had come down and picked them all up. Then they were swished up into the air near the giant's head, whilst he had a good look at them.

'Brownies!' said the giant, in a voice very like thunder. 'Brownies! Oh, the tiny little things!'

'Let us go!' yelled Hop in his loudest voice.

'Oh, he squeaks like a mouse!' said the giant, with a smile that showed enormous white teeth. 'Squeak again, little man!'

'I'm not squeaking!' shouted Hop, angrily. 'I'm shouting at you. Put me down, you're squashing me to bits.'

'Squeak away, squeak away,' said the giant. 'I'll take you home and show you to my wife. What a find!'

He stuffed the three brownies into his coat pocket and strode off.

'Oh, it's like riding inside a camel's hump!' said Hop, as the giant's coat flapped in the wind, and swayed to and fro as he walked.

'What a terrible fix we're in *now*!' groaned Skip. 'How in the world can we get away from here?'

The brownies clung together as frightened as could be. At last the giant stopped, put his hand in his pocket, and pulled out the three brownies.

'Look, wife!' he said in his booming voice. 'What do you think of *these* little chaps?'

'Oh!' thundered his wife in delight. 'Are they real?'

'Real enough!' said the giant, setting them down on a table as big as a field. 'Now then, squeak!' he said, and gave Hop such a poke with his finger that he fell over and nearly tumbled off the table.

The giant's wife was delighted with them.

'We'll give a tea-party this afternoon, and show

them to all our friends,' she said.

'No, no, let us go back and find our broomstick!' begged Skip.

'Listen to him squeaking!' cried the giant in delight, and gave him a poke that sent him head over heels.

The giant's wife carefully put them into a box with some holes punched in to let the air through. She also put in a thimbleful of water and some crumbs of bread. The thimble was as big as a barrel and the crumbs as big as loaves, so that the brownies had more than enough to eat and drink.

They were very upset indeed.

'We seem to do nothing but get caught by someone or other,' groaned Hop. 'If only we could go back to Fairyland!'

'Well, goodness knows what's going to happen to us *this* time!' said Skip, gloomily. 'We're so small, luckily, compared with the giants, that they probably won't eat us. We shouldn't make more than a mouthful!'

'Ugh! Don't be horrid!' said Jump, who didn't like the conversation at all. 'Let's talk of something cheerful.'

All the day the giant's wife kept taking off the lid, and peeping in at the brownies to see if they were all right. She put in three lumps of sugar for them to sit down on, and was very much amused to see them perched up on them. They heard her big voice rumbling all day long. The clatter that her pots and pans made sounded like crashes of thunder.

When the afternoon came, the giant's wife took off the lid of the box and lifted the brownies out on to the table. She put some fresh water in the thimble, and gave them a rag as big as a table-cloth for a towel, and told them to wash themselves and make themselves smart.

'My guests will soon be here,' she boomed, 'and I want you to be a surprise for them.'

When the brownies had washed themselves and smoothed back their hair the giant's wife picked them all up and carried them into another room, where a table was laid for tea. In the middle was a cake, and on top, made of pink icing, were three little chairs.

'Buttons and buttercups!' groaned Hop. 'Look what she's done! We've got to sit on the cake!'

Sure enough they had. The giantess popped each one, bump! on to a chair.

'Now you sit there and don't move an eyelash,' she said. 'Everyone will think you're dolls. When I say, "Now I'll cut the cake," you're to jump out of your chairs and cheer!'

The brownies felt very much annoyed. They didn't like the idea of pretending to be dolls at all, just to amuse a lot of giants.

Skip jumped off his chair crossly.

'No!' he shouted loudly. 'I won't!'

The giantess picked him up and gave him such a squeeze that he felt he was going to choke.

'Now you do as you're told,' she scolded, in her enormous voice, 'or I'll give you to the chickens to peck!'

Skip sat down very quickly on his chair. He didn't like the idea of being given to the chickens at all. Nor did the others. They all sat as still as could be, in case the giantess said anything more.

All around them gleamed great knives and forks and spoons, and huge glasses that seemed as big as houses. From the kitchen came a very nice smell.

'That makes me feel hungry,' said Hop, sighing.

'What about chipping a bit off the cake?' asked Skip. 'The giantess has gone out of the room for a minute!'

'Bite the knobs off the backs of your chairs,' said Jump. 'They're delicious.'

The three brownies bit them off, and very delicious they were. They tasted of honey and sugar, and the brownies were just going to nibble pieces off the back of their chairs, too, when a most enormous noise made them fall off their seats in fright.

It was the guests knocking at the front door! RAT-TAT-TAT!

The brownies began to tremble. It was rather terrifying to have to face a lot of giants at once.

'They're so careless in picking us up and putting us down,' groaned Hop.

'And I *hate* being held tight,' said Skip.

'Sh!' said Jump. 'Here they come.'

With an enormous noise of tramping, talking and laughing, in walked six of the largest giants you could imagine. They were followed by the giantess and her husband, both of whom were smaller than their guests.

'HA!' said a giant, seating himself at the table. 'I'M HUNGRY!'

'HO!' said another. 'I'M THIRSTY.'

The giantess made haste to bring in the teapot, and soon every giant was stuffing himself with sandwiches as big as mattresses. The noise they made too! It sounded like twenty thousand pigs feeding at once.

Suddenly one of them noticed the cake.

'HO!' he said. 'WHAT A FINE CAKE!'

All the giants looked at it, and thought it was very fine indeed.

415

'I've never seen such nice figures before as those you've got sitting on your cake,' said a giant.

'VERY NICE INDEED,' bellowed a giant with an extra loud voice.

All this time the brownies hadn't dared to move in case the giantess should keep her word, and throw them to the chickens. They sat like dummies, staring straight in front of them.

'They look quite real,' said a giant, and bent closer to look at them. Then he took his fork and was just going to poke Hop with it when that terrified brownie leapt up into the air in fright, and gave an anguished yell.

The giant was so astonished that he dropped his fork with a clatter, and sat open-mouthed. All the giants stared at the brownies in the greatest amazement.

The giantess thought it was time to surprise her guests a little more.

'Now I'll cut the cake,' she said.

At once Hop, Skip, and Jump leapt out of their chairs and cheered as they had been told to do.

The giants jumped in astonishment.

'They squeak!' said one.

'They move!' said another.

'They must be alive,' said a third.

'They *are*,' said the giantess proudly. 'They're

brownies. What do you think of *that* for a surprise?'

She began cutting the cake, and the brownies jumped down on to the table. As soon as the giants heard they were brownies they began talking excitedly all at once, and each giant tried to catch a brownie, so as to have a good look at him.

The brownies dodged their great fingers as best they could. They hid behind glasses and under the edges of the plates, and Hop even jumped into the salt-cellar, and covered himself with salt – but it was no good. They were caught and held, and passed from one giant to another.

They hated it, for the giants held them so tightly, and seemed to enjoy giving them a poke now and again, just to see them roll head over heels.

'I shall break my neck soon,' panted Hop. 'That's twice I've been poked over.'

'Let's pretend we're hurt,' said Skip, 'perhaps they'll stop then.'

So Hop lay down on the table and groaned, Skip walked about with a limp and Jump held his head as if it hurt him.

The giantess, who had quite a kind heart, was most upset.

'You've hurt the poor little mites,' she cried. 'Look at them! Leave them alone now, do, or you'll kill them, and I want to keep them for pets, and give them to my children when they come back from their aunt's.'

'Oh!' groaned Hop. 'Did you hear what she said? Goodness knows what giant children would do with us! What a terrible fix we are in!'

The giantess brought their thimble filled with lemonade, and put some cake crumbs on a cotton-reel.

'Here you are,' she said, giving them lumps of sugar to sit on. 'Sit down at this cotton-reel table, and have your tea, while we watch you.'

The brownies sat down and took the cake crumbs. They were as large as cakes and very nice. When they wanted a drink they went to the thimble and sipped the lemonade.

The giants soon grew tired of watching them, and fell silent. The giantess rose and began clearing away the dishes into the kitchen. Then, one by one, the giants fell asleep.

Hop looked round at them.

SNORE, SNORE, SNORE, went the giants, sleepy after their big meal. They breathed so heavily that they nearly blew the brownies off the table.

'I say,' shouted Hop, trying to make himself heard over the snoring, 'let's escape!'

'How?' shouted Skip. 'If one of the giants

wakes whilst we are slipping away he'll wake the others, and they'll all come thundering after us and kill us.'

'Think of an idea, Hop,' shouted Jump.

Hop thought – then he grinned.

'What about the ointment?' he shouted back. 'Shall we use that on the giants whilst they're asleep?'

'Yes, yes!' shrieked Skip and Jump, nearly deafened by the snores of the giants. 'Get it out quickly, Hop.'

Hop got out the boxes of ointment and opened them.

'There isn't very much left of either of them,' he shouted. 'We'll use both and see what happens. Here, Skip, take the purple ointment, and I'll take the yellow. Jump, you keep a watch for the giantess.'

Hop and Skip ran across the table, and each climbed up a giant's arm on to his shoulder. They couldn't reach his forehead, so they rubbed the ointment on to his chin, and hoped it would act just as well.

Then down they clambered, and up on to two more giants' shoulders. Hop was nearly blown away by one tremendous giant, who puffed him nearly off his arm.

At last all the sleeping giants had the magic ointment rubbed on to their chins.

'Now listen!' shouted Hop, whose voice was getting quite hoarse. 'I'm going to say the magic words. The giants will grow smaller and bigger, and they'll wake up in a terrible fright. We've got to escape whilst they're in a muddle. Climb off the table first.'

The brownies clambered down the table-cloth, slid down the table-legs, and landed bump on to the floor. They ran to the door.

Then Hop called out the magic words.

At once three of the giants grew so much smaller that they were only about three times as big as the brownies. The other four grew so much bigger that their heads bumped against the ceiling, their chairs broke with their weight, and they fell on to the floor with yells of fright.

'OH! OH! OH!' they shouted in astonishment. The giantess came running in to see what was the matter. She couldn't believe her eyes.

'What's happened?' she cried. 'Oh, what's happened? Why have some of you grown small and some of you big? Oh dear, dear, dear!'

'Come on,' said Hop, and he and the other brownies ran out of the door.

The giantess saw them.

'Oh, you've worked a spell on them!' she cried angrily. 'I'll catch you, you wicked little things.'

Hop, Skip, and Jump raced across the kitchen floor as hard as they could, and out into the garden. They hid under a large leaf and watched the huge feet of the giantess go clomping by in search of them.

'Good thing she didn't tread on us,' said Hop. Then he saw something that made him shiver in fright.

'Look!' he said. 'There's a giant hen – and there's another one – they're scratching in the ground. Oh my, we've run into the chicken yard!'

The brownies trembled in fear. The hens came nearer and nearer, clucking and squawking as they scratched for grain.

Suddenly one of them saw Hop under the big leaf. She pecked at him. He jumped away only just in time.

'Run!' he cried. 'It's the only chance we have!'

They ran from beneath the leaf and tore across the yard.

'Squawk – squawk!' cried all the hens, and tore after them.

'They'll catch us!' panted Jump.

Suddenly, Hop saw a large hole in front of him. Quick as lightning he jumped into it and pulled the others after him.

'It's a worm-home!' he gasped. 'Come on, it's our only chance of escaping those horrid birds.'

The hens were pecking and scraping around the hole, their beaks sounding like picks and hammers.

But once more the brownies were safe, for the worm-hole was like a narrow tunnel, and they could pass along it easily, one after another.

'I hope we don't meet a worm,' said Skip. 'It would be rather awkward, wouldn't it?'

'I'd much rather meet a worm than a crowd of huge giants, or a pack of greedy birds,' said Hop cheerfully. 'Come on! Goodness knows where this tunnel leads to, but anyway, it must lead *somewhere*!'

Their Adventure in the Land of Clever People

The three brownies went on through the dark tunnel, hoping they would soon find it came to an end. It felt rather sticky, and Hop said it must be because a worm had lately passed along it.

Just as he said that the brownies heard a peculiar noise. 'Oh my! I do believe it's a worm coming!' Hop groaned.

It was a worm, a simply enormous one, for its body filled up the whole tunnel.

'Ho,' shouted Hop in a panic, 'don't come any farther, Mr Worm; you'll squash us to bits!'

The worm stopped wriggling in surprise.

'What are you doing in my tunnel?' he asked.

'Nothing much,' said Skip. 'Just escaping from a lot of greedy birds!'

'Oh!' said the worm with a shudder. 'I know all about birds. I've had my tail pecked off twice by the greedy things.'

'Do you know where this tunnel leads to?' asked Jump.

'It leads to all sorts of places,' said the worm.

'You'll find cross-roads a little farther on, and a sign-post.'

'Oh, thanks,' said Jump, 'Then I think we'll be getting on.'

'So will I,' said the worm, and began to wriggle towards the brownies.

'Stop!' they shouted. 'There isn't room for you to go past us!'

'But I *must*,' said the worm. 'I've an appointment with my tailor at six o'clock. He's making me a few more rings for my body.'

'Oh, *do* go backwards till you get to the cross-roads,' begged Hop.

'I'm going backwards *now*,' said the worm. 'At least I think I am. It's so muddling being able to use both your ends, you know. I never know which way I'm *really* going.'

'It must be *very* muddling,' said Skip. 'But please don't push past us; you're rather sticky, you know, and you'll spoil our suits, and *we* haven't got a tailor like you!'

'Dear, dear, you ought to have,' said the worm. 'I'll tell you what I'll do. I'll bore you a little tunnel to stand in whilst I go past, then I shan't spoil your suits.'

The worm began to make them a little passage leading out of the main tunnel.

'There you are,' he said. 'Get in there, and you'll be quite safe.'

The brownies hopped in. Then, rustle-squelch-rustle! The worm pulled his long body past them, called goodbye, and left them.

'Well, thank goodness, we've got over *that* difficulty,' said Hop. 'Now let's get to the cross-roads before we meet any other worms.'

On they went again, meeting no one but a centipede, who fled past in such a hurry on his many legs that the brownies didn't know *what* he was.

'Must be the fast train to Wormland, I should think!' said Hop, picking himself up, for the centipede had rushed straight between his legs.

Soon the brownies saw a light in the distance. They hurried towards it, and found that they stood at the cross-roads. In the middle was a sign-post with a lamp on top.

'To Giantland,' Hop read. 'Ugh! That's the way we've just come. What's this other way? To the Land of Giggles! That sounds silly. To Cross-patch Country! *That* won't do for us. Now what's this last one?'

All the brownies peered at it.

'To the Land of Clever People,' they read.

'Clever People *might* be able to tell us the

way to Witchland,' said Hop.

'Yes, let's go,' said Jump.

'I hope they'll let us in,' said Skip doubtfully. 'I don't really feel very clever, you know.'

'You're not,' said Hop. '*I'm* the clever one.'

'Yes, you were clever enough to get us all sent out of Fairyland,' grumbled Skip.

'Don't let's quarrel,' said Hop. 'Come on, and see what this new land is like.'

Off they went again, and found that the tunnel they were now in sloped upwards, and was lit by many little green lamps.

'Green for safety, anyway,' said Jump, cheerfully.

The lamps suddenly turned red. The brownies jumped in fright.

'Red for danger!' said Skip in a shaky voice.

The lamps turned blue. Hop thought of an idea.

'I expect it's somebody in the Land of Clever People, showing us how clever they are,' he whispered. Then aloud he said in an admiring voice, 'H'm, blue for cleverness!'

All the lamps turned back to green.

'There you are!' whispered Hop. 'Green for safety again.'

They went on up the slope and came to a corner. Just round the bend was a turnstile, and at it was seated an ugly little man, with an enormous bald head. He wore spectacles, and was writing in a huge book. As the brownies drew near he looked at them over his spectacles. Then he spoke in a way that gave the brownies rather a surprise:

'Good morning. Do I understand,
You wish to enter in this Land?'

'He's talking in poetry!' said Jump. 'Isn't he clever! Are we supposed to answer in poetry too?'

'We can't,' said Skip. 'So that settles it.'

He turned to the turnstile man.

'Yes, we want to come in,' he said. 'You see we ...'

The bald-headed man interrupted him:

'Please talk in rhyme. Unless you do,
I simply cannot let you through.'

'Oh goodness gracious!' groaned the brownies.

'They must be *terribly* clever people,' said Hop. 'Let's see if we can make up an answer in rhyme.'

They thought for some time, and at last they found one they thought would do. Hop went up to the turnstile man and bowed.

'Will you kindly let us through,
There's lots of things we want to do,'

he said. At once the man waved his hand to tell
them to pass, and his turnstile clicked as they went
through. Before they left him he handed them a
book of rules.

'Keep every rule that's written here,
You'll find them printed nice and clear,'

he said in his singsong voice.

'Thank you very much indeed,
I like to have a book to read,'

answered Hop, as easily as anything.

'Hop!' cried Jump, when they had got out of
the turnstile man's hearing. 'Hop! That *was* clever
of you! How *did* you think of it?'

'It just came into my head,' said Hop, quite
as surprised as the others. 'I believe I'll be quite
good at it.'

'What does the book of rules say?' asked Jump.
Hop read it, and told the others.

'Nothing much,' he said. 'Always talk in
rhyme. Make up a new riddle every day. Answer

one. Not much, is it?'

'I don't know,' said Skip doubtfully. 'I think making up riddles is very hard.'

'What happens if we can't make up riddles or answer them?' asked Jump.

'I'll look and see,' said Hop, turning over the page. 'Oh, buttons and buttercups!'

'What, Hop?' asked Skip and Jump.

'Anyone who can't make up riddles or answer them is scolded for being stupid,' said Hop in dismay.

'Oh, I *do* wish we hadn't come here!' said Jump. 'This is *your* fault again, Hop. You're always leading us into trouble.'

'Let's go back to the turnstile man and ask him to let us out,' said Hop.

So they went back.

'Please let us out again, because
We find we cannot keep your laws,'

said Hop, after scratching his head and thinking hard for five minutes.

The bald-headed man shook his head.

'Find rule number thirty-two,
And that will tell you what to do,'

he told them.

Hop found it and read it.

'We can't get out of the Land of Clever People until we think of something that their Very Wise Man cannot do,' he told the others sadly. 'There isn't much hope for *us*, then.'

'Stay here all our lives, I suppose,' said Skip gloomily.

'And be scolded every day,' said Jump, still more gloomily.

The three brownies went sadly up the tunnel. They hadn't gone very far before they saw daylight, and to their joy they found that they were once more above ground. They ran out of the tunnel and danced about in the sunlight. Then they stopped and looked to see what sort of country they were in.

'My!' said Hop. 'It's rather peculiar, isn't it? It all looks so proper!'

It certainly *did* look proper. The houses were set down in perfectly straight lines. All the windows were the same size, and all the doors. All the knockers were the same, and they all shone brightly.

The people looked very proper too. They all wore spectacles, and had very large heads and all the men were bald. If everybody hadn't been rather short and tubby, they would have looked frightening, but as it was they looked rather funny.

Skip began to giggle.

'They don't look as if they ever smiled!' he chuckled.

A fat little policeman came up to them. He put his hand heavily on Skip's shoulder.

> 'You mustn't giggle here, you know,
>   Or else to prison you must go.
>   This is not the Land of Giggles ...'

He stopped and looked at the brownies. The brownies looked back. Evidently he expected them to finish the rhyme.

'Oh dear!' thought Hop. 'Whatever will make a rhyme for giggles? What an awful word!'

The policeman coughed and repeated his lines again. Then he took out his note-book.

Hop began to tremble.

'This is not the Land of Giggles,' said the policeman in an awful, this-is-the-last-time sort of voice.

'How your little finger wiggles!' said Hop suddenly.

The policeman looked at his little finger in surprise. It wasn't wiggling. Still Hop had made a rhyme, so he closed up his notebook and marched solemnly off.

'That was a narrow escape,' said Hop in a

whisper. 'It's a mean trick to leave someone to finish what you're saying, in rhyme. Now, remember, for goodness' sake, don't giggle. We don't want to be sent to prison, or to the Land of Giggles, do we?'

Night was falling. Lamps began to shine in the little streets.

'We'd better find a place to sleep,' said Skip, with a yawn. Another policeman suddenly appeared behind them. Hop saw him in time, and made a rhyme hastily, to fit his last sentence.

'Oh, look at that excited sheep!' he said, pointing behind him.

There was no sheep, of course, and by the time the policeman had discovered that, the brownies had fled down the street.

They came to the neatest little house imaginable. In the window was a card. On it was printed:

STEP INSIDE AND YOU WILL SEE
LODGINGS HERE FOR TWO OR THREE

'*Just* the thing,' said Hop. 'Let us ring,' he added hastily, as another policeman came round the corner and looked at them.

He rang. The door opened, and a kind-faced old woman looked out.

'Would you let us stay with you?' he asked,

hoping that the old woman would finish the rhyme.

'What can you pay me if you do?' she asked, at once.

'Would a silver coin be enough to pay?' said Hop.

'Oh, yes, it would. Please come this way,' said the old woman, and led them inside.

The house was very neat inside. The room the old woman took them to was strange-looking. It had knobs here and there on the wall, and Hop longed to pull them and see what happened.

'This is where you are to sleep,' said their guide, and waited for Hop to finish the rhyme.

'Always look before you leap,' said Hop solemnly. The woman stared at him and went out.

'This rhyming business is making me tired,' said Hop, when the door closed. 'I do hope we find some way of getting out of this land soon. What about pressing a few of these knobs? Look, this one's marked SOUP.'

He pressed it. A little door flew open in the wall, and there stood three mugs of steaming soup!

'Goodness!' said Skip. '*That's* clever, if you like. Let's have the soup!'

They soon finished it up, and began pressing more knobs. The one marked CHOCOLATE brought them three packets of chocolates, and the one marked APPLES a dish of apples. They thought it a very good idea.

'Now, if these Clever People had ideas like this *only*,' said Hop, 'and no silly nonsense about rhymes and riddles and things, this would be a pleasant place to live in.'

He pressed a knob marked BED. Immediately a bed rose from the floor under them, and stood there ready to be slept in. The brownies rose with it, and found themselves sitting on it.

Skip gave a loud giggle.

At once the window flew up.

'Was that a giggle that I heard?' demanded a policeman, peering into the room.

'No, just a cough. Don't be absurd,' shouted Hop. The window shut with a bang.

'There are policemen everywhere here,' whispered Hop. 'For goodness' sake, don't giggle any more and only talk in whispers.'

At that moment there came a knock on their door. It opened, and in came a bright-eyed, prettily dressed little girl.

'Hello,' she said. 'I heard one of you laughing. Are you from the Land of Giggles, by any chance?'

'No, we're not,' said Hop in astonishment. 'Why aren't you talking in rhyme?'

'I'm not one of the Clever People,' said the little

girl. 'I can't make up rhymes properly, so I usually don't talk at all. I come from the Land of Giggles.'

'What are you here for, then?' asked Skip.

The little girl hung her head.

'I was discontented in my own land,' she said, 'and I thought I was too clever for my people. So I came here, and now I can't get away, because I can't think of anything that the Very Wise Man can't do. And I get scolded every single day because I can't make up riddles or answer them.'

'Who asks them?' asked Hop.

'Oh, everybody goes to the market-place and stands in a row for their examination each morning,' explained the little girl. 'Then the Very Wise Man comes along, and you have to ask him your riddle and answer his. If you don't, he sends you to be scolded. It's to teach you to be clever.'

'I don't think it's clever to do *that* sort of thing,' said Skip, feeling sure he would be scolded every day.

'If you can help me to get back to my own people, I'd be so grateful,' said the little girl, nodding her brown curls.

'We'll help you,' said Hop, wondering how they could.

When the little girl had gone the brownies jumped into bed and were soon fast asleep.

Their Adventure in the Land of Clever People (continued)

When morning came, the brownies woke up very hungry. They pressed a few knobs and got a simply lovely breakfast of porridge, honey and cocoa.

'Now we'd better think of some riddles,' said Hop. 'All be quiet and think hard.'

So they thought hard. Hop thought of one first.

'What pillar is never used in building?' he asked.

'Don't know,' said the others.

'Why a *cater*pillar, of course,' said Hop, with a chuckle.

'Very good indeed!' said Skip. 'Listen, I've got one now. What walks on its head all day?'

'Tell us!' said the others.

'The nail in your shoes!' chuckled Skip. 'Now, Jump!'

'What lion is loose in the fields?' asked Jump.

'I know!' cried Hop. 'The *dande*lion!'

'Right!' said Jump. 'Listen, what's that?'

It was a bell ringing.

'It must be to call us to the market-place,' said Hop. 'Come on.'

They all raced outside, and saw a great stream of solemn, fat little people going down the street. The brownies joined them, and soon came to a wide market-place. The people arranged themselves in straight rows. A clock struck nine.

Trumpets blew, and down the steps of the Town Hall came the Very Wise Man. He had bigger spectacles than anyone else, and a very, *very* big head.

Then began the examination. First the Very Wise Man asked his riddle, and then a Clever Person answered it and asked his.

On went the Very Wise Man to the next person.

'Everybody answers all right,' whispered Hop. 'No one's getting scolded.'

Just then the Very Wise Man came to the little girl who had spoken to the brownies the night before. She couldn't answer her riddle, and she was sent off to be scolded by the Ogre who lived in a little house nearby.

Then came the brownies' turn.

'What pillar is never used in building?' asked Hop, rather shaky at the knees.

'Pooh – a caterpillar!' said the Very Wise Man.

'What walks on its head all day?' asked Skip nervously.

'Pooh – nail in your shoe,' said the Very Wise Man.

'Er-er – what lion is loose in the fields?' asked Jump, almost forgetting his riddle, when he felt the Very Wise Man's eyes on him.

'Pooh – a dandelion,' said the Very Wise Man. 'Very feeble. Now answer me this – Why is a toasting-fork?'

'Why is a toasting-fork?' said Hop, puzzled. 'It doesn't make sense, does it?'

'Off to the Ogre's!' roared the Very Wise Man. Poor Hop went off to join the little girl.

'Now *you*,' said the Very Wise Man to Skip. 'Why is a garden-rake?'

'But *that* doesn't make sense either,' said Skip. 'It isn't a proper riddle.'

'Off to the Ogre's!' roared the Very Wise Man again. He turned to Jump.

'Why is a porcupine?' he asked.

'*I* don't know,' said Jump.

'Off to the Ogre's!' shouted the Very Wise Man, and went on asking the Clever People more riddles which they seemed to answer perfectly.

The brownies were well scolded by the Ogre, who was a solemn little man with soft eyes and a sharp voice.

They were very angry about it.

'It's all nonsense,' said Hop crossly. 'He didn't ask fair riddles. I'll jolly well ask him to do

438

something he can't do, and then we'll get away from here.'

'Well, if you can do that,' said the little girl, drying her tears, 'don't forget to take me with you.'

All that day the brownies wandered about the Land of Clever People with the little girl. It was a very solemn, proper land, and nobody laughed or skipped or ran.

Poor Skip and Jump were sent to the Ogre twice for not making a rhyme when they spoke. They felt sorrier than ever that they had left Fairyland. Little tubby policemen seemed to be everywhere, and they soon began to feel that it was dangerous even to whisper.

Next morning they couldn't think of any riddles, nor answer any, so off they went to be scolded again. Hop was getting very tired of it.

'I'll go and ask the Very Wise Man to do something he can't do,' he said. 'Where do I go?' he asked the little girl.

'Go to the Town Hall at three o'clock in the afternoon,' she said. 'You'll find him there, waiting.'

So off went the brownies. They marched up the steps and found the Very Wise Man sitting in a great red chair, studying an old, old book.

'Good afternoon, O Very Wise Man,
   Do what I ask you, if you can,'

439

began Hop.

'Build a castle in half an hour,
With an entrance gate and one big tower.'

The Very Wise Man descended from his throne and walked out of the hall. He drew a wide circle in the market-place, muttered a few words, and waved his arms.

Immediately there sounded the noise of hammering and clattering, although nothing could be seen.

But lo and behold! At the end of half an hour, there stood in front of the astonished brownies a wonderful castle with an entrance gate and one big gleaming tower!

Hop, Skip and Jump were too amazed to say a word. Then, with a wave of his hand, the Very Wise Man caused the castle to vanish completely. After that he turned to Hop.

'Off to the Ogre's,' he said.

So off Hop had to go.

'I'll think of something much more difficult *next* time,' he decided.

For days Hop and the others tried to think of new riddles, and to puzzle out something difficult to ask the Very Wise Man to do. It didn't seem any good at all. They always seemed to be either going to or coming back from the Ogre's.

At three o'clock each day the brownies always went to the Town Hall with something new and difficult to ask the Very Wise Man to perform, hoping that he wouldn't be able to do it.

Once they asked him if he could make a ladder that reached to the stars, and he made a lovely one out of a rainbow. Hop wanted to climb it, but the Very Wise Man wouldn't let him.

'You might escape and that would be,

A most annoying thing for me,'

he said.

Another afternoon the brownies asked him to make a cloak which, when he put it on, would make him invisible. He did it at once, popped on the cloak, and none of the brownies could see where he was. He had disappeared!

'Let us put it on as well,

And try the lovely magic spell,'

begged Hop, who thought that if only he could throw the cloak around himself and the other two, he might be able to escape unseen.

But the Very Wise Man wouldn't let him. He sent them all off to the Ogre's instead.

One evening the brownies were feeling very miserable indeed.

'I believe we shall have to stay here for ever,' groaned Hop.

'So shall I,' sighed the little girl, rumpling her curly head in despair.

'Don't rumple your hair like that,' said Skip, 'or you'll be sent for a scolding again.'

He smoothed down her hair for her, and then picked up a curly bit that had broken off.

'Isn't it curly!' he said. 'I wonder if I can make it straight.'

He pulled it out straight – but it went back curly. He wetted it – but it was still curly. Then he gave it to the others, and *they* tried to make it straight. But they couldn't.

'The Very Wise Man could make it straight in half a minute,' said Hop mournfully.

'Well, I should like to see him do it,' said Skip. 'It simply *won't* go straight.'

'Let's ask him tomorrow!' said Jump hopefully.

So next day the three brownies and the little girl went to the Town Hall at three o'clock. The Very Wise Man was there as usual.

'Your next request I now await,'

he said, leaving Hop to finish the rhyme. But Hop was ready, for once.

'Then make this curly hair quite straight!' said Hop, handing it to him.

The Very Wise Man took it, and looked scornful to think he had such an easy task.

He pulled it out straight, then let one end go. The hair sprang back into curl again.

He wetted it, and pulled it straight once more. It sprang back curlier than ever!

He stamped on it. He clapped it between his hands. He waved it in the air. He put it between the pages of a book.

Not a bit of good did anything do! It only made the hair twice as curly as before!

Then the Very Wise Man called for a hot iron and a cold iron. He ironed it first with one and then with the other.

But the hair sprang back to its curliness, and *wouldn't* stay straight.

The brownies watched in the greatest excitement, their hearts beating quickly.

'I don't believe he can do it!' cried Jump.

The Very Wise Man was so worried that he didn't notice Jump hadn't spoken in rhyme. He couldn't think *what* to do with that wretched hair.

At last he knew he was beaten. He sank back on his throne, mopped his forehead, and asked Hop to let him off.

'Yes, I will,' said Hop, 'if you will do what I want you to do. If not, I'll tell all the Clever People how stupid you are.'

'Talk in rhyme,

All the time,' said the Very Wise Man.

'Nonsense!' said Hop 'I'm not going to talk in rhyme any more. It's silly when you can talk better another way. Now, are you going to do what I want?'

'Yes,' said the Very Wise Man sadly.

'First of all,' said Hop, 'tell me where the Princess Peronel is.'

'In Witchland with Witch Green-eyes,' answered the Very Wise Man.

'How can we get there?' asked Hop.

'Take the Green Railway to Fiddlestick Field,' said the Very Wise Man, 'and ask the Saucepan Man to tell you the way. He knows it.'

'Now the next thing is,' said Hop, feeling he was doing very well, 'you must let this little girl go back to the Land of Giggles.'

'Oh no, I can't do that,' said the Very Wise Man crossly.

'All right,' said Hop, 'I'm going out to tell the people all about how you couldn't make a curly hair straight.'

'Oh, you *are* brave, Hop!' cried the little girl, kissing him. 'Thank you for sticking up for me.'

'Will you let her go?' Hop demanded.

'Yes, yes! Leave me alone!' growled the Very Wise Man.

'And the next thing is, take us out of this horrid land of yours,' said Hop. 'You're not Clever People a bit, you only think you are. You think it's clever to be solemn and proper and never laugh or skip. Well, it isn't. It's just silly.'

'Come along,' said the Very Wise Man, suddenly. 'I'll take you out of the land now. I shall be glad to be rid of you.'

He strode down the hall, out into the marketplace and through the streets of the town. The brownies and the little girl followed him in delight.

At last they came to a high wall, and in it was a gateway and a turnstile. A big-headed, fat little man sat there. He stared at them in surprise.

'Am I to let these people out?' he asked doubtfully.

'Yes, you are,' cried Hop, laughing to see the little man's horror when he heard him speak without rhyming.

Then Hop turned to the Very Wise Man.

'There's just one thing more you've got to do,' he said.

'I will do it,' said the Very Wise Man.

'Well, listen,' said Hop. 'Answer me some of the silly riddles you asked us each morning. Now, why is a toasting-fork? Why is a garden-rake? Why is a porcupine?'

The Very Wise Man hung his head.

'I don't know,' he said.

'Well, you are mean and horrid!' cried Hop. 'It's unfair to ask people riddles you know haven't got answers, and then send them to be scolded because they can't answer them. Now I'll give you just one more chance – Why is a garden-rake?'

The Very Wise Man shook his head.

'All right,' said Hop, grinning. 'Off to the Ogre's with you! Tell him to give you his best scolding!'

The Very Wise Man gave an awful yell and ran away before Hop could say anything more. Hop and the others clicked through the turnstile and chuckled.

'That just serves him right!' said Skip. 'He won't be so keen on scolding now!'

Their Adventure on the Green Railway

The brownies looked around. They were in a bare, open country, with the walls of the Land of the Clever People behind them.

'We'd better see you safely back to your country first,' said Hop to the little girl, who was dancing about and clapping her hands for joy at having escaped.

'Oh, we'll all travel on the Green Railway,' said the little girl. 'I'll get out at Giggleswick – that's my station – and you can go on to Fiddlestick Field if you like, or come and stay with me at my home.'

'I think we'd better not do that,' said Hop, who was beginning to feel that it was far easier to get *into* a strange land than *out* of it. 'We might not giggle enough.'

'Besides, we want to find out the way to Witchland as soon as we can,' said Skip, 'so that we can rescue poor little Princess Peronel.'

'Well, first of all, where's the Green Railway?' asked Jump.

'Oh, it runs beneath the ground just here,' explained the little girl. 'I'll show you how to get to it. Look for a big yellow mushroom, all of you.'

The brownies began hunting all around.

'I've found a beauty!' cried Hop.

'So have I!' called Skip.

'So have we,' said the little girl, running up with Jump. 'Bring them here and set them down in a circle.'

They all brought their mushrooms. They were very big ones, quite as large as stools, and the brownies were able to stand them up straight, and then sit on the tops.

'Hold tight to your mushrooms,' said the little girl, 'while I say a magic rhyme.'

The brownies held tight.

> 'Mushrooms, take us down below;
> One, two, three, and off we go.
> Rikky, tikky, tolly vo!'

cried the little girl.

Whizz-whizz-whizz! The mushrooms suddenly sank down through the ground at a terrific pace. The brownies gasped for breath and held on as tightly as ever they could.

Then bump-bump-bump-bump – the four

mushrooms all came to a sudden stop and tipped the brownies off their seats. They rolled on the ground.

'Ha, ha!' laughed the little girl, who was still sitting on her mushroom. 'Anyone can see you're not used to riding mushrooms. Come along, and we'll see if a train is due now.'

The brownies picked themselves up and followed the little girl, who was scampering through a cave lit by one star-shaped lamp.

When she came to the end of it she stopped, and the brownies saw a little door let into the wall. It opened, and the little girl ran through it. The brownies followed her and, to their astonishment, found themselves on a tiny little platform.

A solemn grey rabbit sat there with piles of tickets in front of him.

'One to Giggleswick and three to Fiddlestick Field,' said the little girl.

'One silver coin each,' said the grey rabbit, handing out the four tickets. 'Next train in five minutes.'

Sure enough, in five minutes there came the rattle and clank of a train, and the funniest little engine ran into the station, dragging behind it a long row of higgledy-piggledy carriages. They had no roof and no seats – only just cushions on the floor.

It was a very crowded train. One carriage was full of velvety moles, who talked about the best way to catch beetles. Another carriage was full of giggling people, who seemed to be making jokes and laughing at them as fast as they could.

'Oh, there are some of my own people!' cried the little girl gladly. 'They're going to Giggleswick, I expect. Let's get in with them.'

So they all jumped in with the laughing people, though the brownies would really rather have got into an empty carriage.

The train went off when the guard waved his flag and blew his whistle. It ran clanking through dark tunnels, and big and little caves. The brownies were very much interested in all they saw and would have liked to talk about it – but the other people in the carriage were so talkative, and laughed so often, that they couldn't get a word in.

The little girl was very excited; she laughed more than anyone, and told all about her adventures in the Land of Clever People. Hop thought she was nicer *in* that land than out of it, because she didn't giggle so much then.

The train stopped again.

'Burrow Corner!' shouted a sandy rabbit-porter.

The moles all got out, and so did the grey bunnies. Then the train went off again.

The next station was Giggleswick. All the Gigglers got out. The little girl flung her arms round each of the brownies and hugged them.

'Do, do, *do* come and stay in my country,' she begged. 'Jump out now, do! We're very merry and laugh all day!'

'No, we really mustn't,' said Hop, who didn't want to go with the Gigglers in the least. 'Goodbye, and we're *so* glad you're safe home again.'

The train rattled off, and the brownies waved goodbye.

'Well!' said Jump, sitting down on his cushion. 'I think I'd rather have to speak in rhyme all day than giggle every minute. What a terrible country to live in!'

'Thank goodness we didn't go there!' said Hop. 'What a lot of peculiar lands there are outside Fairyland! How I wish we could go back to dear old Brownie Town again!'

'So do I,' said Skip, with a sigh. 'But I don't expect we'll ever be able to do that, because we shall never be able to find our goodnesses, as the King said we must.'

'Oh look!' said Jump. 'We're coming out into the open air again!'

The train puffed out of the half-darkness and came to a sunny field. It ran along beside a hedge for some way, and then out on a roadway. All sorts of strange folk were walking there, and all kinds of animals, who looked as if they had been out marketing.

The train stopped whenever anybody hailed it, and lots of people got in.

'We shall never get to Fiddlestick Field,' said Hop, when the train stopped for the fifteenth time. 'Really, people are treating this train more like a bus! Oh dear, what's happened now?'

The train stopped again. The driver was having a long talk with a friend he had met. The brownies got very impatient.

At last Hop got out and went up to the driver.

'Aren't we ever going on again?' he asked. 'We're in a hurry.'

'Oh, are you?' said the driver. 'Well, I'm going to have tea with my friend here, so you'd better get out and walk. This train won't start till six o'clock.'

So saying, the driver jumped from the train, linked his arm in his friend's and strolled off.

All the passengers yawned, settled themselves on their cushions, and went to sleep. The three brownies were very cross.

'Fine sort of train this is!' grumbled Skip. 'Goodness knows when we'll get to Fiddlestick Field!'

'I've a jolly good mind to drive the train myself,' said Hop.

'Oh, Hop, *do*!' cried Jump. 'I'm sure you could. Then we could get to Fiddlestick Field tonight.'

Hop looked at the engine. It really didn't look very difficult to drive, and he had always longed to be an engine-driver. This seemed a lovely chance.

'All right,' he said. 'Come on! I'll drive the train, with you to help me. How pleased all the passengers will be!'

Hop, Skip and Jump ran to the engine, and jumped into the cabin. There were four wheels there, like the steering wheels of motor-cars, and Hop had a good look at them.

Over one was written 'Turn to the left' and over another, 'Turn to the right'. The third wheel had 'Go fast' written over it and the last wheel had 'Start engine'.

'Oh well, this all looks easy enough,' said Hop, twisting the 'Start engine' wheel. 'Now we'll go on our travels once more!'

The train started off, rattle-clank, rattle!

All the passengers woke up and looked most surprised. They hadn't expected the train to go so soon. One of them looked to see why the driver had come back so quickly.

'Good gracious!' he cried. 'Those brownies are

driving! We shall have an accident!'

Everyone looked over the edge of their carriages in alarm. Yes, sure enough, the brownies were driving the engine. Dear, dear, dear!

'We're coming to a curve!' said Skip, who was thoroughly enjoying himself. 'Twist the "Turn to the left" wheel, Jump!'

Jump did so, and the train went smoothly round the bend. The brownies felt very pleased with themselves indeed. Fancy being able to drive an engine without any practice!

'We *must* be clever!' they thought.

'There's a station coming!' shouted Jump. 'Slow down, Hop, and stop, in case anyone wants to get out here.'

But dear me! There wasn't any wheel that said 'Slow down' or 'Stop'! Even when they twisted the 'Start engine' wheel backwards, the train didn't slow down.

Whiz-z-z! The station rushed by and the train didn't stop.

Some of the passengers were very angry, for they wanted to get out, and they began shouting and yelling at Hop for all they were worth. They made him so nervous that instead of twisting the 'Turn to the right! wheel, when he came to another bend in the line, he twisted the "Go fast" wheel.

Br-rr-rr-rr! The engine leaped forward and raced along the rails as if it were mad. All the carriages rocked and rattled, and the passengers' hats flew off in the air.

'Hop! Hop!' shouted Skip, in a fright. 'We shall have an accident. Make it go slow!'

But there wasn't any wheel that said 'Go slow' and Hop didn't know what in the world to do. He twisted every wheel in turn, but nothing happened at all, except that the train seemed to go faster. The wind whistled past the brownies' ears and took their breath away.

Stations whizzed past. The passengers forgot their anger in fear and clutched at the sides of their rocking carriages. A rabbit had his whiskers blown right off, and was terribly upset.

Then the train went up a big hill. It went more slowly, and some of the passengers wondered whether they would risk jumping out. There was a station at the top of the hill, and Hop read the name.

'Fiddlestick Field!' he cried. 'Oh dear, this is where we get out. Oh, can't we stop the train somehow?'

But he couldn't and the station went past. The train reached the hill-top, and began going down the other side.

The engine raced along the rails.

The three brownies sat down suddenly, as the engine started tearing downhill.

'It's like a switchback!' groaned Hop. 'Oh dear! It's climbing up another hill now!'

'And here's another station,' said Skip, leaning out. 'Oh my! Switchback Station! I hope to goodness we're not going to go up and down like this much longer. It makes me feel quite ill.'

The train tore downhill again, then up and then down once more. The carriages followed in a rattling row, while all the passengers shrieked and shouted. Stations raced by, but the train didn't seem to think of stopping anywhere.

'Horrid little engine!' said Hop. 'I believe it's thoroughly enjoying itself!'

'Oh my!' shouted Skip suddenly. 'The engine's gone off the rails! Oh my!'

'And there's a pond in front of us!' yelled Jump. 'Oh!'

Ker-splash! Ker-plunk! Into the pond went the engine, carriages and passengers. Everybody was tumbled, splash! into the pond, and the noise frightened all the ducks away to the bank.

'Splutter-splutter!' went everyone, floundering about in the shallow, muddy water. No one was hurt, but everybody was very, very angry.

'Catch those brownies!' they yelled, and made a grab at Hop, Skip and Jump. 'Take them to prison!'

The brownies scrambled out of the pond as quickly as they could. They began to feel frightened when they heard the angry voices of all the passengers. There were rabbits, moles, weasels, Gigglers, two Clever People, a peddler with a sack, and some peculiar people who didn't look as if they belonged to anywhere.

They all scrambled out of the pond after the brownies and chased them. Down the lane went the three, followed by all the passengers.

'Stop them! Stop them!' they cried.

The brownies raced on. Soon they came to a strange little village, built entirely of large mushrooms and toadstools. They had doors in the stalks, and windows and chimneys in the top part.

Little people came to the doors and looked out when they heard all the noise. They stared in astonishment at the sight of the three running brownies, followed by all the other people.

At the end of the village ran a stream. It was too wide and too deep for the brownies to cross, and they didn't know *what* to do.

'Quick, quick! Think of something!' cried Skip.

Hop looked round despairingly. The passengers were almost on them. Then a clever thought came to him.

He ran to a toadstool, snapped it off, put it upside down on the stream, and jumped into it. Skip and Jump sprang in just in time, pushed off from the bank, and left the passengers staring at them in dismay.

'Ha, ha!' called Hop, feeling very relieved. 'You didn't get us *that* time!'

'No, but someone else will get you! Look behind you!' yelled the rabbit whose whiskers had been blown off.

The brownies looked on to the other bank, and who do you think stood there? Why, three wooden-looking soldiers, all waiting for the toadstool boat to land!

Bump! The toadstool reached the shore. The soldiers sprang forward, caught hold of each of the brownies and marched them off.

'Now, quick march!' said the soldiers sternly. 'You'll go to prison till tomorrow morning, and then be brought before the judge for frightening our ducks, and for using one of our houses for a boat.'

The brownies wriggled and struggled, but it was no good. They were marched into a toad-stool marked PRISON, and there they were locked in for the night.

'Oh dear, dear, dear!' wept Jump. 'I'm wet and cold and hungry. Hop, you've got us into trouble *again*!'

'Be quiet!' said Hop, who was feeling very much ashamed of himself and of his doings in the train.

'Goodnight,' said Skip sadly. 'I'm going to sleep to see if I can't find something to eat in my dreams.'

And in two minutes the bad brownies were fast asleep.

Their Adventure in Toadstool Town

In the morning the brownies were awakened by someone opening their door. It was one of the soldiers. He gave them each a cup of water and some dry bread.

'In ten minutes you will be taken before the judge,' he said.

The brownies shivered and shook. Whatever would happen to them?

'If only we'd waited for the engine-driver to finish his tea!' sighed Jump. 'We'd be at Fiddlestick Field now, and the Saucepan Man would tell us the way to Witchland.'

They all ate their bread and drank their water. Just as they had finished, in came three soldiers.

They marched the brownies out of the toadstool, took them across the stream by a bridge, and into Toadstool Town. Everybody was staring at them and saying they were the bad brownies.

In the middle of the town a round space was cleared. At one end sat the Judge, in an enormous wig. Just in front of him sat a lot of other people in wigs, all writing very fast indeed. All round sat the people of Toadstool Town, and the passengers who had come on the train with Hop, Skip and Jump the day before.

The brownies trembled when they saw them. They all looked so very cross.

'Prisoners,' said the judge in a very loud voice, 'stand up straight and answer my questions. Did you, or did you not, frighten our ducks yesterday?'

'I don't know,' said Hop. 'I frightened myself more than I frightened the ducks, I think!'

'That is no answer,' said the judge, though Hop thought it was really rather a good answer. 'Did you, or did you not, frighten our ducks?' he said again, turning to Skip.

'I didn't see any ducks, so I don't know,' said Skip, who really hadn't noticed any ducks at all.

'That is no answer,' said the judge again, and turned to Jump. 'Did you, or did you not, frighten our ducks?'

'The ducks frightened *me*!' said Jump, who had fallen almost on top of a squawking duck when the train went into the pond.

'That is no answer,' said the judge, who seemed to think nothing was an answer at all. He turned to the people gathered around.

'Did they, or did they not, frighten our ducks?' he asked.

'They *did*!' shouted everybody.

'That *is* an answer,' said the judge in a satisfied voice. 'What punishment shall they have?'

'Scold them!' cried the people.

'Very good,' said the judge, writing something with a big pen in a big book. 'A big scolding for each of them.'

The brownies said nothing. They thought sadly that they seemed to get out of one scolding into another.

The judge stopped writing and looked at the brownies.

'Stand up straight and answer my questions,' he said. 'Did you, or did you not, use one of our toadstool houses for a boat?'

'Yes,' they answered, all together, 'but we didn't know it was a house.'

'Don't answer back,' said the judge.

'We're *not*,' said Hop, indignantly.

'Are they, or are they not, answering back?' the judge asked all the people around.

'They are!' shouted the people, who seemed to be thoroughly enjoying themselves.

'What punishment shall they have for using one of our houses as a boat, and for answering

462

back?' asked the judge.

'Scold them!' cried the people.

'Very good,' said the judge, writing something with a big pen in a big book. 'Another big scolding for each of them. Take them away.'

Just as the soldiers were going to march them off, the rabbit whose whiskers had been blown off stood up and waved his paw at the judge to attract his attention.

'Sit down,' said the judge.

'I have something else to say against the prisoners,' said the rabbit.

'Then don't sit down,' said the judge, beaming at the rabbit. 'What have you to say?'

'Please, your worship,' said the rabbit, 'those bad brownies have done something *much* more serious than frightening ducks or answering back.'

'What?' cried everyone.

'They took one of the Green Railway trains, and drove it!' said the rabbit. 'And they aren't drivers, and they couldn't drive!'

'And they drove it into the pond!' shouted all the passengers. 'And we got wet through!'

'Dear, dear,' said the judge, looking very pleased to think he could punish the brownies for something else. 'This matter must be looked into.'

He turned to Hop.

'Can you drive an engine?' he asked him.

'If I couldn't drive an engine, how could I drive it into the pond?' asked Hop. 'If you drive into a pond it shows you can drive, doesn't it, even if you drive in the wrong direction?'

Skip and Jump thought it was very clever of Hop to say that. Everyone looked very puzzled. The judge scribbled in his book and frowned. Then he turned to the rabbit.

'Do you say these brownies can't drive?' he asked.

'Yes, I do,' answered the rabbit, pulling at his whiskers that weren't there.

'And yet you say they *drove* the engine into the pond. Now this is an interesting point of law,' said the judge, looking very learned. 'The question is – can you say a person drives when he can't drive – no, that's not right – can you say a person can't drive and say at the same time that he did drive, but into a pond?'

Everyone looked at everyone else, and seemed to think hard.

'Well, anyway,' said the rabbit crossly, 'I say they aren't engine-drivers and they shouldn't have driven our train yesterday.'

'How do you know we aren't engine-drivers?' demanded Hop suddenly.

'Yes, how do you know?' asked Skip and Jump.

'Ah yes, how do you know?' asked the judge, looking over his spectacles at the rabbit.

'Well, they aren't,' said the rabbit sulkily. 'Anyone who drives like they do isn't an engine-driver.'

'Prove it!' cried Hop, suddenly getting an idea. 'Let us show everyone here, the judge and all, whether we can drive or not.'

Everyone got very excited, and began talking loudly.

'Silence,' said the judge. 'I have decided what to do. We will stop the next engine that comes to Toadstool Station. If these brownies show us they can drive it, we will give them only a light punishment. If they can't, we will put them in prison. When is the next train due?'

'At three o'clock in the afternoon,' called someone.

'Very well,' said the judge. 'We will all be there. Take the prisoners away, guards, and give them a big scolding each as a punishment for their other misdeeds.'

The soldiers marched the brownies back to Toadstool Prison, gave them a very big scolding, and left them.

'I really do believe we shall be able to get away to Fiddlestick Field this afternoon,' said Hop, sitting down. 'If that silly judge will only let us get in that engine, we'll be off like a shot.'

'Yes, but look here,' said Skip nervously, 'you can't really drive, you know, and I'm getting tired of these adventures that land us into places we keep having to get away from. If you can't stop the engine again, goodness knows where we'll end up at!'

'Well, do you want to stop in Toadstool Prison all your life?' asked Hop.

'No,' sighed Skip. 'I want to go back to Brownie Town, that's what *I* want!'

'Well, we can't do *that*,' answered Jump, 'so we've just got to put up with adventures like this.'

All the morning the brownies sat in the Toadstool Prison and waited for the afternoon. They peeped out through the little barred window now and then, and saw the people of Toadstool Town going about their work, doing their shopping, and gossiping with one another about the three bad brownies.

For dinner they were given a cup of water each and a big crust of bread. They ate the bread hungrily and drank the water, and then peeped out of the window again to see if anything was happening.

People were beginning to gather round to see the brownies brought out to the railway station.

They were talking and nudging each other.

'I don't like the people of this town very much,' said Hop. 'They stare so, and whisper to each other; I think someone ought to teach them manners.'

'Ding-dong,' struck a nearby clock.

'Two o'clock,' said Skip. 'Not much longer to wait, thank goodness! I'm longing to get out of this toadstool!'

At half-past two the soldiers came and took the brownies outside. They marched them through the town, with crowds of people following, all talking excitedly.

'*I* don't believe they can drive,' said one.

'Nor do I,' said another.

'They won't know how to start the engine!' cried a third.

'Then they'll soon be in prison again!' laughed a fourth.

Hop, Skip and Jump began to feel rather nervous. Supposing they *couldn't* start the engine? How awful it would be! Oh dear, oh dear, how they wished they had never had to leave Brownie Town.

'Here's the station,' said one of the soldiers, leading the brownies up some steps on to a little wooden platform.

All the people ran along beside the lines, and looked to see if the train was coming.

'I can see some smoke in the distance!' cried someone. 'It will soon be here.'

Puff-puff-puff-puff! Soon the little train came steaming up and stopped at Toadstool Town Station. The passengers got out, and stared in astonishment at the crowds all round.

The soldiers went up to the engine.

'Hey, you!' they called to the driver. 'Get down a minute, please.'

The surprised driver hopped out, and the soldiers explained to him about Hop, Skip and Jump.

'But look here,' said the driver, 'suppose they go and smash up my engine?'

The soldiers looked taken aback! No one had thought of that.

'Here comes the judge,' they said. 'You ask him.'

The driver bowed to the judge, and repeated his question.

'You should have thought of that before,' answered the judge crossly. 'We've got to go on with this now.'

'Why, I only heard of this plan of yours just this minute,' cried the driver indignantly. 'How *could* I have thought of it before?'

'Don't answer back,' snapped the judge, and turned to the brownies. 'Now then,' he said, 'the time has come to show us whether you can drive or not. Get into the engine-cab.'

The brownies jumped in.

'Drive to that bend,' ordered the judge, 'then reverse the engine and come back. Do you understand?'

'Yes, thank you,' answered Hop, taking a good look at the wheels in the engine. 'Hurrah!' he thought "There's a "STOP ENGINE" wheel this time. I'll be all right, I think!'

He twisted the 'START ENGINE' wheel, and puff-puff-puff, off went the little engine by itself, for it had been uncoupled from the carriages.

'Not so fast!' shouted the judge.

Hop laughed, and twisted the 'GO FAST' wheel. Off shot the engine faster than ever, past the rows of astonished people who were watching all along the lines.

'STOP! STOP! GO BACK!' shouted the crowds at the bend of the line, where Hop was supposed to go back.

'GOODBYE, GOODBYE,' shouted the brownies, waving their hands in delight. 'THANKS SO MUCH FOR LETTING US HAVE THIS ENGINE!'

They passed the last person by the line, and went tearing round the bend. They heard shouts and yells behind them, but they didn't even bother to look round.

'Hurrah! Hurrah!' shouted Skip. 'We've got away! Good old Hop!'

Hop grinned. He was being very careful, for he didn't want to run any risks of being taken back to Toadstool Town. The engine went racing on, and passed one station after another. Jump read them out loud as they passed.

'We ought to be getting near Fiddlestick Field,' said Skip at last. 'Keep a good look out, Jump. Hadn't you better go a bit slower, Hop, so that we don't go rushing past the station!'

Hop twisted a wheel marked 'GO SLOW', and the engine slowed down.

Two more stations were passed, and then Jump gave a squeak of delight, as the engine went up a steep hill.

'Fiddlestick Field!' he shouted. 'Pull up, Hop, quick! We're really here!'

Hop stopped the engine and the three brownies jumped out. No one was about at all. Evidently no train was expected at that time.

'Good for us!' grinned Hop. 'We shan't have any questions asked!'

'I wonder what the people of Toadstool Town are thinking!' chucked Skip. 'They'll know we can drive all right *now*!'

'Come on,' said Jump, running out of the station. 'Let's find someone to ask where the Saucepan Man lives.'

They went down a little winding lane, with honey-suckle hedges on each side. They hadn't gone far when they heard a most curious noise. It was a clanging and a clanking, a jingling and a jangling.

'What in the world is that?' wondered Hop. 'It sounds as if it's coming towards us. Perhaps we shall find out what it is, round the next corner.'

Sure enough they did. They saw the most comical sight – it looked just like a walking mass of jingling-jangling saucepans!

'Goodness gracious!' said Hop in great astonishment. 'What is it?'

'It's a whole heap of saucepans,' said Skip, 'and there are feet at the bottom. I can see them walking!'

When they got nearer they saw a tiny, bearded face peeping out of the crowd of saucepans, and discovered that it was a little man, hung from head to foot with saucepans of all sizes, shapes, and colours.

'It must be the Saucepan Man himself,' said Hop, in delight. 'What a bit of luck!'

Their Adventure with the Saucepan Man

The three brownies ran up to the jingling-jangling little man.

'Hello!' cried Hop. 'Are you the Saucepan Man?'

The little man looked at him inquiringly.

'Hey?' he said. 'What did you say?'

'Are you the Saucepan Man?' bawled Hop, over the jingling of scores of saucepans.

'No I ain't got a sausage-pan!' answered the Saucepan Man, shaking his head so that the saucepans rattled tremendously.

'Sausage-pan! I never said a *word* about a sausage-pan,' said Hop in surprise. 'I said, "Are you the Saucepan Man?"'

'I tell you I ain't got a sausage-pan,' said the little man crossly, 'I only sell saucepans, I do.'

'He's deaf,' said Skip, 'and I don't wonder, with all those saucepans jangling round him all day.'

Hop tried again. 'Are you the Saucepan Man?' he bawled. 'Can you hear me when I shout?'

'Yes, I think there's rain about,' said the Saucepan Man, looking up at the sky wisely.

'Come before evening too, likely enough.'

'*You* try, Skip,' said Hop, quite out of breath.

'WHERE ARE YOU GOING?' shouted Skip.

'Now don't be silly,' answered the Saucepan Man sharply. "Tain't snowing, and you can see it ain't. Don't tell me any fairy-tales like that.'

'CAN WE GO HOME WITH YOU?' asked Jump in his most enormous voice.

'No, my boots ain't new, but what's that to do with you, I'd like to know?' said the little man, looking crosser and crosser.

'Oh, buttons and buttercups!' sighed Hop. 'We'll never make him hear, while he's got all those saucepans jangling round him. Let's follow him and see if he's going home. Then if he takes off his saucepans, we'll try again then.'

So the three brownies trotted behind the Saucepan Man, back down the lane again, and round by the station. There they saw the station-master and the porter, staring in great astonishment at the empty engine standing all by itself in the station.

'Gracious!' said Hop. 'Let's hope we don't get asked any awkward questions!'

The station-master saw them coming and immediately rushed over to them.

'Pretend we don't understand,' said Hop quickly

to the others. 'If we talk a lot of rubbish, he'll soon let us go.'

'Hi! Hi!' called the station-master. 'Do you know anything about this engine?'

Nobody answered anything.

'Are you dumb?' asked the station-master angrily. 'Come now! Do you know anything about this engine, I say?'

'Kalamma Koo, chickeree chee,' answered Hop solemnly.

'Krik-krik,' said Skip.

'Caw,' said Jump.

'*They* don't know anything, that's certain,' said the station-master to the porter. 'They're foreigners.'

'Tanee jug jug jug?' said Hop, in an inquiring voice.

'It's all right,' said the station-master. 'I don't understand you. I'll have a word with this sauce-pan chap.'

'Caw, caw,' said Jump, and nearly made the others giggle.

The station-master poked the Saucepan Man in the ribs.

'Hi!' he cried. 'Do you know anything about this engine?'

'My name ain't Benjamin, and kindly take your

fingers out of my waistcoat,' said the Saucepan Man huffily.

The station-master groaned.

'Come on,' he said to the porter. 'They're quite mad – too mad to know anything about an engine, *any*way!'

They went off to the station again, and the three brownies breathed freely once more.

'That was a near squeak!' said Hop. 'Come on, and let's follow the Saucepan Man.'

On they went again, until at last the Saucepan Man came to a little tumbledown cottage, called Saucepan Cottage. It had old saucepans for its chimneys, and looked the funniest little place the brownies had ever seen. They followed the Saucepan Man inside. He looked at them in surprise.

'What do you want?' he asked.

Hop suddenly saw that the table was very dusty. He quickly wrote on it with his finger.

'We are three brownies who want to know the way to Witchland,' he wrote. 'The Very Wise Man told us to ask the Saucepan Man the way. Are you the Saucepan Man?'

'Course I am,' said the little man. 'Can't you *see* that? Anyway, I don't know why you didn't ask me that in the road, instead of talking about sausage-pans and the weather.'

He took off his saucepans and clattered them into a corner.

'I can tell you the way to Witchland all right,' he said. 'In fact, I'm on my way there tomorrow. You'd better come with me, you'll be safe then. Witches don't touch me, they don't.'

'Why not?' asked Hop.

'Feel hot, do you?' said the little man. 'Well, open the window then.'

Hop sighed. It really was *very* difficult to talk to the Saucepan Man. He tried again.

'May we spend the night here?' he asked in his loudest voice.

'What's the matter with my right ear?' said the Saucepan Man, going to the looking-glass, and peering into it. 'Nothing at all. Don't you be saucy, young man.'

'I can't stand this!' groaned Hop to the others. 'Haven't you got a note-book that we can write in?'

'Yes, *I* have!' cried Skip, pulling out an old note-book and a stumpy pencil. 'Here you are – write in this, Hop.'

Hop quickly wrote down his questions, and showed them to the Saucepan Man.

'Yes, you can stay here for the night,' said the little man, 'and I'll take you with me tomorrow. Find the cocoa tin now and make some cocoa, while I boil some eggs and make some toast.'

The brownies hunted about for the cocoa, filled one of the many saucepans with milk and put it on the fire to boil.

Soon the four were enjoying boiled eggs, toast and cocoa, and the brownies began to think the Saucepan Man was a very jolly little man, for although he couldn't hear very well, he could tell lots of funny tales.

'Now to bed, to bed!' he said at last. 'We've a long way to go tomorrow and we must be up early.'

He showed them a bedroom with a big bed in it, said goodnight, and shut the door.

'Well, I really feel we're on the way to find the Princess Peronel now,' said Hop, as he got into bed.

'Yes, if the Saucepan Man takes us to Witchland, we've only got to find out where Witch Green-eyes lives, and then make up a plan to rescue the Princess,' said Skip sleepily.

'Well, goodnight,' said Jump, yawning. All the brownies lay down and fell fast asleep.

In the morning the Saucepan Man woke them, and they started off on their journey. They walked for miles across the country, calling at little cottages on the way, and selling saucepans.

Soon Hop had a good idea. He took out his little note-book and wrote in it.

'Let us carry your saucepans for you for a little while,' Hop wrote. 'You must be very tired, for the sun is hot.'

The Saucepan Man gladly took off all his saucepans and gave them to the three brownies. They divided the saucepans between them, and off they all went again, clinking and clanking for all the world as if they were saucepan men themselves.

Suddenly, as they were going along, a great shadow came over them, and made everything dark.

The brownies looked up and saw an enormous yellow bird hovering over them. The Saucepan Man gave a frightened yell.

'Run!' he said 'Run! It's the Dragon-bird that belongs to the Golden Dwarf. Don't let him get you!'

The brownies sped away to some trees. The Saucepan Man didn't seem to know *where* to go. He ran forwards and backwards, and sideways, and all the time the Dragon-bird hovered overhead like a great hawk.

Then zee-ee-ee! It swooped downwards so fast that its feathers made a singing noise. The brownies saw it get hold of the poor little Saucepan Man, and then the Dragon-bird rose into the air, taking him in its talons.

'Oh my! Oh my!' cried Hop in despair. 'It's got him! It's got him!'

'Poor little Saucepan Man,' sobbed Skip, tears pouring down his face.

'Look! Look! It's flying towards that hill over there,' said Jump.

The brownies watched. On the top of the faraway hill was a castle. The Dragon-bird flew to the highest window there, landed, and disappeared into the castle.

'*Now* what are we to do?' said Hop mournfully.

'We can't go on and leave him,' said Skip, drying his eyes. 'Besides, we've got his saucepans.'

'Oh, isn't it bad luck that this should happen, just as we were really on our way to Witchland!' sighed Jump. 'Look at that signpost there. It says "THIS WAY TO WITCHLAND" on it.'

'Well, we'd better go to that hill over there,' said Skip bravely. 'We might be able to rescue the Saucepan Man *some*how. We simply *can't* leave him to that Dragon-bird and the Golden Dwarf'

'Come on then,' said Hop, and off they all went, keeping a very sharp look-out in case the Dragon-bird came back again.

The hill was very much farther away than it looked. All the afternoon the brownies travelled, their saucepans clanking and jingling at every step.

'No wonder the Saucepan Man is so deaf!' said Hop. 'It's all I can do to hear myself speak with all this noise going on.'

Presently they came to a little cottage.

'Let's knock at the door,' said Skip, 'and see if we can get some food in exchange for a saucepan. I'm hungry.'

They knocked. A dwarf opened the door and peered at them.

'What do you want?' he said.

'Do you want any saucepans?' asked Hop. 'We've got some fine ones here.'

'How much?' asked the dwarf.

'We'll give you a big one, if you'll give us a loaf, and some milk,' said Hop.

The dwarf fetched them three cups of milk and a loaf of bread.

'Here you are,' he said. 'Now give me your biggest saucepan.'

Hop gave him a fine blue saucepan.

'Who lives in that castle over there on that hill?' he asked.

'The Golden Dwarf,' answered their customer. 'Don't you go there, or you'll be captured by the Dragon-bird.'

'Why does the Golden Dwarf capture people?' asked Skip.

'To eat,' answered the dwarf. 'Didn't you know *that*? Ah, he's a terrible fellow, the Golden Dwarf is, I can tell you. There's only one word that will stop him in his evil ways, but as he lives away up there in his high castle that nobody can enter, he's safe!'

'What's the word?' asked Hop with interest.

'Ho ho! Don't you wish you could use it on the Golden Dwarf!' laughed the dwarf. 'Well, I'll tell you. It's "Kerolamisticootalimarcawnokeeto"!'

'Buttons and buttercups!' said Hop. 'I'll never be able to say that!'

'We'll split it into three and each of us can remember a bit of it!' said Skip cleverly.

The dwarf laughed, and said the long word again. Hop said the first piece over and over to himself, while Skip said the middle bit and Jump repeated the last bit.

'Much good it'll do you!' said the dwarf. 'Why, no one's ever even *seen* the Golden Dwarf since I've lived here – and I've been here a hundred and forty-three years come next November!'

The brownies sighed. Things seemed very difficult. They said goodbye and left the cottage behind them.

'*Is* it any good going to the castle?' said Jump, who was beginning to feel very down in the dumps. 'Suppose we all get caught and eaten.'

'Cheer up,' said Hop. 'You can only get eaten *once*, you know!'

'Don't be silly,' said Jump crossly. 'I don't want to be eaten even once.'

'Sh!' said Skip. 'We're getting near the castle. Better keep a good look-out.'

'Bother the clanking saucepans,' said Hop. 'Shall we take them off and leave them here?'

'No,' said Skip. 'If that horrid Dragon-bird appears again we'll pretend we're just a heap of old tins, and maybe it won't see us then.'

Just as he spoke a shadow fell over them again. At once the three sank down to the ground beneath their saucepans, and lay quite still. The shadow grew blacker, and at last the Dragon-bird landed by them with a flop. It pecked at Skip's saucepans and dented them badly. Then it spread its wings, rose into the air, and flew away again.

'Oh my stars!' said Jump, shaking like a jelly. 'This is the sort of adventure that doesn't agree with me at all. Has that horrid bird gone?'

'Yes,' said Hop. 'It's a nasty-looking thing too, I can tell you. It's got scales as well as feathers, and a long tail. It must have thought we were piles of saucepans!'

'Come on while we're safe,' said Skip.

They ran towards the castle and, panting and breathless, flung themselves down at the foot of it.

'Isn't it a funny colour!' said Hop, looking at it closely. 'It looks just like toffee!'

Skip broke a piece off and licked it.

'It *is* toffee!' he said. 'My goodness! Fancy a castle built of toffee!'

'Toffee!' cried Jump in delight. 'I say, how lovely! I'm going to have a really big bit!'

He broke off a fine fat piece and began chewing it. It was delicious.

'I suppose it was built by magic,' said Hop. 'I can't imagine *people* building it, can you? They'd get so terribly sticky.'

'Well, don't let's forget about the Saucepan Man,' said Skip, looking round about him. 'I expect he's feeling very lonely and afraid.'

'Let's explore round the outside of the castle,' said Hop. 'Maybe we can find some way of getting in then.'

Off went the brownies, after having carefully taken off the saucepans and hidden them under a bush. They were afraid that the Golden Dwarf might hear the clanking if they carried them about.

They marched off round the toffee castle, looking everywhere for a window or a door.

Not one was to be seen.

'Goodness!' said Hop at last. 'No wonder nobody ever sees the Golden Dwarf, if there's no window and no door on the ground-floor.'

'I don't believe there's any way of getting into the castle at all except by that window right at the very top,' said Skip, craning his neck to see.

He was right. Not a door was to be seen, and no windows either, except the big one set right at the very top of the castle, where the Dragon-bird had flown in with the Saucepan Man.

The brownies came back to their saucepans and sat down under the bush.

'Well, that *is* a puzzle,' said Hop. 'We haven't a ladder, and there's no door – so how ever *can* we get in?'

'We can't,' said Jump. 'The only thing left to do is to go back to that signpost, and take the road to Witchland.'

'What, and leave the poor old Saucepan Man to be eaten by the Golden Dwarf?' cried Skip, who was very tender-hearted. 'After he's been so very kind to us too!'

The others looked uncomfortable. They didn't like leaving their friend behind, but they didn't really see what else there was to do.

'Listen!' said Skip. 'If you want something badly enough, you're sure to find out a way. Now let's just keep quiet and think very, very hard.'

The three brownies put their heads on their hands, shut they eyes, and thought.

They thought and thought and thought.

The sun went down. Still the brownies thought.

The moon came up. Still the brownies thought.

Then Hop raised his head. 'If only we could get something to climb up the wall with,' he said. 'But we haven't anything at all.'

'Except silly old saucepans,' said Jump mournfully.

'Yes – saucepans,' repeated Hop. Then his eyes widened as a great thought came into his head.

'*Saucepans!*' he said again, and chuckled. Then he got up and did a little dance of joy. Skip and Jump stared at him in astonishment.

'Are you mad, Hop?' asked Skip.

'Or do you feel ill?' asked Jump.

'No, I'm not mad!' answered Hop. 'I've only got that fantastic feeling you get when you suddenly think of a perfectly splendid idea.'

'What is it?' asked Skip and Jump together.

'Well, here we've been groaning and moaning because we've nothing to get us up the castle wall,' said Hop, 'and we've got the very best thing in the world to get us up there – the saucepans!'

'Whatever *do* you mean?' asked Skip.

'*This* is what I mean,' said Hop, and he picked up a saucepan. He held it upside down and drove the handle into the toffee wall. It went in quite easily, and stayed there, for the toffee held it tight.

'One step up,' said Hop, and picked up another saucepan. He pushed the handle of that one in, a little way above the first one.

'Two steps up!' he cried. '*Now* do you see the idea?'

'Oh *yes*!' cried the other two. 'What a good plan, Hop! We can climb up on the saucepans, if only the handles will hold all right!'

'The toffee will hold them,' laughed Hop, who was beginning to feel very excited.

One by one the saucepans' handles were driven into the wall, so that every saucepan made a step higher than the last. They were quite firm and steady and, as the brownies were little and light, there was no fear of the steps breaking.

Higher and higher they went, until they had almost reached the window at the top. Jump carried the saucepans that were left and passed them one by one to Skip, who passed them to Hop, who drove the handles into the wall.

'What a mercy we had so many saucepans!' whispered Skip.

'Yes, wasn't it!' said Hop. 'I say! We're nearly

at the top. Suppose the Golden Dwarf leans out of the window and sees us!'

'We'll say the magic word!' said Skip. 'I know my bit all right.'

'And I know mine!' said Jump.

'Well, we'll have to join the bits on very quickly when we say it,' said Hop, 'or else it won't sound like a word. Perhaps we'd better practise it before we go any further.'

'Hurry up, then,' said Skip, 'I'm not very anxious to hang on to these saucepans all night.'

Hop said his part of the magic word, Skip said the middle and Jump joined in quickly with the end. After seven or eight times they managed to do it perfectly, and Hop thought they might go on.

They had just enough saucepans to reach to the window ledge. At last Hop could peep over it and look into the room.

He saw a large room hung with golden curtains and spread with a golden carpet. In the middle of it, sitting on a stool, was the Saucepan Man, looking the picture of misery. He was all alone.

'Good!' said Hop, and whispered what he saw to the others. Then he peeped over the ledge again.

The Saucepan Man looked up and when he saw Hop, he fell off his stool in astonishment.

'I must be dreaming,' he said, and pinched himself very hard.

'Ow!' he said. 'No, I'm not.'

He ran to the window.

'Help me over,' said Hop. 'We've come to rescue you.'

The Saucepan Man hauled him into the room, and then they helped Skip and Jump.

Quickly, Hop wrote in his notebook to tell the Saucepan Man how they had come to him.

'You'd better escape at once, with us,' wrote Hop, 'for there's no knowing when that awful Dragon-bird will appear again, or the Golden Dwarf.'

'Ugh! Don't talk of them,' begged the Saucepan Man. 'I shall never forget being carried off in those talons. When I got here the Golden Dwarf came and looked at me, and said I wouldn't be plump enough to eat for a week.'

The brownies shivered.

'Come on,' said Hop, running to the window. 'Let's escape while we can.'

He had just got one leg over the window-sill, when heavy footsteps outside the door made his hair stand on end.

'Oh!' whispered the Saucepan Man. 'Hide, quick! It's the Golden Dwarf.'

The brownies dived behind one of the curtains just as the door opened. In came a peculiar creature, not much bigger than the brownies, who looked as if he were made of solid gold. Hop thought he looked more like a statue than a live person.

'I smell brownies!' said the Golden Dwarf suddenly, and sniffed the air.

The three brownies trembled.

'Remember the magic word,' whispered Hop anxiously. 'It's our only chance.'

'I SMELL BROWNIES!' said the Golden Dwarf again, and strode over to the shaking curtain.

He pulled it aside. Out sprang Hop, Skip, and Jump. 'Kerolamisti –' shouted Hop.

'Cootallmar –' went on Skip.

'Cawnokeeto!' finished Jump.

The Golden Dwarf stared at them in terror.

'The Word! The Word!' he cried, and pulled at his hair. Then he uttered a deep groan, jumped into the air, and vanished completely.

The brownies and the Saucepan Man stared at the place where the Golden Dwarf had stood. Nothing happened. He didn't come back.

'You've done the trick!' said the Saucepan Man. 'He's gone for good!'

'Hurrah!' cried Hop. 'Thank goodness we remembered the magic word! Come on, Saucepan

Man – let's get away from this horrid castle!'

Over the window-sill they clambered, and were soon scrambling down the saucepans as fast as they could go. 'We'll leave them there,' said the Saucepan Man. 'I don't want to waste any more time here, in case the Dragon-bird comes back.'

So off they all went in the moonlight, to the signpost pointing to Witchland.

Their Adventure with the Labeller and the Bottler

They hadn't gone very far when the Saucepan Man began to yawn.

'I'm *so* sleepy,' he said, 'and it really must be very late. What about getting underneath a bush and going to sleep till morning?'

The brownies thought it would be a very good idea. So they all cuddled together beneath a bush, and went fast asleep till the sun rose.

'Wake up! Wake up!' cried Hop. 'It's time to go on our way to Witchland and rescue the Princess Peronel.'

The others woke with a jump. They washed in a nearby stream, picked some blackberries for breakfast and went on towards the sign-post.

Suddenly a great black shadow came over them.

'Oh! Oh!' yelled the Saucepan Man in terror. 'It's the Dragon-bird again. Run! Run!'

The brownies ran helter-skelter to some bushes. The black shadow grew darker.

Zee-ee-ee! The Dragon-bird landed on the ground by them with a thud.

'Where is my master? Where is my master?' it cried in a croaking voice.

'We have said a magic word and made him vanish for ever!' shouted Hop bravely. 'And if you don't leave us alone, we'll make *you* vanish too, you horrid Dragon-bird.'

'No, no!' shrieked the bird. 'Oh, most powerful wizard, let me serve *you*, now that my master the Golden Dwarf, is gone. Let me be your slave.'

'Gracious!' said Hop. 'Here is a to-do! Goodness knows we don't a Dragon-bird always at our heels, begging to be our slave.'

The Saucepan Man, who seemed to hear the Dragon-bird quite well, crawled out from under his bush and walked up to it.

'Go away!' he said. 'If we want you we will call you. Don't come bothering us now, or we will make you disappear, as we did your master.'

'I will come if ever you want me,' croaked the bird sadly. 'I will await that time.'

It spread its wings, rose into the air, and in a few moments was out of sight.

'That was rather a nasty shock,' said Hop.

'I quite thought it would take us all away again. Ugh! I hope we never see the ugly thing any more!'

'So do *we*!' said Skip and Jump.

'Come on,' said the Saucepan Man, and once

more the four set off to the signpost.

At last they reached it, and set off down the road towards Witchland.

'Don't you bother to come with us,' said Hop to the Saucepan Man. 'We can find our way quite well now.'

'No, I can't hear any bell,' said the Saucepan Man, standing still to listen. 'You must be mistaken.'

'Oh dear, you *are* deaf!' sighed Hop, and quickly wrote down what he had said.

'Ho, ho!' laughed the Saucepan Man. 'So you think you could find the way by yourself, do you? Ho, ho! You just follow me, and you'll soon see you couldn't find the way alone!'

No sooner had he said that than the four travellers came to a river. Over it stretched a graceful bridge but, to the brownies' surprise, no sooner did they get near it than the end nearest to them raised itself and stayed there.

'How annoying of it!' said Hop, in surprise. 'What does it do that for? We can't get across!'

'Don't worry!' said the Saucepan Man. He looked about on the ground and picked up four tiny blue stones. He threw them into the river one after the other, saying a magic word at each of them.

At once the end of the bridge came down again, and rested on the bank.

'There you are,' said the Saucepan Man. 'Now we can cross.'

The brownies ran across quickly, just in case the bridge took it into its head to do anything funny again.

They hadn't gone very far beyond the bridge before they came to a forest so dark and so thick that the brownies felt sure they couldn't possibly get through it. They tried this way and that way, but it was all no good – they could not find a path.

The Saucepan Man watched them, laughing.

Then he quickly ran to a big white stone lying nearby and lifted it up. Underneath it lay a coil of silver string. The Saucepan Man took it up and tied one end to a tree-trunk.

Then he said a magic rhyme, and immediately, to the brownies' great surprise, the string uncoiled and went sliding away all by itself into the dark forest.

'Follow it quickly!' cried the Saucepan Man, and ran into the forest.

The silver string gleamed through the bushes and trees, and led the brownies by a hidden, narrow path through the dark forest. On and on they went, following the silver thread, until at last they reached the end of the trees, and stood in sunshine once more.

'I don't know what we should do without you,' shouted Hop to the Saucepan Man. 'We should never have known the way!'

'*Who's* making hay?' asked the Saucepan Man, staring all round about him.

'No one!' shouted Hop, and wrote in his notebook to tell the Saucepan Man what he was talking about.

Presently they set off again. In the distance they saw an enormous hill. As they drew nearer the brownies saw it gleaming and glittering, as if it were made of ice.

'Glass,' explained the Saucepan Man, as they drew near

'I wonder how we get up *that*!' said Hop.

The brownies tried to climb it, but as fast as they tried, down them came, ker-plunk, to the bottom!

'Tell us how to get up!' Hop wrote in his notebook, to the Saucepan Man.

Their guide smiled. He took six paces to the left, picked up a yellow stone, and aimed it carefully at a notch in the glass hill.

As soon as it struck the notch, a door slid open in the hillside and the brownies saw a passage leading through the glass hill.

'It's easier to go through than up,' smiled the Saucepan Man, leading the way.

The passage was very strange, for it wound about like a river. The sides, top and bottom were all glass, and reflected everything so perfectly that the brownies kept walking into the walls, and bumping their noses.

They were very glad when at last they came out at the other side of the hill. In front of them towered a great gate, and on it was written in iron lettering:

WITCHLAND

'At last!' said Hop. 'Now we really have arrived!'

'Here I must leave you,' said the Saucepan Man sadly. 'I cannot go in and I don't know how *you'll* get in either. But you are so clever, that maybe you'll find a way. Now I must go back and make some more saucepans to sell.'

'Thank you for bringing us here,' wrote Hop in his notebook. 'We are sorry to say goodbye.'

'So am I,' said the Saucepan Man, with tears in his eyes. 'Thank you very much for all your goodness to me in rescuing me from the Golden Dwarf.'

'Don't mention it,' said the brownies politely.

Then the Saucepan Man shook hands solemnly with them all, and said goodbye.

'Goodbye, goodbye!' called the brownies, as he went towards the glass hill.

He turned round.

'What sort of pie?' he called in surprise.

'Oh buttons and buttercups, isn't he deaf!' said Hop, and waved to the Saucepan Man to go on.

They watched him disappear into the hill.

'Nice old Saucepan Man,' said Skip. 'Wish he was coming to Witchland with us.'

'I wonder how we get in!' said Hop, looking at the tall gates.

'Don't know,' said Skip. 'We'd better wait until someone goes in or out, and then try and slip in as the gates open. Let's sit down under the may-tree and wait.'

They sat down and waited.

Nobody went either in or out of the gates. The brownies felt very bored.

Hop looked all round to see if anyone was in sight. He suddenly saw something in the distance.

'Look!' he said. 'There's a procession or something coming. We could easily slip in with that when the gates open for it, couldn't we?'

'Yes!' said Jump. 'Let's wait quietly and then try our luck.'

The procession came nearer. At the same time somebody came from the opposite direction. Skip looked to see who it was.

'It's a little brown mouse!' he said in surprise. 'I wonder what a mouse is doing here! He seems to be carrying a heavy sack, look!'

The others looked. The little mouse was certainly carrying a sack that seemed far too heavy for him.

The procession and the mouse reached the place where the brownies sat, just at the same moment. The procession was made up of all sorts of strange people carrying precious rugs, caskets, and plants.

'Going in to sell them to the witches, I suppose!' whispered Hop. 'Look! The gates are opening! Get ready to slip inside!'

But just at that moment the mouse gave a shrill squeak.

The brownies looked round. They saw that the sack had fallen off the little mouse's back, and that hundreds of green labels were flying about all over the place.

'Oh! Oh! What shall I do?' squeaked the mouse. 'I shall be late, I know I shall!'

The brownies jumped up.

'Let us help you to pick them up!' said Hop. 'It won't take a minute.'

'We must hurry, though,' said Skip, 'or we

shan't get in whilst the gates are open.'

The brownies quickly picked up the labels and filled the mouse's sack again. He was very grateful indeed.

'Don't mention it,' said Hop, and turned to the gates of Witchland.

Clang! They shut, for the last of the procession had gone in!

'Oh my!' said Hop in dismay. 'Now we've lost our chance!'

The little mouse looked very upset. 'Did you want to get in?' he asked.

'Yes,' said Hop. 'But it doesn't matter – we'll wait till someone else wants to go in again, and the gates open.'

'I wish we could find something to eat,' sighed Skip. 'I'm getting so *dreadfully* hungry!'

'Won't you come home with me for a while?' asked the mouse. 'I'm sure my master, the Labeller, would give you something to eat, as you've been so kind in helping me.'

'Well, thank you very much,' said Hop. 'But what a funny name your master has – the Labeller! Whatever does he label?'

'Oh, whenever people are crosspatches, or spiteful, or horrid in any way,' said the mouse, 'they are taken to the Labeller, and he puts a label round their neck that they can't get off. Then everyone knows what sort of person they are and, if they're very nasty, people avoid them as much as they can.'

'That seems a very good idea,' said Skip, as the brownies followed the mouse down a pathway. 'Do they have to wear the labels all their lives?'

'That depends,' said the mouse, trotting down a hole in a bank. 'You see, as soon as they stop being horrid, their label flies off, and goes back to the Labeller! If they go on being horrid for the rest of their lives, the label *never* flies off.'

'I say! The Labeller won't label *us*, will he?' asked Hop anxiously, as they all trotted down the hole after the mouse.

'Oh no!' said the mouse. '*You're* not horrid at all – you're very nice.'

The passage was lit with orange lights, and beneath every light was a little door. Each door had a name-plate on, and the brownies read them all as they passed by.

'Here's a funny one!' said Hop. 'The Bottler. I wonder what he bottles!'

'Oh, and here's the Labeller!' said Skip. 'The mouse is going inside.'

They followed him and found themselves in a cosy little room where a bright fire was burning.

By a little table sat a fat old man with spectacles on. He was printing names on labels in very small and beautiful letters.

'Come in, all of you,' he said in a kind voice. 'I don't know who you are, but you're very welcome.'

The brownies said good-day politely and told him who they were.

'Where do you come from?' he asked.

'Brownie Town,' they answered.

'Well, what are you doing *here* then?' asked the Labeller in surprise.

The brownies went very red. Nobody spoke for a minute, and then Hop told the Labeller all about the naughty trick they had played at the King's party, and how the little Princess had been spirited away.

'Dear, dear, dear,' said the Labeller, 'that was a very silly thing to do. Perhaps I'd better label you all silly, had I?'

'No, thank you,' said the brownies quickly. 'We aren't silly any more. We're sorry for what we did, and we're trying to find the Princess and rescue her.'

The Labeller got out some buns and told the little mouse to make some hot milk.

'Sit down,' he said, 'and have something to eat. I'm sure it was very kind of you to help my little servant to pick up all the labels he had dropped.'

The brownies each took and bun and said 'Thank you'.

'And when are you going back to Brownie Town?' asked the Labeller. 'When you've rescued the Princess?'

'No,' answered Hop sadly, 'we can't. The King said we weren't to go back until we had found our goodness – and people can't find their goodnesses, of course – so we're afraid we'll *never* be able to go back.'

'But of *course* you can find your goodness if you've got any!' said the Labeller. 'Why, my brother, the Bottler, can easily give you it if you've any that belongs to you. He bottles up all the goodness in the world, you know, and then, when anyone starts being peevish and grumpy, he seeks out his messenger – my mouse's cousin – to drop a little out of one of the bottles of goodness into something the peevish person is drinking. Then the grumpy person begins to smile again, and thinks the world is a fine place, after all.'

'Dear me!' said the brownies, in the greatest surprise. 'Is that really so?'

'And do you mean to say that if we've done any good deeds, for instance, the Bottler has got them boiled down and bottled up in a jar?' asked Skip in excitement. 'Bottles that we can take away?'

'Oh yes,' said the Labeller, taking another bun. 'With your own names on and everything.'

'Well! If that isn't splendid!' cried Hop in delight. '*Could* we go and see if the Bottler's got any of our goodness bottled up?'

'Finish your milk and buns first,' said the Labeller, 'then you can go.'

The brownies finished their food and jumped up.

'Well, goodbye,' said the Labeller, shaking hands with them. 'The mouse will show you the right door. Good luck to you.'

Off went the brownies in a great state of excitement. They almost trod on the mouse's tail, they were in such a hurry.

They came to the little door marked 'The Bottler'. They knocked.

'Come in,' said a voice.

They went in, and saw a room like the Labeller's. It was full of thousands of bottles standing on hundreds of shelves.

The Bottler was very like the Labeller, except that he was a good deal fatter.

'What can I do for you?' he asked.

'Please,' said Hop in a shaky voice, 'please have you any goodness of ours bottled up?'

'Who are you?' asked the Bottler kindly.

'Hop, Skip and Jump, three brownies from Brownie Town!' answered Hop.

'Hm-m-m, let me see,' said the Bottler, putting a second pair of spectacles on. He walked up to a shelf labelled 'Brownies' and began peering at the bottles.

The brownies waited impatiently. Oh, if only, only, only a bottle of their goodness could be found, they could go back to Brownie Town.

'Ha! Here we are!' said the Bottler at last, pouncing on a little yellow bottle. It had something written on the label that was stuck round it. The Bottler read it out:

'"This goodness belongs to Hop, Skip, and Jump. It was made when they rescued a mermaid from the castle of the Red Goblin".'

'Oh fancy!' said Jump. 'I *am* glad we rescued Golden-hair!'

'Dear me, here's another bottle, too,' said the Bottler. He picked up a little green bottle and read out a label.

'"This goodness belongs to Hop, Skip, and Jump. It was made when they helped a little girl to escape from the Land of Clever People".'

'Buttons and buttercups!' said Hop. 'That's *two* bottles to take back.'

'And here's a third bottle!' said the Bottler suddenly, and picked up a red bottle.

'"This goodness belongs to Hop, Skip, and Jump. It was made when they rescued the Saucepan Man from the Golden Dwarf"!' read the Bottler.

'How perfectly lovely!' cried Jump. 'That's a bottle each! How glad I am that we *did* help those people when we had the chance.'

'Here you are,' said the Bottler, handing them the bottles. 'Take care of them, for they'll take you safely back to Brownie Town. Now goodbye. I'm glad to have been of some use to you!'

'Goodbye, and thank you very much,' called the brownies, and hurried out into the passage with their precious bottles. The little mouse was outside, waiting for them.

'If you like, I'll show you a secret way into Witchland,' he said. 'I'd be pleased to help you any way I could.'

Hop hugged the kind little mouse.

'Please show us,' he said. He put his bottle into his pocket and followed the mouse up the passage.

The mouse ran down passage after passage, and at last went up a very steep one.

'This leads into a witch's house,' he whispered. 'There's a big mouse-hole that comes out into the cellar. You can squeeze through it.'

'Thank you,' said Hop. 'Tell me, little mouse, what is the name of the witch who lives here?'

'Witch Green-eyes,' whispered the mouse.

'Witch Green-eyes!' said the brownies in surprise. 'Just the very witch we want!'

They said goodbye to the mouse, squeezed through the hole, and found themselves in a dark, smelly cellar.

'Well,' said Hop, 'now we'll soon see if we can rescue Princess Peronel!'

Their Adventure in the House of Witch Green-eyes

Everywhere was dark and the brownies had to feel their way carefully, in case they tumbled over anything. Suddenly they heard footsteps, and saw the light of a candle coming down some steps at one end of the cellar.

'It's the witch herself!' whispered Hop in great excitement. 'Keep still, whatever you do!'

Sure enough, it *was* Witch Green-eyes. The brownies could see her eyes gleaming green like a cat's, as she walked down the cellar.

'Now where did I put that barrel of gold?' she muttered. 'Surely it was somewhere in this corner?'

She was coming nearer to the brownies. They shrank back into the shadows in fear.

'I *must* find that gold,' they heard her mutter. 'Now where is it? Ah! Here it is!'

She stopped just by them, and began jingling money in a barrel. The brownies kept as still as still.

The witch began counting out the money. 'One-two-three-four-five.'

The brownies never made a sound. They held

their breath and hoped the witch would soon go.

After she had counted out a hundred pieces of gold she picked up her candle, took the bag of money, and turned to go

She shuffled her way across the cellar floor, muttering to herself. The brownies began to breathe freely again, for they felt they were safe.

But just at that moment something happened.

Skip put his hands over his mouth and nose, and held them tight.

'Whatever is the matter?' whispered Hop.

'I'm going to sneeze!' stuttered Skip.

Now the more you try to stop a sneeze, the bigger it is when it *does* come. And when Skip's sneeze came, it was ENORMOUS.

'A-TISHOO-SHOO!' he sneezed, and nearly sneezeded his head off.

The witch dropped her bag of money in amazement and held her candle up to see whatever was in the cellar.

'Quick – the mouse-hole!' whispered Hop, and the brownies ran to where they thought it was.

But, oh dear me, they couldn't find it *any*where, not anywhere at all.

The witch came down the cellar again, holding her candle up high, and looked as fierce as ever a witch could look.

'Ho! Ho!' she said, as she saw the scurrying brownies. 'And what are *you* doing here, I should like to know?'

'N-n-nothing much,' answered Hop, wondering wherever the mouse-hole was. 'J-just looking for spiders, you know.'

'Looking for my *gold*, more likely,' growled the witch. 'You wouldn't be down in my cellar for *spiders*, you little squiggling brownies. You come along upstairs and I'll show you a better place for spiders!'

She took hold of them and pushed them in front of her.

'Up the steps you go,' she cried, her green eyes looking more like a cat's than ever.

The frightened brownies rushed up the steps and found themselves in a large kitchen.

'Now,' said the witch with a nasty sort of smile, 'you'll find plenty of cobwebs about my kitchen. Just go and look for spiders behind them, whilst I ask my black cat to tell me exactly what you *were* in the cellar for. It's not much good asking *you*, I can see, as you seem to think of nothing but spiders.'

The poor little brownies had to go and poke about in the thick cobwebs that hung in the dark corner of the kitchen. They couldn't bear it, for the spiders were large, and very, very creepy-crawly.

The witch called her black cat.

'Cinders, Cinders!' she cried.

In walked an enormous cat with eyes as green as the witch's.

'Sit in the magic circle, Cinders,' said the witch, 'and tell me the answers to my questions.'

The cat went and sat down in the middle of a circle chalked on the kitchen floor. It closed its eyes and swished its tail about.

'Oh, Cinders,' cried the witch, waving her stick over him, 'tell me, I pray you, what has brought these three brownies here?'

'They come to rescue the Princess Peronel,' replied the cat in a deep, purring voice.

'Nasty old tell-tale,' whispered Hop to Skip. 'Look out for that spider! It's crawling up your leg.'

'Ho! Ho!' laughed the witch. 'To rescue the Princess Peronel! That's a great joke indeed! Now tell me, Cinders, does anyone in Fairyland know they have come here?'

'No one knows,' answered Cinders. 'No one will ever know if you keep them here for ever.'

'I don't like that cat,' said Skip. 'It knows a lot too much for a cat.'

'Ha, ha, ho, ho!' laughed the witch again. 'Thank you, Cinders. Now I know what to do with these horrid little brownies. I'll put them in the High Tower with the Princess Peronel, and I won't let them go till they have made her do what I want.'

She turned to the brownies.

'Come,' she said. 'I will take you to the Princess you want to rescue. I will chain you up with her, and then you shall see whether it is an easy matter or not to come to Witchland and rescue a Princess held by Witch Green-eyes.'

She hustled them out of the room to where a spiral staircase ran up and up and up. The brownies climbed it, and thought surely it would never come to an end. But at last, after Hop had counted two thousand six hundred and eighty-four steps, he saw a low door in front of him, heavily bolted, locked and padlocked.

The witch unlocked and unbolted the door and pushed the brownies inside. There they saw a sight that made their hearts leap for joy – for the little Princess Peronel was in the room, sitting at a window looking longingly out.

She turned as they came in, and the brownies saw that golden chains were round her legs and bound her to a staple in the wall. It made them feel very angry and very sad at the same time.

'Here you are!' said the witch. 'Here's the

Princess you came to rescue! Now just you make her do what I want her to do and I'll set you free! If not, I'll keep you here for the rest of your lives!'

She quickly slipped a chain round the legs of each brownie, so that they were bound to the wall like the Princess. Then she gave a wicked chuckle and went out of the door. They heard her locking and bolting it.

'Hello,' said the brownies to the surprised Princess.

'Have you *really* come to rescue me?' asked Peronel eagerly.

'We came to Witchland to try,' said Hop, 'but the old witch caught us too soon.'

'Oh dear!' said the Princess sadly. 'I wonder if I'll ever be rescued. I've been here such a long time. You *won't* try to make me do what the nasty old witch wants, will you?'

'What does she want you to do?' asked the brownies.

'She keeps telling me I must marry the old wizard who lives next door to her,' sighed Peronel. 'He'll give her a thousand bags of gold if I do marry him.'

'Good gracious!' cried Hop, as angry as could be. 'How *dare* she ask you to do such a thing! We must certainly rescue you.'

'But how?' asked the little Princess. 'I don't think *any*one could escape from this high tower!'

'Besides, we're chained up,' said Hop mournfully.

Jump went to the window and looked out. They were certainly in a very, very high tower. The windows were barred too. The door was locked and bolted, and the prisoners were chained. It seemed hopeless. They would just have to stop there for always!

Hop went carefully round the room, with his chain clanking round his leg, and felt the walls and the door. They were all as solid as could be. The window, too, was far too high for anyone to hear them calling. All Witchland lay spread out below like a map.

The brownies sat down on the floor in despair.

'Tell me how you came here,' said the Princess. 'I've been so dull here all by myself, and I'd like to hear your adventures.'

So the brownies began to tell them. They began at the beginning, and told of the Cottage without a Door, the Castle of the Red Goblin, the Land of the Giants, the Clever People and the Gigglers. Then they told her of Toadstool Town and their adventure on the Green Railway.

Peronel loved it all.

'Go on,' she said. 'Tell me more.'

513

So they told her of the Saucepan Man, and how they had rescued him from the Dragon-bird and the Golden Dwarf.

'And,' said Hop, 'we got an awful fright as we were going along the day after we had rescued him, because the Dragon-bird came *again*!'

'Again!' cried the Princess in horror. 'Did it carry any of you away?'

'No, it wanted its master,' explained Hop, 'and when it couldn't find him, it said it would be our slave, and come whenever we wanted it, if only we'd call.'

'*Well*,' said the Princess, 'why *don't* you call the old Dragon-bird? It might help us, mightn't it?'

'Buttons and buttercups!' squeaked Hop in excitement. 'Oh buttons and buttercups! Fancy us not thinking of that! Oh, Princess Peronel, what a good thing you thought of it! Of *course* we'll call the good old Dragon-bird! It might get us help, even if it couldn't help us itself.'

The brownies were tremendously excited, and so was the Princess. Hop went to the window, and called out as loudly as he could:

'Dragon-bird! Dragon-bird! Come to your new masters! We need you!'

They waited. Nothing happened. No sound of rushing wings came. Everyone felt very disappointed. Then Skip looked out of the window again. He gave a cry of delight.

'I believe the Dragon-bird is coming!' he called. 'Look! Far away, ever so high up in the air!'

Hop looked. He saw a tiny black speck far away.

'I'll call again!' he said. And once more he cried out to the Dragon-bird to come.

The speck grew larger and larger. Then zee-ee-ee! The Dragon-bird swooped down from the sky and landed with a thud on their window-sill.

'Masters, I come!' it croaked. 'What can I do for you?'

'Listen, Dragon-bird,' said Hop excitedly. 'We are prisoners here. Can you find some way of saving us?'

'Let me come into the room with you,' said the bird. 'I can talk with you better then.'

Cric-crac-cric-crac! It nipped each bar at the window with its strong beak, and broke them off one by one. Then, with the window clear of bars, the Dragon-bird hopped through the opening and stood on the table.

'What a peculiar-looking bird!' said the Princess, not at all afraid of the enormous creature. She went up to it and patted it.

The Dragon-bird shivered all over with delight.

'Little lady,' it croaked, 'you are the first person

who has ever patted me! I will do anything to rescue you and your friends!'

'Well, you can rescue us easily enough!' said the Princess, patting the bird again. 'Do you think you could manage to carry us away on your back?'

'I don't know,' said the Dragon-bird doubtfully. 'There are four of you. I've never carried more than one before. I'm not a bus, you know.'

'No, you're an aeroplane!' said Hop. 'Come on, Dragon-bird! Let us tie ourselves on to your back and go. The old witch may be back at any moment!'

The Princess patted the bird again. It was so pleased that it gave a crow of delight.

'Good gracious!' said Hop in horror. 'What an awful noise, Dragon-bird! You'll have the witch here in no time if you do that!'

'What about our chains?' asked Skip. 'How can we get rid of those?'

The bird leant forward and took Peronel's chains in his beak.

Cric-crac! It bit them in two!

'My!' cried Jump. 'What a help you are, to be sure!'

Then the Dragon-bird bit all the brownies' chains in two and they were free once more.

'Now go to the window-sill,' said Hop, trying

to push the bird off the table, 'and we'll get on your back one by one.'

The bird hopped over to the window.

'You needn't tie yourselves on my back,' it croaked, 'I will make four strong feathers stand upright, and you can hold on to those.'

Peronel stood on a chair, climbed up on to the bird's back, took hold of a fine strong feather and settled herself comfortably. The others followed.

'Have we got everything?' asked Hop, looking behind. 'Our bottles of goodness are in our pockets, aren't they?'

'Yes,' said Skip joyously. 'Oh, isn't it grand, Hop? 'We've got the Princess safe, and we've got the bottles of goodness too, so that soon we'll be in our own dear little cottage once more!'

'Hold tight,' said the bird suddenly. Everyone held tightly to their feathers. Then off they went into the air, far above the spires and towers of Witchland, carried strongly along on the big broad back of the Dragon-bird.

It was fine. The bird flapped its wings steadily, and the air rushed whistling by their ears. Witchland was left behind, and the Glass Hill. They were going very fast indeed, and didn't they enjoy it!

They had been flying along steadily for some

time when Hop happened to look behind them. Witchland could hardly be seen – it was just a blur in the distance.

But out of that blur Hop suddenly saw a little black spot come. He strained his eyes to see what it was.

'Look, Skip,' he said, pointing behind. 'Can you make out what that is? Is it another bird, or *what* is it?'

Skip looked, and so did Peronel and Jump, but none of them could make out what it was.

'We shall soon see,' said Hop. 'It's catching us up. I expect it is a bird of some sort.'

'Then it won't catch us up!' croaked the Dragon-bird. 'I fly faster than any bird living.'

'Well, but it *is* catching us up,' said Hop, as the black spot grew larger.

The Dragon-bird looked round to see this fast-flying bird. Then he gave such a jump and such a cry of alarm that his four passengers were very nearly jolted off. Hop just saved Skip by catching hold of one of his legs and pulling him safely up again.

'*Don't* do that,' said Hop to the Dragon-bird, very severely. 'Or at any rate be polite enough to tell us when you're going to do it.'

'I couldn't help it!' croaked the Dragon-bird.

'Do you know what that black speck following us is?'

'No, what?' asked everybody.

'It's old Witch Green-eyes on her magic carpet!' panted the bird. 'She must have missed you and come after you!'

'Oh, quick, quick, quick!' cried the brownies in fright. 'Fly your fastest, Dragon-bird! Quick, quick!'

The Dragon-bird flapped its wings even faster and tore through the air so swiftly that Peronel's hair shot out straight behind her.

Behind them came that horrid black speck, getting bigger and bigger every minute that passed.

'Fly your fastest, Dragon-bird!'

'We can't be very far away from Fairyland,' shouted Hop. 'We must have gone miles and miles already. Go on, brave Dragon-bird.'

On they went, and on and on. But every time they looked behind they shivered – for the black speck was so much larger.

At last they could see quite plainly that it was a witch sitting on a flat magic carpet that raced through the air in a most marvellous way.

'Oh buttons and buttercups!' groaned Hop in despair. 'Fancy, to be so near Fairyland, and yet to be so near being captured, too! Go on Dragon-bird, keep it up!'

'I – can't – go – on – much – longer!' panted the bird. 'I'm – so – tired – and – you're – all so heavy!' He ran the last words together, for he was very nearly breathless. The brownies could feel his heart beating bump-bump-bump in his body and they felt terribly sorry for him.

Suddenly Hop gave a shout of joy.

'Look! Look!' he cried, pointing before them. 'There are the palaces of Fairyland. We're nearly there, we're nearly there! Go on, dear old Dragon-bird!'

The bird's wings were flapping more slowly, but he put on an extra spurt when he heard the good news.

Behind them, closer and closer, came the old Witch Green-eyes on her carpet. She was so excited that she stood up and her hair flew behind her in the wind like long black snakes.

'I'll catch you, I'll catch you!' she shouted. The brownies could just hear her voice, and they shivered.

Nearer and nearer she came. And nearer and nearer came Fairyland.

'I – can't – fly – any – more!' gasped the bird suddenly, and began to drop downwards.

'Go on, go on!' shouted Hop. 'You can, you can! Look, there are the walls of Fairyland; you've only got to fly over them and you're safe!'

The bird made for the walls, tried to fly over them – and just missed them. It sank to the ground just outside Fairyland and lay there exhausted, whilst its four passengers scrambled off its back in dismay.

The Princess covered her eyes as she saw the witch rapidly coming down to them on her magic carpet. She was brave enough not to cry, but she felt very like it indeed.

'We'll fight for you!' said Hop, putting his arm round her. 'Don't be afraid!'

Bump! The witch landed just in front of them, jumped off her carpet, and ran over to them.

'Ho, ho!' she laughed. 'So I've caught you after all!'

The brownies looked at her in despair.

'Keep away from the Princess,' shouted Hop bravely, 'or we'll fight you.'

'Pooh! You haven't anything to fight with!' said the witch, grabbing at the Princess.

'Oh, *haven't* we!' cried Hop, and took out his bottle of goodness. 'We'll whack you with these bottles of goodness, if you dare to touch the Princess!'

The witch turned from the frightened Princess, and stared at Hop in amazement.

'Bottles of goodness!' she cried. 'Where did you get *those* from?'

'The Bottler, of course!' said Hop, swinging his bottle round as if to hit the witch.

'Don't do that — you might break it!' cried the witch. 'Goodness is one of the most precious things in the world, and witches can hardly ever get hold of any. Give it to me!'

'Give it to *you*!' said Hop, 'I should just think *not*! What would *you* do with a bottle of goodness I'd like to know!'

'I could make a wonderful spell!' said the witch. 'Oh, give it to me, I beg of you!'

'We can't get into Fairyland if we give you

our goodness,' answered Hop, 'so we're going to keep it.'

'Then I shall keep the Princess!' shouted the witch in a temper.

The brownies looked at each other in despair. How *could* they give up their precious bottles when they had gone through so many adventures to get them?

But they couldn't, COULDN'T let the brave little Princess be taken off by old Witch Green-eyes again. So with a sigh they knew they would have to give up their bottles of goodness.

'Very well, Witch Green-eyes,' said Hop, in a sad little voice. 'You shall have our three bottles if you will promise to let Peronel go free, and if you will promise, too, not to take us three brownies back with you.'

The witch looked greedily at the three brightly coloured bottles.

'Give them to me!' she begged, stretching out her hand. 'Peronel shall go free, and so shall you, too.'

'Let us see the Princess safely into Fairyland first,' said Hop. 'And if you try to play us a trick, and snatch us all away and our bottles too, we will smash them so that they will be no use to you!'

'Yes, we *will*!' said Skip and Jump, thinking

Hop was very clever and very brave.

'Let her go into the gates of Fairyland then,' said the witch, 'and give me the bottles afterwards!'

So Peronel ran quickly round the walls till she came to where the big gates of Fairyland stood tightly closed.

The brownies and the witch watched her beat at them with her little fists, and saw them open. There was a sound like a glad, astonished cry, and then the gates closed.

'They're shut again!' said Hop sadly.

'Quite shut,' said Skip.

'Now give me the bottles,' said the witch greedily.

They gave her their precious bottles, and watched her whilst she ran chuckling to the magic carpet.

Then, whoo-oo-oo-oo! The carpet rose quickly into the air, and soon the witch had become nothing but a tiny bird-like speck in the sky.

The three brownies looked at each other.

'Our precious, precious bottles!' said Hop.

'We can't go back to Brownie Town!' said Skip in a choking voice.

'Still, we got Peronel back all right,' said Jump, looking in all his pockets for a handkerchief.

Then a croak reminded them that their good

friend the Dragon-bird was still near them.

They ran up to him and praised him and thanked him.

'I'm tired,' he said, 'so tired. Let's all cuddle up here and go to sleep. Then in the morning we will think of our future plans, for I shall never leave you now.'

So the three forlorn little brownies cuddled together into the Dragon-bird, and soon fell fast asleep.

Their Very Last Adventure of All

The sun went down and still the brownies slept. Night came on and still they lay sleeping. They were so tired out with excitement that they didn't even wake when the morning sun shone straight on to their faces.

But they *did* wake when they heard an excited little voice shouting into their ears, and felt someone tugging and pulling at their shoulders.

'Wake up, oh wake up! Oh, please, *do* wake up!' called a voice.

The brownies sat up with a jerk and looked at their awakener.

It was the Princess Peronel!

'Buttons and buttercups!' said Hop in the deepest astonishment. 'What are *you* doing here?'

Peronel was dancing and skipping about in great excitement.

'Oh, I've told everyone all about you and your adventures!' she cried. 'And the King and Queen are *so* glad to have me back. And I've told them how you found your goodness, and how you gave it up to old Witch Green-eyes to save me. And I've

told them I love you, and want you to come back to
Fairyland, so I can play with you sometimes. And
they think you're brave and good, and WHAT
DO YOU THINK?'

'What?' asked the brownies, who had been
listening in amazement.

'There's a royal carriage coming to fetch you
back to Brownie Town!' cried Peronel, hopping
round with excitement. 'It's coming in about two
minutes, and I wanted to ride in it with you, so
I've come out to tell you about it. I guessed you'd
be here till the morning!'

'Good gracious!' said Hop, jumping up and
trying to make his clothes look as if they hadn't
been slept in. 'But, Peronel – how lovely of you to
arrange it all!'

'I'm going to rescue *you* now, you see, to pay
you back for you rescuing *me*!' laughed Peronel.
'And the old Dragon-bird's coming too, of course.
I told everyone how brave he was.'

Well, there was such excitement among the five
of them that they really didn't know what to do
with themselves. They pulled their tunics straight,
smoothed their hair and brushed the dust from
each other a score of times, whilst the Dragon-bird
preened every feather most proudly.

'There's the royal carriage!' shouted Hop

suddenly. Sure enough, there it was, coming out from the gates of Fairyland. Eight white horses drew it, and very grand and sparkling it looked. It drew up when the Princess stopped it.

In she got, and in got the three brownies. The Dragon-bird walked proudly along behind.

Then off set the royal carriage once more. It turned in through the gates of Fairyland, and the three brownies were so glad to be back again, that the tears ran down their faces in big trickles. The Princess was kept quite busy drying their eyes for them.

The carriage drove through Elfland, where hundred of elves were waiting to cheer the carriage as it passed. Then it went through Cuckoo Wood, where scores and scores of woodland folk cheered them and ran after the carriage throwing roses and honeysuckle flowers.

Hop, Skip and Jump were so happy that they really didn't know what to do.

'Fancy being back again!' said Hop.

'*Fancy* being back again!' echoed Skip.

'But just fancy it!' cried Jump in delight.

The Princess laughed. 'It's just as nice for me as for you!' she said. 'I was dreadfully homesick too!'

At last they reached Brownie Town. Hop, Skip and Jump knew every brownie who came running after the carriage, and called to their friends in joy.

'There's Gobo, dear old Gobo!' cried Hop.

'And Pinkie!' cried Skip.

'And Pippet and Gruffles, and Hoppety!' cried Jump.

The Dragon-bird was very happy too. He walked solemnly along behind the carriage, and everyone stared at him in wonder, for they had never seen anything like him in Fairyland before.

'Here's the Palace!' said Peronel, as the royal carriage turned into the gates. It went up the long twisting drive, and at last stopped at the great shining doors of the Palace

And on the steps to welcome the three brownies were their Majesties, the King and Queen.

'Welcome!' they cried. 'Welcome to the brave little brownies who rescued our daughter, and gave up their hard-won bottles of goodness for her safety. All your mischievous past is forgiven, for we know now that you are worthy of being brought back to Brownie Town! Welcome, too, to the brave Dragon-bird!'

'Hip-hip-hurrah!' shouted everyone.

'Don't let us have any more speeches,' begged Peronel. 'Let's get to the feast. I'm sure the brownies are hungry!'

The brownies were really much too excited to

feel hungry, but they were always ready for a feast.

And it *was* a feast. There were twenty different puddings, twelve different jellies, sixteen different blancmanges and fifty different sorts of cake!

There was only one guest there who tried everything – and that was the Dragon-bird, who really had a most enormous appetite.

After the feast, the King ordered three cheers for Hop, Skip and Jump, and one big cheer for the Dragon-bird. Then he took a little key off his watch-chain and gave it to Hop.

'Here is the key of Crab-apple Cottage,' he said kindly. 'I expect you would like to go and get things straight there, wouldn't you?'

So off went the brownies to their dear little cottage and, except for dust, it was all just exactly as they had left it.

'Isn't it *lovely* to be home?' cried Hop, sitting on all the chairs one after another.

'*Isn't* it lovely to be home?' cried Skip, lying on all the beds in turn.

'Isn't it perfectly, absolutely lovely to be HOME?' cried Jump, winding up all the clocks joyfully.

'We'll never be bad again!' said Hop, solemnly.

'*Never*,' said Skip.

'Never, never, *never*,' said Jump.

So they settled down in their cottage again, and dusted and scrubbed, and made it as spick and span as could be. Everybody brought them flowers, and they put them in jugs and bowls, and made Crab-apple Cottage look sweeter than it had ever done before.

And once again the three brownies were happy – especially on Saturday afternoons, for then they always went to the Palace to play with the little Princess.

As for the Dragon-bird, he was much too fond of them all to go away. So they kept him for a pet. Every Saturday he takes them for a fine long fly in the air.

So if you happen to see a big, peculiar-looking bird flying quickly overhead one day, don't be alarmed. It will only be the Dragon-bird, taking his four passengers for their Saturday afternoon ride.

GOODBYE!

And now the three brownies
are happy once more,
And the Princess is smiling all day;
She often comes knocking
at their cottage door
(Usually just about quarter-past four),
And asks them
to come out and play.

But first they have tea,
and they eat jammy bread,
While they talk just as fast as they can
Of the Vanishing Door
and the Hob-Goblin Red,
Of the Very Wise Man
with his very big head,
And, of course,
of the old Saucepan Man.

And Hop laughs to think
of the worm they once met
Who was in such a terrible hurry;

And Skip says he really will never forget
The time when the Green Railway
Train was upset
And put everyone in a flurry!

So they chatter and laugh
while they finish their tea,
Then they think they will go out to play;
And off they all clatter,
as merry as can be,
To take the old Dragon-bird
out for a spree
Away in the air, hip hurray!

They have a fine time
in the sunny blue sky,
And then come to earth with a bump.
And after that Peronel calls out 'Goodbye!
Goodbye, dear old Dragon-bird,
thanks for the fly,
And goodbye to you,
Hop, Skip and Jump!'

EGMONT PRESS: ETHICAL PUBLISHING

Egmont Press is about turning writers into successful authors and children into passionate readers – producing books that enrich and entertain. As a responsible children's publisher, we go even further, considering the world in which our consumers are growing up.

Safety First
Naturally, all of our books meet legal safety requirements. But we go further than this; every book with play value is tested to the highest standards – if it fails, it's back to the drawing-board.

Made Fairly
We are working to ensure that the workers involved in our supply chain – the people that make our books – are treated with fairness and respect.

Responsible Forestry
We are committed to ensuring all our papers come from environmentally and socially responsible forest sources.

For more information, please visit our website at www.egmont.co.uk/ethical